Amulet II

Amulet II

FREDRIK NATH

Fred Nath Books ● Middlesbrough

FOR
HARRY AND TOBI

Contents

THE GALLIC WAR

FOREWORD

In Amulet I, Aulus Veridius Scapula joined the Ninth Legion to fight for Rome and for his honour. The amulet, containing the secret of vast wealth, has been taken from him by his cousin Marcus. This book sees Aulus travel back to Rome and beyond to Gaul where he fights for Julius Caesar still searching for that which was stolen from him by Marcus.

This, the second instalment in the tale of the amulet, brings Aulus full circle and back to his origins. In Pontus he has become a little too complacent, he is comfortable he is in love, he is recovering from his injuries. But Mithridates is coming home and Aulus must move on.

This novel is set in the time when Rome was still flourishing and Julius Caesar is expanding the Roman Empire into Gaul with battle after battle. The finest general and statesman Rome has ever seen is destined for greatness.

Is the same true for Aulus Veridius Scapula?

Read on and you'll see.

BOOK I:
ROME

Chapter I

"The die is cast." – Gaius Julius Caesar.

The news came on a warm and comfortable summer's evening and it snatched me from the arms of the luxurious life I had been living for eighteen months since my return to Sinope from Armenia.

The injury to my head at the battle of Tigranocerta left me with a weak arm and leg but I recovered enough to walk and hold a shield. The doctors told me there would be no further recovery and it made me complacent – content in the belief that I had no need to make the efforts required by a soldier's life.

I understand now what Homer meant when he described the lotus-eaters. Like Odysseus' men I was too content. I was putting on weight. I was eating and drinking a little too well, for a little too long. The lack of exercise was making me flabby and unfit and I should have realised it was too soft a life for a fighting man. That Hypsicratea, Queen of Pontus, did not mind is surprising but it is often surprising what love can do to breed tolerance.

We dined that evening in the garden at the east side of the palace. We lay out-of-doors on the quilted divans and the jugs of wine and water on the table between us were half-empty. The remains of the local fish, roast fowl, olives and bread lay waiting for the palace staff to clear them away in the morning. The sun had long since descended and we were drinking the last of the wine in our cups by torchlight. The servants had withdrawn and we were alone.

An owl hooted nearby from one of the trees in the gardens and the soft smell of jasmine hung in the still, warm, humid air. I noticed it because owls have never been a good omen for me.

'Things seem to have gone very badly for us Romans in Armenia,' I said, sipping the watered wine, which, even watered, was still full of the aroma of cherries and ripe fruit with a faint resinous taste in the finish,.

'No, things have gone very well for us Pontics,' Hypsicratea said with a smile.

'It's all very well for you to laugh, but now the legions have been withdrawn to Bythinia, I have no compatriots left here in Sinope. I am a poor lone Roman in hostile territory.'

'I'm not hostile.'

I paused and looked into her eyes. 'You're everything I ever dreamed of in a woman.'

I stood up smiling, ready to sit next to her and take her in my arms. She looked beautiful in the torchlight, her long raven hair hanging in curls about her shoulders and glistening as she moved her head in the torchlight. Her perfect teeth, a rarity in modern times, reflected the light too and there was a little dimple in her cheek when she smiled. Her large almond eyes with their long cinnabar lashes were like black pools, shiny and deep. I had my mind on love not politics.

'What was that?' I said listening.

'What?'

'I heard someone on the other side of the wall shouting.'

'There's nothing new in that.'

'No, he was shouting something about Mithridates.'

'No, you imagined it. I didn't hear it.'

'Listen,' I said.

She got up. We stood in silence for a moment. I took her hand in mine. Then we both heard it.

'Mithridates is coming. Mithridates is coming.'

It was a man's voice. He sounded elated. There were more shouts. Most of them were unintelligible but we could manifestly hear the name of the Great King of Pontus. We had seemed to be living from day to day in those days, because the politics of Pontus was constantly changing. Since I had begun living in the palace the Roman armies had experienced defeat after defeat and my position as Advisor in Roman Affairs was precarious now. Of course, I was no such advisor. Hypsicratea had invented the position to keep me near, since people talk and talk can be a dangerous thing for secret lovers.

There was a gong at the side of her divan. She struck it. A servant appeared out of nowhere. His name was Eumenides. He had served the King of Pontus from childhood and now he had served the Queen throughout her captivity in the palace at the hands of the Roman army.

'Eumenides, tell me, what is all that noise and shouting?'

'It's the King, Your Majesty.' the servant said. 'He is returning. Have you had no word?'

'No. That is strange. What have you heard?'

'He has gathered another army and marches here even as we speak. I heard in the marketplace this evening he might be here as soon as two weeks from now. I thought he would have sent word.'

'Why has everyone heard except me?'

'I have no such knowledge, Your Majesty. Is it not wonderful news?' He shifted from one foot to the other, uncomfortable.

'Yes, yes. You may go, but keep me informed.'

We sat on her couch and looked at each other. The look on her face was one of intense concentration as she worked out the implications of this piece of news. I dread to think what the look on my own face portrayed.

'We will have to leave,' I said.

'We?'

'Of course. We'll go to Rome and build a new life there together.'

'I cannot do that.'

'But you must. How else can we be together? I can't stay here. I'm a Roman. Besides, all the servants know about us and the pretence of my post as "Advisor in Roman Affairs" is a secret all over the palace.'

'You don't understand. I have a duty to my people and besides, Mithridates is my husband.'

'But I thought it was me that you loved.'

'Love? Of course I love you, but I have a duty to the people. I am their Queen, however hard it may be for us.'

'Mithridates will kill us slowly and painfully since he only needs to talk to any of the servants to know about our nights together,' I said.

'He would never believe them over me. He loves me. I can take care of myself but you will have to leave. You are right about his anger. He once poured molten gold into a man's throat because the man had betrayed him for gold. What he would do to someone who had made love to his Queen I dare not think.'

'Please,' I said, reaching out for her, my arm outstretched. 'I can't go without you. Life would be pointless.'

She sat next to me and stroked my cheek, her touch gentle as the softest breeze. Her eyes, sad and beautiful, met mine.

'Dear Aulus, you must have known it couldn't last? Surely

when we heard about the Senate recalling Lucullus it was obvious that Rome has lost its sway in this part of the world. Mithridates is coming, he will take back what is his, and that includes his wife. My love for you has no place in this decision. I cannot run away.'

I looked at her in amazement. She seemed so collected. We had never discussed what might happen if her exiled husband, long since defeated by the great General Lucullus, returned. I had always supposed she would come with me wherever I went. I had been a fool or perhaps I had shut that sad possibility away in the deepest recesses of my mind, hoping nothing would ever happen. People are like that and I am worse than most.

She was right of course. I can see that but I was loath to admit it even to myself at that time. I loved her and she loved me but she was still right. I had never been anything but a soldier and should never have expected to be living with Hypsicratea in Pontus forever. To this day it astounds me she ever felt for me the way she did.

I suppose the explanation lies in her circumstances at the time. Her husband had fled to Armenia when Rome took over the city. She was lonely and felt vulnerable. There I was; I rescued her from a dangerous situation and we became good friends. We spent a great deal of time together enjoying each other's company. I was thirsting for her and she refused to admit her true feelings even to herself. In the end the boundaries faded and we became lovers.

She helped nurse me through two battle injuries. I had stayed long after my legion had returned to Rome taking my only close friend, Junius Sinna, away with it.

I had no one in Rome apart from Junius and I had no idea whether the Ninth Legion Hispania was even near the city. My parents were both dead and the life I had known in Rome was on the streets as a friendless thief. When an old soldier caught me he forced me into the army and that military nascence had made me and moulded me into a soldier.

'How long do you think?' I said, staring at the ground between us. There seemed an immeasurable distance despite the physical closeness. There was no use denying the inevitable. I suppose I knew that.

'Oh Aulus. I can't bear even the thought of you going, but go you must. If you leave it longer than a week my husband's advance guard will be here.'

'I suppose it will take me six weeks to reach Pergamum by horse, or maybe seven. I suppose I can take a ship from there to Rome. There's a lot of shipping going that way especially with the legions going home. You must come with me – you must.'

'Before we lay plans for you to return home let us at least enjoy the time we have left. It must be this way. I will miss you more than you know but I cannot go with you.'

'I know, I even understand, but it hurts,' I said. I thought I might have enough time to persuade her so I showed no open dissent. I half suspected she was protecting me, offering to stay to prevent her husband sending soldiers after us but she seemed so plausible.

I led her by the hand to the bedchamber and neither of us slept that night. We talked a great deal as well as made love which we seemed to do with desperation as if the sexual act would wash away our imminent parting and separation.

'The thing I will miss most about you Aulus is the fun we've had together.'

'Yes,' I said, 'we do laugh a lot. Perhaps now you will have to be a more serious Queen.'

I reached over and caressed her cheek. She turned her face away.

'My husband is a more serious person, so maybe you are

right. I think he will march on Bythinia next if he has enough men. How he raised an army again I cannot imagine.'

'I hear that he and Tigranes combined forces and Lucullus became overconfident. The string of defeats since has wrecked Roman plans of attacking Parthia.'

'When you leave will you accept a gift of money?'

'Money? No, just travelling money. I have a military pension to claim and there are now two years of back pay to collect. I won't be rich, but I'll have something. Besides, I don't want you to think I wanted you for money, because it wasn't like that.'

'I know why you came back to me Aulus: it was for good wine and good sex.'

'If you don't stop teasing me I'll go tomorrow.'

'Sorry, I didn't mean it. Will you try to get your revenge?'

'What? On Marcus Mettius? Perhaps. I want the amulet he stole. I'm sure it was he who left me for dead with the head injury. If it was then he took the amulet and I must get it back.'

'Do you really think it will make you rich?'

'I don't know, but my father said it contained the whereabouts of those deeds and there must be a reason why a rich man like Marcus Mettius senior would kill to get them.'

'I can't believe Marcus would do that to his own cousin. Leaving you injured like that.'

'Oh I believe it all right. My arm is almost back to normal, but carrying a shield is like holding up a building after only half an hour of practice. I wonder if it will get any better.'

'The physician here said it would never heal any more after two years.'

'What do these doctors know? They said I was going to die when they sent me back from the battle and here I am. So much for modern medicine.'

'Hold me Aulus. I don't know what I'll do without you to talk to.'

'Me too. Won't you come with me?'

'Don't make it so difficult. I can't leave and you can't stay. There are bigger issues at stake than our little lives.'

'There are no bigger issues in life than love. I've learned that lesson now. I thought life was all about achieving rank, fame and position. I'm really happy here with you. What's the point in me returning to Rome if I don't have you?'

'Aulus, love matters and it does not go away but there are things like self-respect, duty and fidelity. I have been unfaithful to my husband but I cannot extend that infidelity to my people. Why can you not understand that?'

'If you loved me you would come.'

She sat up and looked at me. Her eyes narrowed.

'You're being stupid. How can you doubt my love? I have given way over everything and betrayed Mithridates just for you. I won't leave Sinope and I won't discuss it again.'

That damned owl continued to hoot as if mocking me. I knew when I was beaten. We lay in silence in the warm night air and a gentle breeze raised the drapes at the balcony doorway. I got up and walked outside. My heart was sore and I was annoyed. I thought she was being unreasonable. Stubbornness often obscures common sense and that was how it was with me then.

*　　　　　　　*　　　　　　　*

'Aulus.'

It was a woman's voice. A familiar one. I smiled as I turned and greeted her with the informality of long acquaintance. I was standing in the palace courtyard with my horse. He was a tall rowan steed, a gift from Hypsicratea the previous week. The stableman could have tended to him but I wanted him to become used to me before the journey since we would be together for many weeks. I had groomed him and checked his shoes and I was squatting, packing a few belongings into the new, shiny, brown leather saddlebags to save time in the morning. It was a bright sunny morning but it did nothing to assuage my heavy heart. Some sparrows hopped cheerfully across the yard bathing in the horse trough as if all was well in the world. I still had not adjusted my thoughts to the idea of leaving the woman I loved. It all seemed so final, so daunting. I could not understand why she expressed so little emotion at our parting. I often wondered if it was to ease my pain but it only made it worse. She was adamant she wouldn't leave and for me to stay would have been stupid. I learned much later that not all is what it seems in affairs of the heart. Love blinds us but sorrow can mask even more.

'Aripele. I was just coming to say goodbye.'

'You must be very unhappy.' Her eyelids flickered and she looked down.

'Unhappy does not do justice to what I feel, believe me.'

'You can understand how I felt now, when Junius left with you to go to Armenia. I was torn in two.'

She was younger than I was, in her early twenties and half a head shorter. From anyone else's lips, her Greek-accented Latin would have grated, but she made it seem a veritable pleasure on the ear. She was a beautiful woman. Her dark hair and eyes with her full lips made her look like some of the paintings of goddesses I had seen hanging on the palace walls. The loose, red silk gown she wore could not hide the curves of her figure and I had always understood what my friend Junius had seen in her. She had a knack of attracting men. It may have been her femininity for it showed through every movement but even her walk had a seductive sway. Men followed her every movement and I had never met someone who attracted such attention in a market, in a tavern or even walking in the street. She would have been attractive wearing anything and on this day, she looked resplendent.

'Yes, I didn't understand then, but I do now. I hope you don't mind if I pack and talk at the same time. I'm leaving very early.'

'That's what I was coming to talk to you about.'

'I thought I could try to get a message to Junius for you, if he is still stationed near Rome.'

'I don't want you to take a message. I want you to take me.'

'What do you mean by take? You know I can't afford your prices.'

'No, silly, I want you to escort me to Rome.'

I paused.

'I can't do that. I'm travelling on horseback and moving fast, before Mithridates sends his advance party. I can't take you along as well.'

'Please, I have to go with you.'

'But why? Has your nobleman thrown you out? I have a little money if that is any help.'

'No it isn't that. I just have to see Junius again. I can't live without him. Now that you are going home I can come with you. You can protect me on the journey. I have quite a lot of money. I've been saving. I'll give it all to you if you take me with you.'

'It's impossible. I'm riding all the way to Pergamum and then on to Rome by ship. It will be a dangerous journey. They say the storms wreck one ship in ten. You would hate it.'

'Aulus I can ride better than you can. At least I won't fall off all the time like you do.'

'That's only because of the weakness in my leg. The doctor instructed me to ride every day to help my balance. I'm much better at it than last time you saw me on a horse.'

'My mind is made up. I have sold all my possessions and those belonging to one or two of my main customers and I'll follow you all the way if I have to.'

'Why do I have to be pushed and pulled by women all the time? I have Hypsicratea pushing me to Rome and you dragging me there. When I get there, I can't look out for you. I'll be doing, well, questionable things. It would only endanger you.'

'Aulus please. I have been in many dangerous situations. How do you think I used to survive in my line of work in the streets of Sinope if I couldn't look after myself? I wasn't always kept by noblemen in their houses.'

'Do you have a horse?'

'Yes.' She smiled.

'And travelling clothes?'

'Aulus.' She was rolling her eyes now.

'I suppose I can't stop you coming along, but if you slow me down I'll leave you.'

'What will Junius say if he heard that you left me on the road?'

'What if Junius has someone else now that he's returned to Italia? Had you thought of that? What if he is married and has a houseful of screaming children? What will you do alone in Rome?

'Aulus, without Junius I am no one. If I end up alone in Rome I can do the same work as I've always done. It's the same as being alone in Sinope. Anyway, men like me. My work is no different anywhere in the civilised world and beyond. There have been girls in my profession ever since men discovered they could pay for what their fat wives deny them at home. I really can take care of myself. The trouble is, I loved Junius, and he loved me. You can't stand in our way. You simply can't.'

I looked at her face and followed the progress of a single tear trickling down in a meandering journey to her throat, dragging a trail of the cinnabar she used for darkening her eyes. We stood in silence for a moment or two and in the end I smiled and shrugged in resignation. I put my arms around her in a gesture of friendship, offering comfort, but she eased me away and looked up at me with eyes pleading.

I felt manipulated but I gave in all the same. She walked away leaving me pondering whether such a travelling companion would be good or bad. Either way, she was coming and I knew I had to get used to the idea. It was clear she was using me but I had to admit to myself I had used her too. When I returned to Sinope after my head injury she had been my one contact with my best friend, Junius, who had returned to Rome. She understood why I missed him and I understood her loss too. It was our common bond. She was pleasant company and she was one of the few people I could talk to about him. It is true it was an odd friendship with well-defined boundaries, for she loved Junius and I loved Hypsicratea. She had been instrumental in bringing us together when I returned and I was always grateful to her for that.

Travelling fast to Pergamum would be a difficult journey, but with a woman in tow I expected it to be taxing, to say the least.

Chapter II

"When about to commit a base deed, respect thyself, though there is no witness." – Ausonius.

I hate protracted goodbyes. I did not want to prolong the desolation of my farewell to Hypsicratea that morning. I arose from her bed, washed and dressed, my heart sinking with every movement. With clumsy hands, I laced my sandals. It dawned upon me then how it would now always take those few moments longer without my beautiful Queen to help me. It was as if I was already establishing a new routine. I understood too it's the little things after all that herald the pain of grief.

She pretended to be asleep as I leaned over and kissed her forehead, my tremulous hand moving slow and gentle as I stroked her silky, raven hair. I stood up to leave. She stirred then and propped herself up on one elbow looking up at me with moist and sleepy eyes. She looked so beautiful to me in the early morning light filtering through the silken drapes swaying in the warm Sinope morning breeze. It brought with it the smell of the city, one I would never experience again.

'I don't know if I can bear this parting,' she said, her voice a little husky.

'Well it was more your idea than mine.'

'Don't be hard on me. Please.'

'Don't,' I said holding up my hand.

She shifted her position, sitting up, her eyes sleepy but serious. 'I can't go with you. He would pursue me to the ends of the earth and he would have us both killed. I know him. He is a good king but he can be a cruel man and jealous.'

'Come with me. There's still time. We can take money and jewellery and we can live comfortably. I'll make sure you want for nothing, if only we can be together.'

'I can't just run away. I would forever feel that I had betrayed my people. Please go. If you go now I can bear it. If you keep trying to persuade me I don't know what I will do.'

She turned away, her shoulders heaving as she cried almost in silence. I had to leave. If I had stayed longer I might have stayed forever. I knew it would cost me my life if I did, so I walked away. Simple as that. I can't understand how I mustered the strength to do it for I did love her, but circumstance, self-preservation or some machination of the Gods was forcing us apart.

I walked through that palace with lead in my heart. In the courtyard outside, Aripele was waiting with my half-Greek friend Polymecles. He was my friend and landlord and had cared for me when I had returned to Sinope after the battle with the Armenians. He spoke too fast, with deference in his terms of address that he never expressed in his eyes.

'Master Aulus, I am so pleased to see you but it sorrows my heart that my friend, the Roman lord, must make this long and perilous journey to escape the return of the rightful King.'

'Polymecles, I love you but you still annoy me.' I meant it.

Polymecles smiled his Greek smile and put his flat hands out at his sides, shrugging his shoulders. He was a strange man but he was a good friend. I had not realised it when I first arrived in Sinope but he had always been my friend.

'Such things are the will of the Gods,' he said.

'I am bitterly sorry to leave Sinope. I have more here to leave than I have in Rome to return to.'

'Such is fate my friend. You must take good care of Aripele and defend her on the road for she is just a child.'

'Polymecles, she is not much younger than I am. Anyway, she is one girl who can look after herself. Trust me on that one.'

'I have a small gift for you Aulus.'

Polymecles produced a dagger which he had secreted in his robe. A small red stone sparkled in the pommel and it had a beautifully made, long, thin, curved blade such as assassins used in Rome. Red and green stones were set into the silver and wood scabbard and silver and copper wire bound the handle.

'Where did you get this from? It's an assassin's weapon and looks as if it was made in Rome or Italia at least.'

'A previous tenant left it behind and I have had it ever since. I want you to have it. If it saves your life one day I will be well served.'

'Polymecles, you must visit when I am established in Rome – promise me that.'

'I am an old man. I cannot travel, but one day perhaps you will return. I am sure Hypsicratea our Queen will honour you when you do.'

I think he saw the pained look on my face and he desisted from further talk.

I turned to my new travelling companion. 'Aripele, are you ready?'

With a few more goodbyes to Polymecles we embraced him and set off from the great palace of Mithridates. As I looked back I could see my Queen outlined in a window high above. I raised my hand and then we left to take the road to Herakleia, our first stop on the way to Pergamum. My heart felt like it was ossified. We did not speak as we threaded our way through the busy streets.

At the main city gate there was a milling crowd. Guards had shut the gates. They were allowing no one in or out. The guards were not Roman. It came home to me then that we had lost Sinope. Mithridates was taking back all Lucullus had fought so hard to conquer only two years before. The loss of all those lives both Roman and Pontic had been a waste.

A scuffle broke out at the gate then and I led Aripele towards one of the side gates. I was more hopeful we could get out there. This was the first day they had shut the gates and I didn't think it likely crowds would accumulate at all of them.

They had shut the side gates as well. Two guards, both of them armed with swords and spears stood in the deserted street. I recognised one of them for he had been on guard duty at the palace only a week before and I felt certain he would recognise me. He was a broad, squat man in his forties, wearing a leather breastplate and a leather cap. His face showed no recognition.

'Good morning,' I said.

'Is it?' he said.

The tone of his voice was contemptuous. This was going to be more difficult than I had thought.

'I need to leave the city,' I said, my voice even and firm.

'Sorry sir, no one allowed in or out until the King returns. Strict orders.'

'I and this lady have been sent by the Queen to take a message to the King.'

'You can give it to me and I'll see he gets it.'

The other man laughed in the background. I had good reason to want to be out of Sinope before Mithridates returned and realised any lengths to do so would be reasonable. I was not returning, after all.

'Listen, if you obstruct me in my capacity as Advisor in Roman Affairs I'll have you court martialled and brought before the King. Don't stand in my way. Open the gate, there's a good chap.'

He looked at me and grinned.

'I don't care if you're the High Prince of Rome. I have my orders and you will stay here.'

I dismounted and drew my sword. I was a little unsteady because of the weakness in my leg, but my right arm was as good as ever. I swung the sword fast in a single movement as it exited the scabbard and it poked into the soldier's throat. I did not cut him but it must have been uncomfortable.

The second guard stepped forward, drawing his blade as he did so. I prodded with my weapon and the first man warned him off.

'Get your friend here to open the gate. I don't want to kill you both but I will if I have to.'

'Open the bloody gate.' he said.

I walked him backwards with the point of my weapon until he was up against the gatepost. Aripele walked out of the gate leading our horses. She leaped back into her saddle with surprising speed, for she was a fit and nimble girl.

I turned to remount, sheathing my sword. The second man, seeing that his colleague was no longer under threat, ran towards me flailing his weapon. I turned fast. I drew my weapon again in the way Meridius, the legion's sword champion had taught me. The exiting blade struck the blow without pausing. The tip sliced across his throat. It was a way of delivering a deathblow without any gaps in movement. He lay at my feet spurting blood, nerveless fingers clutching the wound. I heard an involuntary gasp from

Aripele as I flicked the blood from the blade and sheathed my weapon.

The second man, seeing his companion fall, drew his sword. He was more cautious as he approached. I stood with my right side forwards. I put as much of my weight on my back foot as I thought it would tolerate. I did not know for certain whether I still had the speed for a one on one fight but I knew my right arm was as skilful as ever it had been. I cursed my cousin Marcus in my mind for the damage he had done me at Tigranocerta. The weakness in my left arm and leg had made every action in life an inconvenience.

The gate-guard was not a swordsman. He approached with cautious steps. He stooped to pick up his friend's wicker shield. I could see the lack of confidence in his eyes.

'Look, you don't want to die too, do you?'

'You killed my friend.'

'He attacked me from behind. I don't want to kill you, but I will if you strike at me. You saw I have the skill to do just that. Don't be a fool.'

'Damn you to Hades,' he said.

I think he must have stopped thinking then. Perhaps it was anger. Perhaps he felt it would be unmanly to retire from the fight. Either way, he came on. I found it odd there was now no fear in his eyes.

In his right hand, he had a long, curved sword. The shield protected him on his left. I stood my ground. He raised his weapon above his head. He struck at me. I parried. It was too easy and I felt sorry for him. I riposted to my right hitting his shield. The shield arm flew sideways and I stabbed fast at his chest. The blade transfixed him. I sidestepped to avoid his descending blade as he fell back. He died very soon after, coughing blood with his last breath. I had not wanted to kill him, but needs must. I was reassured that they had both attacked me first. In one sense,

I was defending myself but I had known all along I outclassed them, despite my weakness. One could argue that it was more like murder than a fair fight. It gave me no pleasure to realise that and so I tried not to dwell upon it.

It took two or three attempts for me to mount my horse, the last of which was successful because I stood on one of my dead opponents, I don't know which one. Using one leg to mount a horse is difficult, since I was unable to use my left to stand and it was stiff besides.

We rode away from Sinope at a speed we hoped would carry us away from pursuit.

After riding all morning we stopped for a meal of bread and olives with a local white wine, which we drank mixed with water. Aripele proved as good as her word for she rode well and I found to my chagrin it was I who most needed the break.

We sat by the roadside without conversing much. Each of us had our own private thoughts. Hers were of Junius and mine of Hypsicratea. We both started talking at once.

'Aripele, do you...'

'Do you think they will come after us?' Aripele said.

'I don't know, but the less time we spend resting the better. Once we get to high ground we can look back and see if there's anyone chasing us. We have to make haste.'

'I know you don't want me along, but I really have to go – to find my Junius. I've thought of nothing else since I heard he'd gone back to Rome. I thought I'd forget about him in time but it simply hasn't happened.'

'I know, I understand. I'll look after you. I want to find Junius too. I'm sorry if my company's glum, but I feel so very unhappy to lose Hypsicratea. You know how I feel. The Fates spin a hard tapestry sometimes.'

'Yes.'

'We need to get on. We can make a camp in about six or seven hours and we should really only take one break before that. If we continue at this pace we can reach Herakleia in two weeks.'

'I'm not very good at camping.'

'You'll get used to it.'

We both smiled and I realised what a pleasant girl she was. She never complained either, which surprised me. It made the journey very different from marching or travelling with soldiers whose lot it is to complain at every opportunity.

I popped an olive in my mouth as we mounted our horses and we rode, not hard but steadily. My weak leg meant that I had to stop periodically to alter my position, or I slipped to the side. I had also had a pressure sore on my buttock from when I had been at my most seriously ill and the scar irritated in the saddle.

I was relieved when we stopped for the night. We had climbed for the second half of the day and reached a high escarpment from which we could see far around us.

We left the road and made our camp a good distance from the main routes, for caution's sake. We sat by a small fire and talked. We were in a gully and I felt it unlikely anyone on the road below would be able to see our fire unless they looked down from the ridge above us. We sat by the flames and warmed ourselves. Neither of us felt like cooking and we ate cheese and bread with olives again. We talked little for my usual headache precluded long conversation and I think she understood.

'Let's hope the Ninth Legion is still in the vicinity of Rome. Don't worry, we'll find him. We have to.'

'Yes, we must.'

'I need to sleep.'

'I'm cold; can I lie close to you?'

I smiled at that. 'Of course, but I'm not paying.'

'You'll be the first for a long time who lies next to me without paying.'

We laughed and cuddled up by the dying fire. It was company and friendship. Falling asleep I thought about Hypsicratea in the palace at Pontus. I missed her and my head thumped.

*   *   *

I awoke early. It had been a long night and I'd had difficulty sleeping. I kept awakening from dreams of battle and blood. It was before dawn and I looked around the camp. Aripele slept soundly and I felt it was a shame to wake her from such deep slumber. She turned over as I stood up and murmured in her sleep.

The sun was beginning to rise. There was dew reflecting the dawn light on the grass and the ground spiders' webs. I climbed to the top of the gully. The air was still and cool. I could hear the first birdsong starting up. It used to irritate me when I was in the palace for it made sleeping late difficult, particularly in the spring, but now at the close of summer they seemed to sing in a milder tone, in concert with my grieving.

I sat on a flat rock, the damp of its rough surface penetrating my tunic, feeling sorry for myself. I looked across the wide field in the valley below. In the distance, westward, there were green hills and I could see the sea beyond them, for we were travelling west along the coast. It was still and beautiful as the sun rose with layers of gossamer mist in the valleys below and I could not help but remember such days when Junius and I and Hypsicratea had been travelling west after a shipwreck, and trying to make our way to Sinope. Such memories were painful now, but like all nostalgia to a grieving man it was an opportunity to wallow in my self-pity. Not that I recommend self-pity. I was a young man and the end of a relationship often causes such maudlin thoughts. I suppose it does no harm.

I thought about the future. It all seemed to be a fog of possibilities. Rome, what a city. With its bustling fora and teeming streets it was the centre of the Empire. I longed for her. I needed her even though there was now little for me to return to in our great city. My parents were dead, my cousin in possession of the amulet and worst of all, me in a damaged and debilitated state with my increased weight and lack of fitness and a weak arm and leg.

I grasped at my stomach and realise how plump I had become. I was a caricature of the man I had been. I had been lean, fast and fit and now, a plump sluggish porker of a man. It irritated me.

'Aulus? Where are you?' Aripele said behind me. She was sitting among the blankets, her black hair awry and her cloak wrapped around her in the morning chill.

'Here I am my little friend.'

'I wondered where you'd got to. I don't like waking up alone.' She got up and stood beside me, drawing her cloak tighter around her.

'I awoke early. I was looking at the sunrise,' I said.

'Well it's the first sunrise I've seen for a long time I can tell you. It's lovely. Perhaps I should do this more often.'

'Aripele, the only reason I am witnessing the sunrise is an acute dose of insomnia. Let's eat.'

'What's that?'

'What?'

'Down there, the dust rising,' She said pointing.

'I don't know. Maybe someone is riding this way.'

'Do you think they're following us from Sinope? You did kill those two guards you know.'

'We can wait here until we can see which way they go. They won't see us up here. We'd better not re-light the fire.'

We waited and identified four horsemen. They rode past below us and seemed in a hurry. They were going in the same direction as us and so we decided to let them get well ahead as a precaution.

We set out around midday. We ate a cold meal again and we rode. We rode and we ate, ate and rode. There was little else in our day apart from travelling and talking. There was no sign of pursuit and I didn't think the death of two gate guards would warrant a full-scale cross-country chase in any case.

The journey lasted eighteen days. My assessment at the start had been optimistic. Our only problem was that the horses required more frequent rest than I had anticipated. I was not a horseman even at my best and the terrain was hard. We rode over craggy hills and hard dry roads and water was in short supply at times. It seemed the more we rode, the shorter was our tolerance of the rigours. By the time we reached Herakleia we were short of provisions and the horses seemed lacklustre and tired. We were caked in dust and looking forward to the bathhouse if indeed there was such a thing in this small trading town. It was much smaller than I had remembered from when I had marched east with the Ninth Legion.

We looked down from a hill at the town. It looked quiet but picturesque, the backdrop of the blue unruffled sea adding a sense of calm. There was a stone wall the height of perhaps two men and the city gate was wide open. In the geographically invidious position in which the city found itself there were enemies to east and west but trading was the lifeblood of the city and so they opened their town to Pontics and Romans alike.

We rode down the hill to the city's approach road, raising dust in a spiralling cloud behind us. Cicadas played their crackly tune and flies buzzed around my head whenever I slowed my pace as we neared the gates .

I did not expect trouble here but something stirred in my mind – a warning, or simply the embers of natural caution unused since I had been a thief in the Subura in Rome. In those days I could smell danger. Time must have blunted that sense or perhaps it was my grief at losing Hypsicratea. Such distractions from the present often rob one of innate prescience. I put away the feeling of disquiet. I had been living in peace for too long perhaps.

Chapter III

"If you wished to be loved, love." – Seneca..

Herakleia was a strange little city. It had started as one long street but as it had grown, the people had built more and more streets and houses without thinking too much about the eventual effects of having all the ways stemming from a single arterial road. It meant that on either side of the wide main street there were myriads of tiny streets and small stone buildings. All the carts entering had to use the same choked thoroughfare.

We made our way down the dusty road to the main square where there was a marketplace There we purchased some provisions for our journey to Pergamum and stowed them in our saddlebags, then we went to a tavern for a cup of wine and a meal. It was the first proper hot meal we had eaten since we had set off, apart from a rabbit I had managed to snare on the way. The snare had been a trick I had once learnt from my friend Junius.

We sat in the corner of the tavern and ate a hot mutton stew flavoured with mint and marjoram and some stuffed vine leaves with fresh bread. I dipped the last of the bread in the remains of the stew and looked around at the people.

Most of them were merchant folk but there were some locals too. The men seemed to stare at Aripele with a look that I can only describe as leering. She was the kind of girl who seemed to attract male attention. I felt alternately proud and irritated to be with her.

Four men entered the tavern. They all carried swords and there was something hostile, almost arrogant, in the way they approached the counter. I knew they were soldiers from their walk. Soldiers have a particular confident, abrasive attitude when they are with civilians.

There was a short, serious conversation in muttered tones with the bartender and they began to look around. Three of them left then for they seemed to have done what they wanted. I hid my face with my hand and looked away. I wondered whether they were the four riders we had seen on the road, and felt it advisable to avoid them.

The remaining man stood at the bar. He was a big man and I could see from his bearing he could look after himself. He couldn't hide that he was a soldier out of uniform.

I leaned to my side whispered to Aripele.

'See him?'

'Who?'

'The man standing at the counter.'

'Yes.'

'I think he's been sent to look for us. We need to get out of here quick.'

She said nothing. We stood up as soon as he had his back to us and made for the door as unobtrusively as we could.

A rough Pontic voice stopped me in my tracks. 'Hey. You.'

I turned.

'Me?' I said in good Greek.

'Yes you. Who are you?' He looked at me with a frown and I could see by the tension of his lips this was not a casual enquiry.

'How does it concern you, my friend?' I said.

'I'm not your friend. Where have you come from?'

'Why do you wish to know?'

'I've been sent to find a man and a woman who murdered two of my men in Sinope. I am a soldier in the army of The Great King Mithridates.'

'I am Simonides, a trader and this is my wife. We are travelling to Sinope. Perhaps you might offer us your protection if you are going in that direction?'

'We won't be going back until we find the murderers. One is a Roman and the other a whore. You seen them?'

'No sir. We have come from Pergamum and intend to visit my cousin, Polymecles a landlord in Sinope.'

'Just one more question,' he said stepping towards me. 'Why would a trader from Pergamum carry a Roman sword?'

He drew his sword and came straight for me, surprising me with his speed of movement. Maybe it was the wine but I was unprepared. He was on my right side. I found it hard to draw my sword in the crowded tavern, or maybe I was slow. He stabbed straight at my chest. I sidestepped fast enough,but he hit me with the sword hilt on the side of the head. I fell to the ground. All was a whirl of flashing, circling spots of light. He stood over me. He raised his weapon.

I'm uncertain whether he had it in mind to kill me or not. I looked up. He fell forward as if hit by a thunderbolt from above. To my surprise, I saw Aripele standing behind him as he pitched across me. She was holding a stool and had felled him with a blow to the back of the head. She helped me to my feet and we staggered outside.

The man's three companions were a hundred paces away talking in an animated way to a trader. One of them looked round and saw us. A chase began. We made it the few paces to our horses. We mounted up.

The whore helping the cripple.

The absurd thought came to me as we rode fast out of the city threading our way through the immobile carts and horses without looking back. We knocked over a fruit stall and some baskets as we fled the city but we could not pause. Their horses could not have been nearby since there was no sign of anyone following as we galloped through the gates. After we had ridden for a while, I was sure there was no pursuit and we slowed down.

'You saved my life,' I said. I looked at her with an involuntary respect. It was a new feeling.

'I thought you were here to protect me. I didn't think I would have to do the protecting.'

'No, nor did I.'

'We make quite a good team don't we?'

'Yes, I suppose so. I can hardly see straight after that blow to the head.'

'Are you all right?'

'No. I have to stop for a moment.'

I all but fell off my horse and vomited on the ground.

'We had better rest here for a while,' Aripele said.

'No we can't. I'm sure they'll follow. I'll manage.'

We mounted up and rode at a reasonable pace for the remains of the day, pausing every couple of hours to rest the poor horses. At nightfall we dared not light a fire and held each other to keep warm. If I had not had such a headache it would have been romantic. She was a beautiful girl.

Morning came, we ate a little and rode until we came to a stream. After watering the horses we walked them in the water for half a mile before leaving the clear icy water, to cover any tracks we might leave for the pursuers. We knew now they would follow.

My dizziness began to clear and my headache went too over the next day, but the bruising extended all the way down to my collarbone on the right side of my head. The blow must have burst a blood vessel and the area was spongy to the touch for days.

We avoided people and farms until we were near Ancyra some three weeks into the second leg of the journey. We were now well into Roman occupied Silicia and did not think that the following soldiers would chase us any further.

We had camped behind a hill off the roadside and made a small pile of wood for a fire. It was turning colder now for autumn was well on the way. There was a clear moonlit sky above us and I could point out Orion, my favourite constellation.

'There, can you see it? Those three are his belt and those at the top are his helmet.'

'It doesn't look like any shape I can make out,' Aripele said.

'Here,' I said, taking her hand in mine and pointing her outstretched finger above us. I looked at her face. She was not looking up at the sky but straight at me. I paused for a moment and as we looked into each other's eyes I think we both realised something that neither of us dared express. I dropped her hand and as it descended slowly to her side, I stepped back and sat down. There was silence then for long moments.

'I'm sorry,' she said, 'I just...'

'It's not you who should say sorry. I hadn't realised how lovely you are. It sort of struck me all of a sudden.'

'Aulus, we have a long way to go and will be spending a lot of time together. What's happening to us?'

'I don't know. I really like you, you know.' My words were lame and inappropriate; I seemed unable to express what I really felt.

'Me too,' she said.

'What about Junius?'

'What about Hypsicratea? You seem to be getting over her rather quickly?'

'I... I'm not over her.'

'But you're looking at me as if you are.'

'You were looking at me too. Maybe we should be more careful. We both have a lot of things going on in our heads.'

'I am Junius' woman and I thought you were his friend. We can't be together in that way – you said so yourself.' There seemed to be a look of regret in her eyes.

'I know. It was just a foolish impulse. Anyway nothing happened,' I said, looking at the ground.

'No but we both thought something we shouldn't.'

'You too?' I said.

'Stop it. Let's eat.'

'Yes perhaps we're just hungry.'

'It would be better if we had something hot.'

'Yes, hot,' I licked my lips.

'It would be better that way.'

'You make the fire.'

'All right, maybe you should... light... it.'

We both looked at each other and began to smile and it happened almost without a pause. I moved towards her and put my open hand on her cheek. For a moment, our eyes met. She touched my hand with hers and I drew her towards me. Our lips met in a gentle kiss. We began to explore each other. The pleasant strangeness of touching her unfamiliar body and her hands touching mine lent a sense of pleasure to the moment that quieted us both.

I heard an owl hooting. Damned birds. They seem always to bring me the worst of life. We stopped. I looked into her eyes once more, in the fading light.

'We can't do this,' she said.

'I'm sorry; I don't know what came over me. Perhaps I was trying to ease my pain. I'm sorry.'

'We're both hurting in our own way and it can't be right to try to relieve it by doing this,' she said.

She pushed me away, looking at the ground. Guilt loomed between us like some large impenetrable fog.

I said, 'No, you're right. It isn't the sensible thing to do. I'm sorry. It was just one of those moments. I would never betray my love for Hypsicratea. I don't know what we were thinking. This will be a hard journey.'

'If I was entangled with you now it would be a betrayal of all I've dreamt about for two long years. It would make a nonsense of my being here.'

'Exactly. I can't understand how this happened. Let's put it behind us and get on with the night.'

'We'll have to be careful.'

My arousal began to reduce and I thought of Hypsicratea as I tended the horses. Aripele lit the fire and we ate in silence. I hardly dared look at her. I was afraid I had ruined a good friendship.

'Maybe we need separate rooms in Ancyra when we get there,' I said.

'Yes, it's no good tempting fate. I'm very fond of you but I can't abandon Junius. If anything happened between us it would be a betrayal.'

'You know I love Hypsicratea.'

'Of course.'

'It's just I thought that I have to put those feelings away somehow. I'll probably never see her again. I can't keep away from women all my life, can I?'

'No, I understand. But I'm not free. With work it was different. There was never any emotion so it was very different. I really like you. Strange isn't it? As soon as you add emotion to it, it's as if it were a completely different act.'

'I don't understand.'

'No, you're a man.' She smiled, her dimpled cheek making her look irresistible.

'Sometimes I feel like I'm only half the man I was.'

'Don't be like that. You can get better.'

'Not according the doctors in Sinope.'

She said, 'What do you want? Sympathy? Isn't there a temple or something in Pergamum that makes people better?'

'Yes they have a temple to Asclepius. There are also very good doctors. Maybe I can get help there.'

'Are we still friends?'

'Of course.'

Sleep was elusive that night. We did not lie next to each other. Perhaps we were both afraid of what had happened but Aripele managed to sleep all the same. I kept dreaming of Hypsicratea and her face became confused with that of Aripele. I awoke once in a sweat and sat up. I thought of Aripele then and my feelings were worrying me. I could not help thinking how beautiful she was.

Surely my desire was only an attempt at distraction from my grief at losing Hypsicratea?

I was becoming confused and when I did sleep it was with a deep and nagging uncertainty prodding and goading me. I admired Aripele. She had a strength that seemed almost obscured by her beauty but I had seen how when it was needed it emerged. But I loved Hypsicratea. I knew I would never see her again. 'Surely I have to start again?' Again, the thought came back. 'If you loved Hypsicratea, how can you feel like this about another woman so soon?' It began to eat away at me. In the morning I again awoke in a sweat. I thought perhaps I was developing a fever but after eating some bread and taking watered wine, I felt better.

We rode hard and only took short breaks. We talked less, as if we were isolating ourselves in our personal thoughts. We camped in a deep gully a short distance from the road and ate, still in virtual silence.

That night was much the same as the last. There was a dampening of our friendliness. It was subdued somehow. We communicated over where we were and what we were doing but avoided anything too personal. My doubts still nagged. It was too soon. Did love mean so little? Was I really so insincere? Every time I looked at Aripele's face I felt guilt. It was borne of a desire growing within. The more I tried to stifle it the stronger it became.

In the morning we ate and finally Aripele broached the subject that we had both been avoiding as we sat by our little fire.

'Are you angry with me?' she said.

'Me? No.'

'We don't seem to be talking and laughing like before.'

'I know. Look, I'm not a weak man you know. I am not so shallow either that I would discard my feelings for Hypsicratea or Junius for that matter. It's just that being near you does something to me.'

'I know.'

'We have to be strong together. I can't betray my friend, it would be a loss of honour.'

'I love Junius too. I couldn't hurt or betray him either.'

'I'm glad we said that. We can get on with our normal friendship now.'

She looked at my face and smiled.

'Yes. Friends. Let's ride,' she said.

She spurred her horse on with a smile on her lips and her dark hair flowing behind in the gentle breeze that came from the west. I wondered at her beauty. I was dumbstruck by it and could only sit and watch as she rode on. The effect it had on me was to dwindle the guilt and make me think of my loss less often. I had thought about Hypsicratea most of the time since I had left Sinope and now that pain seemed to be fading. Was I so shallow that in only a few weeks after leaving my lover, I was thinking of someone else? I think we sometimes transfer our affection to others when we lose someone. I certainly was thinking more and more about the feel of Aripele's lips on mine and the firmness of her breasts as we had embraced only two days before. It was eating away at me and I knew it.

Chapter IV

"Gentleness is the antidote for cruelty." – Phaedrus.

Ancyra seemed an anti-climax to me when we arrived. I seemed to be acting in an odd way. I was more polite than usual and acquiesced to anything Aripele said or requested. I held doors open for her and insisted on buying the provisions from a trader on my own while she sat in a tavern resting after the ride. In short, I seemed to be trying to impress her.

It was a well-garrisoned town. There was a whole legion stationed outside and there was a legionary headquarters, staffed by soldiers and military orderlies. We had to report there when we arrived in order to register as visitors.

'Yes?' the orderly said from his desk without getting up. He seemed a mean-faced man with an expression as if he had sucked a lemon.

'We need to register. We're just passing through on our way to Pergamum.'

'You have a pass?'

'A pass?'

'Yes. You need a pass signed by the adjutant officer.'

'How can we have a pass from the adjutant officer if neither of us has been here before?'

'All the same. I'll have to issue you with a temporary pass if you don't have one,' he picked up a scroll and began scribbling.

'Name?'

'Aulus Veridius Scapula.'

'And your wife?'

'What?' I said.

'What is your wife's name?'

'I'm not married.'

'But you're travelling together?' his eyes narrowed.

'This is Aripele, my companion. She's from Pontus and we are travelling to Rome.'

'Irregular, but if it is only for one night then I suppose it's all right. Are you wanting permission to get married? The legate can give you the documents if you like. We're still under martial law you know and all aliens have to have written permission.'

'No, we don't want to get married. We are only friends,' I said.

'Friends?' He raised his eyebrows.

'Yes, friends.'

'If you say so,' he said looking at Aripele with a keen eye. She was a beautiful girl and I could read what he was thinking. He thought I was mad or lying.

We obtained the written authority and left. It seemed expensive but we had enough money to pay without problems.

'So I'm your companion am I?' Aripele said.

'Well I didn't know how to describe you.'

'Companion is fine. It is at least not as embarrassing as lover.'

'What do you mean?'

She smiled at me and we entered the tavern where we had decided to lodge. We took two rooms. They were adjacent since the tavern had few guests at that time.

We ate a hot meal of beef stew with herbs and hot bread freshly baked at the tavern. It was an excellent meal and we washed it down with liberal amounts of a local red wine which was, as ever, a little resinous for my taste but more potent than either of us was used to. The time passed and we began to relax. It was as if the wine made the self-imposed stress of the last few weeks melt away and we were our old selves again. We were friends, laughing and joking.

Neither of us was drunk but we were far from sober all the same.

'Strange how things turn out,' I said.

'How do you mean?'

'If we hadn't met by chance in the street in Sinope, Hypsicratea would never have known I was back. It was you who told her, wasn't it?'

'Yes. I felt she needed to know and she received me even though she knew I was a street-girl'

'I can't understand how such a lovely girl as you could have ended up on the streets in Sinope, selling her body.'

'It wasn't by choice you know.' She was frowning now.

'Of course, that much even I understand.'

'I don't want to talk about it.'

'Sorry, I didn't mean to upset you.'

'It doesn't upset me. I just don't want to talk about it, all right?'

I downed a cup of wine. 'Look, I'm just a soldier, forgive me if I'm clumsy.'

'You aren't a soldier any longer. A killer maybe, but you aren't in any army now.'

I said, 'No, I suppose even now I'm good at killing, something you could never do, a beautiful girl like you.'

She looked at me with a drunken regard but her eyes

narrowed a little and her voice slurred a fraction too. She poured herself some wine.

'Anyone can kill,' she said.

'Not a girl like you.'

'Oh I could.'

'Don't believe you.'

'Do we have to talk?' she said. She stared at the floor.

'It's getting a bit cooler at night now,' I said.

'What?'

'The weather, it's cooler.'

'Yes.'

There was silence and as it was late I suggested we get to sleep. We had a long ride the next day starting our journey to Pergamum, the last leg. I felt almost sorry to be setting off again. I was not sure I wanted the journey to end.

I took some more wine upstairs with me. Most rooms in traveller's taverns were sparsely furnished and this was no exception. There was a wide wicker cot in one corner under the small window. The bare boards were rough and irregular but worn in the centre of the room where countless sandaled feet had smoothed the splinters away. There was a rough table against the wall but nowhere to sit. It was, all the same, a bedroom.

I had not slept with a roof over my head for so many weeks it seemed palatial to my eyes. I put the wine on the table and poured a cup, then spread my blanket on the cot. It sagged a little in the middle and squeaked when I knelt upon it as I stared out of the window. The night was starless and there was nothing to see in the deep dense blackness outside. I had removed my sandals when there was a soft knock on my door.

I opened it a crack, peering out. She stood, legs slightly apart, with a determined look on her face. I remember the feel of the rough floorboards under my feet and thinking they were cold.

'Yes?' I said.

'What do you mean 'Yes'?'

'What can I do for the mistress, my companion?'

'Oh, stop it. Let me in.'

I opened the door and she marched straight past me to the cot and sat down. I closed the door and there was a soft click as I dropped the catch.

'And to what do I owe the pleasure of your company at this time of night?'

'Aulus, you touched a nerve when you asked me about my time on the streets in Pontus.'

'I'm sorry but it was just casual conversation. I didn't mean to offend you.'

'No, it's not that. I thought maybe I should tell you.'

'No, you don't have to tell me anything, Aripele. Anyway, your speech is slurred.'

'All the same, I want you to know I am not the sort of girl you might suppose. When it comes to relationships I am as faithful as a king's bodyguard.'

'Look, you don't have to tell me anything. We're friends.'

'My father died when I was only six – of a fever.'

I said nothing and stepped across the bare boards to sit beside her. She looked so pretty but forceful: a fighter, defending herself. Surely not from me?

'After my father died, my mother took up with a big man who liked his wine, if you know what I mean. He was often drunk and when he was drunk, he was usually violent. He beat us children and beat my mother too.'

'It's all behind you now. You don't have to tell me you know.'

'You don't understand what it was like to come home after playing out at the age of seven, to be confronted by a huge man, drunk and scowling. He would ask me where I had been and what

I had been doing, his voice booming, threatening. I knew that whatever answer I gave it would be wrong and he would beat me. There was no one to help, nowhere to run.'

I poured her a cup of wine. I wondered if it was coincidence that the tavern-keeper had given me two cups.

'You won't understand the helplessness I felt, but it made me strong in the end. I realised very early that in truth we are all alone when it comes to it. We're alone when we come into the world and alone when we leave it. My mother depended on this man, yet he beat us all. Maybe she loved him, I don't know, but I cannot forgive her for staying with him. I hated him. Once he beat me so badly I couldn't get out of bed for a week.'

'You poor thing. It must have been terrible.' I meant it, the wine was making me emotional.

She was right of course I did not understand. How could I? My childhood was so different from hers. Yes, we both shared the loneliness and isolation but the circumstances were so different.

She was becoming agitated. She gestured with her cup and a slurp of wine spilled on my tunic. Neither of us reacted. Perhaps it was because we were both drunk. Perhaps it was because of the urgency with which she wanted to impart her story.

'Aulus, in the end he raped me. He was an evil man. He raped me.'

Her eyes were moist as she looked me in the face. I had no idea what to do. If we were threatened or in a fight, I could cope. Hearing how she had suffered, I was lost.

I reached out and touched her shoulder. She looked so vulnerable. I wanted to kiss her but I was strong. I knew it would be wrong. I felt then I had moral fibre; I would not yield to worldly pleasures when there was honour at stake.

'One day when I was sixteen years old, I took a knife and stabbed him when he slept.'

'You what?' I stiffened and sat upright.

'I stabbed him hard in the chest. He opened his eyes briefly then they closed and he groaned. Blood covered my hands and my tunic; it flowed onto the floor, dripping from the edge of the cot. I ran. I wandered the streets and eventually a man took me to his home. I thought he was kind. He fed me and gave me a room to sleep in.'

'Then you were safe?'

'No. He raped me as well and then he locked the room and other men came. It became a repeating pattern. Several men every night. I ran away in the end. I began to sell myself in the street. I had no other way to survive. Men really like me you know. I earned money and had no one to pay for the privilege of being a prostitute. I saved money and in the end, I met Junius. He was the first customer whom I really liked. More than liked.'

She stopped almost breathless and looked at me.

'I didn't understand at first,' I said. 'In the end he told me he was fond of you.'

'Yes he promised to come back but never did. I wrote to him but he couldn't reply, being on the move with the legion and all.'

'He can't write, actually.'

She ignored the information and went on. 'Junius was the only one. If it wasn't for him and the chance of being with him as a respectable woman in Rome I don't know what I would have done after he left.'

Tears came then. Bitter tears. To me she seemed scared. She was more frightened of the future than I had realised. Frightened and vulnerable. I put my arm around her and she sobbed those bitter tears into my wine-sodden tunic. I smoothed her hair with my weak left hand and after a few moments she looked up at my face.

'I never told Junius the whole story. I tried, but there was always something stopping him listening.'

'He's a really good friend but he's not a very emotional man you know.'

'I know.'

'I wish I could just wave a hand and make it all go away for you,' I said.

She smiled through her tears. I had never seen her so vulnerable or so beautiful. I could resist no longer. I reached over and placed my lips on hers. She kissed me back uncertainly. I had always seen her as confident and strong. This seemed to be a very different girl as if having told me of her past she could discard it.

I reached for her and we began caressing each other. It was a gentle pleasure enhanced by the long anticipation I had been feeling. I touched her breast with my fingertips and felt her breathing escalating, urgent.

'Aulus, we shouldn't.'

'I know. Aripele, I love you.'

I said it with the earnestness and fervour that belongs only to a young man, but it might have been the wine. The words seemed to come without difficulty. Her eyes flashed but she said nothing and we made love, not with passion but with gentleness, as if the very act of love was a comfort to our tortured minds. Love illicit – more exciting than love.

We lay in each other's arms, enjoying touching, caressing. I rested my head on my hand, leaning on my elbow.

'Aripele, I love you.'

'Don't be silly, we were just drunk' she said.

'No, really I do. It takes more than a little wine to make me drunk.'

'And what about Hypsicratea? You wanted to give up everything to be with her. Don't you remember? If I wasn't here and she had come with you instead, you would be saying the same thing to her, you silly boy.'

'Perhaps you can love more than one person at a time?'

'No you can't, Aulus.'

'But I do.'

'And if you had to choose between us?'

'Whichever of you asked, I would say it was her, perhaps?'

She looked at me and smiled. She turned and slapped me in the face. Not as hard as she might, in fact not as hard as I deserved.

The conversation left me thinking. She turned over and seemed to sleep. I looked at her in the lamplight. The gentle even movement of her left breast as it rose and fell with her breathing made me smile and aroused me too.

Then I thought of Hypsicratea. Would I abandon her for Aripele? Aripele, who was my best friend's woman? The Queen of Pontus who had saved my life by taking me in when I was badly wounded and whom I had worshipped for almost eighteen months?

I began to think how shallow I had become. These feelings were a strange road for me to take who once had been a warrior, a swordsman and a Legionary of Rome. Where amongst all this mixture of emotion was the old Aulus? Was he not somewhere deep inside trying to re-establish himself? The man who wanted to be a proud and successful soldier of Rome? My great grandfather had been a consul and had led armies. Was I so much less – so much weaker than he had been?

I became sleepy and nuzzled into her. She responded by wriggling in a seductive way and I realised she was not sleeping and we made love again. It made all the thoughts disappear. I knew then that being with her was the best thing I could imagine. I wanted to be with her forever. Eventually it would not be my choice it would be hers. She had waited for an opportunity to find my friend again and she would choose in the end but I knew if it was possible I would take her into my life with all the strength and love that I could give and I would always want to be with her.

I put the future away. Facing Junius in Rome was the last thing I wanted to think about and with any luck we would never go. I had no real reason for returning apart from the amulet. I unconsciously reached for it at my neck. I half smiled remembering it had been stolen by my cousin. I focused on what it had meant to me. It had been a gift from my father and I had owned it all my life. I knew it contained the secret to the location of some deeds but was this now so important? If I could stay with Aripele I did not mind if I was poor. I was torn between the thoughts of revenge and the pressure of a new love. Sleep came gradually but that moment was one that lingered.

Chapter V

"Nature herself has never attempted to effect great changes rapidly."
– Qunitilian.

Aripele and I waited in the courtyard of the temple. I had paid an aureus for the appointment. With two more, I could have bought a slave. The doctor was reputed to be the best Greek physician in Pergamum and that meant one of the best in the empire. His fee seemed to reflect that but such things are deceptive. A knave could set his fees high in the expectation that those who paid them would assume the advice was cast-iron and not nonsense because of the exorbitant fee.

A slave called us through. He was not a servant for he had a bulky waist-belt, a token of enslavement.

'Step this way and Erasistratus of Chios will see you shortly.'

The doctor had been a royal physician to one of the Seleucid kings before he retired to Pergamum and he came recommended to us by a merchant who worked in the main forum of the city. We had talked to several such men and we were confident that

Erasistratus could not have bribed them all to recommend him. On the other hand, perhaps he could, considering his fees.

He was a tall man, elderly and bald as a marble statue. He had a broad, stooped frame and was no doubt the remnant of a big man rendered smaller and thinner by the ravages of time.

He asked me some questions and the detail was irritating. I kept my temper because I was paying for his time but I thought he should have known what I wanted from looking at me.

He laid me on a couch and prodded my stomach. He moved my arms and legs and hit my knees with a tiny hammer. They jumped and I thought he was playing silly games to impress. The whole business began to annoy me.

'How long were you unable to move the arm and leg after the injury?'

'I don't know. Maybe four weeks,' I said as he at last let me up from the couch. He shook his old head slowly. He had an odd habit of moving his mouth as he thought and I expected him to lick his lips at any moment, but he didn't.

'You were a fit man and a soldier, were you?'

'Yes I was, but my injuries have stopped me from training and my arm is weak.'

'Nonsense. You have become a fat boy because you are lazy.'

'What?' I said getting irritated.

'Yes, you have sat on you widening backside wallowing in your self-pity and the effects of your injury for far too long.'

'I didn't come here to be insulted,' I said and made to leave.

Aripele held on to my arm and made me stay.

'You had a terrible injury and you want me to give you medicaments to make you the same man you were before this all happened to you. It is not as simple as that.'

'What?' I was not at my most fluent, for my temper was finally getting the better of me.

'People come here expecting to get medicines to cure every ill, my boy. I am afraid that I do not do that. I tell the truth. I know people do not like it, but I am a physician of integrity. It is always disappointing to hear the truth but I will tell you precisely what to do to get the most out of what is left you.'

'Left me?'

'Yes, exactly.'

'You can't help me then?'

'I can help you if you listen closely and take my advice. If you do not, you will remain just as you are – a fat weak man with a weak arm and leg.'

I began to calm down. He was not saying it was hopeless.

'If you are lugging all this weight around it is no wonder you feel weak. You are eating the wrong things. Eat mainly meat and fish. Vegetables are good also but avoid fatty things. Never leave the table with a full stomach. You must exercise vigorously every day. I suggest you run for one hour each day and use your arm muscles for a similar time daily as well.'

'I have no time to exercise.'

'Then make time, sleep less and exercise instead. If you want to stay as you are then do so. Sexual activity is good too.' He smiled to Aripele when he said that and she grinned. 'I have given you my advice, whether you adhere to it or not is up to you.'

'Do you not have any medicine to give me?'

He looked at me as if I was some kind of crushed beetle stuck to the sole of his sandal.

'I am not one of those doctors who gives people false potions in the pretence that they will cure them. It is a sign of a charlatan that he not only gives false hopes but false remedies. Look, Aulus Veridius or whatever your fancy Roman name is, the injury has damaged that bit of you that used to control that arm and leg. It will not get better. You must train the rest of your brain to do what you want your weak arm and leg to do. Can I put it any simpler?'

'No sir.'

I had lapsed into a legionary's response. His personality seemed so forceful it pushed me into military mode.

'Should I sacrifice to any particular Gods?'

'You haven't heard me have you? Perhaps the injury has made you stupid too. There is nothing the Gods can do that exercise and the right diet can't.'

I thanked him though I don't know why. He was rude and had pushed me to the limits of my tolerance. Aripele however, was of an altogether different mind.

'He's very good isn't he?'

'He's lucky I didn't stick him with the knife Polymecles gave me. He was rude and did nothing to make me better.'

'You can't judge that until you've followed his advice can you?'

'Has he paid you? He wasn't an ex-customer of yours was he?'

Aripele ignored the barb.

'We will stay here for a while and see if he is right. If he isn't then we can come back and ask for the fee to be returned.'

'Simple as that?'

'Of course,' she said and she smiled one of her enigmatic smiles, leaving me, as usual, uncertain whether she was joking or serious. She was a puzzle and I loved it.

We remained in Pergamum for a month. We had planned to stay only until we could find a ship to take us to Rome but we changed our plans. Aripele insisted on staying to see if Erasistratus was right.

In desperation, I visited the temple of Aesculapius and paid to bathe in the hot spring in the temple. It did make my arm and leg feel looser and more mobile but of course, the next day it was all the same.

Aripele pushed me out of bed to go running every morning and no doubt enjoyed the extra hour in bed on her own. I had not run for more than a few steps in the last eighteen months and the first day, I walked more than I ran. Over that month, I gradually, almost imperceptibly, increased my abilities and after only two weeks found myself running for longer and longer. I discovered all the winding streets of Pergamum and the locals looked at me as if I was mad. There was no Campus Marius and no track where athletes trained regularly, so all I could do was use the streets.

At the end of three weeks I noticed an improvement in my gait. I had practised with sword and shield every day as the physician had told me and indeed felt some very mild improvement in my finger function and strength.

Aripele said that she noticed a difference in me. She said I was walking better and that my stamina when we made love was better. I had no complaints about that and nor had she.

A month after we saw the doctor I knew I was on the right road. I would have hugged him if I had seen him again, but at those prices, he could keep the money and I would reserve the hugs for Aripele.

At the end of that month we booked passage on a trireme bound for Rome as part of a convoy of coast-hugging ships carrying returning soldiers from Pergamum. The ship was not due to leave for another two weeks and I began to realise I did not want to go.

'Aripele, I think I could stay here with you for the rest of time.' I said one night. It was late and we had both drunk plenty of the local wine.

'Here? We can't stay here,' she said.

'Do you really want to choose between me and Junius?'

'Oh Aulus. I chose long ago. I love him. I think I love you too. You once said to me that you could love me and Hypsicratea and I scorned you. I know now that one can love two people, but a person has to choose. If I stayed with you then I would always wonder if it was really Junius that I needed. When we reach Rome our love affair must end. I promised Junius I would seek him out if I ever got the chance and that chance has come. I don't know how I feel about us. I have found you to be the most wonderful man I have ever met apart from Junius and I have been with many, believe me. I cannot betray the trust of a man who loves me.'

'Aripele, do you not think that leaving me is a similar betrayal?'

'No, Aulus, we both knew the cost and the consequences. I am with you but I will leave you because I promised. I really do love you but I love him too and have given my word. The word of a whore maybe, but it means much to me.'

'Aripele, I don't have the right to ask, for Junius is my friend, but can't we just stay here in Pergamum? I would give up all thoughts of revenge and getting my inheritance back to be with you. We can make a life here, you and I.'

'Please don't ask again or we will quarrel. I must go. It is my destiny. There is no more to say.'

We were unable to sleep together after that. The disappointment I felt meant that I found it difficult to be in her presence. I spent more and more time exercising, until it began to distract me from my new grief. I started to think the Gods had engineered the whole situation and that they were laughing at me. How could I feel like this? I had pined for Hypsicratea before my return to Sinope and now I faced the same feelings for Aripele. I could make no sense of it all.

Chapter VI

"Rule your mind or it will rule you" – Horace.

It took two months to reach the port of Ostia from Pergamum. We had slept on the deck of the trireme under an awning erected by the ship's crew. Even at sea it was warm enough at that time of year. There was no privacy on the ship so there had been no chance of any physical contact between us, even if that was likely to happen. Our affair had petered out as suddenly as it had begun.

We talked about what was to come rather than dwelling on the past. It was the most positive feature of our friendship. Neither of us betrayed to the other whether we were hurt by the end of our love affair. We directed the mounting tension between us towards facing Junius if ever we found him. We both had guilt-feelings and for good reason. We resolved the problem in part by once talking about it and agreeing that it would be best if Junius were never to know.

No one on the ship knew anything about the Legions or where they were and I realiszed my enquiries would have to await our arrival in Rome. I would have to go to Legion Headquarters to arrange payment of my pension. I had no one to look up in Rome in any case, it had been a friendless place for me since the death of my parents and as the ship docked, I wondered why I felt it was home.

The quay was busy with men carrying sacks in a long line from a newly arrived ship – one of those that came from Sicily carrying African grain. I could see the slaves sweating in the morning sun. There was a smell of fish, and when the wind gusted I could smell the odour of the Tiber carried in the air. It was a familiar smell and one bringing back memories. I could almost feel the weight of my shield and helmet as I recalled the last time I was in Ostia. We were boarding then, not disembarking, but the sight of the docks held the same aura and evoked memories so clearly in my head it was like travelling back in time. We stepped back to dry land and it seemed as if the ground rose and fell beneath my feet after the long sea voyage. I could see a temple where three priests stood arguing about something outside.

'What place is that?' asked Aripele, indicating the round temple.

It had deep red-coloured wooden columns around a square inner temple. Above the entrance was a triangular stone relief depicting Hercules slaying the Nemean Lion and in the background was a Medusa's head. The Medusa's head reminded me of a ring my father had once made for the Chief Vestal. He was murdered before it could be delivered but I discovered afterwards that it had been sold by one of Marcus Mettius' slaves to a jeweller, and when I found out, it explained a lot.

'I don't know. It wasn't here when I left.'

When I enquired, they told me it was the new temple to Hercules built by Lucilius Gamala, the town Mayor. He was a supporter of Marcus Tullius Cicero, the brother of my old commander when I first joined the Ninth Legion.

'What happened to the walls?' she enquired as we walked through the crowded streets. where a stonemason was mustering fifty or so sweating slaves , himself looking flustered and angry.

'They were thrown down originally by Marius when he invaded the town in the old Marian-Sullan war. Then some pirates invaded only a few years ago but Pompey destroyed them. I suppose they're still building and repairing them. It may go on for years.'

'I want you to tell me all about Rome as we see it.' She was excited and I was glad to show off my knowledge. I realised then how I was a Roman to the core because I took such pride in telling Aripele about the history of Ostia as we walked to the northern edge of town, surrounded by busy, happy people. The sounds of the port were like music to my ears after the long sea voyage in which the only sounds had been the sailors talking or shouting and birds crying overhead, high above the sound of lapping waves on the side of the ship.

We passed street vendors plying their wares, children playing and groups of people talking quietly, or loudly gesticulating with their arms and hands as only Romans do. Carts laden with grain bound for the city passed us in long lines wending their slow, tortuous way to feed the people of Rome.

It was wonderful to be back especially to be back as a free man and not as a soldier. I did not have to march with the men or stop when instructed. The freedom seemed odd. I was only in my mid-twenties yet I felt as if I had been a legionary for most of my life, the habits were so ingrained in me.

'How far away is Rome?'

'About a day's march for a soldier. Longer for us unless we ride. We can hire horses if you like. It would be better than walking all that way. We will need to spend tonight here in Ostia. There are plenty of taverns where we can stay.'

'Aulus, it will be our last night before Rome.'

'I know.'

'It will be strange.'

'Not so strange. We both have different futures and we have accepted that, haven't we?.'

'We still have tonight to say goodbye.'

'Yes, tonight.'

We looked at each other and both understood. She was intuitive and read my needs easier than I had a right to expect. It was late afternoon and it was cold, for winter was upon us. Wrapped in our cloaks we found a small tavern where we could eat and take a room for the night. I baulked at the cost, for prices were not only much higher than Pergamum, they had risen even since I was last home.

We sat in a corner next to a brazier and as the day waned, we ate a meal of bread and fish. We drank a delightful local white wine grown on the slopes of the south-facing hills nearby. Some legionaries on an adjoining table were laughing and tussling in high spirits. One of them overbalanced and grabbed our table, tilting it and spilling my wine.

'Hey, you,' I said. 'Better spill blood than my wine.'

He looked at me and then realised I was joking.

'Sorry about that. Can I buy you some more?'

'No it's all right. You can give me some information though.'

'Of course.' he was a grizzled veteran of maybe forty years old. A scar adorned hi forehead and his left arm showed a deep scar. He smiled at me as I spoke.

'I wonder if you know where the Ninth Hispania is stationed. I've been away a long time and need to make contact with some old friends.'

'You were in the Ninth?'

'Yes, for almost five years before I got injured.'

'So you were at Artaxarta?'

'No I was at Tigranocerta and my injuries prevented me rejoining my legion. I heard all about it though and wish I hadn't missed it.'

He leaned forward in his seat, pointing a finger at me for emphasis.

'I know what you mean. Well, I don't know exactly where the Ninth would be now. Last I heard they were north of Rome and marching to the fight with the rebels.'

'Rebels?'

'Yes haven't you heard?'

'I've been on a ship for two months. Tell me.'

'A senator called Catalina has raised an army and is trying to take over the government. There are two legions on their way north and two legions moving south from Segesta to finish him off. No cause for alarm. It's a foregone conclusion that the Senate will win.'

'You think the Ninth is one of the legions moving north then?'

'Probably. You can find out once you get to Rome; everyone is talking about it.' He turned to his comrade beside him and said, 'That's right isn't it Laetus?'

His friend nodded and drank his wine. We chatted some more about the Pontics and Armenians and I passed on the little news that I had. Aripele and I stood to leave.

'Your wife?' enquired the soldier looking at Aripele, with admiration.

'Er... yes, that's right,' I said.

'You're a very lucky man. Take good care of her.'

Aripele smiled and he smiled at her too, which I found irritating. I wondered why I felt so jealous. She was, after all, not my woman.

Alone in the tavern's bedchamber we undressed and made love. It was the first time for two months and we both clung to each other as if it was the end of more than a passing relationship. I think neither of us could have explained how it came about but it seemed natural and in a sense it was an easy way of saying goodbye. We wanted each other. It was as simple as that and we both knew we could not be together once we reached Rome and found Junius.

In the morning, we hired horses. My heart was heavy.

'Deliver them back to my partner at the Servian Gate. If you don't know where that is, then just ask, it's well known. If you ask for Barbato I'm sure you can find him.'

'I know the Servian Gate well.'

'By the way, not that I don't trust you, but horse thieves are sent to the arena just so you know.'

'Do I look like I would steal a horse from you?'

'No, but the last one who tried was a patrician called Mettius and I had to hunt high and low before I got the horse back.'

'Marcus Mettius?'

'Yes he's one of the Costa family. Very rich but just decided not to return the horse. Said he forgot. I had the job of Perseus to get the nag returned and had to resort to the law courts in the end.'

'When was that?'

'Only a few weeks ago. Let me see... It was about a month after Saturnalia so it was about five weeks ago.'

'I'll return the horses, don't worry.'

We rode to Rome. It was a long and winding road leading east then north from the port. We wore our cloaks since the weather had changed and it was cold with a bitter wind blowing from the north.

'Marcus Mettius, is he the one that you were going to find?'

'Yes I think it was him who hit me on the head and stole my amulet.'

'Why is the amulet so important to you?'

'Inside it my father carved directions to where some property deeds are hidden and this Mettius fellow wants them. I don't quite know why the property is so important to him. As far as I can recall, it's just a small estate near Ariminium.'

'Was he in the legion with you?'

'Sort of. I had no choice but to join the Ninth Legion when I was caught stealing.'

'Yes I know.'

'Well I came across him in Sinope. He'd joined as a tribune but I have no idea whether it was just luck or design.'

'It seems a bit beyond co-incidence.'

'Yes maybe someone recognised me. Either way, he has my property and I intend to get it back.'

'How?'

'I haven't worked that one out yet. I don't even know if he is still in Rome or with the Legion.'

It took five hours of solid riding to get to the Servian Gate where, with some difficulty, we managed to leave the horses with the right stableman. He insisted on checking every anatomical part of the nags we had ridden and kept trying to suggest we had mistreated them. I gave as good as I got and he desisted in the end. He wanted money I suppose but he got none from me. Everyone in Rome seemed to want to rob you or overcharge you. Nothing had changed.

We passed through the gate where the familiar sights and sounds evoked nostalgic. It brought back recollections of my former life, some good and some bad. I knew exactly where to go to find accommodation. There was a well-known tavern on the edge of the Forum Boarium not far from the entrance to the Subura that was still there and thriving.

I told Aripele all the history I could as we walked and began to feel like a tour guide. I discovered I knew a lot about Rome for I had a good teacher in my youth and I soon began to feel at home in the city.

We made our way towards the Subura which I knew well from my days on the streets of Rome as a thief. We hired a room and ate downstairs in the tavern. We drank wine and, I thought to the envy of the tavern's customers, went to bed early.

'Aulus. Now we are in Rome we cannot remain lovers any longer.'

'Why?'

'Because whatever I feel for you, I now have to face Junius.'

'We might not even find the Ninth Legion for a long time.'

'True, but I am Junius' woman. Not yours.'

'But I need you Aripele.'

'We've both let him down by our behaviour on the journey and we can't continue. Be sensible.'

'But I want you above all other women. I mean that. You aren't married to him anyway. You haven't seen him for two years. I'm here now.' I said.

'No. It's finished. You can't sleep with me now. Surely we don't have to have separate rooms, do we?'

'No, but I don't understand.'

'Rome has to be for me and Junius if he and I are to be together. If I continue as your lover it will spoil it all for me. I will have memories of us and it will interfere. You surely care enough for me not to spoil my life here don't you?'

'I think you're being unreasonable. We're together and we feel for each other, yet you won't let me near you. You're chasing a dream. Even if we find him, he's in the legion for another thirteen years. Had you thought of that? He'll be away most of the time and will leave you playing house in the cheapest part of Rome or else you can become a camp follower. Is that what you want?'

'And what are you offering? You have no work, no land, the army thinks you are dead and all you have left is hopes of revenge on an impossible target. Wake up.'

A cloud of dust rose in the air between us as I thumped my hand on the bed.

'Women. Who can understand you. Not me.'

She put her hand on my arm.

'Aulus, can't we be friends anyway? We have been through much in the last few months. It shouldn't end with anger.'

She looked so pretty. I tried to take her in my arms and she pushed me away. My frustration rose and fell but remained there between us like a wall that neither of us could scale. It pushed us apart and left me with my feelings of rejection, frustration and longing.

The night passed and I think neither of us slept well and we did not speak even when dawn brought its first grey nimble rays through the cracks in little window shutters. I had pondered on my dilemma all night and concluded I had to have her. I knew also it could not happen and decided to go to the Campus Martius to exercise. It was my only release from the pent-up emotion. She seemed to be sleeping when I closed the door.

I returned in a more cheerful frame of mind having mulled over the entire predicament. The exercise had done me good in that respect for I was determined to remain friends if she would offer me nothing else. She was allowing me to peep over our barrier but not vault over it.

We went to the baths together. Aripele had never been in a Roman bathhouse. It was one of the large public thermae near the Circus. They did not allow men inside until the early afternoon and women used it in the morning. I had to bribe the slave at the door to let me in to the men's facility which was of course, empty. Aripele went into the women's entrance and as she entered she paused half turning and gave me a little wave. I wondered whether the unfamiliar routine to which the slave was introducing her to would make her feel daunted.

I had to hire sandals to insulate my feet from the heated floors and also hire a slave with a strigil for I had not been to the baths for so long I had none of the accoutrements. I began with a scraping and massage. The slave scraped my skin free of the oil and dirt while I pondered what to do next now I was home in Rome. I needed to find the Legionary Headquarters and let them know I was still alive. I hoped Junius would have entered my name on the roll of missing soldiers and it would be a simple matter to claim my pension. It was enough to live on but I would need work.

Swimming in the ice-cold water of the frigidarium, I realised the movement on my left side was almost back to normal. Because it was so much better, I had hardly noticed the improvement. Any weakness was imperceptible now. It occurred to me how unjust I had been over the advice I had received from the Greek doctor in Pergamum.

I had no clean tunic with me so I had to don the one in which I had arrived, despite which I felt clean and refreshed. I waited outside for Aripele. The lady citizens came and went for one could bathe for several hours in the state owned thermae for only one copper *as*.

I looked around and it dawned on me that although I was no stranger, I knew no one in the city. A good thief makes no friends. I wondered what had happened to my neighbour Julius with whom I had play-fights all those years ago when I was growing up. Probably untraceable. In any case what was there to say to him apart from that I was there?

Aripele emerged from the baths with a smile on her face and a rosiness to her cheeks I had not seen before.

'Aulus. It was wonderful. I met some really interesting ladies. They were really friendly and some of them were rich. I have been invited for a midday meal by one of them. Should I accept? Her name is Flavia Ostoria. She gave me directions to meet her at the Forum Romana. Where's that?'

'Hey, wait a minute. Not so fast. You may need to stop for breath sometime. Anyway it's Forum Romanum, you made it feminine.'

'Well whatever it's called I want to go.'

'All right, I'll take you. It's near where I have to go to enquire about my pension. They owe me two years back pay on it.'

'I need to buy a new gown like the ladies here wear.'

'Don't worry we can do that this morning. I can delay my trip to the military headquarters until then. Have you money? I'm running out.'

'Yes I still have plenty left. How long it will last I do not know.'

I knew the army owed me money. It all hinged on whether they had kept me on the books or not, but I was hoping there would be a record of my injury and whereabouts after Lucullus had defeated the Armenians. My ignorance of financial and military matters still amazes me.

If the pension did not materialise, I had no way to keep a roof over my head, unless I allowed Aripele to pay for me and her money had to last her until she found Junius. My pride would never allow me to accept her charity and anyway I was confident the army would not let me down. I must have expected life to be easy. I could not have been more wrong.

Chapter VII

"Lawyers are men who hire out their words and anger." – Horace

We walked around at the northern end of the Forum Romanum before parting company. It was the biggest and busiest forum in Rome. Situated in the very centre of the city, between the Capitoline and Palatine hills, it was always crowded during the day. It bustled. There was an atmosphere of community in the place. Here and there were street vendors selling anything from food to clothing. There were small podia for political speakers and there were queues of people waiting to enter the temple of Castor and Pollux to pray. Everyone went to the forum, to gossip, to relax, to eat and generally to participate. It was the hub of Roman life and the sounds and smells had not changed at all. The scent of people, food and incense, all mixed to produce an odour of humanity that was characteristic. I loved it and it brought back memories of my childhood when I had visited with my parents.

'Look over there' I said, releasing her hand and pointing.

'What's that?'

'It's the Basilica Sempronia. They built it on the site of a house owned by the Scipio family. The chap who built it was the father of the Gracchus brothers.'

'Who?'

'The Gracchi were brothers and part of a famous family linked by marriage to Scipio Africanus but they all died violent deaths. This building is almost all that survives of them. That's the Regia, over there,' I said pointing.

'Regia? What's that?'

'We had kings a long time ago and they lived there.'

'It doesn't look very big. If I was a king I would have built somewhere bigger – more palatial if you know what I mean.'

'In those days their engineering skills were not as good as ours are now. They didn't know how to build big buildings. These days it's only the Pontifex Maximus, high priest of Rome who lives there, a chap called Gaius Julius Caesar. He's a pen pusher and there were some amusing rhymes about him having a naughty relationship with the king of Bythinia.'

'Really?'

'Well yes, I think it was long ago when he was sent there on an embassy.'

'What was the rhyme?'

'No, it's rude.'

'Please, tell me. You can't keep quiet now.'

'I only know the first four lines. It goes:

"*What'ere Bythinia and her lord possess'd,*
Her lord who Caesar in his lust caress'd",

'I won't repeat the other two lines. Even I, a crude soldier, don't find them appealing. A chap called Calvus Licinius wrote it. Made Caesar a laughing stock, but didn't stop Caesar becoming Pontifex Maximus or Consul.'

'There are a lot of man to man relationships in our society. They don't consider it shameful in Greece either you know.'

'Well we do. Anyway, enough history lessons for one day. You're wearing me out. You need to go up there and I'm going this way.'

I was feeling a little awkward. My Greek tutor had once tried to seduce me and although I had pushed him away and run to a life of crime in the Subura afterwards, some of my thoughts about that had made me ashamed, for they occasionally haunted me. I know that at the time I was horrified, but later I had moments when I had almost felt attracted to him in my thoughts. It later made me question the quality of my friendship with even Junius, for we had been very close through all those year in Pontus and Armenia. It was never a physical affection but much lurked in the mud I suspect. I have never felt strongly about men being together but it is not something that has ever really attracted me either. It never formed part of my life. I'm not Greek after all. All to their own, I suppose.

I left Aripele to find her new friend and gave her instructions for her return journey. She seemed too excited to take it in but I knew she was resourceful enough to manage. I walked across the Forum towards the Viminal where the military headquarters were. There were records of all enlisted soldiers there and I hoped they had records of my pension.

The building I sought was next to the Library of Bacchus. Most of the archived information about the army was kept in the library and highly qualified slaves manned the Military Resource Centre. I entered and a uniformed slave with a white tunic dusted with chalk, greeted me. He seemed to have an air of pride and arrogance. I assumed he was the man in charge.

'Excuse me,'

'Yes?' he said, looking down his nose at me as if I was a beetle he was about to step on.

'I was injured in Armenia and left behind. I have now recovered from my injuries and want my pension, which I believe should normally have been paid since the Battle of Tigranocerta.'

'Really?' he looked me up and down with the same disdain.

'Who do I see about pensions?'

'Well I can deal with it.'

'What do I do?'

'Come with me.'

We went inside a large colonnaded room, to a desk at which the slave seated himself. There was only the one chair and I remained standing in front of the man.

'Name?' he said taking a wax tablet from under the desk.

'Aulus Veridius Scapula.'

He scribbled.

'Rank?'

'Decurion.'

He looked at me with doubt written all over his face.

'You don't seem old enough to be a Decurion.'

'I was promoted after my tribune was killed. I survived a battle against corsairs near Sinope and they promoted me. Look, will this take long, I have to meet someone.'

'No, not long at all. I just have to check what you say against the register of missing soldiers and verify your identity.'

'My identity?'

'Well, obviously. Anyone could come in here and claim to be you.'

'What?'

'Anyone could say they were at Tigranocerta two years ago and expect us to be stupid enough to give them a pension. Couldn't they?' He began writing.

'Well, yes I suppose so. How do I prove who I am?'

'Have you no identification of any sort? Letters, bills of lading, a signed statement from your commanding officer? Oh, yes you said he was killed, didn't you?'

'No not at Tigranocerta. That was earlier. My commanding officer was Gaius Valerius Procillus and Gaius Calvus Vegetius was my centurion. I was in the first century second cohort of the Ninth Legion Hispania.'

'But you can't prove it?'

'There must be some record?'

'Yes, we have records but the Ninth Legion is now half way to Aretium and I have to have documentary proof of identity or I can't pay you a pension. You can understand that, can't you?'

'How about this?' I drew my sword to the alarm of several slaves nearby who hid behind the stone pillars. 'It's the sword the Legion awarded me after a sword contest here in Rome.'

It was illegal to have a bladed weapon inside the city walls, but I had hidden it beneath my cloak since I thought I would need it.

I showed him the forged letters on the blade: LEGIO IX HISPANIA.

'That's very nice,' he sounded impatient now, 'but it could have been taken from anyone.'

'You have written records then? Reports, lists of soldiers?' I sheathed my sword. I thought I would get away with it.

'I will check those as a routine. Is there no-one who can vouch for you?'

'Well yes, I suppose so. Would it be enough to talk with an ex-Prefect of the Ninth who knows me?'

'Only if he produced a sworn document ratified by the courts that your identity is genuine.'

'How long would that take?'

'Let me see,' he consulted a scroll in front of him on the desk, 'Next Ides. The Aedile who deals with documentary validation is away visiting his relatives in Croton and won't be back until the Ides. Annual leave is always a problem.'

I counted on my fingers. It gave me two weeks before I could even start to get any money.

'I'll run out of money if I wait until then. Surely, you wouldn't let an old soldier languish on the streets, penniless and starving. There must be some emergency provision?'

'Of course. The Legion can give you money direct from the legionary funds they carry with them.'

'But you said they were on their way north.'

'Yes, you could try to catch up with them.'

'On foot?'

'You have no means of transport?'

'No, of course I don't have means of transport. I've just arrived from Sinope you bastard.' I gripped the hilt of my gladius, then dropped my hand to my side. It was becoming ridiculous. Nothing but red tape and delays.

'There's no need to lose your temper,'

'You must give me something.'

The man shook his head, 'I'm sorry sir, but we have regulations and I cannot transgress them.'

'What can you do then?'

'All I can do is make a file of the information you have so far provided and keep it to hand. I will search our archives personally. You must come back with something in writing for the Aedile to co-sign then we can apply to the Military Services Commission for the payments. That takes a while, maybe two weeks and then the pension is yours. Simple.'

'Don't you understand I could starve to death before then?'

'I'm sorry sir but that's all I can do. Anyway, no one starves in Rome, you know that. The free bread ration allows everyone to eat, doesn't it?'

'I'm a crippled soldier damn it. I'm no beggar,' I said but my words were becoming unconvincing even to myself.

I thumped the desk with my closed fist. The slave indicated to two Town Guards at the other side of the room and they approached. I had one on each side as they walked me to the entrance.

I descended the steps wondering what to do. I had no one in Rome who could verify my identity apart from my cousin Marcus and the man who had forced me into the legion when he caught me stealing. It was Marcus who had crippled me in order to steal the amulet, so asking for his help for a pension was as useful as a manicure to a dead horse.

That left only Quintus Cerialis the old retired prefect of the Ninth, but I did not even know if he was alive. I knew where he lived: I had tried to burglarise his house. It was how he caught me. Either I went to him or I tried to reach the legion. With no choices left, I decided to try Cerialis.

I walked to the Quirinal. The large flat cobbles with their ground-in grouting of horse manure were uneven beneath my sandaled feet as I looked up at the street markers on the corners. Nothing had changed in Rome, not even the smell of the Tiber. Cerialis had a small house there, dwarfed by the mansions all around. It was what had attracted me to the house in the first place. It stood apart and a little isolated. Easy housebreaking. Looking at the exterior, it was clear he had not bothered too much with the upkeep or maybe he had not been able to afford to keep the walls whitewashed and the cracks filled.

I rang the bell. He had not had any slaves when last I had been there. Returning brought back to mind the dread I had experienced when I had first seen him. He had prodded me with his gladius and I had thought that he was going to kill me at the time.

I waited. Nothing happened for a long time and I was in two minds whether to leave or continue ringing the bell, when I heard a noise from inside.

The door opened with a sudden movement. He swung it wide. He wore a breastplate. He carried a sword in his hand. He moved fast and before I could react, his sword was at my throat.

'I warned you.'

'Hey, wait a moment.'

I found myself struggling against a vice-like grip on my arm and a gladius impressing my throat.

'What?' His one eye looked quizzically at me. The long scar from his forehead to his chin shone white as it crossed the opaque eye and trailed away across the corner of his mouth. I had never seen it quite so clearly. It must have been a horrible injury; how he had survived it, could only be the Gods' intervention. I thought he looked mad. Not raving but just a little mad. His one good eye glared at me.

'What?' he said again.

'I'm Aulus Veridius. You haven't spoken to me in seven years.'

'What?' he said again, puzzled.

'Aulus Veridius. Don't you remember me?'

'No. Who are you?'

'The thief. I'm the thief. You caught me and made me join the Ninth. It was years ago. You must remember.'

A look of recognition seemed to flicker across the gaze of his eye. His grip relaxed a little and the sword tip wavered enough for me to straighten my head, bent back as it was, by the pressure of the gladius.

'You with them?'

'Who?'

'The thieves.'

'No, I was with the Ninth until about two years ago when I was injured. I've just got back to Rome.'

'Just returned to Rome?'

He had a look of complete incomprehension on his scarred face.

'Look let's start again. I'm Aulus Veridius Scapula. I was a thief and you caught me. You made me join the Ninth and I have been with them ever since. Now do you remember?'

He let go of me and sheathed his sword seeming almost reluctant to do so.

'Sorry, I thought you were somebody else. Don't get many visitors. Hope I didn't hurt you.'

'No, I've had worse,' I said with a smile. 'Can I come in?'

'Yes, yes.'

I followed Cerialis into his home. It was a scene of complete destruction. Someone had piled up the sparse furniture in a corner and I could see it had been damaged and broken up. The alcoves in the atrium in which we stood were empty, except for one which held a statue of a soldier holding aloft a sword. There were no other statues nor tapestries or death masks on the wall, as would have been usual in a Roman home. The floor tiles were broken and the mosaic ripped up.

'What happened here?' I asked.

'Robbers, that's what. I thought you were them, coming back. That they didn't kill me was a wonder. I grabbed my statue and barricaded myself in the bedchamber upstairs then challenged them to come up but they didn't. They wrecked the place and shouted they would return. I thought you were one of them. Sorry.'

'That's terrible. I'll help you clear up. I need some help from you but it can wait.'

'Clear up? How do you mean?'

'The furniture. You can't leave the place looking like this. Some of it can be mended. What were they after?'

'I don't have a lot of money. Enough, yes, but not a lot. They must have thought that with living on the Quirinal I was rich. If they come back I'll kill them.'

He was a man who would have been too young to retire from the legions although he had achieved the highest possible rank short of Tribune. The Primum Pila or first spear was Legionary Prefect, the man who ran the legion. He was a sort of super centurion, who oversaw the other centurions and their work and had a hand in discipline and logistics. To achieve that position was to be the General's right hand man. Cerialis had risen through the ranks both because of his fighting skills and his organisational ability. He was short, broad and tough. He had a strong sense of honour and was not an unkind man. I knew this from my previous encounter with him.

We cleared up as much as possible, separating that which was broken from that which was not and ended sitting in the peristylium, the colonnaded garden, in the winter sunshine. He produced some wine and looked at me, pausing before he spoke.

'So what happened?' he said.

'In the legion you mean?'

'Yes.' He took a sip of wine and stared hard at my face.

'You were right.'

'Oh?'

'Yes, the legion taught me all those things you said I needed. I was in Crete to put down a rebellion and then went to Pontus under Lucullus. I fought at Tigranocerta but was badly injured and they sent me to Sinope to die. I didn't. Here I am.'

'More detail please.'

I told him the whole story. I held nothing back, not even how I was sure it was Marcus, my cousin, who had left me for dead on the battlefield. I told him of the loss and significance of the amulet. He only said 'Oh' and 'Ah' in various places and seemed thoughtful.

'Meridius is dead is he?'

'Yes. He was a good man.'

'Yes, it was Meridius, who saved my life when I got this,' he pointed to the unseeing eye and the scar on his face. 'Yes. I'm glad he trained you,' he went on, 'he was the champion of the legion. I never saw a man who could wield a sword as well as he could. You said you needed help?'

I explained what I needed.

'There's no problem there. I can deal with the identification problem and we don't need an Aedile to countersign anything. I have contacts.'

'What was the reason for the men breaking in? They didn't steal anything.'

'No, they didn't even get the statue you tried to steal.'

I smiled in reply, remembering our first meeting.

'One of my neighbours,' he went on, 'has been pressurising me to sell the house and it may have been something to do with that. He's complained over and over again that my boundaries overlap his which they don't.'

'Can't you go to the courts?' I asked.

'He's a lawyer himself. It would be useless without a very powerful attorney which frankly, I can't afford.'

'I can help if it's a fight. I owe you that much for putting me in the Ninth.'

'Owe me? No lad, you owe me nothing. A little comradeship as a fellow pensioner from the legion maybe, but nothing else. I would appreciate the help though if they come back. All my friends are away with the legion straightening out this Cataline conspiracy.'

'I heard something about that. Who is this Catalina?'

'He's a senator and a top rank patrician. He's raised an army of veterans and malcontents and is marching to Rome. Tried to start an armed uprising in the city too but Marcus Tullius Cicero found out and quashed it. The lads are moving north to deal with the Cataline army.'

'Who's leading our men?'

'Antonius Hybrida. He's quite experienced but I heard he was part of the Cataline conspiracy in the first place so I don't quite know what's going to happen. He's an animal. He tortured people and stole when he was in Greece after Sulla left to return to Rome. He's still facing charges.'

'What do I need to do about the pension?'

'Nothing, leave it to me. You've been recorded by that pompous git in charge of records have you?'

'Yes, he wrote about me on a wax tablet and said he would look out my details.'

'You won't have to do anything then. I can take care of it.'

'I need to thank you though. We're staying near the Forum Boarium.'

'We?'

'Yes I have a friend with me. It's a girl. She came with me from Pontus to find a friend of mine whom she fell in love with when we were stationed there. Her name is Aripele.'

'Pregnant is she?'

'No, nothing like that, she just wants to see him and get married I think.'

'You can both stay here if you like. That way if those brigands come back we can together give them a run for their denarii.'

'You're very kind. I'll ask her tonight. I'm sure she won't mind.'

'That's settled then. All this talk makes me thirsty. More wine?'

'No really, I must go and find Aripele. She should be back by now and the light is fading. Perhaps we could come tomorrow?'

'Tonight if you like. This business of the break-in has me more rattled than I would have thought possible. It's not like me after all the fighting I've done in my time, but there you are.'

'Don't worry we'll see to them. If not tonight, then tomorrow.'

I left the house wondering how I had come to such friendly relations with Cerialis. He was a hard, dangerous man, and from my previous exposure I hadn't imagined I would ever befriend him. They had still talked about him in the Ninth when I was in Sinope. The Prefect had held off a band of Marcomannii on a bridge to allow his men to get away. He killed more than twenty single-handed and in the end was badly wounded. A picture arose in my mind of the first time I had seen him. He had tied me up and threatened to torture me. I was only a boy then and it worked. My fear had made me compliant and respectful – and incontinent. I regretted my life of crime and found myself in the legions. I had so wanted to become a successful soldier and there was always a background feeling that I wanted to live up to the expectations thrust upon me by this fearsome retired soldier. I had little prescience. If I had, I would have seen that I would not let him down.

Chapter VIII

"Remember when life's path is steep to keep your mind even." – *Horace.*

I walked down the Vicus Longus towards the Forum Boarium as dusk was approaching. Rome always had a threatening air after dark because the street lighting was negligible and these days that was true even outside the Subura, the most lawless part of the city. Our laws forbade weapons inside the inner walls of the city or Pomerium. I had only carried a stout stick, although I had the dagger that Polymecles had given me hidden beneath my tunic next to my sword.

Aripele was not there when I reached the tavern. I went to the room and changed my clothes. I hid the sword under the cot. Then I sat down and waited. I began to worry. Minutes passed. I donned my cloak and went downstairs to find the tavern-keeper.

'Have you seen the girl who travels with me?' I asked.

'No, I thought she left with you this morning.'

'Yes, she did but she went to the Forum to meet a friend and I've had business elsewhere. I don't know whether to go out to look for her or wait. I don't like the idea of her wandering around Rome in the dark.'

'You would be wise to find her. She's quite a pretty thing. A lot of nasty people around here at night.'

'Would you keep an eye out for her? I'm going to look. If she returns could you make sure she stays here.'

'I could send my son Verus with you if you like; he's handy in a fight.'

'No, it's all right; I can look after myself thanks.'

He gave me an odd look as I walked out of the tavern with the intention of retracing our steps to the Forum Romanum. I walked quickly. I wondered whether I might have been wiser to take the tavern-keeper up on his offer. It was very dark and although light filtered from the tiny tenement windows anyone could waylay me in the streets.

I'd walked for maybe ten minutes when I saw her. She was unmistakeable even in the gloomy moonlight but it may just have been my familiarity with her body and walk. What I did notice was she was not alone. About fifty paces behind her were three men outlined in the moonlight. They kept their distance at first, but seemed to quicken their step all at once.

I speeded up and called to her.

'Aripele. Where have you been? I've been worried sick.'

'Aulus,' she was more than a little drunk and she threw her arms around my neck.

'Where have you been?' I said.

'I had a wonderful time. I forgot how much I missed female company. You're lovely but you make a poor woman,' she giggled until she hiccoughed and she stroked my face with her hand.

I could see over her shoulder how the three men were closing in. My presence seemed not to bother them. I felt for my dagger and grasped my stick.

'Let's go,' I said. The prospect of getting in a fight with a drunken girl in tow was not attractive.

'But Aulus, it's such a lovely night, can't we walk for a while.'

'I thought you could take care of yourself?'

'I can, but I had a little more wine than was wise and got a bit lost on the way here.'

'Don't look behind,' I whispered in her ear,. 'There are three men following you.'

'Only three?' she waved her outstretched arm in a dismissive gesture. 'I can take them on. They don't know a real woman when they see one.'

I grasped her around the waist and we began to walk back the way I had come. I was hoping there would at least be a few people still around in the streets.

A little rain began to fall. It was not a cold rain but a vertical soft shower, out of place in Rome's winter. I thought to myself it felt like a spring rain as we walked, but I was just distracting myself. I could feel my heart beating and noted the speed of my breathing. The prospect of taking on three men armed with Gods know what, on wet cobbles, did nothing for my confidence. Had I been alone I could have run away and taken each one singly but I had an inebriate Aripele with me and she was not running anywhere.

We rounded a corner and I quickened our pace. The cobbles were slippery underfoot and the poor light left us tripping and slipping as I tried to get us back to the tavern.

I heard them run behind me and realised I had to stand my ground.

I turned, gently pushing Aripele ahead and to one side. She turned too and stood blinking and swaying a little as she watched. I heard her hiccough again. The three men, armed with cudgels, came at me all at once. If my fears of a weak left arm were real things would go against me. I drew my dagger with my right hand and had the stick in my left to use as a shield. I backed fast to one side as they approached. They had to come at me in turn then, or fall over each other in the narrow street.

The first man aimed for my head. I parried with my stick. I stabbed him in the chest. Left arm up. Right arm forward. It was very fast, almost reflex. He went down. There was a warm wet feeling on my chest.

The other two stepped back. They had not expected to fight an armed man.

Then they both attacked at once. Each used his club sideways. I leapt back and as they missed, I hit the left hand assailant smartly on the forehead. It broke the stick, so it must have been a hard enough blow.

He stumbled and fell to his knees. I forgot about him. The last man came forward swinging his club from side to side. He launched himself at me. He raised his cudgel above his head. I stepped forward much as one might with a sword. I stabbed him in the midriff. The club descended anyway. It caught me on the right shoulder. An old wound was there; the scar hurt me. I let go the dagger. He stumbled away, the knife handle protruding from the front of his tunic.

The second man was on all fours to my right. I knelt with my knee in the small of his back. I slipped my good arm around his neck. I twisted underarm until I heard a crunch. He collapsed under me and lay still. He wasn't breathing.

It was over. I felt my heart racing. I was alive and almost unscathed. I knew then that I really was the killer that Aripele had painted me as in Ancyra. Their deaths meant nothing to me. Taking their lives had been physically hard but I felt nothing. No remorse, only a grim satisfaction borne of the certainty that had it not been their deaths it would have been mine.

Aripele had sobered up enough to realise what was happening. She approached me and attempted to help me up. It was unnecessary.

My shoulder felt as if it was on fire because of the old healed wound there, but I knew there was nothing broken. I was out of breath but needed my knife back – it was a parting gift from Polymecles after all – so I dragged Aripele away by the hand and we followed the dying man. We found him sprawled in a doorway and I was able to reclaim my weapon. I searched him but found nothing of interest, merely a few copper *as* that I disdained – I'm no thief.

'Let's hurry,' I said.

'Are there more of them?' she said, looking around.

'No, but it's illegal to have a bladed weapon in the city.'

'But they attacked you.'

'Makes no difference; if the authorities knew I had a dagger then they'd call it murder.'

'What if anyone saw us?'

'We just have to chance that. Come on.'

I grabbed her hand and we ran as fast as we could, Aripele a little unsteady, and I, limping from the effort.

The tavern's proprietor came to us as soon as we entered. He was a plump, genial, balding man of a pleasant disposition. We were soaking wet and must have looked alarmingly bedraggled.

'Are you two all right?' said the landlord, hurrying forward. A few disinterested heads turned towards us as we entered the tavern but no one stared.

'No we aren't all right,' Aripele said.

'We were attacked but managed to fight them off and they ran away.' I said.

'Ran away?'

'Yes.'

'Looking at your tunic that one didn't run anywhere. I presume it isn't your blood?'

'I gave one of them a head wound and it must have bled a lot in the struggle.'

'If you say so. No one around here will ask any questions in any case and I won't tell anyone. The streets aren't safe and we all know it. Don't worry.'

'I'm grateful; could you perhaps bring us up some wine? I suppose I need to change my clothes.'

'Of course sir.'

We sat on the edge of the straw mattress in silence at first. I still wanted her, you see. Whenever I was with her, it invigorated me with an excitement that would not go away. Call it love or infatuation;, I wanted her to be happy. I also knew she had the idea that it could only be Junius who could give her what she needed.

The landlord knocked and brought in some fresh bread, olives and wine with two cups on a tray.

'Look sir, if there are bodies to be found, the town guard will be here in the morning. It would be helpful if you both left early, you know. Some of my regulars saw you come in and tongues wag. Oh, how they wag in a tavern. You know what I mean?'

'Yes, thank you,' I said.

'Do you want to settle up now?'

'Of course,' I said, 'How much?'

'Two *sestertii* each please.'

I paid him and he left us to the wine and bread.

Aripele looked at me as soon as the door shut.

'What do we do now?'

'I have a friend, no, more of an acquaintance really, but he'll put us up. That's where I've been this afternoon.'

'An acquaintance?'

'Sort of. He's the one who made me join the Llegion. I visited him on the off chance he might help me get my pension.'

'Why in Hades would he help you?'

'He's an old soldier and he sees us both as pensioners from the army I suppose.'

Aripele poured the wine.

'Look,' I said, 'we'll have a place to stay and all he wants from me is some help protecting his property.'

'In the morning then?'

'Before dawn, my girl.'

She smiled. We changed our clothes. Dry and comfortable, we both slept. It felt as if we were both resigned now to friendship instead of love.

I hated it.

*   *   *

'We can't wake him up this early. I don't know what time he gets up,' I said as we left the hostelry.

'What do we do for the rest of the morning then?' Aripele said as we walked along the cobbled roadway avoiding the central gutter. It stank.

'We can go and eat. I could do with a shave and you can bathe if you wish. Men aren't usually allowed in most of the thermae in the mornings. The one we went to yesterday made an exception.'

'Why?'

'I paid the door slave a bit extra. I don't have the resources now.'

'I have some money.'

'No, I'll take you to the therma and then I'll get a shave; I can afford that. I'll wait outside with our things.'

I took her to the Thermae Decianae – one of the two large thermae on the Aventine. By the time we arrived at the house of Cerialis it was late morning.

We waited at the door for him to answer the ringing bell. I was not surprised to see him appear sword in hand.

Aripele looked at Cerialis but his terrible scarred face seemed to produce no reaction in her whatever. She smiled.

'Quintus Cerialis, I am Aripele. I am from Pontus. I am delighted to meet you. I have heard how brave and honourable a soldier you are. I am very grateful for your kind offer of hospitality.'

Cerialis smiled as best he could. It was more of a contorted grimace but it was the most animated I had seen his face since he caught me stealing.

'Please come in. It's wonderful to have such a beautiful woman grace my home. It has not had a woman's presence for many years since my wife died of a fever. Here, let me take your bag. I'll be pleased to show you to your cubiculum.'

I caught myself standing in the doorway with my mouth open. It was the most polite conversation I had heard from his lips since I had met him and his communication skills seemed suddenly much better with Aripele than with me.

They left me, to my irritation, standing on the doorstep as if I was baggage waiting to be deposited somewhere. On the other hand, Aripele and I were lovers no longer and if anyone knew the effect that girl had upon men, I did.

We ate fresh figs and drank watered wine in the Atrium since it was drizzling outside. The room was a little dark and Quintus sat in the darker part of the room away from the window perhaps to hide his face, I don't know.

'I apologise for the mess miss, but I had burglars recently and they caused a lot of damage. I haven't gotten round to tidying up properly.'

'I'll do that. It would short recompense for your kindness in letting us stay.'

'Wouldn't hear of it. Aulus and I can finish that off later. Did he tell you there might be a further visit from the burglars?'

'Yes, but I can take care of myself – mostly,' Aripele said, glancing at me, a secretive smile on her lips.

'Quintus,' I said, 'Aripele and I have some things we need to do now we're in Rome. We need to find my friend Junius, a decurion in the Ninth. He is the reason Aripele is here.'

'And the other?' Quintus said.

'Well, the amulet.'

'What about it?'

'I need to get it back. I will then have land, I hope. I can use my pension for farming maybe. I hadn't really thought about it.'

'So you want to take risks getting back this amulet and you have no idea what to do with it once you get it? Bit addled aren't you?'

'No,' I said, 'it's all I have left from my family. I'll get it back, whatever happens.'

'Seems to me you're feuding rather than trying to get anything material.'

'Maybe, but I can't let it go. Marcus Mettius left me for dead and damaged me. I want my revenge.'

'I understand that, but don't lose sight of your aims lad. It isn't really about an estate, was all I was saying. Here, more wine.'

He leaned forward and poured more of the wine into my cup.

'Perhaps you're right,' I said, 'First things first, I need to find the Ninth and let Junius know that Aripele is here and that I'm still alive. He may be surprised.'

'Perhaps you should go alone. There's a battle brewing with the rebels and I don't think it will be safe for a young lady like Aripele on horseback near a battle.'

Aripele said, 'But I must go too. I've waited to see Junius for almost two years. I don't intend to sit here now when I'm so close.'

'No,' I said, 'I'll have to go alone. I can't protect you in a battle but I can manage not to get involved if I'm alone. Listen to me this once, please,' I said.

'How can you leave me after all we've been through to get here? Besides, if the burglars or bandits or whatever they are come back, I may be in just as much danger.'

'Do you want me to delay until that quarrel is over?' I said. 'They may never come back. I could be here forever.'

'I can look after Aripele while you are away. I don't think they'll send anyone else to attack me, certainly not while there are others here,' Cerialis said.

'Quintus, you're a good friend and I have done nothing to deserve such help. I'll repay you somehow, I swear.'

'Just find your friend and that's enough. We can't have a beautiful young lady like Aripele, languishing all alone in Rome. Anyway, I'm glad of the company.'

'How about the beautiful young lady having some say in the matter?' she said.

We both turned and looked at her.

'I want to go too,' Aripele said. 'If Junius leaves from there to go to another country I might miss him entirely.'

'You'll have to take that chance. I'll make sure he knows you're here and he may well be able to come as soon as the battle is over, that is, if there is a battle.'

She clenched her fists in her lap and said, 'Aulus please.'

'No, no and treble no. I'm going and you're staying. Quintus will see you safe until I return. No further arguments, please.'

Aripele stood up and strode into her room without another word. She slammed the door.

'Beautiful and lots of spirit too. What a woman. If I was twenty years younger I'd throw you out and keep her,' Quintus said.

'If you were twenty years younger I would never trust you with her.'

Quintus looked at me. He frowned. Within seconds he considered what I had said and we both grinned.

The next morning I hired a horse at the Salarian Gate and left, riding north on the Via Salaria. The thought I had betrayed my honour with Aripele stabbed at me still but I had to find Junius. I wondered then whether he was indeed still with the Ninth. He had to be. I had to find him – had I not promised?

I had that much honour left at least.

Chapter IX

"When we cannot hope to win, it is an advantage to yield." –
Quintillianus.

I had never been a good judge of horses. I think it was because I had grown up in the city and had never ridden a horse until I was a young man. The one I hired had a narrow chest and lacked stamina. He had short stocky legs and slight cow hocks.

The broad Via Salaria ran north in a straight line for some ten miles and then petered out into a paved road, in places too narrow to accommodate carts going to and from Rome at the same time. There were paved areas at the side of the road where one could stop and wait for the oncoming traffic to pass.

Even ten miles from Rome, the countryside was much less urban. There were farms and copses of trees to left and right. Drizzle fell most of the time but it was not cold enough to make a cloak necessary.

I rode for four hours and had to stop for a wide-loaded wagon to pass. There were three soldiers behind it.

'Greetings,' I said to the tall legionary at their head.

'Greetings.' He looked at me with a smile and wiped sweat

and rainwater from his brow beneath the edge of his helmet as looked up at me.

'Do you know where the Ninth have gone? I'm looking for some friends in that legion. I have messages for them.'

'The Ninth? You've missed them by a few days. They were here only five days ago but they had orders to march north to bring Catalina to battle.'

'Any idea where they went?' I said, shifting in my saddle.

'Don't know, but a huge number like that won't be missed by anyone you ask.'

'You seem to have missed them.'

'Very funny. We're just escorting this wagon to the outskirts and then re-joining our legion as soon as we can,' he spat on the ground. 'Any wine on you? I'm parched.'

I reached down behind me for my leather bottle and he passed it around. The wine was watered and they drank deep, but I had more.

'Do you think it will be a battle worth watching?'

'Frankly no. Catalina has a lot of men, maybe ten thousand. Hybrida has two legions, the Ninth and the Tenth. The Tenth is a new one formed for the invasion of Gaul by that Caesar chap and Hybrida's nephew Marcus. I think Hybrida will wipe out the rebels like swatting flies. Sounds bad. They're all Romans and you know how we hate to fight each other. Rankles somehow.'

'I'll probably catch up with them in two days or so then. They won't be marching very fast I guess with all their baggage.'

'Two days sounds about right. Ride north and then head for Pistoria, you'll be able to ask anyone even if you're too short-sighted to follow a trail that's two centuries across.'

We smiled at each other and I rode on. I got into a routine of stopping every couple of hours and walking my horse, for he seemed fatigued in the afternoon. The miles passed and as night fell, I made a little camp by the roadside hoping no brigands would find me. I had in fact little need to worry – the lowlands of Etruria were safe enough.

I passed vineyards, brown and wilted, waiting for the warming touch of the spring sunshine. I saw slaves moving herds of cattle and carts, endless carts bearing goods to the Great City.

I thought about my future. I felt relieved to have one. I had sustained an horrendous injury at Tigranocerta and knew that having faced my own mortality I had changed. I'd learned to value my life and try to enjoy whatever part of it was left for me to experience.

Aripele had become part of that warm, cheering part of life and I was sad to have abandoned the physical aspect of that relationship. I understood however; I had a choice between my friendship with Junius and trying to seduce his woman again and even I had enough honour left to recognise the right course of action.

I drifted off into a fitful sleep. As Somnus took me, I thought about the amulet and how I might get it back. As Quintus had rightly surmised, it had ceased to be the means of obtaining any deeds. It was now what it represented to me. It was a symbol of revenge on the people whom I was sure had killed my parents. They had allowed me to be cast out into the streets as a child, to fend for myself.

It was not the principle I struggled with, it was the mechanism. I could not break into the Mettius home and search. There had to be a way to entice Marcus to reveal the amulet's location. But how? I could think of no leverage I could bring to bear on my cousin. He held the dice and I seemed to be only one of the players.

I rode for a further day and at the end of the morning of the third day, I saw the legions. They had stopped for a midday meal and a short rest and must have had a long march already for they seemed to be well established where they were.

Even when stopping on a march you can tell where to find almost any individual in a Roman camp. The order of things was so constant that anyone could see the officer's areas and the various Ccohorts and Ccenturies with minimal training.

I looked for the bull standard of the Ninth and saw it as I entered the valley, where they had stopped by a small stream that trickled past with a merry tinkle, untroubled and clean. I made my way to where I thought the Second Cohort was and I found the First Century without difficulty.

Few faces looked familiar, and those that I did seemed not to recognise me. I thought perhaps I had changed but it could have been because I had not been part of this brotherhood for almost two years now. I was supposed to be dead after all.

Then I saw him. Junius was a big man and a head taller than me. He was broad with curly fair hair and a beard framing his ready smile.

Dismounting, I approached. I was limping a little having been in the saddle for three hours that morning already. The mud squelched beneath my sandaled feet and I threw the hood of my cloak back.

He looked at me with no signs of recognition at all.

'Junius.' I said.

'Yes?' he said and then his face changed into a portrait of surprise and pleasure, 'Aulus? Is it you?'

'Yes you great big ox. So, bloody farmers don't even recognise their best friends.'

He stumbled forward and threw his arms around me in a bear hug that left me gasping for breath.

'Aulus, is it really you? I can't believe it. Back from the dead. I have grieved and thought so often about what happened.'

I looked at his face and could see tears appear in his eyes. It seemed uncharacteristic; I had never thought of him as an emotional man.

'Junius, I recovered. Not completely – my left leg is a little weak but otherwise I'm now better. When Mithridates returned to Sinope I had to leave but it's a long story. What about you? How is life treating the Decurion?'

'Decurion? I'm an Optio now. Got promoted after the battle of Artaxarta. After that they ordered us back to Rome. I had no way to return to Sinope so I couldn't go back to find out what happened to you. I wrote.'

'Yes I got one letter but all the ones I wrote were returned because you were moving around so much. What happened to Titus?'

'His head wound got infected and he died a few days after you were sent to Sinope. It's so good to see you alive. I really had thought you would have joined Titus.'

'Junius, a bit more good news. Aripele has come to Rome looking for you. We travelled together and she's desperate to see you.'

'What?'

'Aripele. She's here.'

'Where?'

'In Rome, not on the battlefield. What's the matter with you?'

'My Gods.'

'My Gods?'

'It's just... It's just....'

'Come on man, out with it. I've dragged the poor woman all the way from Pontus just to see you and all you can do is stand there with your mouth open. Aren't you pleased?'

'Aulus, I don't know what to say.'

'I can see that.'

I looked at his face. It was not the expression of ecstatic bliss that I had expected. He began to flush and said nothing. I could see he was thinking hard.

'Junius, it's so good to see you. What's the problem?'

'I'm married.'

'What?'

'I'm married. She's a wonderful girl. You must meet her. Her father owns a tavern in the Subura and a vineyard in Ostia. Oh Jupiter. What am I going to do about Aripele? Can't you tell her you couldn't find me? No, tell her I'm dead.'

'Are you serious? That girl loves you. She's been pining for you since you left and now when she felt she couldn't live without you any longer she's sold everything she has to travel here to be with you. I'm not lying to her.'

'How come you're so bothered? You never liked her anyway. I remember you telling me it had to be all business and she couldn't possibly be involved with me?'

'That was different. After I was recovering in Sinope she was very kind to me. So was Polymecles.'

'That grasping little half-Greek fellow? What about him?'

'He really missed us you know. He tended me for months. He thought the world of us both. He still thinks we saved his life when he got shot by that bowman in the night.'

'It's as if you've led a completely different life in another world to the one we shared when we were in Sinope together. We'll have to talk all about it later. What should I do about Aripele? The last thing I want is for her to run into Aemilia. I don't ever want to run the risk of them meeting. I never told her about Aripele you see.'

'This gets worse. I thought I was going to bring her word that you would be seeing her soon.'

'What in Hades do I do now?'

'You'll have to speak to her yourself. I can't do it.'

'Aulus, are we not the best of friends? Can't you do that small thing for me? I beg of you.'

'She won't believe me. I.... I have feelings for her and she knows it. She will think I've made it up.'

'What do you mean "feelings"?'

'Well I wasn't going to tell you but there's no harm in it I suppose. We got a little confused about boundaries on the trip here and... .'

'I see. So you've been playing me false all the way back to Rome,' his furrowed brow and the look of anger as his eyes flashed made me step back. I recovered quickly and said, 'It wasn't like that. I was grieving about leaving Hypsicratea and she comforted me. That was all there was to it.'

'You betrayed me with the woman you thought I loved.'

'Yes, but you didn't love her did you?'

'That's beside the point. You betrayed me,' Junius said. He looked hurt.

'Oh for the love of Mercury. This is stupid. You weren't interested in Aripele anyway. You're married to Aemilia. What do you care?'

'Aulus.'

'Does any of it matter?'

Junius studied me and for a moment, I thought it might end in a fight. Then the look on his face passed as fast as it had arisen and he smiled a faint smile.

'Actually, do you think she might want you instead? If so, it solves my problem. You and she can be together and no one needs to be unhappy.'

'I had thought of that. I think Aripele might have something to say about it. She is not easy to persuade to anything. She made the choice between us on the way here. I can't see her changing her mind, you know.'

'Look Aulus, of the two of us I always knew more about women than you. Trust me. It can all work out well.'

I looked at my friend with doubt. He could be right but I had a feeling deep inside that Junius and I might get it wrong. We could both lose out. Damn my weakness.

'Do me a favour Junius.'

'Of course.'

'Tell Aripele about your marriage and I will take it from there. Don't tell her you know about me and her will you?'

'No of course not. I can see that. Well now that's behind us we can catch up on all the events since I waved goodbye to you on that cart bound for Sinope.'

'I think there may be a bit of a fight for you to get through before we get the chance.'

'Catalina. Yes of course. I had almost forgotten. Just seeing you again wrecks my focus. I have always thought of you as my brother.'

'Me too. After the battle, will you be allowed to get some leave and return with me?'

'I'm sure of it. Procillus is still our Tribune and he's a really good fellow.'

'Procillus. That's good news. I should look him up.'

'Yes, he'd like that. He's often talked about you.'

'Really?'

'Yes, seems he valued you more than either of us knew. He was always impressed with your ability with a sword. Are you still just as fast?'

'With the sword? Yes but I'm a bit slower moving around since my left arm and leg don't work as well as they used to.'

'Seem all right to me.'

'You don't change. You're still not a doctor.'

'We have to march shortly. What will you do now?'

'I'll just follow and watch the battle if I can find a place with a good view. I'm a civilian now you know.'

'Pensioner you mean. Considering you're only about twenty-five that's an odd thing to be. After the fight we can talk and drink some wine. I can't get over the fact that you're still alive. It's the best news I've had since leaving Pontus. Aulus back with us. It's wonderful.'

'You really mean that, don't you? I feel the same. Make sure you don't get killed in this battle. It would ruin it all.'

'Very funny. We'll slaughter them. Bit sad really, they're all Romans like you and me, just misguided.'

'I'll find you after the battle.'

We embraced and I made my way to the rear of the army since they were getting ready to leave. I wondered what he would tell Aripele. I hoped she wouldn't go to pieces. I also had a feeling of hope that somehow I might now be able to be with her. It raised my spirits; the problems eating away at me on the journey seemed to be resolving themselves.

Chapter X

"True nobility is exempt from fear." – Marcus Tullius Cicero.

I rode to one side of the rear-guard. I did not intend to become the victim of all the flying mud the two legions were churning up on the march. I was free to move around as I wished and stopped when I wished to as well.

Above, an overcast sky with grey rain clouds foreshadowed a downpour and the temperature was dropping. The army was marching three centuries abreast with an ala of cavalry at either flank. They came to a shallow valley with wooded hills on either side. The column of march was readjusted to fit the gap and this led to some delays. I had no idea at that time where the enemy might have positioned themselves and I thought it would be better to go around the hills ahead. I cut away to my right and skirted the wooded hill ahead of me.

There was soft mossy turf under foot and light forest ahead. A rabbit scuttered away, oblivious of the vast numbers of men readying themselves to kill or die so close at hand.

I entered the tree line but failed to notice the riders. They came from all sides, fast. There was no way to escape. The nag I was riding would have been incapable of escape in any case. That, combined with my poor riding skills meant I had no options.

The riders were equites, well mounted and holding spears. They seemed ill equipped. One had no breastplate, another a bronze tipped spear the like of which I had never seen but guessed it was of more historical interest than use. Their shields varied in size and design and I realised they belonged to no ordinary army. It seemed clear to me the rebels were going to be no match for the two legions under Hybrida if their equipment was as bad as that of my captors.

'Spying were you?' the leader of the equites said. A clean-shaven young man of my own age and well spoken, he wore an old helmet without a horsehair plume although the central ridge which under normal circumstances held such a decoration was still present.

'No, I'm a civilian.'

'What are you doing here if you're not spying?'

'I'm following the army because I have to try to get some back-pay and I have friends in the Ninth Legion.'

'Kill him and be done with it Gaius,' a rider to my left said. I did not take my eyes off the young man in front of me; he seemed to be the leader.

'We're just here to reconnoitre but if we found a spy we would kill him, you realise that?' Gaius said.

'Yes of course,' I said. 'I'm not a spy. Besides, what benefit would it be to the two legions over there to know that twenty horsemen are in this wood? You would hardly be here to attack their flank would you? I don't think they care where your army is, they intend to march on until they make contact and then fight. The outcome is in the hands of the Gods rather than in any information I could impart,' I said.

'I'm sure you're right,' he said, 'but I can't take a chance.' He turned and said to a man on his left, 'Vibius, tie him up and gag him then with two men take him to the General, he may want to question him.'

They tied my hands then roped my legs to my hands under the horse's chest. The gag was a piece of filthy cloth stuffed into my mouth and held in place with a length of cord. They led my nag away somewhat circuitously, with me astride, to a high hill a mile away where a group of soldiers sat on horseback looking down into the wide valley. The far end of the valley was where the Roman Legions would emerge and at this end an army had drawn up with part of them on the slopes of the hill and the remainder on the approach to it.

The mounted men paid me no attention at first. I looked at the army below. There were at least two legions but they were not all in uniform and their equipment was not regular either. There carried archaic shields and swords and none of them had pila of the usual design. They had spears but they varied in length and weight. Their armour varied from none at all, to leather hauberks and occasional rusty loricas. I saw one man with a homemade wooden breastplate. I suppose it was better than nothing, but I thought this homespun army stood no chance of even denting the front ranks of the Ninth and Tenth Legions.

Catalina's rebels may have had poor equipment but they stood their ground and were in well-organised cohorts and centuries. I realised many of them were veterans of the legions, long since retired and as rusty as their armour. There were few mounted soldiers and maybe a hundred Gauls whom I had heard were all the Allobroges tribe were prepared to provide.

'What's this,' said a tall thin man with a red general's plume adorning his helmet. He pointed at me. One of my captors spoke.

'Caught this one about a mile away. Thought maybe he's a spy, sir.'

'A spy? Seems a bit unlikely. Why would they need intelligence when they are only half a mile away?'

'Yes sir. Maybe he's an assassin?'

'Dressed like that? Take the bloody gag off him and let's see what he says.'

They removed the gag and I spat out the piece of cloth. It left a foetid taste in my mouth. I looked at the general in front of me. He had a small scar on the left side of his face and laughter wrinkles at the corners of his eyes despite his sagging mouth.

He frowned at me. 'I am Cassius Manlius, General and second-in-command to General Catalina. Were you spying?'

'No, sir. I'm a military pensioner. I was injured at Tigranocerta when I was in the army of Lucullus sir. I was simply following the army because I have friends in the Ninth Legion and I need to see them after the battle.'

'You seem to think it's a foregone conclusion.' he said, frowning. 'What makes you think any of your friends will survive?'

'I have no knowledge of that. I'm not a spy. What useful information could I give that Hybrida's scouts couldn't give better and quicker?'

'Maybe you're an assassin?'

'No one can assassinate anyone in the thick of a battle.'

'True. Maybe you're telling the truth. I'll deal with you after we've defeated this lot.'

He turned his back on me then and pointed to the first cohorts of the Ninth and Tenth Legions who had begun to appear across the field. The man standing next to him was older, broad in the chest but of medium height. He had a clean-shaven face and no scars. He was arrayed like a general and I assumed it was Catalina himself. He turned and looked at me, his eyes both serious and sad. I wondered if he really believed in his army.

'What's your name boy?'

'Aulus Veridius Scapula sir.'

'I seem to remember a family of that name. One of them was a consul and a general many years ago.'

'Yes sir, I think that may have been my great grandfather. My grandfather was a general in the army of Marius as well.'

The expression on his face changed. he looked disapproving. 'Marius eh? I fought against that bastard's army under Sulla. We won you know.'

'Yes sir I know. Sulla took everything we owned and my grandfather was killed in the proscriptions. '

'And now you're here.'

'I'm only an observer. I have no part in this fight.'

'Every man must take a side. I take the side of the poor oppressed people of Italia. People are starving in the provinces while rich men get richer in Rome. Someone must stand against the rot. If I'm successful every poor man in the country will thank me.'

I decided not to argue. I had heard Catalina was corrupt and cruel, but of course I had no real knowledge of the man.

'You will see now that although my men are not well armed they have spirit. They are mainly veterans and they know how to fight. They've all sworn an oath to me and I know they will not run. Anyway, there's nowhere for them to run to is there Cassius?'

Both generals grinned and turned away from me and I could see from my perch on the horse how the Ninth and Tenth drew up in battle order and began advancing.

'Have the men advance,' I heard Catalina say.

His tribunes rode away with the message to their various commands and I sat on my horse, my feet tied beneath me. They had tethered the irritating creature to a gorse bush, giving me a view of the battle from the hill. It was unfortunate that I was at best a poor equestrian and my steed was no better trained than I was. He turned every now and again and I was unable to get him to move as he grazed, ignoring my foot movements and the approaching battle. I therefore lost sight of the field on occasions, to my intense frustration, and could not persuade the nag to move at all.

I did see the start of the battle though. Catalina had ridden down to the front of the battle-line. It surprised me; I had not gauged him to be that type of commander.

The light infantry engaged first. They threw a few pila but most of the fighting was hand-to-hand in a loose formation. They had no velites on either side who would have engaged first with their light throwing javelins. Catalina had dismounted and was fighting and shouting encouragement to his men.

The Ninth Legion Principes – heavily armed and armoured veterans entered the fray. I could see their front line. The ranks of adjacent shields were raised. They clashed with the opposition. The battle line was stationary for long moments with neither side giving way.

At this stage, my horse decided it was easier to graze facing in the opposite direction on the other side of the brow of the hill. I lost sight of the battle for almost twenty minutes or so. I kicked in a feeble way since my feet were still bound. I cursed but the horse refused to budge. In the end, I had to turn as far as I was able despite my bonds. All I could see was the right flank of Catalina's troops.

What I saw surprised me. The ranks of the rebels, despite all their disadvantages, held firm. They stood and fought shield to shield. They stabbed with their swords as did the legionaries they fought. Men fell and were replaced by the men behind. The numbers only dwindled slowly. The legions seemed to be making no headway.

Grudgingly I felt an admiration for these men; they were fighting against overwhelming odds against a superior force. They were facing death with little hope of victory. I wondered what had spurred them on to the fight. Was it Catalina and his dreams of glory? Was it simply that men want to struggle against poverty and perceived injustice even if it costs them their lives? I had no time to analyse what I felt because the scene before me kept changing as my horse roamed – at least the little I could see of it.

I kept kicking the damned beast. In the end he did turn back again no doubt tired of grazing on that side of the hill and I was able to witness the whole battlefield, the fight unfolding below me. I could identify Catalina, his bright armour and red plume marking him out in the front of the battle line. As far as I could see the loyal legions' commander was not there, perhaps a mark of his confidence, perhaps feeling his men did not require him in the front line. It brought home to me that a general fighting in the front lines gives his men such a boost they fight like Furies, giving no ground. I could see how the rebels died where they stood and gave no quarter in return.

Then came the sound of the cornua blasting a charge. At last, I could see the Roman commander with his century of praetorians. They were handpicked for their size and fighting capability – veterans all. They charged the centre of the rebel forces. They attacked with such vigour and fury I could see at last that the rebel line began to buckle and give way before them. They weren't routed. They continued to fight.

Catalina's comment that there was nowhere for them to run to, came to mind. They were rebels and could look forward to little mercy if they gave in. I thought Hybrida would have any prisoners crucified and it therefore didn't surprise me how these men preferred to fall on the battlefield rather than endure the slow and agonising death awaiting them.

I found out later that Hybrida was not present and the general I had seen entering the fray was Marcus Petreius, his second in command. It was rumoured that this was because Hybrida was enmeshed with Catalina and couldn't face him but some said he was ill.

I could see how in one small section of the front line, Catalina and Manlius, both identified by their crimson plumes forged ahead with a handful of men. They cut their way through the front line of the Tenth. They were engaging the second and third lines with a force and determination I found both surprising and enthralling. This could not be the man I had heard so many bad things about. His reputation was of a corrupt and greedy coward who had sought to take Rome for his own avarice. He did not seem a mean or cowardly type to me at all. I began to feel admiration for him as I watched. I was to learn in the end however that all men have both good and bad and we are all capable of both.

The next row of loyal troops made a fresh sally all along the line. The rebel line still did not fragment. They were fighting in close, but with very thinned ranks. It was then I saw Catalina fall. I saw both red horsehair plumes borne by Catalina and Manlius sink and disappear in the melee, downtrodden, forgotten as the slaughter progressed.

I wished I could get free but they had trussed me well and my bonds would not budge. A few of the rebels had now formed a shield wall in a square pattern but the numbers of the Ninth and Tenth Legions became overwhelming and the square contracted until it melted away like a summer cloud in a bright sunlit sky.

A group of loyal legionaries were running up the hill towards me. What they would make of me I did not know. They looked wild-eyed and bloodied. They ran at me. All at once, they stopped and I recognised a face. It was Junius. He was laughing. He pointed at me and said something I didn't catch, but I could see his companions convulsed in laughter and pointing in my direction. It began to annoy me because I realised they were laughing at me. No man likes to be the butt of a joke.

'Bloody well get up here and untie me will you, you grimacing Saturnalian. There's nothing funny about being tied up.'

'I'm sorry. It was just that...' he burst into more peals of laughter. I was frowning.

'What's so damned funny? They captured me and tied me up. Cut the rope.'

Junius gradually regained control and although he was smirking he had enough possession of himself to do as I asked.

'I'm sorry Aulus, it's just that you were sitting up there all through the battle and we thought you were Catalina or one of his Generals. It just seemed so funny to see that it was the last person we expected in the entire world.'

'That's not even funny.'

'Maybe not to you but we fought all the way to this hill because we thought you were a general and now we find it was you instead. When one of the chaps said it was a rum way to get your pension and we all just folded with laughter. Sorry. We fought like demons to get here that's all.'

He started to laugh again and it spread like an infection. If I were an enemy, I would have slaughtered the lot of them. They were powerless with laughter at my expense.

Once their laughter died down and they had untied me I too began to see the funny side of the situation. I was the only person in the battle who had no commitment to either side but I was the only one they had captured.

Dismounting, I led my horse down the hill with Junius. The

legionaries were beginning the clearing up process. Bodies were being cleared, wounded were being tended and of course, bodies were being stripped of their possessions. I saw one legionary staring at what I took to be the body of a slain rebel, judging by the body's clothing.

'What's the trouble?' I asked.

He looked up at me with a look of grief. There were tears in his eyes.

'You all right?' I said.

'No. It was a bad fight. This man is my brother. I don't know what he's doing on the field.'

'Your brother?'

'Yes, he must have joined the rebels. He was a poor man with mouths to feed at home. He believed in Catalina. He maybe thought Catalina would relieve the poverty of the people. He paid for that mistake and it doesn't make it easier to bear.'

'There is no joy in killing fellow Romans,' I said. 'The wounds of civil strife cut deep, as someone said once.'

'Yes,' he said.

He looked at me with his moist eyes. I felt perhaps there were many dead on that field whom the legionaries would recognise in the clearing up process. I could feel his pain, it was almost tangible.

Junius and I saw many similar little scenarios as we walked back to the camp. I had no real place there but I had to wait somewhere for Junius to arrange to return to Rome with me. I was almost at the point where the camps were being set up when a familiar voice behind me spoke.

'Aulus Veridius. Is it really you?'

I turned and saw a young tribune astride a white stallion. He had fair hair and a long sunburned, freckled face. He dismounted and approached us. He was tall and thin but his pleasant disposition showed in his good-natured, unassuming expression.

'Tribune Procillus. How good to see you after all this time.'

'Aulus, we thought you were dead. I am so glad you made it. You look well enough. The surgeon's prognosticating was clearly wrong, old chap.'

'Yes, it's taken me until now to recover. I was lame and couldn't move my arm and leg for a long time but I exercise and run and I can wield a sword now.'

'Well, well. I'm so pleased. What will you do now?'

'I need my pension. I've run out of money and they won't pay me without proof of identity. They owe me two years' pension and I can't get an *as* from them for a month.'

'Nonsense. Drop by my tent in an hour and the legion's adjutant will pay part of your pension straightaway. I will see to it personally.'

'The Tribune is most kind.'

'Don't you be so bloody formal with me. Don't you remember how drunk we got together after we put down the mutiny on the way to Tigranocerta, that time when Lucullus had the mutineers crucified?'

'I remember it well sir. I think I still owe you for that last wine skin, if my memory serves me right.'

'How is your sword arm?'

'Good as ever sir, it's my shield arm that bothers me. It's a little weak.'

'If you use your sword arm like you used to, you won't need your shield, will you?'

'No sir.'

'My uncle is chief of the Town Guard. If you need work I can write a letter of introduction.'

'Town guard? They're just the dregs of the army and the ones who aren't fit for duty. I was hoping for something better than that.'

'Well if you change your mind let me know. Hello, what's this?' He pointed to a body lying sprawled among several dead Ninth Legion bodies.

'It looks like Catalina's body. I saw him before the battle,' I said. 'Look, all his wounds are at the front. He wasn't a man to run after all, I suppose. I think maybe we misjudged him as a man. A foolish fellow, but brave.'

'Yes he fought like a Barbarian. He got cut off from his men and died fighting. Cicero denounced him as a coward and a traitor to the Senate but I see no evidence of cowardice.'

'No, I think he won't disappoint his ancestors when he greets them in Hades.'

'Well, I'll see you later Aulus. So good to know you are alive.'

He instructed one of the legionaries engaged in the clearing up process to cut off Catalina's head and take it to the command tent. He looked over his shoulder at me and he was smiling.

'The Senate wants to see his head to make sure he is dead. Perhaps they mistrust someone. Damned strange way to run a country.'

He rode away and Junius and I walked on. We sat outside Junius' tent and ate the porridge of mashed wheat kernels that was standard legionary food.

'You always liked him didn't you?' I said.

'Yes,' replied Junius, 'He's not as relaxed as Meridius was but he's pleasant company when he's in his cups.'

'You don't change do you?'

Junius smiled.

The kinship I had always felt for him still warmed me. It seemed at last I had come home. It was as if home is where the people are, not the bricks and mortar of our existence. And the legion of course; this was where I belonged and now I was not part of it any more. All I was, was man apart. A damned civilian, unwanted and useless.

Chapter XI

"True friendship ought never to conceal what it thinks." – St. Jerome.

We entered Rome from the north at the Salarian Gate; the sun was setting and the alleyways were in shadow as we walked to the stables. I cursed as I stumbled on a lupanar sign. The phallus carved into the flagstone tripped me. I realised my preoccupations over Aripele were making me drag my left foot. With an injury like mine, even thinking deeply distracts enough to make my leg weak. We stabled our horses. I was glad to return mine to its owners. It had been a contrary beast and when I said so to the stableman, he grinned.

'I don't know why I had to pay so much for a nag that won't obey me,' I said.

'Well I suppose I could have warned you, but you wanted a cut-price rental and this is a cut-price horse.'

'But it doesn't do what you want it to.'

'Funny, that's what the last chap said, but it does what I want it to. It earns me lots of money.' He thought this was funny and sniggered at his own joke.

'I've a good mind to ask for my money back.'

'Look, you paid to rent this horse. If you had any sense you would have ridden him for a bit before you rented him. You can't have any money back I'm afraid. We don't do that.'

Junius seemed to find the matter as amusing as the stableman so I desisted from further argument. We walked through the city.

'Aulus, the tavern is almost on the way to the Quirinal you know.'

'No it isn't. You said it was in the Subura, that's across town.'

'Well maybe not on the way but it's not far.'

'Look my friend, you promised me you would face Aripele. I can't do it for you. I wish I had never brought her with me.'

'So do I. Believe me.'

'I don't want this to interfere with our friendship.'

He slapped me on the back. 'Agreed. My mother always said that the two things in life you must look after, are small cuts and old friends.'

'Which am I? A small cut or an old friend?'

We looked at each other and smiled. It was as if the old humour had re-established itself between us. A two-year gap is as wide as the Tiber in some respects, but in others, we had picked up where we had left off. It's a sign of real friendship. Had we not had our formative years together as raw recruits?

I told him who I thought had injured me at Tigranocerta and about the theft of the amulet.

'I'd forgotten about that amulet of yours. I've not seen very much of your cousin in the last year. Come to think of it I haven't seen anything of Bassus either. I do know he was wounded at Tigranocerta. He apparently killed a Persian prince and got rewarded with a medal from Lucullus after the battle.'

'He didn't kill the prince, I did. Then Bassus attacked me and I stabbed him in the thigh. Marcus sneaked up behind me and hit me on the head, leaving me for dead.'

'That explains a lot. So that's the end of your amulet and the buried will?'

'Deeds. It's not a will.'

'Well whatever.'

'I need to get it back.'

Junius shrugged. 'It could be anywhere.'

'It's either in his house here or with him as he travels with the army. If it's round his neck I might take his head off first to get it.'

'You could never get close unless you joined up again. Then you won't get your pension at all.'

'I suppose I could just return to my post and claim my back-pay.'

'I thought you said you weren't fully recovered?'

'I am, near as anyone can tell. The arm's a bit weak but with exercise I can keep it strong enough to fight.'

'It would be good to have you back. We're being sent to Gaul you know.'

'Gaul? More guard duty in the Cisalpine province?'

'No, apparently Gaius Julius Caesar has been given the Proconsulship of all of Gaul and rumour has it he intends conquest. Funny choice really, he's Pontifex Maximus and a bit of a pouf. I can't see the high priest of Rome being much good at conquering anybody to tell the truth.'

'No, it'll take him many years to conquer Gaul. It's huge.'

'Well I suppose I'll find out in the end.'

'No my friend, we'll find out. I must have that amulet. Here, that's the house.'

I rang the doorbell of Quintus' house. It seemed a long time before anyone answered. Quintus emerged, as ever holding his sword. The introductions over, he invited us in.

'So you're the chap Aripele has been talking about. She goes on and on about you. I'm afraid she's out visiting one of the lady friends she met in the baths. She knows well enough not to stay after dusk so she should be here any minute,' Quintus said.

There was a ring of the doorbell. Then a loud banging on the door as if someone was impatient to be admitted.

'I'll go and answer that. Now where did I put that sword?'

Quintus grabbed his sword and went to the door. The next few moments blur into an instant in my memory. We heard a scuffle in the vestibulum, then the sound of steel ringing against steel. We rounded the corner with swords drawn.

Figures of men crowded the tiny space at the entrance to the vestibulum. Quintus stood stabbing with his gladius; the thick oak of the door protected his ight side. I could not see how many men there were but one lay twitching at Quintus' feet and another was parrying with a short sword.

I stabbed that one in the neck with my blade. He fell onto his dying comrade. Two more filled the gap. Junius was behind me, and taller than I, was stabbing over my head with his weapon. We were three against an unknown number but in that confined space we might as well have been a hundred.

Quintus parried a blow to his head. He stepped backwards. He kept stabbing and parrying and we did the same. We backed away needing more space to move. We ended with Quintus and Junius standing side by side on the right of the impluvium. I stood on the other and the shallow pool between us protected my right side as we fought in the atrium. There were at least six of them but they could only come at us three at a time in the small room.

A broad stocky man jabbed at me with a short sword. I parried with ease. My blade flashed in the lamplight as I returned the stroke. I felt it make contact. He still fought. His blade flashed too as he wielded it in quicker strokes. I was fast that day. Right side forward I plied my trade. It felt good. Right, left, stab, thrust. It was the old way. I had learned it years before. It had never left me. He kicked at me. I cut his thigh. I smiled. I was an artist in killing. Now I knew it. He stabbed again. I sidestepped enough, but it was close. Right to left, I sliced through his throat and he fell back, half in the pool. I saw a look of surprise on his face, fingers clutching, blood spurting. Dead or good as. Blood reddened the rainwater in the pool.

A second took his place. He fared no better. It took only one parry and a stab to his groin and he was down. I penetrated his throat as he fell and he was gone before he hit the ground. I was aware of my friends fighting on my right as another man came at me.

This one was good. He feinted to my left. I ignored it. He kicked with his left foot and stabbed at the same time. I stepped back a little looking for an opening in the dull lamplight spreading across the fight from behind. He came forward. I too stepped up. I held back my sword arm and I grabbed his wrist with my left hand as he raised his sword to strike. I half turned twisting to my left. I used all the power of my back muscles. My gladius penetrated his chest. He died quick, gasping, bright red blood trickling from the wound onto my hand.

A fourth man was swinging his gladius in fast strokes. In the poor illumination, it seemed made of fire, his blade reflecting. He aimed at my head, right handed. A downward stroke. I parried. I failed to see the knife in his left hand. It flew upwards towards my midriff. I had already stepped back enough for it to only scrape though my tunic and cut me across the ribs.

I let out an involuntary yelp. The pain drove me to fever pitch. I swung my sword at him and he stepped back. I followed, aware of my companions fighting on their side of the pool. My sword moved fast. I stabbed at his face and he moved his head. I cut his cheek to the bone. He stabbed at me with his knife, but I was the faster. The blade in my hand struck as I stepped back. It hit the right side of his neck and it was over. Blood poured from the wound. He staggered with his left arm and leg going limp and flailing as he sank to the floor. I thought in an odd detached way how I knew that feeling well.

Then all was quiet. I heard some passing people outside laughing and shouting in a drunken revel as if nothing had happened inside the house as they walked past. They must have missed the two bodies in the vestibulum since the front door must still be open.

'By Mars.' Quintus said, 'more bloody clearing up.'

We looked at each other, blood-soaked and breathless. We laughed. Whether it was at Quintus' obvious irritation at clearing up, or relief at the conclusion of the fight I cannot tell.

'You did well there my friend. How many did you kill?' Junius said.

'Four I think. It all happened so fast. Yes, four. I got cut though.'

'Here, let me see that,' Quintus said.

I showed him the wound. It was a hand's length and right through the skin, one edge of it hung exposing corrugated, bloody, yellow fat in a dependant, semi-circular flap. It had exposed my ribs and a cut right across one of them was visible. It began to hurt. I had not felt much pain during the fight, but as I calmed down it came on. I had sustained plenty of wounds before and this one was nothing by comparison.

Quintus took me by the arm.

'Look, I'm not dying.' I said snatching my arm away. 'I don't need help to walk. I'm not a bloody cripple you know.'

He looked at me and smiled.

'The why do you want the pension?' he was still smiling.

'Sorry, just joking. If you follow me to that cubiculum off the peristylium, I'll stitch it for you.

It was a minor procedure and Quintus clearly had a lot of practice in suturing. In half an hour, I had a bandage around my chest soaked in wine and oil over the stitched wound.

'What do we do with the bodies?'

'Not a clue. I don't normally have a lot of dead people to get rid of at home, do I?'

'I know where I can get a cart. We can take them to that place outside the city wall where they dispose of the poor. No one will see if we do it late tonight,' Junius said.

A short scream interrupted us, a feminine scream. We looked at one another and realised it was Aripele.

We ran to the atrium where the fight had taken place. She stood in the entrance; her was face pale. She was supporting herself with an outstretched arm, hand against the wall. She looked up as we entered.

'Junius?' she said, her voice soft.

She ran to him and stood on tiptoes with her arms encircling his neck.

'I thought one of the bodies was you. Oh Junius, how I have longed for this moment.'

Quintus tugged at my arm and we left them alone together.

'This is going to be a problem.'

'What is?'

'Junius. He's already married.'

'What?'

'Yes, he thought he would never see her again so he got married. I persuaded him to come here to tell her the truth.'

'Gods. I don't know what she'll do. She's besotted. Mind you, what can people expect these days? Civil strife, wars all over the place. A soldier's life is no good for a married man anyway. She's better off without him.'

'Try telling her that.'

'You serious? You can't tell her anything. I've never met anyone with such a strong will. I had to threaten to tie her up to stop her from following you.'

'Good job you did. I was captured by the rebels and nearly killed for a spy.'

'Really? Tell me about it.'

We sat and talked about the Catalina episode and Quintus seemed to know a good deal about it already but where he got his information from, I have no idea. Presently, Aripele appeared in the doorway her face strained and drawn. She walked past us into her bedchamber without a word, shutting the door slowly and quietly behind her. I got up to go to her but Quintus grabbed my arm.

'Leave her alone. She doesn't need you right now.'

'No...'I said, turning back. 'Maybe not.'

'I don't know much about women,' he said looking sideways at me. 'So don't ask.'

'Quintus, the Primum Pila knows everything in the legion, but you are probably the last one I would ask for advice as far as women are concerned.'

'I was married once, you know.'

'All the same.'

We lapsed into silence just as Junius appeared in the doorway. He looked wistful but nothing more. I wondered what would happen next and I wondered what had transpired, but dared not ask. I was intending re-joining the legion. Where would she go now? Junius sat down in silence. He looked pensive.

'Quintus,' I said.

'What?'

'How long can Aripele stay here with you?'

'Why?'

'I was thinking of re-joining the legion. You can see I can still fight.'

'Then you can't claim a pension can you?'

'No but they'll owe me back pay.'

'I can arrange that if you want. I'm grateful to you both for your help with my little domestic disturbance earlier.'

'If I'm back in the legion, I'll be able to find the amulet, assuming Marcus Mettius has it with him.'

'If he hasn't, you'll be stuck in the legion and he will have kept it here in Rome.'

'Who knows what the Gods plan for us? If that is the road ahead then I must follow it.'

'So be it. I'll fix that one for you. I need to cancel the pension arrangements I made for you yesterday. Remind me – my memory isn't what it used to be.'

'Oh, sorry. Didn't realise you'd already done it.'

'No bother really, it's just another conversation. If I had been alone tonight I would be dead.'

'Will they send more men?'

'Doubt it. They've failed twice. It won't help them to send even more. This is Rome after all. I'm going to ask the Town Guard to keep a watch when I report this incident tomorrow.'

'Report it?'

'Yes, of course. Not doing so, would be criminal. All I have to do is leave the bodies where they can be inspected at the city burial pits and let them know. Some of the men may have had relatives who will want the bodies for burial.'

'Do you care?'

'It would be impious to ignore the wishes of even these men's families.'

'Yes perhaps,' I said.

'Look I'm going now,' Junius said.

'Go where?' I said

'To Aemilia.'

'We need that cart.'

'Oh yes,' he said as if his mind were elsewhere, 'I'll do that.'

The three of us spent most of the evening clearing up the debris of the fight. Scrubbing away bloodstains was not my idea of a pleasant evening but there was no use complaining. It reminded me of my mother admonishing me for not tidying up. Aripele stayed in her room. I think my heart was in that room with her too.

She was never far from my thoughts.

Chapter XII

"Accept the things to which fate binds you, and love the people with whom fate brings you together, but do so with all your heart." – *Marcus Aurelius.*

'How are you?' I asked.

'What do you mean?' Aripele said. She was sitting on the edge of her cot staring down with her gaze fixed on the rush matting in front of her. Her serious face looked tired and unhappy. It was a sharp contrast to her usual cheerful demeanour.

'As I say, how are you?'

'I'm all right, I suppose. I was foolish not to realise that a Sinope whore deserves no better than to be alone.'

'That's not true. You're beautiful, strong, and resourceful and we are still friends.'

'Yes Aulus. When did you find out he had married?'

'In the camp.'

She said, 'And I suppose you were glad?'

'Look, I didn't know this would happen did I? I still love you.'

'Why didn't you tell me? Why did you have to bring Junius with you?'

'I thought it would be better if he told you, it's between you two. Not my business.'

'How can you say that? I suppose now you think I'm yours, do you?'

'No, but I want you to know I am here if you want me.'

I leaned on the door-jamb. Then I stood straight. I had no idea how to handle all this, but I knew I wanted her even if it sounded contrived. In the end, I sat down beside her and put an arm around her shoulders only to be pushed away as if I was a plague-carrier.

'I don't know what I feel now. I feel alone and you aren't helping.'

I left her to it. I had no persuasive answers, no clever phrases. I wished I could communicate better on her level. I went to the atrium where Quintus sat attacking a bunch of grapes.

'Want some?' he said, 'they're fresh. Very sweet.'

'No thanks, Quintus. Are we going to the Military Resource Centre?'

'Ready when you are.'

'Will they take me back in the legion?'

'They will on my recommendation. I just need to cancel the pension arrangements.'

'I'm grateful to you.'

We left Aripele in the house. Quintus solved the matter without difficulty since he was a violent man with a reputation. The slave in charge of records knew him, prepared a seat for him and was almost obsequious.

'When do I join up again?'

'Well sir, that depends upon you. If you ride out to Pistoria, you can join as soon as you arrive. Otherwise, you can wait for the legions to come home. We are expecting them in about a week from now. You will find them on the Campus Martius. Of course your pay does not start until you have re-joined your century.'

We left and I felt almost elated. I was back in the arms of the legion and could leave all the troubles of Rome, my love life and poverty behind.

'Quintus, will you look after Aripele for me?'

'I'll look after her but not for you.'

'What then?'

'For her. She can stay as long as she likes. I like having her around. Makes me feel young. Not had a woman around for a long time.'

'I love her you know.'

'Don't you start. What's all this love nonsense? I put you into the legion to make a man of you not a lover. You're supposed to be a warrior'

'Yes of course. Sorry.'

'Sorry. Don't apologise like you're some child stolen a biscuit. Be a man Aulus.'

'Sorry.'

'And stop apologising.'

He was not smiling and I knew better than to speak. We walked in silence and I began to wonder if he was right. I had serious business to attend to with my cousin Marcus and I could ill afford for feelings of love and romance to distract me. I wanted to put all the rest of my life on hold and get my revenge.

It was raining as we walked up the cobbled street to Quintus' house. We entered and there was an unusual stillness in the house. The silence was oppressive.

'Seems quiet, wonder where Aripele's got to?'

'I'll see where she is.'

I crossed the peristylium and knocked on her door. There was no answer. I entered. She had gone. The blanket on the cot lay in a crumpled heap but otherwise the room was empty. That emptiness hung in the air and I was gripped by a feeling of loss deep inside me.

'She's gone.'

'Where?'

'I don't know. She was very unhappy. Maybe I should go and look for her?'

'Where would you look? Rome's a big place.'

'I don't have any idea really.'

'Better sit tight and she might re-surface when she realises that Rome's streets have little to offer a lone woman.'

'I think she can look after herself but I want her back. She might have gone to the Thermae'

'You can't spend all your time hanging around the baths. They'll think you're pestering some young woman. People are sensitive these days you know.'

'I can't just leave her to it. I have to know. I still have a couple of weeks before I have to join the legion. I want to make sure she's all right.'

'You're mad. She's a lovely girl but you're wasting your time.'

*   *   *

The year was turning. I sat in the autumn sunshine. It was quite cold for that time of year in Rome, but the sun was warming and the sky blue and clear. I sat on the wall that marched in a circle around a little fountain in the square, outside the baths. The rough flagstones undulated and I reflected in a detached way they needed re-laying.

I had decided I would look out for Aripele each morning at the Thermae Decianae, the one I knew she favoured. I knew she had made some friends there and I thought she might return for that reason at some time.

I could see the women arriving for their ablutions. They were people of all shapes, sizes and wealth. Some arrived in sedan chairs and the others who were young, arrived in groups, giggling, pushing and playing around. I attracted little attention apart from an occasional inviting stare but I was not there to attract women.

Once the initial influx had slowed, I went to get a shave. It was cheap and cost a copper *as* although I could afford to splash out now that the legion had released some funds to me thanks to Procillus. There is something special about a good shave. The oil that my barber used was imported and it left my skin feeling soft and smooth. It was better than the usual olive oil I had always had before.

'What oil is that?' I asked.

'Well it's a special one. Imported from Parthia. They make it from palm trees.'

'I thought we were at war with Parthia?'

'No, where have you been for the last five years?'

'What?'

'We've had a treaty with Parthia for three years now. We get regular imports from the east. Palm oil is lighter than olive oil and smells better too.'

'I heard rumours in a tavern the Senate was planning war with the Parthians.'

'Hope not. This palm oil is cheap and goes down well with the customers.'

'Well let's hope the only war is going to be with the Gauls. We don't get anything but slaves from there.'

He said, 'True.' He smiled and I paid him a little extra for the excellent shave. It made me feel ready for anything. No wonder he liked the Parthians.

I walked back towards the Quirinal, and then I saw her. She was walking out of the baths and it was clear I had missed her going in; how, I could not guess, but I had missed her. She was making for the north end of the Forum Boarium and heading towards the Subura. I followed. I did not accost her in the street for I wanted to know where she was staying.

I followed her to a tenement, and after a few minutes, I entered the building. There was an old lady on her way out and I asked if she had seen a dark beautiful girl, and where she stayed.

She indicated a doorway. I knocked and she came to the door.

'Aulus?'

'Aripele, come home now.'

'Home?'

'Well, back to Quintus's house. I have to leave in a week to join the legion again but I need to know you're safe. Quintus will look after you.'

'Why should I? I'm not your woman. I can go back to my normal business and you go to the legions and there is an end to it.'

I looked at her face. Her eyes were strained and unwilling. I knew the words were not what she was feeling, so I tried again.

'Aripele. I love you and I don't want to be parted from you – ever. You will come with me if I have to put you across my shoulder and carry you. Whoring on the streets of Rome is not what I want for you.'

'And what alternative are you offering? You want me to marry old Quintus? I really believed I was coming to Rome to marry Junius. You don't offer me any better prospects than I already have in this rented room.'

'Aripele, if I come back alive from Gaul I will marry you. I promise.'

'You mean that?'

'I would never lie to you. I really will marry you. I am as much in love with you now as I was the first time we made love on the road to Pergamum.'

She looked at me. There was doubt in her eyes. She was in pain. I stepped forward and took her in my arms.

'Say you want me,' I said.

She looked at me with large, dark tearful eyes. I looked right back.

'Say you want me.'

'I want you.'

It was a faint mumbled sound. I resisted her weak efforts to push me away.

'Say you want me always.'

'I want you always,' she said with a sigh.

I pressed my lips to hers as we stood before the open door of the little room. Almost unwilling at first then surrendering to my mouth and hands, she yielded and I shut the door. It closed with a soft click and my heart skipped

Chapter XIII

"One wanders to the left, another to the right. Both are equally in error, but, are seduced by different delusions." – Horace.

Is it not strange what risks men will take for a matter of principle? Logic would have demanded of me that I wait until I knew where the amulet might be before trying to obtain it. It was pride of course, foolish pride.

I was impatient too and such feelings tempt a man to recklessness. I told no one of my plan. I was confident I would find the amulet if I could only gain access to the Mettius home. I went out alone and walked along the Vicus Patricius towards the house. It was a cool night and there was a light drizzle dampening my cloak and making it heavy.

That house had been a gift from Sulla to Marcus Mettius Senior as a reward for his support both as a military commander and as a political ally. I felt this made the Mettius Costa family doubly guilty. It was the proscriptions promulgated by Sulla that caused my grandfather's death and plunged our family into poverty – all except for a single estate near Ariminium in the north.

There was a high wall all around the house. It had a wide perimeter of gardens and a long paved road leading from the janitor's hut at the front gate up to the house.

I sneaked along the outer wall and ran through the layout of the house in my head. Although there was no street lighting, rays of moonlight lit my path. My steps were silent on the stone roadway as I hugged the wall, but if I could see my way ahead, then I was sure any passing observer might see me too. I took the risk in any case; I had to have the amulet.

I had a good mental picture of the villa dredged up from my memories of being there as a child, and felt certain I could enter and search undetected. I had experience at thievery, after all.

There was an alley at the back of the house with a tree close to the wall near the slave quarters. It had a thick overhanging bough. I had seen it before and I knew I could almost reach the pendulous branch. The night was still and the high wall shaded me from view so I took a few moments to collect myself before I jumped and reached the tree branch, grasping with my right hand. I managed to pull the branch down and hand over hand with feet scrabbling on the brickwork, reached the top of the wall.

I looked down. I was at the side of the outside slaves' quarters. Some shrubs and trees stretched between the peristylium and my perch. I jumped down and ran across. I climbed the wall of the peristylium with no difficulty for a vine had overgrown the entire surface. It was dark as an Egyptian's eyebrows when I dropped to the tiles on the other side. I recognised the place. There was no nostalgia. I had never enjoyed being there as a child. Marcus had bullied me with a relentless passion during the three years I attended lessons. In the end we had fought and my natural ability in a fight had come out – to my horror. I recalled the feeling of hitting my tormentor on the chin even though he was two years older than I was. His head shot back as he fell backwards onto the flagstones. He lay quite still and at first I thought I had killed him. Our tutor, Gennadius came out as Marcus was coming to. When my cousin turned over and vomited I ran all the way home chased by trepidation and fearing I had brought down terrible trouble on my parents. It was the last time I attended the villa. Gennadius came to my home after that.

I made my way to the stairs. It seemed unlikely the amulet would be downstairs, for slaves and servants were the main occupants of the cubicula opening out onto the peristylium.

All was quiet and I assumed everyone was asleep. I hoped Marcus would be home. I knew then that given an even chance to do so I would kill him without hesitation or remorse. After what he and his family had done to me and mine I thirsted for vengeance. It was also clear to me that the amulet was central; it was the lynchpin of that retribution. It was mine; it would belong to me again. Depriving Marcus of it was a matter of pride and satisfaction to which I looked forward almost more than his death.

I reached the top of the stairs leading up from the atrium and began to feel my way along the passage in the gloom. Nothing stirred but the darkness made me jumpy. I made slow progress. I placed each footstep in complete silence on the wooden floor. Once a board creaked and I froze with the shock of it. That tiny sound was like an army marching past, in my ears.

I was halfway along the corridor when I heard a noise from downstairs. There were men and a woman talking. She was laughing and the men, how many I could not tell, were talking. I peered down the stairwell. The sounds came closer. Their almost spectral shapes appeared and I saw three men and a woman at the foot of the stairs. They were laughing and one of the men had his arm around the woman's waist. They seemed to be drunk and they swayed as they ascended the stairs.

There was no chance of killing all of them in silence. I was not inclined to do so in any case, for my quarrel was with Marcus alone. The man with his arm around the woman released her and began mounting the stairs. He was in front and they were still laughing with inebriate humour. One of the following men groped the woman's buttocks. There was nothing negative in her reaction but she emitted peals of laughter almost falling back on top of the two men behind her. I took the opportunity to duck into the first room I came to and looked for a place to hide. Fortuna was watching over me for there was no one in the room. If there had been, I cannot say whether or not I would have killed them but I was anxious enough for the tension to make me react fast. I was sweating and my heart beat a rapid tattoo in my chest. I surveyed the room in the faint moonlight filtering in through the window opening.

There was a large chest in the far corner exposed by a pale illumination from an open doorway leading to a balcony. The cool night air swayed the drapes towards me as I crossed the room. On my left was an empty cot. I had no clear idea of what to do. To try to search an occupied house in the night had turned out to be a piece of foolishness of monumental proportions.

I pushed the billowing drapes aside and stood on the little balcony. Peering into the peristylium below, I could see two men whom I took to be slaves from their dress, crossing the courtyard below. I flattened myself against the wall and waited. To my left was another balcony and moments after I had hidden, I heard the revellers in the adjoining room.

'More wine Marcus. Must have more wine.'

'Yes, more and it's a shame we don't have more women.'

The voice was familiar. I knew then the tall man was Marcus. I could feel my anger rising but I was in total control. This was not the time to fight. Stealth was the requirement and it declared itself with ease in my thoughts.

A door slammed.

'Where's he gone?' one of the men said.

'You wanted more wine so I suppose he's gone to get it,' Marcus' voice said.

'Well we can always amuse ourselves,' the woman said. She sounded mature but I had only glimpsed her on the stairs.

'Flavia darling, come here,' Marcus said. There was a long silence then, followed by a gentle, barely audible feminine moan. I felt stupid and angry. This was not the robbery I had planned. I made no noise as I slipped back into the room I had come from.

There was not much light and it was only with difficulty I managed to fumble the catch on the chest. I was listening all the time. My nerves were taut as a ship's hawser in tow. If I had heard anything behind me, I would have jumped like a cat.

The lid opened without a sound. I thanked Fortuna for the good Roman workmanship of that chest. I lifted everything out. There was an assortment of clothes and sandals; there were three scrolls and some writing materials.

I put the scrolls into the leather pouch at my belt and smiled for I had almost neglected to bring it. There was of course no amulet. Even if it were in the house, there was no way I could find it. The house was full of people and none of them seemed inclined to sleep. I had to get out. The drop from the balcony was too great so I knew it would have to be the stairs. I decided to wait until the man who had left returned. I opened the door in silence. There were lit oil lamps in the corridor now and I could see it better. I waited for what seemed an eternity.

The man returned. He was carrying a half-amphora, which I assumed contained wine. I licked my lips, an involuntary reaction. I could just do with a cup of wine, I thought.

I gave him a few moments to re-enter the other room and

moved with silent stealth towards the stairs. It was my first mistake.

'Hey, you.'

I heard the sound and it made me jump. I ran for the stairs. There was a sound of pursuit for a moment as I gained the stairwell. The pursuer must have fallen in his drunkenness for I heard a crash behind me; I began to descend the stairs three at a time. To my horror, a slave was at the foot of the stairs and I crashed into him to the accompaniment of the sound of breaking pottery as the cups he was carrying shattered on the floor.

At that moment I realised the man carrying the wine could not possibly have been carrying cups as well. A half amphora is too large to carry with a handful of cups. Stupid mistake. It all passed through my brain in an instant.

We both fell, I on top of the slave and he struggling in a panic beneath me. I picked myself up quickly. I ran for the vine in the corner of the peristylium. I climbed. I scaled the wall in seconds. I ran as fast as I could heading for the tree where I had entered the garden. There was a growl to my right.

Dogs.

I could not run any faster nor could I look to the side without bumping into something. It must have been a big dog. The creature flung itself at me from behind as I ran. I felt its paws clawing my back and its slavering jaws snapping next to my ear. I gained the tree. I launched myself into it and climbed like a demon. The dog had grabbed my sandaled foot in its teeth and was shaking its head from one side to the other, the fangs sinking deeper with every shake.

I was hanging on with both hands. I knew I would fall if this continued. I kicked hard with my right foot and must have connected with some tender part because I heard a yelp and then I was free. I scrambled to safety as slaves and others crossed to the tree. The dog barked and growled. I dropped in pain to the cobbles below. I ran as best I could. I ran south towards the Subura. No one in his or her right mind enters the Subura after dark. It was always full of criminals but at night they roamed the streets unhindered, looking for victims to rob.

There was no pursuit. I slowed to a walk and shook my head, mumbling to myself how stupid I had been. I had not researched whether Marcus was home. I had not gained any intelligence concerning the amulet and worst of all they would now have raised the level of their security.

I looked for a street marker in the moonlight and saw a small square image of a half-moon and realised where I was. I had a good half-hour's walk and the pain from the dog-bite was escalating, making me limp. My foot was bleeding and beginning to swell. It became more and more painful until in the end I had to stop and examine the damage in the light from a window. There were puncture marks and a short open wound, but the foot and ankle had swollen from the bruising.

I limped home. I let myself in and I bathed the foot in a mixture of hot water and wine and oil. It soothed it and I crept into bed with the soft sounds of Aripele's sleeping breath.

*   *   *

We sat in the sunshine in the peristylium having our morning meal. There was a cold breeze, not unexpected for that time of year. We wore our cloaks. The trees above us leaned as they bent in the wind with soft whispers. They were bidding farewell to the long, hot summer perhaps.

We ate our favourite breakfast. I dipped the fresh bread into the watered wine and smiled at Aripele. Quintus emerged from the culina bearing a small plate of fresh figs and sat at the low table opposite us.

He looked straight at my eyes. 'So where were you last night?'

'Well, I err....'

I thought Aripele might be angry.

'You weren't at the tavern. We missed you.'

'No, I paid a visit to the Mettius house.'

'You did what?' Aripele said, putting down her cup.

'I broke in.'

'Is that why you're limping?'

'Bit of a problem with a dog.'

'A dog?' she said.

I could see from her expression this was not going my way.

'As I left it went for me, as a matter of fact.'

She said, 'We'll have to bathe it in oil and wine.'

'Not now,' I said with an impatient tone in my voice. 'Anyway, I did that last night.'

'What did you do that for on your own?' Quintus said.

'I just thought I could search the place, that's all.'

'You could have been killed,' Aripele said.

'I take it you didn't find your damned amulet then?' Quintus said.

'No, I ended up being chased by dogs. The house was full of people. Marcus was there having an orgy.'

'What did you expect to happen? An invitation to join in?' Quintus said, chewing with a frown on his face, the long scar making him look fierce.

'It isn't funny. I never got a proper chance to search. All I picked up were some old scrolls.'

'Scrolls?' Aripele said.

'Yes, I haven't read them yet. I'll get them.'

I limped into the cubiculum and emerged with my leather pouch.

'Let's see what we have here,' I said.

I began to read.

'Read it out loud Aulus,' Aripele said.

'Oh, sorry. They're letters.' I held up the rolled papyrus in front of me and began to read.

'To Marcus Mettius Costa.

From Marcus Mettius Costa the Elder, Consul, Proconsul of Raetia, Censor.

Marcus,

My physicians have expressed grave concerns over my health. I have not been well at all while you have been away. It seems to be some affectation of the heart but you know what these doctors are like. They pray a lot and give nasty potions but they achieve little. I am still very breathless despite all they do.

I have now been to Ariminium as you suggested. I searched the archives and you were quite right. It was as I had suspected all along. The property is vast. There is a distinct possibility that the deeds indicate not only ownership of the estate, but also half of the town of Ariminium. If that is so, the sale of the land back to the current occupants will accrue a fortune of fabulous dimensions.

I am very excited by the archives that I have searched and my doctors say I should be more careful to avoid excitement. It seems unlikely now, after all I have been through to fix your future inheritance, that I will see it to fruition.

You will recall what Cerberus said when he returned from the house of the Veridians. The location of the deeds is recorded on that amulet around your cousin's neck. Cerberus couldn't get Gaius to wake up again, and if the woman had known she would have talked. We would have known where those deeds were hidden if only

Cerberus had not been so heavy handed. Pity the boy was not there when he broke in.

I never understood him turning the boy away from our gates afterwards if he knew about the amulet. He said the boy had someone with him and he thought he could find him later when he was alone but he failed miserably in that. I should never have bought him from that gladiator school for I fear he is a fool.

This time I expect you to do your duty to the house of Mettius Costa. Do not fail me. You must at all costs find that cousin of yours and get that amulet back to Rome so we can examine it together.

When you have it, send word and I will write to Lucullus and ask him to release you because of my health.

I know you were angry when the Veridians were killed, but it had to be so. If we had let them live they would have hidden the documents somewhere else and we would never have been able to find them.

Do what you must to get that amulet. Cerberus told me that Gaius cursed us before he died. Such curses are nothing in the scale of things. The two of them were as nothing compared to the house of Mettius, or at least the heights that our family will rise to when we are the wealthiest in Roman history. Wealth like that might even allow you to declare a permanent dictatorship, for you could buy the entire Senate.

I am sending you an amulet in the likeness of Hecate, to guard against that curse. It does not hurt to be careful.

I hope this letter finds you in good health.

Your Father,

Marcus Mettius Costa'

When I had finished, I had difficulty speaking, for my emotions strangled any sensible speech.

'You were right then.' Quintus said.

'Yes,' was all I could say. Anger had the better of me.

'What do the other letters say?' Aripele said.

I gathered my wits and read.

'From Marcus Mettius Costa the Elder, Consul, Proconsul of Raetia, Censor.

To Marcus Mettius Costa.

Marcus,

I am sorry to disturb your time in Herculaneum. You must be enjoying the sunshine and the new villa. I have just received news of the whereabouts of your cousin Aulus Veridius. It seems he has joined the Ninth Legion while it was stationed in Rome. He was seen on the Campus Martius by Cerberus and he brought me the news immediately. Aulus was in a sword contest and Cerberus saw him on the podium getting a prize from his legate. From there your cousin went to Crete with the Ninth and now has been sent to join the legions of Lucullus.

I have arranged for you to join the legion as a tribune and you will need to join in Sinope, capital of Pontus. All arrangements have been made.

You should be able to get the amulet from your cousin. He is apparently just a legionary and your position will make it easy.

I will write again when I have seen the archive in Ariminium as you suggested.

Marcus Mettius Costa

'I think you have the letters out of order. That one goes before the first one,' Aripele said.

'Yes,' I said. 'There's another one.'

'From Marcus Mettius Costa the Elder.

To Marcus Mettius Costa.

Marcus,

My health is failing. The physicians hold little hope for me to see the spring. If it is the will of the Gods that I should leave you and join your mother then there is nothing to be done.

All I ask of you is that you obtain the amulet and find those deeds. It will preserve the house of Mettius Costa for eternity and it will be a suitable tribute to my life if you can do this thing.

Stop at nothing. The deeds must be ours.

Your father,

Marcus Mettius Costa'

The third letter was the last. I had it all now. I understood that the amulet contained much more than I had expected. I knew now who was to blame for the death of my parents and why they killed them. The thought of them being tortured for a piece of land filled me with rage and sorrow but most of all with a wish for revenge.

'I'll keep the letters. I can use them as evidence if I need to,' I said.

'Don't be daft man. If they were ever found in your possession you would be off to the galleys in no time.'

'Beats me why he didn't destroy them himself. He must be insane or stupid. They incriminate him in murder.'

'No they don't,' Aripele said. 'They implicate his dead father not him. His sole involvement seems to be that his father told him of the crime.'

'True, but he did try to kill me in Armenia and that's almost as bad. He thought I was dead and he left me there. I still want him dead.'

'Here,' Quintus said, 'I'll burn them.'

He stood and took the scrolls from me and went into the culina.

'Aulus you have to be more careful. These people are killers,' Aripele said.

'So am I,' I said, my mind racing. The revelations of the letters were eating away at me now. I felt restless and angry and involuntarily reached to my throat for the amulet. I let my hand drop with irritation. It was gone, lost perhaps forever, but I had Aripele and if it all came to nothing at least we were together.

Wearing the amulet through all those years had made me give it a special status. It had become part of me and whenever I had thought of the good things in my life, I had sought the feel of its ridged silver wiring and remembered my father's round, pleasant and smiling face, as he had placed the bulla around my neck. I missed him. I missed my mother too even now as an adult; I wanted to tell her of my day; to feel the unreserved affection that she had for me. I wanted them back. I sighed as I realised I could never go back and that despite my love for Aripele I was still alone in many ways.

Chapter XIV

"Go forth a conqueror and win great victories." – *Virgil.*

'Barbus?' Quintus said in a surprised tone.

We squelched though the mud on the Campus Martius in the sloping rain as we approached the Ninth Legion encampment. There were no fortifications since that was unnecessary outside the very gates of Rome. It was raining and we were both damp by the time we reached the encampment.

'Quintus Cerialis. By Jupiter it's good to see you. It must be three years at least.'

The speaker was a squat, broad stocky man, built like a bull, with a thick black beard. His voice a deep growl, he stepped towards us and embraced Quintus like an old long lost friend.

Quintus turned to me.

'We go back a long way. We joined the Ninth together many years ago. We fought together with a centurion called Calvus for many years.'

'I know Calvus, he was my centurion at Tigranocerta,' I said.

'I know you. You're the one who Meridius was always talking

about. He said he was training you for something special. How come you're with this disreputable fellow?'

'If anyone else spoke of me in that way...'

'Ease up old friend,' went on Barbus, 'It was a joke, you know. You remember jokes?'

'What happened to you? Where are your medals and vine cane?'

'Lost 'em.'

'What?'

'Like I said. They almost crucified me but Procillus spoke up for me at the court-martial and they just broke me to the ranks.'

'What did you do?'

'I slapped a stupid chicken-hearted tribune around a bit when he tried to retreat from the field, taking the whole of our right flank with him. We lost the battle anyway, but at least it wasn't my men who caused that.'

'You hit a senior officer?'

'Couldn't resist it. Po-faced bastard. He lied to the legate and I got arrested after the battle.'

'Who was it?'

'That bastard Mettius. If I get a chance to get even without endangering myself I will.'

'Marcus Mettius Costa?' I said.

'Yes. Bastard.'

'He's my cousin. We hate each other.'

'Then I don't envy you. He can make your life hell you know. I heard though he was hoping for a transfer to the Tenth anyway. They're the apple of Caesar's eye. His favourites and he takes them everywhere. They've already left for Gaul and we're to march north in a few weeks' time.'

'Who's the legate?' Quintus said.

'Cicero, you know, the brother of that senator.'

'He has a good reputation,' I said.

Both men looked at me.

'It all depends on what you mean. He's good at leading men and in a battle; he fights at the front. He's a bit humourless for my taste but fair though,' Barbus said.

'Barbus, you're not going to marry him you know. Anyway you don't choose your Legates in an election so you just have to get on as best you can,' Quintus said.

'So this little chap here is a decurion?'

'Yes, that's right. I was promoted in Pontus.'

'Do something special?'

'No, just fought well against the corsairs in a sea battle. The one where Meridius was killed. I fought alongside him.'

Barbus regarded me with a look that might have been respect. That fight was one which had been widely talked about in the Ninth Legion even after Tigranocerta.

'I thought maybe you would have been at Tigranocerta.'

'I was, but got injured and they sent me to Sinope. It took me a long time to recover.'

'Well, you're back with us now. I'm in the second cohort first century,' Barbus said, scratching his beard.

'That's my old century. The optio and I are close friends.'

'It makes a change from the fifth cohort I was centurion in. If it wasn't for the rank, it would be like a promotion.'

We all smiled at that and walked to the centurion's tent at the second cohort headquarters. Quintus raised the tent flap without ceremony and shouted into the tent.

'Hey. You. You fat, old goat.'

A growling sound came from inside and with frightening speed Gaius Calvus Vegetius appeared with a snarl on his face and a sword in his hand. He had clearly been woken from sleep.

'What the..?' he said as he looked at us, 'Quintus, you old dog.'

Calvus too, embraced Quintus as if he were a brother, home from the wars. I looked at the three of them, Quintus, Calvus and Barbus and thought they could almost be brothers from their appearance. They were hard, dark, stocky, muscular men; each as dangerous and irascible as the other. These were the backbone of the Roman army. Tough men, strong men, whose lives were threatened time and again, but who always survived. They were natural born-to-the-fight killers.

'Veridius. Welcome home. We were all very sad when you were killed in Armenia. Now you're back of course there won't be any special treatment you know that don't you?'

'Didn't expect any, sir.'

'Just joking. You know that cousin of yours Marcus Mettius? It was him who told me you would desert before we left Sinope and that was why I was so rough with you. You've proven yourself since. I am glad you're with us.'

'He did me a lot of harm. It's a personal matter however between us.'

'I realise that. Optio Sinna is over there. You may wish to see him about quarters. I suspect there is room in his tent for an old friend.'

'Yes sir.'

I saluted and bade farewell to Quintus. 'When I get a chance I'll visit if that's alright with you.'

'Of course, but I don't think you will have much time if the legion is moving on. Isn't that right Gaius?'

'Yes, we have pretty intensive training and no one is getting any leave at the moment, even your friend Junius.'

I left them there, the three friends. They began laughing and swapping stories as they sat by the meagre fire burning outside Calvus' tent.

Junius was not there. I found his tent and dumped my gear in front of it. I had Quintus' shield in its leather cover and a spare pair of sandals. Quintus had insisted I took his shield. He said he had no further use for it anyway and it had served him well in his time in the Ninth. The rest of my gear consisted of clothes and the knife Polymecles had given me. He had said that if it saved my life even once he would be happy and it had indeed done that when Aripele and I were attacked. I wondered whether he was alive and well, but knowing him, a change of rule would make little difference to his life. There are those who can cope with any change of government and still turn a profit and he was one of those.

I pondered also, what had happened to Hypsicratea. I wondered if she was now happy with the return of her husband, the King. I hoped she was, but I knew I would never see her again and my heart was twice as heavy at parting from both her and now Aripele.

'Hey, Decurion.'

I turned to face my friend with a smile on my lips.

'Junius. I'm now back. Maybe it will be like old times but a lot of things have happened since last we shared a tent.'

'Share a tent? I'm an optio now; I don't share a tent with anyone.'

'Oh, come on.'

'Just kidding. Where's your sense of humour?'

'Not funny, I'm still getting used to the idea of sleeping on the ground in a military tent. I haven't done that in over two years you know.'

'How's Aripele?'

'Fine.'

'How is she?'

'Fine, she's staying with Quintus and is practising sewing. She thinks that if she makes tapestries she'll make money and Quintus encourages her.'

'Tapestries?'

'Well apparently she learned it from her mother as a child and thinks she can turn a profit.'

'I meant, is she really upset?'

'How can she be upset when she's got me?'

'Well I've got you now and I'm unhappy.'

'Oh be quiet. What are you unhappy about, you've got a wife.'

'That's the problem. Try telling a wife you're away for months or years. She's very upset.'

'I don't relish being away either but it's something we have to get used to. I've got another thirteen years to go. I've had a very comfortable year this year too.'

'Well you're back now. Better get used to it.'

'What's on tomorrow?'

'Drills and more drills then mock fights and weapons practice. Then guess what? Drills. The usual stuff. It's all getting pretty serious now though. Only a few weeks to go before we get to Gaul and start fighting the Barbarians.'

'To be honest, I'm looking forward to it. I joined the army to make a reputation and get promoted and frankly, the time we had in Pontus bored me stiff. The only decent battle I had was Tigranocerta. I missed all the others.'

'You didn't miss much I can tell you. We won at Ataxarta and then we started to lose. Battle after battle we found that they had superior numbers and although we'd thought we knew all about fighting their armoured cavalry it turned out they were harder to kill than we thought.'

'Sounds hilarious. What are the Gauls like?'

'Rumour has it that they're big and tough but not well organised. The men don't seem too confident I must say.'

'What about this Caesar chap?'

'Him? He's a pen pusher. He had a short spell in Spain, put down a rebellion there and made huge amounts of profit out of their mining. No one thinks he can do much in Gaul and that's why they've given it to him. Pompey's on his way to Asia Minor to trounce Mithridates and we end up with this Caesar chap. I ask you.'

'Well if no one's heard of him, maybe he's going to turn out to be a great leader. We should give him a chance.'

'All I've heard suggests he's a womaniser and a religious one too. You know he's Pontifex Maximus?'

'Yes I heard that. Why is the main religious leader of Rome going off to Gaul?'

'Don't know. Rumour has it he's bought himself five years as Proconsul and aims to conquer Gaul. Impossible in five years if you ask me. We'll find out soon enough.'

'Let's share a jug of wine and stew on it.'

'The perfect end to a perfect day?'

'Something like that.'

I had started another journey. It was a journey of hope. I wanted the amulet and had to find Marcus to get it. Where was it? Had he really taken it with him?

Back in the arms of the legion I was restricted, but so was Marcus. He could no more escape me than I could now escape my destiny. As I closed my eyes, I hoped that the Fates would lead not just to the amulet but to a military glory such as I felt my ancestry deserved. I dreamt of battles and glory that night.

BOOK 2:
GAUL

Chapter I

"As a rule, what is out of sight disturbs men's minds more seriously than what they see." – Gaius Julius Caesar.

An icy rain fell from a dull, overcast sky leaving the ground in front of us a sodden field of greasy mud. Two crows cawed overhead, circling before soaring off west as a gust of frigid breeze took them away. In the ordinary course of things we might have seen it as a bad omen but not today. Today we were confident. Like all the others in my century I felt I had trained to a honed perfection. We had drilled for weeks before leaving Rome. Junius and I had bidden farewell to our women and it felt as if a chapter had closed.

They had detached us from the main body of the Ninth as a vexillation. There were five hundred of us and they had sent us to deal with a group of Gauls who were moving north to join the Gallic and German armies who were gathering. It was my first real battle since we had arrived and I was finding it hard to get used to the cold weather, for spring in Rome was a warm season but here it seemed as if it was always cold.

The Gauls, dressed in furs and skins over the bright-coloured leggings of which they were so fond, had lined up ten ranks thick. They stood glaring at us in no apparent order, the men in the front rank still, those at the back waving black banners with circular red motifs. They were chanting in deep slow voices, menacing and fierce. They were a large war band almost a thousand strong, and since our vexillation numbered less than half their force we knew we would have our work cut out.

To the Gauls' right was a group of horsemen; one could hardly call them cavalry. Like the Gallic infantry, they stood in no particular order. I thought they were a rabble who would run. I was proud to be a Roman on that day in that place fighting for both the honour and glory of Rome and the bull standard of the Ninth Legion, borne high above me by the standard-bearer, next to the Vexillium. Of course, we were too small a detachment to carry an eagle but a Vexillium is almost as precious to us.

The enemy became silent as if a curtain had descended upon their chant and a tall bearded warrior stepped out of the front ranks. He held a long sword and carried a green-painted shield. Bellowing at us, he stode towards our ranks, beating his shield with the hilt of his weapon. He was shouting, his voice high pitched but loud. Crossing the space between us he kept screaming. When he stopped, he faced us then began to strut up and down all the while bellowing in his strange language.

I suspected he wanted to fight someone single-handed, challenging the might of Rome in the hope of killing our best and demoralising us. It was wasted on us however. We were a disciplined troop and no one would now break ranks for such nonsense. Besides, he looked foolish standing alone with no one coming forward to accept his challenge. We ignored him and after what seemed like only moments, the battle began.

The velites went in first. I often puzzled how these skirmishers managed to run with such quick, light steps in the mud, loosing their javelins at the Gaul's front rank and stepping back without a scratch. They were fit and nimble I supposed. It was after all, a young man's section in the army and they seemed to be able to keep up this skirmishing all day if the infantry would let them. I saw the Gallic champion fall, skewered by a pilum. It hit him in the face and he stopped shouting then. The man on my left laughed. It was a bad way to die but the man was foolish. We don't play by their rules; we make our own and so Fortuna smiles upon us, for we are strong.

The velites' one real vulnerability was cavalry, but as long as they were well supported by the infantry they could fall back with most of them unscathed. The Gauls possessed few archers and these had difficulties with the moving targets presented by our velites. besides, the wet weather made the bowstrings much weaker so our lads were having an easy time of it to-day, I thought.

Once we had softened them up our staggered centuries of hastatae moved forwards in grim silence. I was at the front of the second cohort since I was in the first century. The big rectangular shield Quintus had given me was as good a protection as a man could have, but it was heavy and my arm tired easier than I would have liked. I wondered why the Gauls had not yet learned that shields, unbroken ranks and discipline always won.

Twenty yards from the advancing Gaul army, we released our first pila. Our javelins had hardened tips that would bend on impact on the softer metal in the haft. The damaged tips rendered the pila useless to the enemy if they tried to throw them back. The volley tore gaping rents in the undisciplined ranks of the Gauls but they were brave men and proud. They came on at a run. Their blue and balck-painted faces grimaced and their tongues protruded as they screamed their war cries.

The next volley of pila forced the second rank of Gauls to clamber over the writhing, bleeding, dying forms of their comrades. They charged again although our missiles had reduced their momentum. They hit our front rank with incredible force anyway. I had never imagined the volume and violence of that first impact. The long barbarian swords scythed down in wide slashes. They dented shields and helmets, ringing against our Roman steel. I remembered my training. Push with the shield. Stab with the sword. The teaching was to maintain a grim silence. It created reflex action and killed the fear, for the fear was what paralysed men. Every movement was one we had practised until it became mechanical. When your man is down, stab at the man to your right; protect the man on your left. Silence and order.

That familiar feeling gripped me. It was anger – a rage. A red rage. The smell of blood in my nostrils and the cries of men dying, fighting, struggling. Blood, flesh and death. I loved it; I don't know why. I stayed in line but I stabbed and kicked and thrust my shield forward in a frenzy.

These Gauls were big men but they died all the same. We presented a solid wall. Gladii stabbed forward in the press. Barbarian after Barbarian fell. They had no room to swing their swords and we were like the prow of a ship, pushing forwards into the water, slicing through the waves of the Gallic ranks. I lost count of the kills. My mind raced. I looked forward to the next opponent as we stepped forward over their bodies, our sandaled feet squelching in the reddening mud. Gore smeared and covered us. It pervaded our hair, our faces, our armour and perhaps our very shades.

Their cavalry formed up and charged into our left flank. They had beautiful horses. The beasts were small but feisty and they fought like their riders. The cavalry were in a wedge and their riders stabbed down with long spears. Our response was contemptuous. The shields closed as our men turned. The front rank knelt. The second rank held their shields up. Impenetrable.

Staunch and hard we held them. Many horses fell whinnying as our Roman gladii sliced and stabbed, hamstringing and disembowling.

Soon, the Gauls ran, scattering into a wood behind them. Of the thousand men we took on, only about half survived. At last, we broke our silence. We raised our swords and shields and jeered at them as they ran. There was little pause in our ranks as we wandered among the vanquished, slitting throats and stabbing the wounded men. We took no prisoners. I wondered then what the survivors would say to their commanders. Did they simply say they had lost yet another battle? Did they blame their Gods? It was becoming ridiculous. We always beat them.

We collected and kept all the useful and valuable things they carried for the legion's coffers. There were silver arm rings, torques and of course, weapons. We collected our dead and wounded. Across the churned and rutted mud, orderlies crossed back and forth, binding wounds and lugging stretchers amid the groans and cries of our wounded and dying men. Above all, there was a smell of death; offal stinking and bodies covered in blood, excrement and urine. Battles are never pretty.

We formed up into our centuries in the sloping rain and the wind whispered across our helmets as we marched to the camp we had built the day before. It might seem odd that the general mood was not one of great elation. This was business. It was work to us. We were a machine. A war-machine. There was little emotion expressed. We knew the next day would bring much the same as the last. Barbarian armies, war bands, big battles and small, it was all the same to us. We were Rome. We were the conquerors and victors of the known world. The glory of Rome was our business and we did it well.

We made our way to our tents. The morning fire was still smouldering and I added some wood as we sat next to it trying to absorb the little warmth it threw out. The sweat of the battle was cold on my skin now.

'Of course you realise that was just a skirmish, don't you?' smiled Junius. 'The real battle is yet to come.'

'Seemed like a battle to me,' I said.

'The ones we fought to-day were only some Gallic allies of the Germans not the real army. Boii I think Calvus said. Ariovistus, the Suebi king, is marching his army to a place up the river and it looks like he he's got a lot of German allies who've crossed the Rhine to support him.'

'I heard they were up north somewhere and we can't find them.'

'Calvus was telling me the Bald Eagle's sent Procillus and some other tribune to trace where Ariovistus has gone. We're following and I think he wants to take on their whole army. I don't mind a fight but if they take you prisoner they cut off your bollocks and burn you.'

'So, it doesn't sound like a Saturnalia party, but the General's not made a bad decision yet and he looks after his men. And you called him a pen-pusher.' I said.

'No. you're right. He's no pen pusher. I heard some of the men are talking about refusing to fight. It's a bit like before Tigranocerta. Morale seems rock-bottom. Doesn't help that the General favours the Tenth so much either,' Junius said.

'However big these Barbarians are, they can't match Roman discipline. We fight as a job of work but they fight as if it was some sort of game. We always win. That's the Roman way.'

We saw Calvus approaching. He had another centurion in tow as he picked his way among the tents.

'That was a tasty fight. They outnumbered us two to one. Such odds are nothing to us of course,' Calvus said.

'We were just saying, our discipline can defeat any German

bear, however big he is and that's the Roman way. We don't get the impression morale is very good though.'

'You're quite right lad. There's been some seditious talk in the camp, that's why I'm looking around now. As for the Germans well, we faced the Armenian cavalry so I think we can stand against any barbarians no matter how big they are. By the way, if you hear any words of dissent, you must tell me at once. We can't have a recurrence of the breaches of discipline we had in Armenia.'

'I'm sure it won't come to that. If we hear anything, we'll let you know.' I said.

Calvus slapped me on the arm. 'You're always a sound lad Aulus. At the third hour there'll be a briefing by the General and all officers are to attend. That means you two, since even decurions are invited.' Calvus said.

He grinned, not the most pleasant sight since his teeth were stained and his breath foetid. He poked me in the chest with his vine cane. 'We've got a big battle coming up against Ariovistus and we'll need that sword arm of yours. Don't get hit on the head this time.'

'No sir,' I said.

Calvus continued his rounds and Junius said, 'We'd better get some food and report for the briefing. It'll be about the battle with Ariovistus. After all, the whole bloody German army and the local Gaul chieftains too are marching this way.'

'We don't need any allies, at least not Gauls. They're unreliable and seem to turn on us all the time.'

'The Aedui are still loyal and we've got almost a thousand horsemen from them. Mind you, they can't even say discipline let alone demonstrate it that lot.' Junius said.

'Strikes me we really aren't here to help the Aedui defend themselves from the Germans you know.'

'No, I think the General has plans to see off the Germans and stay. Maybe the Aedui will regret asking for help. You know that fable about Old King Log and that. Think their cavalry'll be any good?'

'Who knows? At the least they can still ride down the stragglers after we've smashed the infantry,' I said. 'The Germans even try to fight in phalanx formation so one of the officers was telling me. They clearly don't understand how funny we find their vulnerable flanks. About as well informed as the Greeks.'

We both smiled at the thought. The Roman army had long since realised that phalanx formation was very strong from in front but very weak on the flanks. Such formations were ponderous at turning to the side unlike our mobile and more versatile Roman legionaries. By staggering the centuries we Romans always defeated the Greeks since we could attack from in front and from the side at the same time. The idea that the big Germans might employ Greek tactics amused us. We cooked and ate some cereal porridge, wondering what the General had in mind for his briefing.

'We might be able to civilize these creatures, but it looks like we'll be in for a long haul in trying' I said.

'There are at least twenty different tribes in Gaul, and all of them on a war footing. Rumour has it we're going to take them all on, but that way, we can flood the slave market at home and we'll all get rich. There may be more Gauls in Rome than Romans in the end.'

Chapter II

"If I cannot influence the Gods, I shall move all hell." – Virgil.

Quintus Cicero, the legate of the Ninth Legion stood with Caesar facing the assembled officers. He called for silence as Caesar climbed to the rough wooden platform. Cicero was the son of a senator but a man well-liked by the rank and file of the legion. He had shown his leadership skills many times in both battle and in training. He was Caesar's right-hand man – hard and inflexible despite his background.

His men loved him. He had led them through many battles and they responded to his leadership giving their lives and their limbs for the glory of Rome at the command of their legate.

The sun shone behind the proconsul sending a faint cold light streaming across the barren, trodden, muddy parade ground. A faint pastel rainbow hung in the air to the west, spectral almost in the drizzle falling from the grey sky. Above him, a bird circled and crowed then flew away to the west. A gloomy silence fell upon the assembled legionaries. Crows are bad luck as anyone knows.

There were many in the legions who talked about refusing to fight and some of the men had openly voiced their dissent.

Floggings had taken place almost every day and I wondered how the Bald Eagle would be able to turn these events around and inspire the men. Across the silent drizzle-soaked senior officers Caesar projected his voice with a confidence and volume that made many look up.

'Men, I, who am your Proconsul and Governor of Gaul and Pontifex Maximus of Rome, greet you. I am your General, your leader and your priest. The signs are good for a battle.'

Silence still diffused the scene. Some men looked at each other but most stared at the ground. The balding general looked down at us.

'That bird was an omen. Yes. An omen.' He paused for a moment and then went on. 'It circled the Praetorium three times and flew to the west. He scorns our enemies and so should we. He has left us a sign; yes, a sign from the Gods which hangs there in the sky as a giant coloured bow. It is a message from Venus, from whom I am directly descended and whose blood flows in my veins. We will use that bow against Ariovistus.'

A longer pause followed to allow this piece of spontaneous augury to sink in. We Roman soldiers are notable for being superstitious and Caesar had played upon this throughout the campaign. He was the only one in the assembled company who had the religious status to perform augury, examining the entrails of sacrificed animals to read the future. Elected to the highest religious office in Rome as Pontifex Maximus four years before, he knew how to take advantage of his men's beliefs.

'Our scouts tell us of a great host encamped to the north and that bird heralds a great victory to come. I know this because I am your priest. I am Pontifex Maximus. These rebels are Germans – Barbarians as big as any we've faced in our campaigns here in Gaul. They are truly worthy opponents. Their king makes light of the power of Rome. He scorns us, mocks us and invites us to attack in spite of the senate calling him Friend of Rome. He thinks he is invincible but we, brave Romans, know better. They don't like us and they fear our pila, our gladii and our discipline. We will crush them in silence and see them flee before us and hear the wailing of their women – for – we – are – Romans.'

Weak cheers arose from some of the men but most were from the direction of the Tenth Legion officers. I could see that Caesar felt his speech was not going the way he had planned. I listened and found my admiration for his ability to improvise was involuntary.

'I know there is talk among you that we are out-numbered but what are their numbers against our solid Roman discipline? There is talk that the enemy is fierce. Are we not more fierce? There is talk of defeat but we have lost no battles in this place. There is even, so I hear, talk of torture if they are victorious. Well, hear me.'

He paused for dramatic effect again and his voice rose to a volume and depth that seemed to command the men's attention.

'We'll crush them.' Another pause. 'If I hear talk that you, my men, will not follow me, then I will go alone, taking only the Tenth, my loyal troops, who fear no Barbarians and whose valour has been proven time and again. The rest of you can stay here and witness a great victory, to which you will have given nothing. Is that what you want – or do you want the glory of Rome?'

Calls from all parts of the Praetorium responded to Caesar's hard voice with, 'No. We follow the Eagle' 'The Eagle.' 'The Eagle.'

'Then let it be so,' bellowed the General. 'For to-morrow we march and tomorrow we add another glorious victory to the scrolls of the history of Rome'

Amidst tumultuous cheers, Caesar left the platform and stepped into his leather tent followed by Titus Lepidus who held open the flap then entered, followed by Marcus Antonius and Quintus Cicero his most trusted legates.

'Optimistic bugger isn't he?' I said.

Junius smiled and put his mouth close to my ear, shouting above the noise, 'Sounds like we all have to be optimistic now. We've got a fight on our hands and the boys liked his speech.'

'Damn the Tenth – they really are his favourites. Well, we can match them,' I said.

'Maybe so, but this Ariovistus seems to be a dangerous man.'

'Yes they say he's as big as a bear and he's succeeded in uniting a lot of tribes for this war.'

'I thought he was invited by the Alobroges?' he said.

'Sort of, but I think he wants to stay as much as we do. I wouldn't want to be a Gaul. It's like two eagles fighting over a rabbit. We're fighting Gauls and Germans in one go. If morale holds up we should win.'

'Isn't that the point?'

A voice behind us interrupted the shouted conversation.

'So it's you.'

The sound of that voice made me stop in my tracks. It was a familiar high-pitched southern accent behind me. I turned, knowing who it was. The man was fat, unkempt and hairy. His brown beard, tangled and matted, obscured his red throat. He wore a centurion's lorica perched upon his fluctuant torso and he wore a medal of the army of Lucullus. It was not a hot day but he had beads of sweat on his upper lip.

'Centurion Bassus. Haven't seen you since Armenia. My last memory of you was when you were sat on your fat arse on the ground with your helmet over your eyes at Tigranocerta. I see you're limping. Perhaps my cut has improved your walk.'

'You call me 'sir'. As for the limp. It is from a war wound I got from an Armenian prince whom I killed honourably in battle.'

'You didn't kill him, I did. You know that.'

'If no one knows but you knows it, it's only my word against yours, isn't it?' Bassus said. 'Funny how things work out. I got this medal for that.'

'You...'

'Now, now, Veridius, you wouldn't strike a senior officer would you?'

Junius grabbed my arm.

'Aulus, have some sense.'

'Yes, Veridius, have some sense. You should listen to your optio. Don't worry though; we'll have an opportunity to settle things before long.'

Bassus grinned. I wanted to kill him. He was Marcus' henchman and a vicious killer. I had fought him before my injury and had every reason to want him dead. Junius pulled me away.

'Now you've done it,' he said.

'No, that man deserves to die. He tried to kill me at Tigranocerta and set me up for Marcus to take the amulet.'

'I know all that. You whinge on about it endlessly. It's lucky for you he's in the Tenth, we don't mix much with them except in town. If he was in the Ninth I wouldn't give much for your chances. Centurions have a lot of power.'

'Maybe, but I'll get him one day.'

'I wish you luck. I think he's untouchable. Forget him.'

'Forget? I can't forget what he and Marcus did to me. I want them both dead.'

'You won't get anywhere if you carry on like this. Go slow and you make time, as my dad used to say.'

I shrugged and we walked into Bibracte for a drink and to meet our men whom we had arranged to find at one of the taverns.

Chapter III

"In other living creatures the ignorance of themselves is nature, but in men it is a vice." – Boethius.

The night air had a chill to it and I wrapped my cloak around me as we walked with plodding footsteps through the mud. The tavern was a mud and wattle building but big enough to accommodate a cohort. There were three central stalls where they served wine. The place was stuffy and smelled of vomit. They hadn't changed the straw on the floor since the previous night, but this was the norm as the place was seldom empty enough for cleaning. Some of our men drank the local beer, acidic and strong, but it was not a drink favoured by many as long as there was wine to hand. On this particular evening there was wine and plenty of it. The tavern was packed and it was a struggle even to get a drink. We bought jugs of wine to avoid queuing more than once.

Junius and I pushed our way through the crowd and found Barbus and some of our lads seated at a table in the corner. It was like fighting my way through a battle but with no weapons drawn. Swords were forbidden in the town unless on official business, although we carried our knives in our belts openly. Some had knives almost as long as a gladius in any case, which served to prove what a stupid rule it was.

'Junius. Aulus. Over here.'

Barbus stood up shouting at the top of his gravelly voice. He gesticulated with both hands for us to join him. Seated round the table were a half dozen of the lads from my own Contubernium. I nodded as we joined them and they moved along the benches to accommodate us. There was a small brazier under the table and a blanket that overhung the table edge to keep in the heat.

'Manlius here was just talking about us going off up north to fight the Germans, isn't that right Manlius?'

'Well it's no bloody secret,' I said, raising my voice against the tumult all around us. Men were laughing, shouting and joking.

'No. There are no secrets in this army, I can tell you,' Barbus said. 'Manlius hears everything you know. His ears are so long they can listen round corners.'

'Well there's no harm in my telling you about the briefing; we're marching north tomorrow to take on that German king, Ariovistus. The Tenth are keen but everyone else seems upset with the supposed size of the Germans.'

'As that prostitute round the corner says all the time, "Barbus, size really does matter after all" but I'm not sure the same thing applies in a fight.'

The surrounding men burst into laughter. I smiled and took a mouthful of wine.

'We can take on any size of German, can't we?' I said.

'That's what the whore said,' Calvus bawled at me.

We all laughed at that. I said, 'As long as we hold the line and fight like we're trained to do. You were the one who told me that.'

'I know. No one here is frightened, are we?'

He looked at the men and they were still smiling but I couldn't tell if it was the wine or their real feelings.

'Junius, did you see that girl outside?'

'No.'

'Maybe she's gone. She was asking after you.'

'Me?' Junius said.

'Yes, she asked if I could get her a horse instead next time.'

The men laughed again and Junius frowned. He didn't like them laughing at him and he was of a size making it unwise to upset him. I put a hand on his shoulder and he shrugged it off. He seemed to know a joke when he heard one.

We passed the evening drinking and the hours went by rapidly enough. Men began to leave and I decided to go back to the camp. Junius wanted to stay so I left him there and began the long trudge back across the muddy tracks. I came out of the doorway and turned to follow the path. Bibracte was dark and silent as a Cretan Labyrinth and I had not walked more than a few yards when a large figure loomed ahead.

I stepped to the side to let the man past and felt a blow on my head powerful enough to throw me to the ground. I remember feeling the mud against my cheek before two big men picked me up by both arms and dragged me struggling, into the gap between two huts.

I was dizzy but conscious as I felt a fist hit my stomach. It was forceful, as if a mule had kicked me. I vomited. My breath came back in gasps and I lifted my head. Although it was too dark to make out his features clearly I knew it was Bassus from his shape. He leaned close to me and his breath smelled of rotting things.

'I'm going to kill you this time. You survived last time because you were lucky, this time nothing will save you.'

I heard him draw a weapon; it was a soft leathery scraping sound.

'My friends know exactly where I am. They'll be here any minute.'

'Well even if they are, they'll be too late.'

He raised his hand. I presumed he was holding his knife. I had to do something. I had no intention of dying here. They held me upright in a vice-like grip on either side. I knew I couldn't access my weapon. Bassus was close up to me. He was gloating. If there is one thing a killer has to learn, it's not to gloat and not to talk but to get on with the task at hand.

I brought up my knee hard. It was a very hard blow. It caught the centurion between the legs and he emitted a wheezing high-pitched sound as he missed me with his blade. By instinct, I pulled to my right, to avoid the knife. The blade must have struck the man on my left, because as Bassus fell doubled-up onto the mud my left arm was free for a moment. It was long enough. I hooked my fist into the throat of the man to my right. Pivoting in his grip I stepped fast to my right. I was free and I ran. I ran towards the tavern and all but floored an inebriate Barbus coming out with the men.

'Quick. I've been attacked.'

'What?' Barbus said.

'I was just attacked by three men, follow me.'

I backtracked but it was too late. I heard a scuffling sound from the back of the alley between the huts but it was too dark to see anything and although we went in we found nothing.

Junius slapped me on the back.

'You all right? No wounds?'

'No I'm fine. My head hurts and I vomited all that wine but otherwise I'm still here.'

'Did you see their faces?'

'I can't see your face, let alone anyone else's. I know who it was, though.'

'Bassus?'

'Yes.'

'I'd better watch your back from now on. It seems a very stupid thing to do, attacking you so close to the camp.'

'I think it just means his thirst for revenge has got the better of him or maybe it's Marcus who's the driving force.'

'From Marcus' point of view there is no advantage in him killing you now. He's got the amulet anyway. Probably you're right and Bassus is acting alone. Lucky he's not in the Ninth anymore.'

'Venus, my head hurts.'

'I never thought that part of you was so sensitive. Are you sure it isn't your pride that's hurting?'

'Maybe you're right. Perhaps I should kill the bugger.'

'You'd only get caught and crucified. Why don't we wait and see what happens?'

We talked as we walked to the camp, but when we got there neither of us could recall the password.

'I can't let you in without the password, you know that,' the guard said.

'Do we look like Gallic spies to you?' Junius asked.

'No, but I have my orders and Calvus is in charge.'

'You let the other men in. What's your problem with us?' I said.

'Like I said, I don't recognise you with all that mud on your face and I'm very cautious of Calvus.'

'What do you suggest we do?'

'Don't mind. Don't care either, you're not coming in.'

'You'd better go and get Calvus then hadn't you? He won't be pleased to be woken.'

The guard shut the gate to the accompaniment of a string of invectives from both of us. Barbus and the others would laugh when they caught us up but at least they would know the watchword. We waited.

'Well, what have we here then?'

It was Calvus. He wore his lorica and looked the same as he did in the daytime.

'I'm sorry sir. We forgot the watchword and this guard wouldn't let us in, even though it's obvious we're with the legion.'

'Lad's just doing his duty Aulus. If everyone here did their duty we'd have no problems at all. Get in here.'

Barbus joined us as the sentry opened the gate. He knew the watchword, to my irritation. We should have been patient.

'Calvus, my friend,' he said, 'we had a good night in Bibracte – you should have been there.'

'Guard duty tonight. Letting in soldiers too stupid to remember their watchword.' He glanced sideways at me.

'Well it happens.' Barbus said. 'How about a drink?'

'I don't have any in the camp.'

'No, but we have. Here, Manlius, show him what you're carrying.'

Manlius had a whole amphora of wine on his shoulder. How he had managed to carry it all the way was a complete mystery to me but where there is a will there is a way I suppose. Within only a few minutes we were ensconced in Calvus' tent and were drinking again. I told Calvus about my encounter with Bassus.

'He's a nasty piece of work alright. Caught red-handed embezzling funds and they let him off on a technicality. Man can fight though, despite his fat gut.'

'I fought him in Armenia after I had killed that Armenian Prince. He got all the credit.'

'Yes,' Calvus said, 'that was because you were dead.'

They all laughed and the conversation moved on to more mundane things but at the back of my mind I kept a place for vigilance. I knew there would be more attacks, but how they would come I could not fathom. I figured Marcus wanted me dead and Bassus had no qualms doing it for him.

Chapter IV

"Ambition is a vice, but it may be the father of virtue" –
Quintillianus.

It was still dark. The cornua sounded all around the camp. I
awoke with a foul taste in my mouth and the grandfather of all
headaches. The night before came back to mind. We had drunk
wine until very late in Calvus' tent. I managed to find my tent,
although I did stumble into someone else's at one point. It almost
resulted in a fight. It was early morning after all and the sleeping
optio awoke fighting fit as I sat on him.

I thought of Aripele. I missed her. Her dark eyes, her black
hair. I wondered when I would see her again and worried in case
someone else would overwhelm her with his advances. She had
promised me that no other men would exist to her. She had been
a whore and I suspected it had put her off men rather than the
converse. I think she was relieved not to have to ply her trade and
that may have been what stimulated her to seek a more stable life
in Rome in the first place.

I had no real fears for her in Rome. I knew Quintus would
look after her as long as his warring neighbour sent no more

ruffians to kill him. He had left the house on the Quirinal to Aripele in his will. It had surprised me for I had not realised they were close and he had known her such a short time. He had no other family I suppose and he told me it could not go to better hands if he was dead. A hard man that, the tough outer shell of a killer, but a softer more emotional interior than I would ever have imagined.

The cornua blasted again jolting me back to reality. Time to move on. A soldier's life was like that I reasoned. Damp, sweaty smells and not enough to eat. As a decurion my sole privilege was that my men had to be on parade before me. If they were absent my privilege was to be disciplined. I rubbed my face and sat on the straw bed I had made three days before. I swung my legs over the edge and tried to assemble my thoughts. A louse itched my beard. Wine. Oh Gods, what was that wine? The throbbing in my head reverberated in my consciousness.

Junius stirred in his bed.

'Hey you sir, my Senior, my Boss; about time you raised that ugly face of yours and roused your men,' I said using my parade ground voice in Junius' ear.

'Oh Jupiter Optimus Maximus. Do you have to do that? I was dreaming of this Treveri girl I met at Bibracte, the one with the big puppies. I was just about to...'

'Never mind that, the trumpets have been blaring for ages and we haven't eaten yet.' I was feeling testy and anxious to get on the road.

'Alright, I'm ready' Junius said. He had a love of the simple life as a soldier. It was his view of an easy time. He smiled in silence to himself as he buckled the lorica over his tunic. Glancing down, I could see that he was still thinking of his dream and the unfulfilled sexual acts he had anticipated.

Within a few minutes we had emptied the tent and the line

soldiers were packing it up ready for the ox-driven carts to pick up all of the camp's tents. The whole army was marching and marching to war; there was no time for stragglers.

The biggest annoyance was the mud. It was a damp, cold place at best and we were used to the wet. It was the mud that clung to everything, even the food. It speckled all our gear and there was little time for washing unless we were in a town with a bathhouse. That of course was a rarity. The nearest town with a bathhouse was Bibracte in the south and of course the whorehouse was even more popular. The tavern took second place and the baths seemed to dwindle to the end of the list. It was the army after all.

Our century formed up ready for the march. Calvus approached trudging through the mud followed by the senior optio. To my annoyance he showed no signs of feeling worse for wear. He had taken a skinful too but must have been made of steel. I thought I could hate a man like that.

'Aulus Veridius, where do you think you're going?' Calvus said as he rapped me on the helmet with his vine cane.

'To join the century for the march, sir.' I replied, standing to attention.

'Wrong; you seem to have a very convenient memory for a decurion. I told you to remember to report first thing to the Praetorium or have you forgotten? It was after the third jug of wine as I recall. I told you your orders and you seem to have forgotten. Do you know what happens to soldiers who forget their orders, you miserable excuse for a Roman legionary? Well?'

'They get reminded?' I said, uncertain whether Calvus was serious.

Calvus chuckled, 'No you laggard, they probably end up senators. Seriously, though, I did tell you. The legate of the Tenth has some special instructions for ten men of the Ninth and I suggested you. A donkey could do this job – that's why I thought of you.' Calvus appeared to think this so funny the grin on his face seemed embedded.

'Sir.' I saluted and marched, no doubt looking smarter than I felt, down the Via Praetoria. My head hurt and I needed to visit the latrines more than I needed a visit to the Praetorium.

I stopped outside the legate's tent and waited. A beautiful white horse stood tethered close to the tent. It urinated a whisker's breadth from my sandal. I looked down in distaste. An orderly came out in moments and asked my name.

'Aulus Veridius Scapula, Decurion of the Ninth, First Century, Second Cohort,' I said as I stood to attention.

'Look I'm just the orderly, I only want to know what your name is, all right?'

I flushed, embarrassed; he had taken me by surprise and I was feeling jumpy.

'The legate will see you now,' the orderly said. He went inside the tent shaking his head.

I followed. The legate sat at a wooden table which had some scrolls and a sword upon it. Its surface was the only smooth thing in sight. Next to him, stood Marcus Antonius, one of the three Antonine brothers, a legate and brother to two tribunes in our army. Antonius Hybrida was his uncle. I felt as if I had the stature of a mouse next to these giants of the army. I marched forward and saluted. I stood to attention.

'Aulus Veridius, Decurion, sir.' I said.

'Who the hell are you?' Marcus Antonius said.

'I, err... I was told to report here sir.'

'It's all right Marcus, he's the chap we were talking about,' Cicero said looking up. 'You could always leave this bit to me Marcus, couldn't you? Julius has fully briefed me on the map.'

Cicero was a man of medium height, with short, curly, black

hair and a frowning serious face. In appearance he was the antithesis of Caesar whose frontal baldness had become the butt of many jokes and humorous rhymes in the army, since 'Caesar' means curly, and one could imagine no greater living oxymoron.

The legate, Cicero, seldom smiled and some of the men said he had no sense of humour. He had led the Ninth in Crete six years before against a rebel army soon after I had joined up. We knew him well in the Ninth therefore and we remembered him as a good general who fought with his men at the front line. The men knew he could be trusted to be just and scrupulously fair.

Cicero's father had come from humble beginnings to become one of the foremost lawyers in Rome and with that success had come wealth. Wealth meant an almost certain commission in the army for Quintus his second son and a seat in the senate for himself. Despite his wealthy and some might think soft background, Quintus had joined Caesar in Gaul and fought alongside the Proconsul revealing a talent both for war and for managing his men.

As legate of the Ninth Legion, he had distinguished himself in the early battles Caesar had fought. In the first battle against the Helvitii he had driven the enemy left flank into a rout and brought his men back to attack the centre of the enemy infantry from the rear. The move won the battle and as far as we knew, Caesar had considered Cicero his most trustworthy officer ever since.

Marcus Antonius smiled. He was a man with a handsome but brutal face, clean-shaven and dark-skinned.

'If you like, but it was my plan you know, even if our illustrious leader embellished it,' he said.

'Full credit to you then,' smiled Cicero.

Marcus Antonius walked towards the tent flap, held open by the orderly, since Quintus and he seemed to have reached an understanding. He glanced over his shoulder at me and smiled a cold smile.

'You'd better be good, that's all I can say. Let me down and you'll find yourself in the arena'. Prophetic words as it turned out and they made me cringe. I began to wonder what I was doing in the legate's tent.

I looked straight ahead. Although I had no idea what was going on I had an uncomfortable feeling I was in over my head.

Sink or swim.

Cicero stared at my eyes for a moment.

'You can stand at ease Decurion.'

He unfolded a map.

'You know the geography around here?'

'No sir,' I said.

'Well you had better bloody well learn about it because I need you to perform a mission, young man.'

'A mission sir?'

'Yes. I'll tell you the background. We, well the Proconsul really, sent two men accompanied by five Aedui horsemen to keep an eye on our friend Ariovistus. We thought he might be moving his army towards us and planning a surprise attack. They're two tribunes, one from the Tenth Legion and the other from the Ninth, by the name of Marcus Mettius and Gaius Valerius Procillus. Briefly, we don't know what happened to them and we think the Suebi or maybe the Marcomannii who ride with them, have captured our men. We need some volunteers to find them at the end of the battle and Gods help you if they're dead. You've been volunteered, is that clear?'

All I could come up with was 'Yes, sir. Permission to speak sir?'

'Make it short will you Autus or whatever you name was, err, is.?

'Aulus Veridius, sir. It's just – well – why me? I hope you don't mind my asking sir?'

I wondered if I was overstepping the mark but Cicero seemed so relaxed I thought I might be able to ask.

'Well maybe it's because you are expendable and don't matter.'

The Legate looked up then and grinned. It was humourless grin all the same.

'No, just my sense of humour old boy. It's actually, because Tribune Meridius was a friend of mine. He and I grew up together. Lucullus told me that Meridius had trained you in Pontus. He also told me you saved his life on the battlefield at Tigranocerta. There can be no better recommendation. When Calvus suggested you I felt you'd be perfect.'

I was surprised at the answer. Pontus and Armenia were a whole world away as far as I was concerned and much had happened to me since.

'Yes sir,' I said.

'Well what are you waiting for? Oh yes, here's a map, it's only a crude copy but it should give you a rough idea of the layout of the land. You can read, can't you?' frowned the Legate.

'Of course' I said. 'Do I go now?'

'Well of course you bloody go now. By Mars, all you have to do is wait for the end of the battle then kill a few Germans and get our chaps away from the torturers. Go to the Aedui auxiliary cavalry and they'll fill you in on what to do. Take your twenty best men and ask the Aedui politely if they will lend you ponies and off you go. Understood?'

'Yes sir, right away sir'

I turned about and marched to the tent flap.

'Wait a minute.'

'Yes sir?'

'Weren't you in a sword contest on the Campus Martius a few years back?'

'Yes sir I came second, Meridius beat me. You presented me with this gladius sir.'

'Now I remember. You were just a boy then. Your sword work was very good. Still as fast?'

'Maybe sir.'

'That's the spirit. Don't forget, as soon as you see those Germans routing or retreating you mount up and fight your way into the German camps and find our men.'

'Yes sir.'

I saluted again and left.

Jupiter, Mars and Venus, had they all gone crazy? How could I have been picked for something like this?

I had no confidence in my riding ability; that was the trouble. There was an even chance I would fall off with my weak leg. There was nothing for it however; I would have to do my best.

It was Marcus Mettius who had stolen my amulet and left me for dead. The irony did not escape me. I now had orders to save him from torture and death. The Gods indeed do strange things to us. I decided to search Marcus' tent for the amulet before the battle since he was not there, but I didn't think there was any strong likelihood he would have left it behind. He thought he'd killed me in getting it. The chance of him leaving it in his tent was remote.

I went to find the latrines. It had been a long night's drinking and I was paying for it now.

Chapter V

"Forgive many things in others; nothing in yourself." – Ausonius.

'Junius,' I said.

There was no answer.

'Junius.'

'What is it? You've woken me up.'

'I need some help.'

'Aulus, it's the middle of the night, for Somnus' sake. Can't you even take a piss on your own? Go to sleep.'

'I need your help to search Marcus' tent. It has to be now, at night.'

'What on earth do you want to do that for?'

'I need to know where the amulet is. It probably won't be in his tent but I need to check. I want you to stand guard,' I said.

'How about tomorrow night? I'm totally weary.'

'No, tonight.'

'Oh, all right. If you get caught I'll deny all knowledge. What do you want me to do?'

'All I need from you is for you to stand outside and whistle if you see anyone approaching. It's not much to ask, is it?'

We trudged through the camp towards the Tenth Legion

encampment trying to look casual. Wood-smoke filled the air from fires smouldering still outside the tents. The guards were not looking for intruders inside the camp and they fixed all their attention on the ground outside around the palisade. To anyone looking on, we were just a couple of legionaries walking in the camp.

We located Marcus' tent without difficulty. I had made some enquiries during the day, pretending to be looking for him. He was after all my cousin and no one seemed to think it was strange I was looking for his tent.

It was a moonlit night but cold and there was intermittent cloud drenching all in a sooty blackness when it obscured the moon. I heard the sound of growling from beyond the palisade and then a squeal of pain. Wolf or fox, it had found its prey and I wished I could do the same with mine tonight.

Junius stood outside the entrance to the tent and I crept around to the back where I felt no one would see me. I took my dagger and slit the leather enough to get in. The tent was empty, to my relief. It would have been a problem if Marcus had shared his tent with anyone.

I peered into the gloom. There was a cot at one side of the tent-space and a small travelling chest next to it. There was an oil lamp hanging from a hook on the central tent pole and I took it down. There was no lock on the chest and as I lit the oil lamp, I saw nothing else of interest. I opened the lid and began to rummage around inside. There were clean clothes folded in a neat pile and some spare sandals. I lifted them out and continued my search. There was a little money in a leather bag but I left that. I was not a common thief now as I had been in my youth.

When I had emptied the entire chest I realised there was no amulet. I was not particularly disappointed since I hadn't expected it to be there. I had to search the tent to be certain. The amulet was either on Marcus' person or in Rome. If it was in Rome, there would be nothing I could do about it. If he had it on him, then I hoped the rescue would be too late and I could retrieve the amulet from his dead body.

A whistle.

I remained crouching, motionless for a moment, waiting. Moments passed. The whistle came again. I replaced the clothes with hurried movements and shut the lid. I put out the lamp. I reached for the cut flap of tent and stepped out. I kept low to avoid detection. I could hear Junius in conversation with someone at the front of the tent. I remained squatting behind it to avoid them seeing me.

A light drizzle had started and it added to the discomfort of the cold as I crouched. The voices ceased and I deemed it safe to move. I could see Junius outlined by the torches on the Praetorium.

'Junius.'

'Aulus, I just had a long conversation with a centurion of the Tenth Legion. He seems to think we'll contact Ariovistus and his German army in the next day or two.' He lowered his voice, 'Did you find it?'

'No. Be that as it may, we need to get out of here.'

'No one thinks it odd that we are here wandering around in the night you know.'

'No?'

'Well I said I had trouble sleeping to the chap and he said he always had the same problem before a battle. He recommended drinking more wine. Nice chap really.'

'You'll drive me crazy, Junius.'

'Why?'

'I'm doing a burglary and all you can do is pass the time of day with the Tenth Legion's commanders. What if he remembers you?'

'He won't. I told him I was you.'

'Oh, thank you. Thank you, for your loyal help.'

'Oh, come on. I'm here at least.'

'Yes all right. Let's get back now before you start chatting up the guards as well.'

We found our way back to our tent without difficulty and with no further encounters. Junius closed the tent flap and was soon sleeping. He snored.

I lay on my straw palette deep in thought. Thoughts of the letters I had found in Marcus' home began to enter my mind. They made it plain how my parents had died. Until that morning when I read them aloud to Quintus and Aripele I'd been guessing. I felt as if, on that morning, I had emerged from the ignorant dark into the bright daylight of certain knowledge. I knew what secret the amulet and the deeds held and what might await me if I could find it.

A vivid picture of my father's smiling face appeared in my mind. He reached forward placing the amulet around my neck with the words, 'You do know what Etruscan is don't you Aulus?'

Perhaps Marcus didn't know. I couldn't read Etruscan but I knew there were people in Rome who could and it would be possible to get a translation provided that one had that knowledge. If Marcus had been able to decipher the message on the amulet, I doubted that he would still be with the army. He would have obtained such fabulous wealth he could have bought his way out with ease.

He had never been a good student and I remembered that Gennadius, my Greek tutor had been close to despairing of ever teaching Marcus anything. The chance of Marcus recognising Etruscan was therefore remote. Perhaps it was not too late to get the amulet and use its secret.

But was it wealth that drove me? I think it was revenge more than the thought of riches. It was indeed as Quintus had surmised. It was a feud and a wish for revenge. I thought of my parents tortured and burning. I could not sleep for the anger welling up from the very depths of me. Marcus must die. I wanted him to die in pain like my parents had and he was here, nearby. I was his shadow and would keep him close.

What had the letter said? Marcus was angry that Cerberus had killed them. I wondered what that meant. He was a coward and a backstabbing fool but perhaps his irritation at my parent's death showed some spark of goodness. I would kill him but perhaps I should do it in a fair fight after all.

My thoughts meandered in this way for hours until sleep came. It was a brief sleep and I did not wake refreshed. I had to focus on a day of marching, with battle near too. I had to bury the turbulence of my emotions and hide my unconscious thoughts deep, as was my custom. I never was one to face up to deep emotions. It was symptomatic of the traumas of my life. I knew I could not get on with day-to-day life if I ruminated.

We marched at a blistering speed that day which Caesar insisted was the norm as he wove his way through our ranks on his white stallion. The tension was mounting. Ariovistus was ahead and we would be killing Germans soon. Some of the men still held that the enemy were fearsome but Junius and I tried to maintain calm among them. We chanted a song called 'The Suburan' as we marched. It was crude old ditty about a man, a donkey and a whore and it kept the men cheerful. Crude, vulgar humour was the best cure for what ailed them. I was to discover later in the campaign that when Caesar spoke to the rank and file he was no better himself. Some of the things he suggested we do to the enemy would make a lupa blush. The lads were jumpy all the same and I could see how their hands often played with the hilts of their gladii and they looked around far more than usual as we marched. They had stopped complaining and when a soldier does that it is only because his mind is elsewhere. They were steeling themselves to meet a fearsome enemy and not all of them took it well.

When we rested at midday I had time to talk to Calvus.

'Excuse me sir. Do we know what the plan is yet?'

'Yes we do, but there is no general order issued so I can't tell you the details.'

'Is there anything I can pass on to the men? They're getting a bit jumpy and some information would probably settle them.'

'Well it seems the Germans have gathered an army about twice the size of ours. They're a migration not just a war band. By tomorrow, we should be able to locate them. Our scouts say they've camped on a hill overlooking a deep valley and we're to attack them where they are. Don't know any more details. We'll probably be briefed tomorrow and as soon as I know, you will too.'

'Thank you, sir. It's enough information to pass on. Facts are better for the men than rumours I suppose.'

'Did the legate give you your instructions?'

'Well yes, but I'm a bit puzzled really.'

'Oh?'

'Well he's ordered me to take two Contubernia on horseback to enter the German camp after or during the battle and rescue the two captured tribunes. I can't work out whether I'm supposed to be in the actual battle or not.'

'For an educated chap you seem to be remarkably dense at times. No, you won't be in the battle and yes, you will be mounted. The reason for that is that once you get off the bloody horses you will be a proper fighting team unlike those damned horse puppies who can't fight anybody once they're on their feet.'

'Why me? I wanted to be in the battle line. This is only the second real battle I've been in since Tigranocerta.'

'Tough. Stop whingeing and follow orders.'

'Yes, sir. May I report to the Auxiliary Cavalry officer to arrange the horses?'

'Yes, do that.'

I walked to the far side of the field in which we had made a temporary camp, so as to find the Roman officer in charge of the auxiliary cavalry. I found him lying with his eyes closed and his head on his saddle.

'Excuse me sir,' I said.

'What?' he said, without looking up.

I saluted. 'Decurion Veridius reporting, sir. I've come about a mission entrusted to me by Legate Cicero.'

'Oh, yes I remember,' he sat up then and smiled. 'You're the chap going to find our tribunes tomorrow eh?'

He looked as if he had just emerged from the therma. His hair was short and neat, his lorica evenly lamp-blacked and his tunic new and clean. He was a good-looking man too, with fine-chiselled features and blue eyes. I was sure he was the only clean, neat fellow in Caesar's army. He made me feel nervous for some reason.

'Well I don't know if it's tomorrow. It will be after the battle with the Germans, sir.'

'Yes, that's right.'

He stood up and lifted his saddle onto his shoulder. It was a heavy contraption, with a high rise at the front and back to stop the rider falling off.

'How will we get the horses, sir?'

'Well at the start of the battle you come and ask me before the equites and auxiliaries charge. We'll furnish you with steeds. Leave it late and you'll have to walk. We've plenty of spare nags since a number of the Aedui have deserted.'

'Deserted sir?'

'Yes, they heard you were coming and they fled.' He smirked. 'No, seriously, they were frightened by the numbers we're facing and about a hundred a day are legging it.'

'Will it make a difference, sir?'

'Not really. They have no discipline and they're best used to chase down a fleeing enemy than a co-ordinated attack.'

'How will I find you sir?'

'Just ask for Publius Crassus and all will be well.'

'Yes sir,' I said.

He walked away and I realised to whom I had been speaking. I hadn't previously seen him up close. His father was reputed to be the richest man in the civilised world. I thought I recognised Publius from a cavalry charge when I was in Armenia but I had never met him before. I guessed he would be reliable. The last thing I needed was to turn up with my twenty men and not be able to get a ride. I wandered back to my Cohort cursing my luck. It may have been an opportunity to find Marcus – maybe even kill him, but I wanted to be in that battle too. Such was not my luck however and I had no more control over my movements than the slaves we would take on the morrow.

Chapter VI

"Ambition is a vice, but it may be the father of virtue." –
Quintilianus.

We marched the next morning to the vale where we heard
the Germans had encamped. We were about half a mile from them
when our officers called us to a halt.

A cold sun shone above us, hardly clearing the horizon and
the ground was as muddy as all of us had become used to in Gaul.
It was something to do with the clay that was everywhere. Despite
the late morning sunshine there was a cold east wind rattling and
biting through the halted troops.

Calvus summoned me as soon as we stopped.

'Veridius, I want you to take the two contubernia and join the
auxiliaries on the left flank. Take ten from our first century and
ten from the first century of the third cohort. We can't reduce our
numbers too much. You will march with the left flank and help
make a fortified camp. We're making a camp here. There'll be two
legions in the forward camp. Your men and the auxiliary cavalry
are to cover operations while the camps are built.'

'I don't understand. Why make a forward camp and divide the forces?'

'The chance of the Germans attacking is small. They're a dull lot and they'll need time to work out what is happening.'

'When do you think the battle will be?'

'Probably tomorrow by all accounts. We're advancing early but you must stay back with your men. As the Legate explained, you have to enter the German camp and rescue the hostages.'

'There seem to be a lot of Germans.'

'Yes, as I told you, they outnumber us about two to one.'

'We've faced worse odds, I suppose.'

'Yes.' There was no smile on his face.

'Good luck for tomorrow. May we both live.'

'It'll take more than few Germans to kill me, I can assure you.'

'All the same, may Fortuna follow us.

It sounds foolish, but I was convinced a passing horse smiled as Calvus turned away. I made my way to the second cohort.

I took my contubernium and asked the third cohort commander if I could have ten men who could ride. I explained the mission. He lent me the men as if he begrudged giving them to me. Barbus was among the men from my century, the rest I did not know well.

'Don't relish salvaging that bastard Mettius,' Barbus said, as we trudged across the muddy camp area.

'No, nor do I and he's my cousin.'

'He wounded you in Armenia you were saying.'

'Yes but he thinks he killed me. I'm going to surprise him. He'll think he's seen a ghost if he hasn't become one himself already. If he has, I won't worry.'

Barbus scratched his beard. 'He may welcome it after being captured by these Barbarians. I hear they're fond of torturing their prisoners. The more they scream the more power they think they obtain from the torture.'

'I'm not sure who I hate most, the Germans or Cousin Marcus.'

'You'll soon find out I suppose.'

Barbus looked at the ground. 'Actually, I don't hate them. I have no particular feelings about them at all. It's just work to me. If they want to fight, well, I'll fight.'

'Not thought about it that way,' I said.

'Well if you don't get emotional about it and keep your temper in the fight, it makes you more efficient.'

We found the cavalry unit again and advanced with them. It took half of the afternoon before we could see the vast German camp. They had spread out over a grassy hill overlooking a wide valley. A small stream crossed at the foot of the hill and I could see forest high up on the slopes above them and to the north and west.

We built a camp on the far eastern side. The cavalry are not much good for such work but the two legions who accompanied us had the palisade up in only two hours and a trench dug in half that time. There was nothing left to do then but wait and shiver in the cold, inhospitable weather. I wondered what Junius was doing and I envied him being in the battle proper.

After a restless night in the new camp my men and I mustered in a separate group from the rest of the infantry. We stood behind the legions looking as we felt, small and insignificant. We must have looked as grubby as we felt small. Barbus scratched his beard like a man possessed. He told me it was a habit of old whenever he was going into battle.

'It makes the lice jump. Maybe they smell blood,' he said.

Crassus rode up to us looking smart and clean, brave and young. He had fine features for a large man and he often smiled. I always like men who smile, although common sense dictates such men are as likely to be fools as they are to be friendly.

Publius Crassus was no fool. I had seen him lead an ala of Thracian cavalry against Cataphractii in Armenia. The Thracians were outnumbered and lightly armed but they attacked the Armenian heavy cavalry so fast the enemy crumpled after only one lancinating charge. I knew he had guts and talent and admired him for it.

'If you chaps go over there,' he indicated to the massed cavalry, 'they'll give you your mounts. Once you get yourself organised walk them up to the top of that hill and I'll join you. It's a good place to see the battle from and I can decide when and where to attack.'

He turned his horse before I could reply and we did as he ordered. We sat mounted on the small hill on our side of the stream behind the left flank. My horse was a skittish beast and hard to control. It kept stamping its feet and every time I pulled up on the reins it sidled into the horse next to me. When Crassus joined us my mount took a dislike to Crassus' beast and began snorting then stepping sideways. I always seem to pick the worst mount.

'Sure you can manage that one?'

'I'm not very good on horses,' I said as I drew in the reins and tapped with both feet.

'You'll be fine. They read you, you know. If you're nervous so will your mount be. Come.'

Crassus gestured to the top of the hillock. I followed and looked out at the enemy.

'Veridius, you can see the enemy nicely from here can't you?'

'Yes sir.'

'They don't look too fearsome after all, do they?'

'No sir, they don't. I would rather kill them than Cataphractii.'

'Cataphractii?'

'Yes sir, like in Armenia.'

He said, 'You were there?'

'Yes sir.'

He looked at me raising one eyebrow.

'You were there? When we fought the Cataphractii?'

'Yes sir. I saw the Thracians cut right through them and we came behind, killing what was left.'

'Good fight that. Shame about Tigranocerta though. Lucullus had them beaten so fast; most of us rode around killing the fleeing enemy as if they were fish in a barrel. Poor buggers. We only lost a handful of men and Tigranes lost thousands upon thousands once it became a rout.'

'I remember looking across the river at their army. There was on big man, heavily armed but he avoided my gaze. I could tell they were frightened. Lucullus knew it too.'

'These Germans don't look frightened,' he said, 'but you know, they should be. Most of our men are veterans and after that battle with the Helvetii our reputation should have reached even the ears of Ariovistus.'

We looked down upon the valley. Caesar had brought up his four legions to our right and the cohorts formed up in triple line formation.

A dog barked somewhere in the distance though where it came from was anybody's guess. The rising sun began to cast long shadows as it cut though the predawn light and I looked at the dark sky. It seemed odd to me that on a day when men would die and lives would end there were creatures living their normal lives. The sun would still rise and rain still fall whatever happened on this battlefield. It was as if all these lives counted for nothing in the whole vast scheme of things.

The Roman ranks below us were silent. A business-like silence. This was, as ever, a piece of work to the legions. They fought as one man not heroes, not individuals either but as one huge machine oiled by the blood of their adversaries.

'See how our legions have drawn up facing west along that dirt track?'

'Yes, sir.'

'Notice how the German armies are backed by that line of crude wagons? Their women are standing on them. The German women accompany their men to the battles to show that if they are defeated the tribe loses everything they value. Mind you the women are fierce too by all accounts.'

'I can hear them wailing and screaming. It seems to give the valley a bit of a ghostly atmosphere, I suppose. Our men seem calm enough though.'

'Perhaps they've heard women scream before. Heard them silenced too, I don't doubt.'

'I know what you mean.'

'There will be no quarter given today. We'll end the Suebi threat here in this valley for good and all.'

'Not just the Suebi,' I said.

'No, they've brought all their friends to the party.'

'Do you know what tribes they are? I don't know their names at all. They all look the same to me.'

'They're roughly in tribal order. Harudes, Marcomannii, I think those are Tribocii and those are Suebii on the right facing the Ninth and Tenth. It pays to study your enemy you know.'

Our legionaries stood side-by-side readying themselves for the battle to come. Most of the German cavalry lay at the northern end of the massed Barbarians. The Germans fought with no reserves that I could see. Perhaps they were confident that one savage charge would carry the day because of their huge superiority in numbers.

The Suebi troops were tall, tough warriors with bearskin

cloaks bearing long spears and shields but the Ninth and Tenth Legions were the fighting heart of this Roman army. Staunch, loyal men as courageous and strong as they were loyal to their leader.

This was not a battle to send in skirmishers; both battle lines were near enough to each other to see expressions on faces and details of dress and weapons. I could make out Junius as optio standing to the side of our century, his job to close the ranks and order men forward to replace the soldiers who fell.

The triple line formation was a conventional way to give battle. The first two lines were to fight and the third acted as reserves. When your right arm grew tired from the slaughter, men in the rank behind would move forward and take over. And there would be slaughter for not a man among us watchers doubted the Roman war machine would crush the Germans now they had come to the fight.

Our legions are drilled and trained to work like an automaton. All of it was routine to these tough stocky Roman fighting men handing out the death and destruction I knew was about to unfold. I could feel it. I could almost touch the tension, my mouth dry and my heart beating fast. I wished I could be in the front rank of my century. I wished I could enjoy once more the feeling of blood lust that had taken me at times before and held me in its clutches like some soaring eagle holding its prey.

We had ballistae mounted on wagons behind the troops and I watched as they began to fire into the massed Germanic forces. The heavy bolts skewered shield and man alike and sometimes penetrated two Germans at a time. The Germans had to pull their wounded back and I witnessed some of them killing their own wounded, perhaps to put them out of their misery. The ballistae were concentrated behind the Ninth and Tenth so it was the Suebi who took the brunt of the missile attack.

I heard the cornua sounding two blasts and then three more

indicating right, two legions and advance. The Ninth and Tenth Legions advanced closing the gap between them and the Germans. The Suebi attacked fast. They ran with incredible speed considering their armour. There was no time for the legionaries to launch pila. It forced them to join in hand-to-hand combat sooner than they would have wished.

Caesar had instructed all the tribunes to stand with their legions and cohorts.

'The General said it was to encourage the men. I wondered personally if it was to stop the men running away. There's a lot of bad nerves at play in the ranks,' Crassus said.

'I know. There've been many rumours that the Germans are very big and very fierce.'

'Rubbish man. They fall just like any others.'

'We'll see now won't we sir?'

'We will indeed,' Crassus said. He looked thoughtful then, as if he might have doubted the crux of our conversation. Even from that distance I could hear the German war cries filling the air as they charged beneath the sea of their banners onto the readied Roman lines, like a wave on a troubled seascape. All along the Roman front rank our men had drawn their swords and the advance halted as the Barbarian onslaught began.

The left flank wrenched my gaze back again. Those men were now advancing on the enemy's right. The two legions below us walked with unhurried calm towards the waiting Germans. It was a beautiful sight. The unbroken lines of shields, the glinting swords and the silent order could only have been terrifying to the enemy.

The Germans charged here too. They whooped and screamed. They waved spears, axes and long swords as they came. They hit our front rank hard. Within moments there was a crush as the Germans behind pushed their fellows forward. The men in their front line, packed tight, were unable to wield their long weapons.

The short gladii of the legions' front rank flashed almost in unison. They bit into a solid wall of flesh. Flesh that fell, flesh that bled.

Apart from the Cataline defeat I had never seen a battle from a distance and I wondered at the purity and beauty of it all. This must be the way a general experiences battle – involved but distant. Men were dying, screaming and bleeding. The legions pressed forward. They had difficulty keeping their balance in the bloody red and grey mud as they slipped and clambered over the German bodies. They kept advancing, stabbing, thrusting at the densely packed foe.

Few Romans fell. The Germans couldn't fight back, pinioned as they were in the press of bodies. The progress of our forces was inexorable. It took about an hour for the Germans to turn and flee as best they could across the blood-slicked mud. Our men remained in formation but jogged forward killing the slipping and falling enemy.

'Right, well, it's time for my lads now to pursue. Don't dawdle, there's a good fellow, will you?' Crassus said.

'What?' I said, woken from my reverie.

'Now's the time. Ride through that lot of running Germans and find their camp. Then search it. Of course, if you can kill a few on the way, that's all right with me. I'm off.'

He turned his horse away and joined his men. The auxiliary cavalry charged in a tight wedge below us and then broke formation into a loose-knit group, thousands strong. They reached down with their spears among the fleeing Germans and killed one after another. The enemy died by the thousand. It took my mind back to Tigranocerta. The cavalry's role there was similar. The riders with their bloody spears annihilated the retreating enemy.

We rode down. By contrast, we were not a beautiful sight. We had no training and were a simple group of individuals on horseback. We would have looked laughable to the cavalry if they had looked back over their shoulders at us. We carried our shields slung on our backs and held the reins with both hands. I knew I could not wield a sword as well as stay on my steed so I concentrated on the business of riding. We cantered across the battlefield a furlong behind the real cavalry and up the hill towards the German encampment.

There were three camps to search. The first was empty apart from a few wounded Germans crawling on the ground. There were cook-pots hanging over lit fires and empty leather tents. The Germans had erected a rough shelter from brushwood in one corner. We searched all the tents but found nothing. We rode on to the second camp.

It was here we encountered our first real resistance. Not soldiers – women. They looked savage. Their fair hair was wild and they wore bearskins like their men. They screamed as we came to the edge of the centre of the camp. The Germans had cleared a wide area and erected tents and shelters around it.

We dismounted fast. We were twenty men and we faced maybe twice our number of wild wailing women. They hefted axes, some of them short for throwing and we formed up as fast as we could, shields together expecting a hail of missiles. None came. They rushed straight at us and although I would have baulked at killing any woman we all knew these fierce, tall, blonde Furies could be deadly.

We fought them off without difficulty but they kept coming back until we had lost three men and only a handful of the women remained. They turned and ran and we began our search in earnest. This camp was behind the middle of the German forces in the battle. They were not Suebi and I couldn't remember despite Crassus' lesson to which tribe the camp belonged. We found no signs of our tribunes, not even bones.

'Barbus, I don't know if we can even find their bodies. They would hardly have left them alive.'

'They might have taken them with them as they fled. They might try to use them to bargain with.'

'Possibly. We have one camp left, that big one over there behind the German left flank.'

We made our way there. We had to leave three good men dead in the clearing. We promised each other we would return and reclaim their bodies. Two were from my own contubernium. I felt, with sadness, they had died for nothing.

We crossed the narrow strip of grass that separated the two camps. This was much bigger and we guessed it was the Suebi camp. They had built three large huts out of mud, wood and thatch in the short time they had been there and I assumed it was because Ariovistus himself had been here.

It all seemed abnormally still. There were a few dying Germans huddled together next to one of the huts as if someone had laid them there to die. We drew near and one of these men tottered to his feet and approached leaning on a spear and with a sword in his right hand.

His face had the pallor of a dead man and blood stained his drooping moustache as it leaked from his mouth with every breath. He stared straight at me and his gaze seemed to penetrate my skull as he looked me in the eye.

'Wuotan, ' he cried, his voice weak and deep.

He stumbled forward and aimed a blow at me with his sword. I had not the heart to kill him. It would have been a travesty. I knew he was dying; a child could have parried the blow he tried to land. He followed through and he fell at my feet, still grasping his sword.

I put my foot on the blade and looked down. I surprised myself with the thought that this was a brave man who wanted to die as he had lived. Sword in hand, fighting an enemy whom he saw as evil. I felt sorry for him. I kicked his blade from his grasp and I strode away as we began to search around the camp. I learned later I had done him a disservice, because the Germans believed they could not enter their version of Elysium if they died without a sword in their hand. I hope now he managed to crawl to his blade. I had not meant to condemn him in that way.

There was still no sign of any Roman prisoners and I began to wonder if we had missed them in one of the other camps.

'No sign of anyone, Aulus.' It was Barbus. He was shaking his head.

'Perhaps they took them with them as they escaped east.'

'We'll have to go back and report.'

'We can't do that without some indication of what happened. Procillus is worth saving,' I said.

'I know that but we don't have enough men to pursue a war band and they've killed them as likely as not.'

'Barbus, we have our orders. Even if we die in the attempt we have to follow them.'

'It'll be suicide. Can't we let the cavalry do it?'

'No. It's our job, not theirs,' I said.

'Our job to die for Marcus Mettius?'

'Yes. Mount up.'

'This is stupid Aulus, but I'll follow you even though you don't know what you're doing.'

Barbus grinned. He had far more experience than I, but he knew I was in charge. Like any good soldier, after he had said his piece, he would follow me to the grave if that were his destiny. The trick with Barbus was to let him have his say, I think.

We mounted up and rode east in the direction the fleeing Suebi would have taken to get to the Rhenus. The Rhenus separated Gaul from the Germanic lands and the routed army would head there to try to get across and escape Caesar's wrath. I knew that if they were in large groups we could do little but I was determined to achieve something that day. So far we had failed in our mission. My only thought was to try to salvage something. A mental picture of Antonius' face haunted me as I rode.

You'd better be good.

Yes, I'll be good, you bastard.

Chapter VII

"Either do not attempt at all, or go through with it." – Ovid.

We entered a forest. It was not a dense forest, more like a thick copse of tall pine trees with a number of tracks meandering through it. There were low bushes and thickets under the trees and we had to be cautious in case there were fleeing soldiers hiding in them as we went up the slope.

At the top of the hill we could see down into the next valley and realised that the way east was a series of slopes and vales.

'Look there.' Barbus pointed and shaded his eyes although the sun was not shining. Maybe he was short-sighted or something.

'I see them. How many do you think?'

'About fifty. They outnumber us by more than two to one.'

'But they have no horses.'

'Wonderful. Have you ever fought on horseback?'

'No.'

'Nor have I,' Barbus said. 'Mind you, it looks easy enough I suppose.'

'With these stupid saddles I'm surprised our cavalrymen don't fall off.'

'That's the point – they usually do. I wish there was some way to stay stable.'

'There's nothing for it. We have to attack them. Do you see what I see?'

'Yes, red tunics,' Barbus said.

'Now I know we have to attack. The Germans don't know we're infantry do they?'

'No, suppose not.'

'They won't like it if they think we're cavalry. They're scared of our horse puppies aren't they?' I said.

'If you say so. You're in charge; I must give you the field.'

'Let's surprise them. Any chance we can ride in a wedge?'

'Only if we're walking and leading the horses.' Barbus smiled.

'Draw swords men,' I said, trying to sound confident. 'We ride them down and kill them. As soon as we can, we dismount and form up.'

My men looked at me as if they thought I'd gone mad. Not one of them demurred however and we began a charge in greater disorder than any of us would ever have admitted to. It is true to say that infantry make no better cavalry than the converse. We rode into the back of the Germans in silence and I'm proud of my men to this day. They swung their swords and since most of the Germans were facing away from us, we had a good start. We must have killed or injured at least fifteen of their number in that first charge.

I had to lean to my right in the saddle as much as I could, to stop myself falling off and swung my gladius, striking a man on the shoulder. It was a cruel blow and he fell bleeding in the turf. I realised the horse's momentum had aided me.

We rode through them and formed up twenty yards from the enemy. Not one of us had fallen from the saddle. They no longer outnumbered us by two to one. We dismounted. There was a large rock the height of two men on our left and we used it to prevent them from out-flanking us.

They had tied the two prisoners hand and foot and gagged them. The Germans were dragging them along the ground like sacks. They dropped their captives behind them and all turned to face us. Most had shields and spears although some had the long German swords they seemed to like.

We stood in two lines. I was in charge and stood to one side like a centurion with his century – without the aid of comrades either side. That was why, after most battles, there were prospects of promotion. Few men lasted very long in the centurionate unless they were exemplary fighters – like Barbus or Calvus.

The enemy were readying themselves to charge but they looked frightened and tired. They breathed hard and they were sweating. There was a huge Barbarian in their midst. He was shouting orders. He wore a pointed helmet and a massive thick bearskin. The chance of penetrating that skin with a quick stab was minimal and I guessed it was part of his armour.

He wielded a great spear but had no shield. He had a scar like Quintus. I felt a faint smile on my lips as I saw the similarity. The scar extended down from his forehead, to his chin but had spared his right eye. The wound had healed leaving a contorted scar, even worse than the one that Quintus bore. It drew his face into a malevolent grimace as he encouraged his men in the guttural language these Barbarians speak.

They attacked us faster than I had expected. The grassy tussocks did nothing to impede their sandaled feet as they bounded across the turf towards us. They bunched up, which I thought was a ridiculous way to attack. If they had advance in a line, they could have enveloped us and attacked front and rear but Germans don't fight that way. Full frontal attack or nothing. The big German came straight for me.

He was a huge bear of a man like his cloak, or maybe the cloak made him look bigger than he was. He seemed to tower above me wielding his long spear as if he was reaping corn. I raised my shield and took the blows. It was my weak arm but it held. Perhaps he was not as big as I had thought or maybe he had already fought in the battle and was finding it hard to muster his strength.

I held him at bay without much difficulty. I pushed forward with my shield and stabbed when opportunity presented itself. Fortuna failed to smile upon me that day for I spent the entire time battling this big hunk of a man and did nothing else. I was aware of the clamour and battle sounds to my left but had no time to look. I could smell blood and offal. The fight was progressing I thought.

Barbus told me later how the Germans, exhausted as they were, tried to force our men back but the lads kept their discipline and held the line. The German soldiers tried to reach over the shields with their spears but they were outmatched. Their numbers dwindled until a handful remained. Those remaining turned and ran for all they were worth towards the woods from which we had attacked them.

My huge adversary managed to push me to the ground and run in the opposite direction to his men. I mounted my horse to pursue him. I had killed no one today, apart from a blonde Amazon woman who had fallen screaming in the camp skirmish and I was eager to kill this war chief.

To my intense frustration it took me so long to mount the horse with my weak leg he got away. Mounting a horse was the sole act of soldiering I could not do with ease. I lost precious moments and by the time I was ready to pursue he had reached a copse of Rowan trees growing near a stream. I gave chase but to my chagrin he vanished into the treeline. That huge bear of a man melted into the wood with no visible trace. It was as if some magic possessed solely by the German's Gods intervened to save him.

One of the surviving enemy told us the escaping man was in fact Ariovistus himself. Years later I found out that he escaped back to Germany across the Rhenus but he never raised another army and his power was gone forever.

I rode back to my men. They had untied Procillus and were releasing Marcus Mettius. I knew it was him. I recognised that shock of black curly hair and the cleft chin immediately. He still had a gag on his mouth and as I approached, sword in hand I was tempted to run him through. There were too many witnesses and I couldn't count on the men who were not in my century to keep quiet so I resisted the temptation. I pushed my fellow legionaries aside and helped him to his feet. He didn't recognise me as I released his gag – I was wearing a helmet with cheek-guards so it does not surprise me. I felt all around his throat for the amulet. To my intense disappointment it was not there. He had no pouch or belt so clearly it was not there either. If the Germans had taken it then I would never see it again. I wondered what to do. He spoke.

'By Venus and Mercury, I thank you for your timely arrival.'

There were tears in his eyes and two of my men had to hold him up. Procillus behind me was weeping and seemed unable to speak in a coherent fashion.

'They cast lots,' Marcus said, 'whether to burn us then or later. They were going to burn us alive. If you hadn't saved us we would have died in their fires for their revenge.'

'Well, you're free now,' I said.

'Which brave soldier do I thank for this courageous rescue? I will report it all to Caesar. It was a great victory. An oak leaf crown will be yours at the least. I owe you my life,' Marcus said.

He looked at me with no recognition in his face at all. I knew it was too much to expect for this experience to have humbled him but I was glad of the opportunity to shock him. I took off my helmet. I delight still in remembering his face as it dawned upon him that a ghost had been instrumental in his survival. His jaw dropped and he gazed at me through his tear-stained eyes that widened more and more by the moment.

'Cousin Marcus? Don't you even recognise your own blood kin?'

I said it with intense smugness and pleasure. I had not participated in the battle, nor had I killed Ariovistus but that look on Marcus Mettius' face made the whole day worthwhile. His face went paler, that is if there is a shade of pallor whiter than white. His knees began to tremble and sag. I loved it. I hated the man and my pleasure at seeing him so disadvantaged was obscene, but enjoyable.

'But...,' was all he could say.

'Yes, cousin that's right. This is all a dream and you will wake soon....'

'But....'

Since Marcus seemed unable to speak again, I turned to Procillus, but he too was mumbling incoherently and I felt it wise to evacuate them both as soon as possible. We had lost four men in the fight. We tied the bodies onto two of the horses and helped the tribunes into the saddles of the remaining two.

We rode west. We had accomplished our mission but at the cost of seven of my twenty men and the disappointment of not being in the battle. At least I now knew the amulet was probably in Rome and its pursuit would have to wait until the legions returned home.

Chapter VIII

"The wish for healing has ever been the half of health." – Hyppolytus.

The sunshine above me seemed as ever, half-hearted, meagre and cool as I made my way through the churned-up mud in the Ninth Legion's encampment. I began to wonder if Gaul ever experienced the sort of sunshine we had at home, where you sweated as you walked and everything around you is bright and clear. This place was dull and grey, dull and cold and worst of all the mud clung to everything. It splashed on your legs and arms and even into your food.

The camp was busy. Men were cleaning blood from their equipment and weapons. The relief squads were still bringing in the wounded men and despite the tiredness we all felt there was activity everywhere. The Legate had ordered me to give my report in person in the evening after, Caesar had addressed us.

Our tent was in the same place as it might have been in any other camp. Outside it there smouldered an evil smelling little fire with Junius' cook pot hanging from a wooden tripod we had made together only days before. The one missing ingredient was Junius.

I took off my armour but as I had done so little killing, there was not much to do to it apart from cleaning my sword.

Every day, the blade had to be cleaned and oiled. Missing one day could mean the appearance of rust and the loss of the edge. By good fortune, the steel of my gladius was hard compared to even the best legionary weapons. Hispanic smiths had tempered and folded the steel and I had won it on that day when I was second in the sword contest on the Campus Martius; second only to Meridius, the legion's champion.

I cast my mind back to that day. So much had happened since then, yet so little time had passed and I was after all, not much older. I looked at the blade as I cleaned it. Cut into the blade was a script, 'LEGIO IX HISPANIA.' It made me proud to have earned it but I knew that a blade is only as good as the man who wields it. How would it matter if a fool has a wonderful or even magical blade? What would he do with it besides cutting a few things or killing a few men?

No, I knew even then when I had won my blade, the quality of the man is the important thing. A skilled swordsman can fight with any sword, even a rusty, bent weapon, ages old. Speed of foot is good, speed of thrust and parry is good too, but experience and anticipation are the Gods of any swordplay. Know your opponent and read him was what Meridius had taught me. He had shown me many different techniques, patterns of movement and combinations of strokes but he always said the one thing above all is to read your opponent.

There was one other thing he had taught me that few people knew or practised. It was a particular technique for drawing the sword. It comes out of the scabbard so fast and strikes as it is drawn – all in one movement. Using that technique one can defend oneself when attacked from any direction in a very quick, effective and deadly way.

He had taught me also that unlike a gladius a longer sword is a cutting weapon not a cudgel. Strike but draw the sword towards you as you do. Use the edge to cut as you strike. I can almost hear him say it.

I sat and wished he were here. He had tutored me, taught me and shaped the man I had become. I began to ponder what kind of man that was. I had started as a thief in the Subura and the legion had taught me to kill. Then Meridius had trained me in how to use those killing skills with all manner of weapons and not just swords.

I can hear him say it with startling clarity in my head. 'You can defend yourself with almost anything if you just think ahead. Even a simple stick can be useful. Break a stick and it has a point – a sharp point. It can parry and stab. Look for the right places to stab and you can disable or kill anyone. We all expose our weak spots in the end. The throat, the groin and the chest all are good killing points.'

I was deep in reminiscent thought when Barbus approached. I heard him as he sat down beside me.

'So where's your mate, the optio, then?'

'Who? Junius?'

'Yes,' he said.

'I'm not sure. Calvus may have detailed him to bring in the wounded or burn the bodies. Last I saw of him he was fighting with the Ninth against the Suebi.'

'Should be back by now. All the retrieval teams have returned. There's only the cremation squads out there now.'

I had a sense of foreboding. I wondered if he might be among the dead. No, surely not? He was a big man and a fierce fighter and one who I would have expected to be able to look after himself more than any man in the legion.

'Maybe I should go and look for him.'

'Yes, perhaps wise. I'll come with you if that's all right?'

'Of course, should we go to the battlefield first?' I said.

'That seems to be the best idea. I hope he hasn't fallen.'

'No, he's a tough man.' I stood up and sheathed my sword.

'Even the toughest can meet their match in battle you know.'

'There are few men who can fight like him, Barbus.'

'Maybe, but I've see the strongest of us fall in battle.'

Barbus began telling me about some of the battles he had been in over the years and I realised that compared to him I knew little. He had fought in Hispania, Africa, Pontus, Germany and now Gaul. Most of his time had been as a centurion and he was a man who even I would have been wary of fighting.

Men were clearing the battlefield of bodies and some were erecting a podium for our General's speech. Caesar was to address the whole army but how his voice would reach across such a vast expanse was a puzzle to me. They had separated the dead into piles. They dragged the Germans down towards the stream and left those on the opposite side.

The cremation squads laid our men with reverence on pyres of wood for there was no way to bury such a large number. We do not like to touch or handle the dead. It is bad luck and until a Libitinarius – a priest of the dead, purifies the bodies, there is a risk of angering the Gods, for one would have become unclean. On the battlefield however, we were rather more pragmatic and we ignored the usual rules.

We had lost several hundred and one of the men clearing up the field thought there must have been about a hundred wounded. Carts had taken them away to the camps for treatment by the camp surgeons.

I had seen such a place before, after a battle against the Armenians and still recalled how the smell and the blood had revolted me. The last time I sought an injured comrade in the surgeon's environ I had vomited.

We walked to the Ninth Legion surgeon's tents. It had its own palisade, which I had never seen before. We entered and an orderly, whose job it was to carry out triage of the stretchers and walking wounded, accosted us.

'Are you injured?' he enquired.

'No,' I said. 'We're looking for a friend.'

'I'm afraid you'll have to wait sir.'

'I just need to know if he's alive. He's our optio and we need to know for the proper running of our unit.'

'Sorry, surgeon's orders.'

'Look, we have to find out if our optio is still alive. Don't you keep a roster?'

'Of course we don't. Half of our admissions are unconscious. They can't tell us their names. We do a list later when we've treated them and done the prayers.'

'Prayers?' Barbus said.

'Yes,' the orderly said. 'It is an integral part of treatment. If you don't pray, evil airs enter the wounds and the patient can die. Prayer has to purify the wounds and then it is up to the Gods. Most seriously injured men die anyway.'

'So the prayers don't work then, do they?' I said.

'Of course they work. We wouldn't have the recoveries we do, if we didn't pray. It would be impious not to pray and it would anger the Gods.'

I drew my sword.

'Do you know what this is?' I said.

'Look there's no need for that. It's my job.'

'I intend to enter and find my friend. You will not interfere.'

'I'll get the surgeon. He won't like this.'

'Off you go then,' Barbus said as the orderly scurried away to make his complaint.

'Let's have a look around,' I said, sheathing my weapon.

It was a large compound. There were five large huts erected at the far side of the circular enclosure. There were four tents in the centre distanced from the huts and there were stretchers with wounded all around them.

We walked across to the first. There was a queue at the largest of the surgeon's tents. The walking wounded stood in the fading sunshine waiting for the surgeon's attention with little enthusiasm. There was no way to control pain and one could guarantee any treatment meted out would be unpleasant.

The smell from the tent was enough to deter anyone with a minor injury from entering. It stank of death; a mixture of bowels, urine and blood. Flies, even in this cold climate swarmed rather than flew. The blood-stained surgeon's table in front of the tent was empty now apart from flies and the crude blood-caked and smeared instruments discarded on its rough, scored top. I looked at the instruments with disgust.

'May Jupiter keep me from returning to their clutches,' I thought, with a sincerity that burned in my mind like a furnace.

I looked into the tent. The dim lighting made it hard to distinguish detail inside but I could hear groans and whimpers from the injured men within.

'Aulus,' a weak voice pierced my consciousness.

I peered inside but recognised no one.

'Aulus it's me you blind bastard,' the thin, attenuated voice said again.

It was Junius. He lay on a blood soaked straw bed inside the tent. With a sinking feeling, I crossed to the tent. The orderly from the gate had returned and he took my arm.

'You can't go in there; this is a medical tent, and we don't need dirty, bloody soldiers disturbing the patients,'

I shook off the attendant's hand and pushed him aside. I saw my friend's face imbued with a gruesome pallor. Junius was breathing fast as if hungry for the stale and foetid air around him. With a feeling of horror, I took in what had happened to my friend. His left arm, from immediately below the elbow was gone, the stump covered in a blood soaked rag. The full horror of the injury began to dawn on me. I found it hard to speak over the tension in my throat.

'What happened, Farm Boy?' was all I managed to say.

I had to lean close to Junius' mouth to catch the words.

'A sword cut. A bloody sword cut. It was Bassus. We were fighting close to the Tenth and a group of them detached to support us. I raised my sword for the next charge and he hit me. Fucking bastard. No one saw either. Almost clean through. The surgeon took it off. Very quick he was, but oh Aulus, the pain. It's almost more than I can bear. They said it would ease but it hasn't. Gods, it hurts.'

What he said made sense. Bassus had tried to kill me and he must have known Junius would watch my back. Removing him laid me open to any schemes he cooked up in the future. I swore. Revenge came into my mind only to dissipate as I looked at Junius.

A cold sweat soaked him; beads of it on his forehead stood out like dew on a leaf and his breathing was speeding up with the effort of speaking, but his clear brown eyes remained fixed on my face.

I knelt at my friend's side. 'But you lived, Junius. You lived. It will heal.'

'It feels as if my arm is still there. It feels like it's in a vice. I can't bear it.'

'Give it time Junius.'

I hoped the tone of my voice might disguise my own pain and bitterness. A soldier with one arm was no longer a soldier; fit only for shipping back to Rome, for a life of begging in the streets, penniless and bereft. I had seen many such old soldiers seated at the city gates with wooden cups outstretched hoping for an occasional passer-by to throw a coin to them. The thought of this happening to my friend filled me with a mixture of shock and anger.

'What's the point, I have nothing now in life, who wants a one armed man?' whispered Junius.

'You'll get through this. You'll see. Just don't give up. Think of Aemilia.'

The orderly pulled at my arm 'You really must go, or I will have to have you removed.'

I stepped back from the tent opening. 'I'll be back, Junius, I promise.' I left the tent trembling. I looked at the orderly and asked, 'Will he live?'

'They often don't. He lost a lot of blood, he's very weak, and that's when the wounds turn putrid. He looks strong though so maybe he'll survive. There's nothing you can do for him. Not much we can do either, I suppose.' The orderly turned and walked away leaving Barbus and me to ponder why the Fates did this to the little people. The rich never suffered like this. I had not the heart to tell Barbus who had wounded my friend. If I did there would be no one in the legion who would have been able to stop him killing the fat centurion, or so I reasoned at the time.

*   *   *

The rest of the day passed with interminable tedium. The army rested. There were no drills, no marches just a celebratory day of rest. Caesar had declared the following day a rest day as well and most of us concentrated on drinking wine and anything else alcoholic we could lay our hands on. The whores in the camp followers' tents made vast sums because they put prices up as was customary after a victory.

I had experienced grief before in my life and it all seemed to return with the feelings of loss over my friend. Mixed with the emotions of fear and worry over Junius were thoughts of my dead parents and even the death of Meridius my mentor. Junius was at death's door. Throughout all I had experienced in the army Junius had been there, staunch, loyal and strong. To see him fighting for his life in the surgeon's clutches made me distraught. It revealed my vulnerability and the frailty of human life and I had no wish to think of such things; I who only two years before had faced my own mortality. The bitterness was even greater knowing that it was Bassus who did this to Junius. I convinced myself it was all my fault. Junius was my staunch supporter and now the fat centurion thought he had removed my only protection. I vowed to kill him and Marcus one day.

I tried to concentrate on cleaning my equipment and cooking a meal for myself but felt listless and down. Our noble general was addressing us in the afternoon and I had to report to the legate afterwards.

I walked to the battlefield and joined my men. It seemed strange and empty without Junius. His absence ay this time emphasised how much I had depended upon him. A surgeon had once said to me in Armenia that it was unwise to make friends in the army, for friends often died. He may have been right but Junius was a kindred spirit and we had done much together. We had both grown to manhood in the legion and change had come to us both in different ways but together all the same.

The podium which now stood on the battlefield rose tall and sturdy in the afternoon sun. Our generals had arrived on their splendid horses. They dismounted and Caesar climbed to the platform.

He prepared to address his men. We stood before him, many of us still battle-stained and exhausted, screwing up our eyes in the afternoon sunshine. Our helmeted heads looked up at the man on the podium whom even we could recognise as one of Rome's greatest generals. The men had fought hard; they had bled and had triumphed over their enemy. They had seen the Germans flee before them like rats in torchlight and witnessed the cavalry finish the slaughter they had begun. It was a great day.

I felt odd being there. Junius was not with us and to make matters worse, I had not even participated in the battle. I felt as if I didn't deserve words of praise from our general. I looked carefully for Bassus among the Tenth Legion officers but could not see him. I think had I done so I would have had trouble controlling my urge to violence even with everyone around me watching.

I stood and looked up with the rest in awe of the great man. He had brought us victory against a German army twice the size of our own force and I knew there were few men in the Roman world that could have done this. Two thirds of the German forces were dead or wounded. Of the remainder those who had fled to the forest had escaped back to the Rhine but crossing the freezing river after a rainy autumn left few alive to fight again.

The proconsul stood with a smile on his face and a helmet in his hand. His purple-edged tunic was creased and sweat-soaked from sitting in the saddle from morning to noon. His breastplate reflected the sunlight and flashed across the faces of his assembled men. He smiled in triumph as he looked out on his army and waited for silence. Centurions stood next to their men ready to relay the general's words to those behind.

The cornua blared again and Caesar spoke. 'Men, there is little to say, for you have done much, and it is the action, not the talking that matters to men such as you. Brave men need few words, so I won't keep you long. The Spartans never asked about the numbers of the enemy only where they were. With men like you, I could take all of Gaul and Germania too! The Germans...' he paused, 'are annihilated.' Tumultuous applause rose to the sky, vying in volume with the roar of the crowd in one of Rome's arenas.

'I don't think they will be back for more, do you?'

This time the roar of acknowledgement reached gargantuan proportions.

'You are my family. We have on this day, shown the whole civilised world just what a Roman legion is worth and of what a legion of brave comrades can do. For we are the most formidable army this world has ever seen. We have more battles to fight, but I know we will be victorious for no general could ask for better men. The two thousand slaves will make you rich men. In years to come, when you're all farmers in Italia, never forget this day. It will have given you your living.'

Caesar turned and left the podium to the sound of further cheers that seemed to hang in the air for an eternity. The tumult subsided, the centurions dismissed the assembled centuries and the army dissolved like grains of sand from a sieve.

I stood a while longer as the field emptied, gnawed by a feeling of tension. Would Junius live? Was any of this worthwhile? To lose lives, health, everything, for the sake of gaining land and power over others? It was more than that, for I did believe in the glory of Rome, our Mother City and the centre of the known world. I felt deep inside it was worthwhile to die for one's country, one's home and all it stood for. I had faced death to try for a chance of glory, to become a real soldier and revive the name of Veridius Scapula from the ashes and dust it had become in that house fire set by my enemies.

The contradiction of having saved Marcus Mettius from torture and death at the hands of the Germans when at the same time I wanted him dead by my own hand, made me thoughtful. I cared not a fig whether he lived or died in truth, but I now needed him alive to trace what he had stolen from me. I hoped he had not brought it with him and left it in Rome. I had no way of knowing which of us would get back to Rome first but whichever of us it was, he would be the one to retrieve the deeds I was sure. It occurred to me that Marcus could have hidden it anywhere in the city for all I knew. A little more burglary would be required to find out, but I was good at that. Had I not practised for years as an adolescent? I looked back at my leaving Gennadius, my teacher, and how I became a thief in the Subura. The Gods had given me that experience with a clear purpose. I felt trained and practised at what was necessary and thought that perhaps I could express my gratitude to Fortuna with a sacrifice. I turned and walked back to the tent Junius and I had shared.

In that moment, I missed him. I missed Aripele too. It would be a long and lonely night.

Chapter IX

"Where there's life, there's hope." – Terence.

I sat outside the leather tent wondering how my friend was doing but knew there was nothing I could do. I was no surgeon but I also knew there was not much the surgeons could do for Junius either.

It was time for me to see the Legate. An orderly appeared and was leading me to Cicero's tent. The time of the evening meal was approaching and I was hungry. I passed Barbus as I walked out of the second cohort's encampment.

'Where are you off to?'

'I have to report to Cicero and brief him on the mission we undertook.'

'Good. Tell him I was very brave and we killed many Germans. He might promote us both.'

'Is that likely?'

'Well no, but it doesn't hurt to embellish a bit. A shy retiring man goes nowhere in this army, just remember that.'

There was a smile on his face as I walked away. The sun was sinking, casting long shadows in the camp. The shadows darkened the muddy ground in patches and the depth of the mud was difficult to judge. The orderly swore as he put his foot in a deep puddle to ankle depth.

'Damned place,' he said. Wish I could have stayed in Rome.'

'Why's that?'

'I had it good in Rome. I was an orderly in the house of records but I dropped a bit unlucky with the senior clerk. He had me transferred to the Ninth Legion and here I am. It's cold, it's unpleasant and worst of all muddy. Hate the place.'

'I know what you mean, but for me it's the best chance I have of making a proper military career.'

'The way things are going, you'll get a lot of chances. We're wintering south of here near Bibracte and then next season Caesar plans to take on the northern savages.'

'Which ones?'

'The Belgae, they're the most war-like of the Gauls.'

'Not till next spring?'

'No, I think the General wants to go back to Rome. He has to raise money for the campaign. It's an expensive business this conquering, you know.'

I had no time to enquire where he got his information from as we had arrived at the Legate's tent. I assumed he overheard all the legate's meetings.

'Wait here, would you?'

'Fine,' I said.

'What was your name again?'

'Aulus Veridius Scapula,' I said it with pride. It was all I had and I was proud of it.

Presently, he appeared again and showed me into the tent. He announced me to Cicero. The Legate sat at his desk with his sword on the flat surface and some scrolls before him which seemed to hold his interest more than my entrance.

I stood to attention in front of him for a few minutes and he eventually raised his head and looked up at me. He smiled.

'Welcome, Veridius,' he said. 'I'm glad to see you're in one piece and even more pleased to see that you managed to salvage our two tribunes.'

'Yes sir,' I said, uncertain what else to say; he was my general, after all.

Two oil lamps that flickered and smoked upon the desk illuminated us with an anaemic light. I noticed a movement in the dark corner of the tent and realised there was someone else present. I guessed it must be Marcus Antonius come to see whether he should send me to the arena or not.

I gave my report. I did not dwell upon the rescue but concentrated on the events leading up to it and of course out of loyalty, I mentioned Barbus' role in the fighting.

'So Barbus saved the day did he?'

'Yes sir, to a large extent. I was glad to have such an experienced and resourceful soldier with me, sir.'

'Shall I tell you about Barbus?' the Legate said. He leaned back in his chair and regarded me, looking up with winter-cold eyes.

'Sir?'

'Barbus is a powerful soldier. He rose through the ranks with a speed few men could emulate. He distinguished himself in battle and had a good way with the men. It is indeed unfortunate that he is undisciplined and insubordinate and will never make centurion again if I ever have anything to do with it.'

'May I speak frankly, sir?'

His words rankled; it was an injustice and I felt he was applying an unfair prejudice.

'Yes, but keep it short.'

'He's a good soldier and he serves Rome and the legion well.

He is one of the men who is the backbone of our legion and makes us successful in war. He's wasted as a ranker. One would no more put Barbus in the ranks than one would put Leonidas among the Helots, in my opinion.'

Cicero frowned, almost scowling. There was silence for a moment and his speech was slow and deliberate.

'Your opinion eh? Barbus is a good soldier, but he's undisciplined. He's a man who cannot be relied upon to obey orders when there is serious necessity for him to do so.'

I cannot explain it but I proceeded with no caution, perhaps I was still irritated by his prejudice.

'I hope you will forgive me for saying so, but if that is based upon reports from inexperienced tribunes then it isn't true. I've fought next to him in battle and I know the man. But who am I to say so? I am only a young man and only a decurion. I do know though that if Barbus, like Calvus, gave me an order I would want to follow it. He is a true Roman, sir.'

'How dare you lecture me you insignificant little toe rag? I am the Legate. You forget yourself. Damned plebs. What right have you to...?'

A voice interrupted him from the corner.

'Quintus, Quintus my friend. Not so hasty. He is only expressing his loyalty to one of his men. If we all had such nobility, Rome would triumph all over the known world.'

Cicero stood and looked embarrassed. He glared at me. I had cut my bridges.

Gaius Julius Caesar walked into the circle of light. I realised what a mistake I had made in speaking with so little thought. I wanted to sink into the muddy floor and disappear. If only, at moments like that, some kind God could beam me up to Olympus life would be so easy. It is not, however, that easy. Once we have opened our mouths and spoken, the words are as immutable as the stone carvings on the Acropolis.

He was shorter than I had imagined him. I had only ever seen him on a podium addressing the troops. Close up, Caesar was a balding, thin, athletic looking man no taller than I was. The frontal baldness was striking for a man of his age for he must have been only forty or so years of age. The impressive thing about Julius Caesar was his eyes. They were hazel in colour but they had a piercing quality that seemed to look though you, through to your very soul.

How I wanted to be somewhere else. I was confronted by one of the most powerful Romans in the Republic and I had said too much. He looked straight at me and I felt more nervous before those eyes than if I faced a century of Ariovistuses.

'You talked of Leonidas. Do you know who he was?'

I stood to attention. I looked straight ahead.

'Sir, he was one of the greatest Greek Kings and a great soldier from Sparta.'

'And do you know what he did?'

'Yes sir.'

'Well?'

'He saved Greece from Xerxes the Persian king. He took three hundred men and he fought off a Persian army of a million men,' I looked at Caesar and it was clear that he wanted me to finish.

I went on. 'He showed the rest of the Greek states and even Sparta that to die for Greece was noble and his sacrifice made them unify and gather afterwards to fight off the Persians. He created a kind of national conscience through sacrifice, sir. His death salvaged democratic thought.'

'Yes, that's quite right. How do you know this story?'

'I had a Greek tutor in my early life sir.'

'What was his name?'

'Gennadius sir.'

'Well, never heard of him, but he seems to have taught you all the right things. I will tell you that loyalty has always impressed me. You seem very loyal to this man Barbus. Why?'

'I genuinely believe he is good soldier and good at leading men, as well as fighting. He argued with his tribune in a battle and when the tribune wanted to retreat, he beat him up and continued to fight. It's the Roman way sir.'

'The Roman way? The Roman way? I can't believe what a tactless young bugger you are.'

Caesar began to laugh. He not only laughed, he guffawed. He turned to Cicero, pointed at me and laughed uncontrollably. He continued to laugh until both Cicero and I, could not prevent ourselves from laughing too. It was involuntary. It was like battle rage. It possessed me.

There are moments in our lives when laughter is infectious and it catches us all. This was such a moment. Each time Caesar looked at me, he burst out laughing. I too, was powerless to control myself. I looked at Cicero and he was crying with laughter. It ceased for a moment, but as soon as I looked at Caesar, and he looked back at me, we began laughing again and it became hopeless. Three grown men, bent over with tears in their eyes bursting with merriment. Where was gravitas? Where was the chain of command? For one short moment, we were just men, laughing over something stupid and trivial.

It continued for minutes. Every time it stopped, Caesar looked at me and it began again. In the end, Caesar waved me away. He had no choice. Nothing sensible could take place that night. He was propping himself up with an outstretched arm on the desk and he pointed to the tent flap. I had to go. He couldn't speak for laughter. I was still laughing as I left the tent. Whenever I thought about the ridiculous conversation, I laughed. I had to stop thinking about it as I walked back to the tent in case to some observer I might appear to be drunk or crazy. I could hear my seniors and betters still laughing behind me in the command tent as I walked away and I began to wonder if I had made the biggest mistake of my career.

It was then I saw him. Bassus. He was staring at me from across the Via Praetoria. He was fully armed as I was, but he didn't attempt to approach me. He stood stock-still and stared at my smiling face with a look of utter malevolence. It abolished the humour I had been revelling in moments before as quick as a wink. I realised I hated him and wanted him dead as he deserved. If he did not attack me then I would find a way to get even with him for what he had done to Junius as well as the events in Armenia.

I walked up to him. He backed away at first then thought better of it.

'You're still a lucky man.'

'Yes and you're a dead one,' I countered.

'Well that big blond bastard you hang around with won't interfere any more, will he?' Bassus smiled and my hand went to my gladius, but I did nothing. He was a centurion and I was a grunt. If I killed him I had no evidence against him and no one would believe me. I stayed my hand.

'The only reason I haven't killed you already,' he went on, 'is because your cousin Marcus seems to think that he'll be cursed if I do. He's superstitious. He even thinks you surviving the tap he gave you on the skull was some kind of divine intervention. Saw an oracle it seems.'

'He must have seen your death then. Believe me, it's coming.'

'Dead men don't kill their quarries. Don't forget I'm a professional killer and I'll see you in Hades for that cut in my thigh. It's left me with pain and a limp for the rest of my days.'

'Don't worry, it won't be for long.'

'You'd better be careful Veridius. Your parents died in pain and I intend for you to meet them in the same condition.'

'You're a fool. I could kill you where you stand with about as much difficulty as picking a grape from a vine.'

'We'll see.'

He backed away until he felt it safe to turn and limped off into the night leaving me standing outside the now silent Legate's tent.

I went back to my tent and sat outside it. I was hungry but lacked the volition to start cooking my usual porridge of corn and water. The fire had gone out and I lit it again with some kindling Junius had gathered the day before. Barbus joined me.

'Poor old Junius,' he said.

'It was Bassus.'

'What was?'

'He wounded Junius, during the battle.'

Barbus stood up. There was thunder on his face. He turned to go but I grabbed his arm.

'You can't do anything about it.'

Pulling his arm free, he said, 'Just watch me. I'll skewer him like the fat pig he is. Nothing's going to stop me.'

'Suppose I tell you that you will be crucified and it will all be for nothing. It's my right to kill him, not yours. Junius is my friend and I've sworn an oath to kill Bassus. Would deny me that pleasure?'

He looked uncertain then. 'What you waiting for then? You can't just sit here while the creature still lives. Come on. We'll do it together.'

'No. It isn't the right time and the risk is too great. I'll bide my time.'

'And Junius lies dying while you tolerate the man who did this?'

'He's with the Tenth. He has men protecting him and I have other things to do as well as get vengeance on Marcus and Bassus.'

'And if Junius dies?'

'He may still live, if the Gods have planned for him to do so,' I said.

'Losing a limb in this world is not the ideal way to leave even this army.'

'No.'

'If he survives, they'll take him back to Rome.'

'I know. He's married and his wife's family own a tavern and a vineyard. He'll be all right.'

I spoke but had no real belief in what I said.

'I told the Legate you fought bravely but he doesn't seem very pleased with you.'

'I told you that Cicero was a humourless bugger. Pass the wine.'

He looked as if he had calmed down but I knew him. I had to get him drunk before that could happen; even then he might go berserk and cast all caution to the winds to get revenge for my friend.

'Well actually, the atmosphere in the tent was getting pretty difficult until Caesar intervened.'

'Who? Caesar?'

'Yes. He was sitting at the back of the tent and when he heard what I had to say about you he burst out laughing and since none of the three of us could string three words together for laughter I had to leave.'

'What?'

'Well yes. Even Cicero was laughing so hard he had tears on his face.'

I thought of the silliness of it all and almost began to laugh again myself.

'You were laughing at me?'

Barbus growled, bestial anger forming on his scarred face like a storm brewing on the horizon..

'No, not at you, at my ridiculous reply.'

'What did you say?'

'Well basically, I told him that you beating Marcus Mettius up was the Roman way.'

'You did what?'

'The Roman way.'

It began all over again. Barbus laughed almost as much as Caesar and we drank the rest of the wine amidst more hysterical laughter. I think it was a form of grieving – a mild escapism. The loss of a comrade whom we valued – it seemed to have heightened our emotions or maybe it was a wish to be free of our thoughts. We were escaping from Gaul and all the trouble it brought to us Romans. Years facing death, maiming and grief; without some relief we could never have come through it.

We drank the rest of the wine and it was late when the night ended. We were both relieved that the next day had been designated a rest day. I would never have survived a drill.

If you don't laugh, you cry I suppose.

Chapter X

"True nobility is exempt from fear." – Marcus Tullius Cicero.

Despite the headache and nausea, I arose at dawn the next morning. I had woken several times thinking about my wounded friend despite the initial drunken coma that had descended when Barbus left. I crossed the camp heading for the surgeon's camp. I walked straight in as there was no orderly at the gate this early in the day.

I went to the tent where I had seen Junius the day before but they had moved him to one of the huts. I plodded across the compound and entered the low-roofed building.

It was dark inside but clean and window spaces in the walls provided ventilation, allowing a cold breeze to waft away the foetid smell. Low wicker cots lined the walls and there were two in the centre of the hut separated from the others. My friend occupied one.

Junius was no longer awake or talking sense. My mood began to plummet. Even I could recognise he was feverish and confused, if not delirious. There was an orderly on the far side of the hut and as I stood next to Junius' cot, he approached.

He shook his head and said, 'I told you it would go putrid. It's up to the Gods now. If you were close, you might consider a sacrifice.'

'Don't tell me, a white bull.'

'Why yes, how did you know? That is exactly the one that pleases Aesculapius the most. I saw a most remarkable recovery from a terrible wound last time they did that, but of course where you would get a white bull around here I can't tell you.'

'Not much bloody use then is it?'

I felt like hitting the man. It was of course not his fault that medicine involved all these stupid religious practises. We had inherited it from the Greeks. Many throughout the Republic still thought they were the best in the medical field. I thought back to the Greek physician whom I had paid to see in Pergamum. It seemed an age away and shrouded in the mists of recollection. I felt my left arm with my right hand. I realised there was much that doctors did not know. I had all but recovered from the terrible head wound and I was sure that there must be a remedy for the putrescent wound on my friend's stump. I could not believe it was his destiny to die here. I walked back to my tent.

I sat outside the tent and was deep in thought when Calvus approached, vine cane in hand.

'Seen Barbus?'

I stood to attention.

'No not since last night, we had a skinful and he may still be sleeping it off.'

'Go and find him would you? I need to speak to you both at my tent in a few minutes. Bring your full gear.'

Puzzled, I went to find Barbus. I knew my performance in front of Caesar the night before had been an unmitigated disaster and guessed some punishment was due. When my sleeping friend had awoken we stood to attention outside Calvus' tent and waited.

Calvus emerged and looked us up and down.

'Smarten up chaps. We've got company arriving any minute.'

'Company?' I said.

'Yes, just mind your manners.'

Moments later, I saw him. It was Caesar accompanied by Cicero, Lepidus and Antonius. They were walking in a relaxed way accompanied by Manius Ostorius our camp prefect. The entire general staff had arrived and what I thought would turn out to be a simple punishment hearing was turning out to be my worst nightmare.

I groaned inside. I must have done something serious if it required all the top generals to witness my punishment. It seemed so unfair. Both the legate and the proconsul had been laughing too. Why single me out? Insubordination perhaps? I tried in desperation to recall what the punishment was for insubordination to the Proconsul of Gaul. I could not guess.

Caesar stood before the tent and smiled.

'Aulus Veridius Scapula. I have a duty to do.'

I was quaking. My knees knocked and my bladder cried out to be relieved.

'The general staff and I have discussed the report you gave yesterday to the Legate Cicero and we have decided that some kind of action is required in your case.'

I knew it.

'You have led a mission that required skill and determination in the face of an enemy who outnumbered you by almost three to one. Despite their numbers, you rode and attacked them and in doing so risked your life to save two of my tribunes, both of whom owe you their lives. It is with great pleasure I award you with an oak-leaf crown in recognition of your valour.'

I looked straight ahead. I could not believe what I was hearing. An oak-leaf crown. It was one of the greatest honours for bravery the legion ever gave and Caesar was awarding me with one. I was speechless and I think my mouth must have gaped, for Calvus reached forward with his vine cane and placed it under my chin pushing up my jaw.

'This army is a family and I regard all my men as part of that family. Your bravery and leadership skills have saved two members of my family and that loyalty and courage will be rewarded. You are also recommended to Centurion Calvus for promotion. Whether he chooses to promote you within his unit or not, is of course up to him, but I would hope that he will consider it as a favour to me.'

'Finally, ex-centurion Barbus. Step forward.'

Barbus did as he was told. Caesar looked him in the face. I think Barbus must have wished he had had a chance to wash for he was grimacing as if in torment. Caesar continued. He was the only one speaking but there was no one present who felt inclined to comment.

'You assaulted a tribune on the field of battle. I remember the case well for it was much discussed. I realise you thought it was for the best at the time. You were punished for it. Yesterday you saved the life of the very man you assaulted. Some would say that was adequate recompense for your crime, but that I cannot do. You have to work your way up to centurion again by yourself. I will recommend that you be promoted to decurion, if Calvus here is willing. You can consider that to be the first rung of a long ladder. You owe this to the loyalty expressed by your future optio and you will need to give him due respect. Do you think you can do that?'

'Yes, sir,' Barbus said.

'Very well, you're both dismissed,' Caesar said.

'It is the Roman way, after all, don't you think, Veridius?' Cicero said and I for one, avoided looking at his face for I knew he was daring me to laugh.

We turned and walked back to our tents. I was hungry and needed to eat something. Barbus was grinning.

'You know Aulus; I was only joking when I said to tell them I fought well. Thank you. I owe you one.'

'Don't mention it. I must say I'm impressed with the proconsul. He really does reward his men. I thought we were there to be punished.'

'Punishment parade is an altogether different circumstance, I can tell you. When you are subject to it believe me, there is no doubt in your mind where you are.'

*   *   *

It was the end of October. The year was drawing to a close and there was now no further time for campaigning. The army had to seek winter quarters. At the face of it, it might have seemed an easier life but for me it meant continuous and boring winter training, building of fortifications and a cold, cold season in Gaul. None of the men looked forward to winter. The bitter weather and the poor food held little attraction for us Romans, but someone had to do it. We became the guardians of Gaul and the Cisalpine approach to Italia.

The standing orders were for two legions (the Thirteenth and Fourteenth) to remain behind in Admagetobriga, near where we fought the battle with Ariovistus, in order to ensure there was no seepage of Germans across the Rhine. A further two legions were to be stationed at Cebelionum further south and they were there to construct a winter camp to support the two legions left behind nearer the Rhine. The two remaining legions were to return to Bibracte and encamp there, the aim being to keep the tribes both north and south from encroaching on the new Roman borders.

The Ninth and Tenth Legions were the ones stationed at Bibracte. It was no more than a small crude mud-hut encampment but I had fond memories of a night with Junius in a tavern there.

The evening had begun with a drinking contest between Junius who could take a drink or two and a huge Gaul with a blond beard dressed in leggings with bright red and green stripes. The Gaul seemed to have the capacity of an ox. They had drunk gallons of the local beer which of course Junius was not used to. After twenty large cups of the filthy brew, Junius had vomited on the floor. The Gaul had insisted that he had won the contest which was fair. It was unfortunate that he then followed up the statement with a number of insults to the weak little Romans who couldn't hold their beer.

The ensuing brawl ended with the arrival of the legionary marshals who broke up the fight and both Junius and I ended up on latrine duty for two weeks. We had enjoyed the fight though and despite the punishment had laughed about it so often that the anecdote had become a favourite.

The whole army was mobile now. The legions staying in the Saone valley had the original camp in which to establish a base but the rest of us had long marches before we could make permanent camps. Caesar had decided to return to Rome but we all understood the need since politics was always uppermost among our topics of conversation, like fat on a stew. Even the enlisted men listened to their junior officers who always boasted they knew about the complex machinations of the political world.

Aripele was much in my thoughts. I missed her badly and wanted nothing more now than to go home with Junius. I could still not quite grasp that he might not live to return to Rome.

Before we departed for the winter camps, I returned to the surgeon's tent to find out what had become of him. My heart sank as I approached, for I expected the worst. The wounded were to be transported in the camp wagons with the tents and it was rare for those with serious wounds to survive. The bouncing around caused wounds to re-open and bleeding to start again and infection was the rule, because of contamination with soil on the battlefield and infected material spread from one wound to another by the orderlies.

The camp was being dismantled and I saw the orderly who had sent me away two days before.

'How is my friend Optio Junius Sinna?'

'Who?' he said.

'The man who lost his arm in the battle. Did he die?'

'Oh yes, I recognise you. No, not yet but I can't promise he won't. There's no absolute time that you can say exactly when they go to Hades. He's over there.' The man pointed to a stretcher in the queue to be put onto a wagon. I approached dreading what I would see. I looked down at my friend. Junius lay quite still. The brown colour of the bandage on his stump had green areas. I leaned forwards and sniffed at the bandage. It reeked of purulence.

'Hey you,' I said indicating to the orderly. 'What are you doing about this? The bandage stinks.'

'It's putrid that's why,' the orderly said. 'He won't be with us long after it spreads up the stump to his chest and I don't have enough fresh bandages to waste on the dying'

'Can't you do anything?' I said.

'The only thing that may work would be myrrh but we ain't got none, so he won't get any, will he?' There was a hint of contempt in the orderly's tone which rankled.

It was a couple of hours yet before I had to return to march my men out of the camp and I felt there must be something I could do for Junius. I walked over to the auxiliaries' camp on the off chance they might have some homespun remedy. Barbus had always sworn by their poultices and liniments.

I encountered the large Gaul called Ventires whom I had seen a few times since the brawl in the tavern at Bibracte. 'Hey, you. Yes, you, you big ox,' I called.

Ventires turned and smiled, 'Better a big ox than a little Roman bitch.'

We both smiled at our insults, for it was clear that they revealed the comradeship we all had in this army.

'Do you remember my friend Junius who you tried to drink to death in Bibracte?' I asked.

'Of course I do Roman, he's the only one of you who can punch,' he said rubbing his jaw in reminiscence and smiling.

'He lost an arm in the battle and the stump is rotting. It's spreading up his arm. The bandage smells bad and he lies still as if he's about to die. I wondered if you Gauls had any treatment that might help. The Roman surgeons don't seem to have any remedies that work,' I said.

'Ursen has something his grand-mother taught him which he swears works on wounds. I don't get wounds myself because I kill my enemies, but I hear it works. He won't give it to you of course,' Ventires said.

'Why not?'

'Well he might, if you give him an arm ring, it's the only thing he values.'

'Look you old goat, I don't have any arm rings. I'm a Roman and we don't wear that kind of thing,' I said. I felt like a man with a boil and the barber kept talking politics instead of lancing it.

'Then tell your friend he will die. He might take that sword as payment,' the big Gaul said.

'I can't part with that whatever happens,' I said. 'Take me to him, please, I don't have much time.'

Ventires turned and led me across the auxiliaries' camp. It was untidy and disorganised by Roman standards, but the big Gaul seemed to know where he was going. Here and there men stood talking, laughing and gesticulating. There was a smell of horses – not dung but that odour you get close up – a leathery ripe smell.

Some men stared at me as we threaded our way through the camp as they sat outside rough tents, lighting cooking fires in the mud. Soon we came to a small tent with a fire and a small cooking pot suspended upon it. A diminutive, dark-haired, wiry Gaul in a green tunic and striped leggings sat cross-legged before the fire roasting a piece of fowl skewered on a knife.

'Are you Ursen?' I enquired.

The man looked up with narrowed eyes and then smiled. The smile was one of pleasant good humour, which seemed almost out of place on his scarred and rough looking features. He had two tattoos, one on each side of his forehead in the rough shape of two snakes facing each other and on each arm he had four silver arm rings. His hair hung in dark pigtails either side of his head. I noticed small bones tied into them but what kind of creatures they came from I could not tell.

Ventires pushed me forward and patted my shoulder. I think he meant to reassure me but all it did was overbalance me. He was a big man after all. I stumbled to my right then corrected myself.

Ursen looked up at me, his brown eyes full of humour. 'Roman, have you come to eat?'

Unbidden, I sat down and crossed my legs. I scrutinised the Gaul, who looked back at me as if he had all the time in the world.

'I need a favour,' I said.

'A favour from a Gaul? I don't do favours for Romans. They killed relatives of mine amongst the Boii last summer and I only came on this little picnic because I hate the Germans more than even I hate the Romans.' He laughed at that, and continued roasting his bird on the fire, stopping now and again to examine how it was cooking.

I was silent for a few minutes, wondering how to tackle the request for help. 'I have a sick friend,' I said at last.

'How sick, Roman?' asked the Gaul, his face expressionless.

'Very sick, he has lost an arm and the wound has turned sour.'

'That sounds very bad. I am sorry for you. It hurts to lose a friend; not as much as losing family but all the same, it hurts. Believe me I know.'

'Ventires said you might have a remedy that could help.'

'Yes I might have something, but tell me Roman why should I help you? Would you help me if I needed you? I think not. You would leave a dying Gaul for the crows wouldn't you?'

The Gaul had a more serious look on his face. I couldn't work out whether the conversation was going well or not.

'I really need your help and will be of help to you one day perhaps,' I said.

'I doubt if there is anything you could ever do to help me. I don't even trust you to try.'

'Am I wasting my time or do you have a price?' I asked.

'No, I will help your friend but not because you ask it. It is because we are all in the same war band. We all fight the Germans who are evil men and torturers. If your friend fell fighting that scum I will be pleased to help,' the Gaul said.

'Will you come with me?' I asked.

'Yes, one moment please,' the Gaul said, laying down his intended meal. He went inside the tent and emerged with a bundle of cloths in his hand. 'Let us go, Roman.'

I led the way to the surgeon's tent. Neither of us spoke. It seemed as if we had reached an understanding. Ursen knelt at the cot side.

'Oi! What you doing to my patient?' the orderly blustered when he saw us. 'You mustn't interfere with his treatment.'

'What treatment? You've left him to die; this man may be able to help, and surely we won't lose anything by trying an old Gaul remedy?'

'He's dying, leave him in peace.'

'I'm telling you. There isn't anything to lose is there?' I said.

A look of doubt descended on the man's face. 'I suppose not, but be quick,'

Junius lay on the stretcher, quite still. Ursen knelt by his side and pulled the stinking rags off the stump. He tutted and sucked his teeth.

'Butchers,' he said. 'We never keep the wound dry like this. He unwrapped the bundle that he had carried from the tent. To my disgust, it contained layer upon layer of what looked like mouldy bread.

'What are you doing with that?'

'The mould contains something which heals the wound. It has been in use for many generations in my tribe and I know that it works,' Ursen said.

He cut a clean length of rag from his bundle and bandaged some of the mouldy stuff over the infected stump.

'It needs changing twice a day and must be dampened with oil and wine. Good luck.'

With that, the Gaul stood up in a casual fashion and sauntered away without looking back. I wondered if I had exchanged one fatal remedy for another. I picked up the mouldy bread and rags and stuffed them into my belt pouch. There was nothing more I could do until evening, but I was determined to come back then to change the bandages. I went about my duties with a heavy heart that day.

Throughout the day's march, my thoughts kept returning to my injured comrade. When all was quiet, I returned to the surgeon's wagons, on which they were transporting the wounded. It seemed as if Junius' life hung by a thread. He was dry as a cockroach. I tried to force some watered wine into his mouth but to no avail. All he could do was cough and splutter.

'We've been trying to get some broth into him all day but

he can't take it. He still has a raging fever,' the orderly said. 'The surgeon will do his rounds in the morning.'

'Could you dress his wound with this stuff? I'm no doctor,' I asked 'it doesn't look good, but the Gauls swear by it,'

'All right, but it's against my better judgement. I suppose if he's going to die anyway then it won't make a difference. He can't get worse, whatever you insist upon,' replied the orderly who seemed much more forthcoming on this occasion. There was faint smile on his lips when I left.

The following morning the army began its second day's march to Bibracte. I was delighted to note that Junius was less fevered than the day before, but he remained in a delirious state. The orderly felt there was slight improvement.

On the third day, Junius showed slight signs of recovery. He opened his eyes to the sound of my voice and was able to take a little watered wine. His recovery continued at a very gradual pace during the ten-day journey back to Bibracte. It had taken Caesar seven days to march his men to the battle site to stop the Germans and the return was less urgent and at what seemed a more reasonable pace.

All the way I was thinking about how our surgeons could be so wrong. Junius was going to live even though I never found that white bull to sacrifice.

Chapter XI

"A word once sent abroad, flies irrevocably." – Horace.

It was a long tiring march to winter quarters. The prospect of being cooped up all winter with the men irritated me. I wished I was back in Rome and in Aripele's arms. I thought of her often. It was as if now that I was unencumbered by the day to day acts of war, I could afford to think of softer and gentler things.

I wrote regular letters on the usual wooden tablets but their delivery was a hit-and-miss affair, I discovered later. All such communications had to be vetted by the legion scribes before being packed and sent with the ships leaving from Massilia on the south coast. There was never any guarantee they would even be shipped.

I received only one letter from Aripele. The Greek script had faded in places and the papyrus must have become wet at some stage. It was not an expensive papyrus scroll and it had unravelled here and there as well, making it hard to read.

From Aripele to Aulus Veridius Scapula Decurion Ninth Legion Hispania.

My dearest Aulus,

How I miss you. It seems such a long time since I even saw you but I think of you all the time. Quintus and I regularly sacrifice for your safe return. He sacrifices to Mercury and I to Hecate for I think her magic may surround and protect you.

We are well. I am earning a small fortune selling tapestries. They are easy to make but take time. There seems to be a market for them in Rome and I have employed some people locally to do some of the weaving.

We hear about the exploits of the Ninth Legion from time to time and all Rome is fascinated by Caesar's success in his campaigns in Gaul. He seems to be very popular here amongst the ordinary people and captures their imagination. Have you met him? I suppose you won't have. I can't wait for you to come home but as you said in your last letter, it could be years.

Quintus is very kind and looks after me. He fusses like an old grandfather although he is not really old. Don't worry. I'm not returning to my old trade.

How is Junius? I met his wife Aemilia at the thermae. She seems very nice. We talked a little about him and about you and we have arranged to meet again. She helps her father run a tavern called The Old Soldier in the Subura. They have a wine business as well, with vineyards in Ostia.

This sheet of papyrus is ending now and since it is so expensive, I can only afford one.

I love you, come home soon.

Aripele

It was not much of a letter but Aripele was no scribe or poet and I knew there was much more to say, but left unsaid.

*   *   *

When we reached the camp we began preparations for building wooden buildings in readiness for the winter. The two legions, Ninth and Tenth, had separate encampments which were identical in layout but twenty yards apart. I was glad of that for it made it unlikely I would run into my cousin Marcus. I had not seen him since the day I freed him from the Germans. Procillus had recovered well and was almost his normal self though at times, he would stare off into the distance as if re-living some bad moment. The attacks would stop and he would force a smile but they became less frequent as time passed.

Both camps had surrounding fortifications of staggered ditches containing wooden stakes so that an enemy would have to criss-cross to approach the walls and would be limited in the numbers who could approach. We strengthened the palisade inside and a platform supported on wooden supports made our wall-walk allowing the sentries to see over the top.

During this construction, there was a great deal to do. We needed all our skills to build and source the raw materials. We even built two bathhouses which, although crude and limited in size, were good enough for general use. The officers had one and the enlisted men had the other.

Junius had at last recovered enough to stand and walk but he remained unsteady on his feet. The first shipload of injured and maimed soldiers was due to leave and Junius had to go with them.

'No-one needs a one-armed soldier I guess,' Junius said.

'What will you do when you get back?' I said.

'I don't know. I can't imagine Aemilia will want a cripple for a husband. I can't earn much of a living and I can't even return to farming with one arm.'

'Look, my friend, when I was recovering from that head wound I had to learn to fight with myself. I was as down as you are and could see no future either. I got through it by being determined and letting time pass. I never gave up hope, nor will you. You hear?'

'But look at what I've lost.' There were tears in his eyes. 'Look what they make you give.'

'I thought I had lost Hypsicratea because I could not imagine her wanting to be with a cripple. In the event, I misunderstood her love. It was beyond my physical shortcomings. I'm sure Aemilia will be happy as long as you go back to her.'

'But I can't earn a living.'

'You can work in the tavern. Just think what tales you can tell. You've been to Pontus, Armenia, and Gaul and seen battle in all of those places. The place will be packed with people wanting to hear your stories. Trust me.'

'Do you really think so?'

'Of course. You need to be angry. Don't fight it Junius, use it. Believe me, I know – it's what I did.'

'You really are a good friend Aulus. I'll be sorry to leave you to the mercies of the Gauls. Who will look after you now?'

'If you ever looked after me before it would mean this is all your fault.'

'Seriously though,' he said, 'you will have to find me when you return and we will share a few jugs of wine on the house.'

'Take care my friend.'

We parted and it was long time before we met again.

*   *   *

Caesar and most of the tribunes were wintering in Rome with the promise of bringing back artillery and troops and of more importance, obtaining funding for the war in Gaul which had become an astronomical expense. Titus Lepidus was in command in Bibracte. Lepidus was a man of middle years, well connected in political circles and a staunch supporter of Caesar's campaign.

I felt as if I was kicking my heels in the camp. I knew that the amulet was not in Gaul and I needed only to bide my time until we returned to Rome, if we ever did. Separation from Aripele and my lack of success with the amulet was getting on my nerves. The boredom didn't help either.

It was in this state of mind that Procillus found me.

'Aulus. Good to see you.'

'Good? What's good about it? It's freezing and there's nothing for a soldier to do, sir.'

'Well there's no need to be like that.'

'Sorry Tribune. I'm just bored and since Junius left to return to Rome I have only Barbus for company and you know what he's like.

'Is he over-refreshed again?'

'Well let's put it this way, he drank himself to sleep on the local beer and it's now morning and I don't think he would take kindly to being disturbed.'

'Pity, he was one of the men I wanted with me.'

'Oh?'

'Yes the Legate has summoned me and asked me to bring some of the officers who I feel are reliable. He was very cloak-and-dagger about it I must say. Curious?'

'Yes, sir.'

'Come along if you like. I'm meeting Calvus and Publius Crassus at the command hut.'

We walked side by side through the slush and mud. My toes were numb within minutes. Aripele had sent me some socks a few weeks before but the wool soaked up the wetness of the mud and that did nothing to keep my feet warm.

'I've been meaning to ask you; have you been in any trouble lately?' Procillus asked.

'No, what do you mean?'

'Someone was making enquiries about you, that's all.'

'Who?'

'A centurion from the Tenth. He had orders from the legate of the Tenth to see the books. I told him it was none of his business and he said he had to look in the books for some records. Then he asked after you.'

'Asked after me?'

'Yes, he said he thought you had retired from the legion and wondered how come you had re-enlisted.'

'What was he like sir?'

'Fat fellow, looked mucky somehow. Dirty black beard that needed a wash. Frankly, he looked as if he hadn't seen the inside of a therma for years. He didn't smell much better than that either.'

'Bassus.'

'Yes, that was his name. Friend of yours?'

'No sir, quite the opposite. He didn't say what he was looking for in the books did he?'

'He may have done but I don't recall what it was. I was just keen to get him out of my tent. His smell seemed to linger.'

I walked with Procillus to the Legate's quarters. It had snowed a little during the night and a biting wind blew the light snow into drifts against the huts. I pulled my cloak around me but it was becoming threadbare and I couldn't afford to buy a new woollen one. I hoped to pick up a cheap one in Bibracte but there was a ban on entering the town at the time since one of my fellow soldiers had picked a fight with one of the Gauls and almost killed him.

Publius Crassus was waiting with Calvus outside the General's hut. It irritated me a little that he was always so clean and well turned out. Every time I saw the man, he looked well groomed. I wondered how he managed it in this hellhole.

'Veridius. You've come to this mystery party too, have you?' Calvus said.

'Yes, sir. Tribune Procillus invited me.'

We entered the vestibule of the hut into which the two rooms of the building opened. One room was an office and the other was a sleeping room. It was warm and dry and it was the first time I had been anywhere dry for days.

I heard a deep voice call, 'Luventius. Is that chap Procillus here yet?'

Luventius, the General's orderly appeared at the door of the office and bade us enter. Lepidus was a short, dry, serious man, with a weak narrow chin and fair, straight hair. He stood to my shoulder in height and his features were small and delicate. He was a sharp contrast to the General. Lepidus was big. He was tall, fat and broad and had a headful of dark brown hair combed with immaculate care. His ears stuck out through his straight fair hair and his chin was narrow and weak. He wore a red tunic and had wrapped himself in a thick crimson cloak to keep the cold out. He stood in front of a brazier filled with hot coals and managed to block most of the heat from his officers as we stood before him to attention. He scratched under his arm and looked at us in silence.

'Procillus, I told you to bring a reliable second in command not a whole bloody cohort.'

'Sorry sir,' Procillus said. 'You did say to bring reliable men. Positive attitude, you said, so I used my initiative.'

'Initiative, eh?' Lepidus looked at his tribune with a slow nod. 'Well at least someone has some redeeming features around here.'

'Sir?'

'I had a good day's hunting yesterday. I think the only thing worth doing in this miserable place seems to be the hunting. Do you hunt, Procillus?'

'Yes sir. When I was at home I used to hunt with my uncle who is legate of the Town Guard.'

'What about you?' he said, poking me in the chest with an outstretched finger.

'No sir, afraid not. Apart from Germans that is.'

Lepidus ignored my attempt at humour. 'Nothing like hunting, you know. I took two boars yesterday. The first from horseback using my father's boar spear. The sport went easily. The boar tried to run across open ground and although most horses would shy away from pursuing a boar, Bucephalus, my palomino stallion fears nothing.' He made a stabbing gesture with his right arm, almost clipping Procillus across the face, 'I managed to thump the heavy spear into the creature's humped back. Finishing the creature with my sword presented no problems as it tried to scramble forwards using only its front legs. What do you think of that then?'

'It must have been a good day for you sir,' Procillus said.

'Oh it was. The second, I took in a thicket whilst on foot. I used slaves as beaters and they'd driven the boar towards me by banging on pots and shields. The creature charged and do you know what?'

He looked at us each in turn, his eyes wide. He seemed possessed by what he was telling us, as if it was some great battle. I felt like groaning with boredom.

'Well,' he continued, 'the force of the impact knocked me to the ground but as the boar launched itself at me I braced my spear against a tree trunk. The tip struck the beast in the chest and I skewered the oncoming creature with all the force of its own momentum.'

There was silence as none of us dared speak. I wondered when he would get to the point.

He stared at us. 'Momentum. Yes, that's the thing, momentum. Where would a hunter be without it, eh?'

'I believe you had a mission for us, sir?' Procillus said.

'Mission? Oh yes. I got carried away. Hunting here is really pretty good you know. Perhaps we should all go for a hunt when you get back?'

'Get back sir?'

'Yes, from the mission.'

'Yes sir, the mission.'

There was another pause. I began to realise that the General seemed only to have a slim hold upon reality. I supposed it might have been the enforced loneliness of the command or something like that. I had heard of people going mad with isolation, but never when they were surrounded by people.

'I have a little job for you Procillus. There's been a problem you see,' Lepidus said.

'Sir?'

'It's a raiding party of Nervians. They burned an Aedui village killing many of the inhabitants, torturing some and enslaving all of the remainder who had not escaped. What do you think of that?'

'A great pity sir,'

Procillus seemed nonplussed by the way the meeting was going.

'Yes, quite. The Aedui, poor chaps, are allies and friends and being under the protection of Rome means that retribution for such transgressions has to be swift. An attack on one of Rome's allies is tantamount to an attack on Rome herself, don't you think?'

'Of course, sir,' Procillus said.

'The Nervians live immediately to the North. They're sandwiched between the Viromandui and the Atrebates and have a crude tribal culture based on fighting and not trade. In fact there is precious little for them to trade with since they farm poorly and most of what they have is derived from raiding and herding. They are among the least advanced of the Belgic tribes but their war-like qualities make them ferocious enemies. I need you to sort the problem out.'

'Err. Yes sir.'

'I need you to teach them a lesson but I want to avoid a war. I can tell you now I am not imbued with the same leniency as our commander-in-chief Gaius Julius. I do want to settle this matter as bloodlessly as possible though. We have a choice. I could on the one hand, send troops to attack Nervian villages to make an example of them but the risk of a protracted situation of attacks and counter-attacks is likely to ensue. On the other hand, an envoy might be able to exact some compensation for the Aedui and the matter could be settled.'

'An envoy sir?'

'Yes, that's you.'

'But you said to ready some troops, sir.'

'I want you to negotiate through strength. It's the only way with savages.'

'Yes sir.'

'And do try to settle the matter without starting a bloody war. We don't want the Proconsul to return to find us in a bloody mess, do we?'

'Of course not, sir. What do you actually want me to do?'

'Damn it man, I want you to take two cohorts – the first and second will do, oh and an ala of horse and some auxilliary cavalry, to the Nervii leader Boduognatus. Make it clear that we, as Rome's instruments, take a pretty dim view of his nonsense. If he won't release the slaves he's taken and compensate our allies then explain that we'll slap his backside. Understood? Eh?' Lepidus said.

'But I thought you didn't want a war sir?'

'Of course I don't want a bloody war, I just told you.' Lepidus said, irritation creeping into his voice.

'But then... Yes sir.' replied our puzzled tribune.

'Off you go there's a good chap. Simple really. Pop along then.'

'Yes sir.'

We all turned with military smartness and followed Procillus from the room.

'I must say,' Procillus said, 'there was no point in arguing, but I have definite reservations about how a war-like chieftain will respond to Roman threats to slap his bottom. I suppose anything must seem simple for a dyed-in-the-wool patrician legate.'

'He has a strange demeanour but he is in charge I suppose,' Crassus said.

'I think we can do this. If we negotiate by killing them all it won't take long,' was Calvus' only comment.

We walked away and I began to wonder why Caesar had left Lepidus in charge. It may have been that he would have messed up the Proconsul's political machinations in Rome. Lepidus after all, was not the sort of politician one would want dealing with delicate matters.

Chapter XII

"A thing is not necessarily true because badly uttered, nor false because spoken magnificently." – St. Augustine.

By morning, our vexillation was set to move out. There were two cohorts of infantry comprising twelve hundred men and an ala of cavalry and a similar number of Gallic horsemen on their small horses. Although such a squadron of cavalry varied in size, there were one hundred and twenty Roman equites armed with cavalry spears and swords. The cavalry protected our flanks and served as scouts and advance parties. Our force was not a complete legion so we didn't carry the prized eagle of the Ninth, though we did have a standard-bearer in each cohort who carried our standard of a bull's head, the sign of the Ninth. The aquilifer carried the bull and his second carried a vexillium, a triangular pennant as well.

It was a ten-day march to the Nervian territory. There were no roads after the first day and marching across country in the snow and slush made progress tough but not too difficult once we got going. I marched next to my century keeping the ranks in line but it was an impossible task on the uneven ground which was broken here and there by the remnants of last year's scrub and vegetation. It occurred to me we would not be in a good position at all if we were ambushed since the main strength of a Roman century was derived from keeping in formation to take advantage of the shields which formed an almost impenetrable barrier to attacking infantry and cavalry.

It was a bleak landscape. Hills covered by pine forest were broken up by valleys and dips with frozen streams and boulders. Our cohorts marched eight hours each day, with flanking pickets most of the time and a scout force of twenty cavalry, with a similar sized rear-guard. Publius Crassus led the cavalry.

At the end of the first day we were tired with the long march since with the enforced lack of exercise, winter quarters left a man with less energy and fitness. It was therefore with some effort we dug the trenches in the frozen ground and built the palisade before setting up our tents in the places marked out with wooden pegs by the advance guard. We adopted the same routine each evening to ensure we were protected from surprise attack. Each of us carried a wooden spar for the palisade and was responsible for its arrival at the next camp.

It was late when I got to my tent. I had supervised the fortifications with Calvus as each century took its turn at that duty. I was walking along the reduced scale Via Praetoria when I saw Crassus walking the other way talking to Procillus. The two men were having an animated conversation and smiling. They saw me and slowed down.

'Well, Decurion. How are you getting on after today's little excursion?' Publius Crassus said.

'Just fine sir. Glad to be out of barracks to be honest.'

'Aulus here,' Procillus said, 'is one of the finest swordsmen in the legion. He came second only to Meridius in a sword contest on the Field of Mars, did you know that?'

'No, I hadn't heard that. He saved your bacon though didn't he?' Crassus was smiling.

'Aulus, you certainly did save me. I saw you fighting with Ariovistus that day. I wished you had killed him. The Germans drew lots as to whether to put us in their fires before or after the battle. Fortuna smiled upon me and Marcus that day, I can tell you.'

'It's all behind us now sir,' I said.

'I hope so. The Gauls don't torture their prisoners, they enslave them. They're not as inhumane as those Germans bastards.'

'All the same we'll have to treat them the same if it comes to it,' Crassus said with a smile still softening his features.

'You did well in that battle yourself,' Procillus said.

'Well yes, I'm pleased to acknowledge it. Caesar seemed to think so.'

'What happened sir?' I said.

'Crassus was returning from the rout with his ala and saw the right flank beginning to fall back. He ordered the rear rank into the fight, and leading his men around the side, charged the cavalry into the enemy flank.'

'I thought only the senior officers were allowed to give orders like that?' I said.

'Well yes, that's true but instead of punishing him, Caesar rewarded him. He values initiative. I think I'm going to have to display a bit of that myself, but I don't think Lepidus is the man to recognise it.'

'No, nor do I,' Crassus said.

'Can we really persuade the Nervians to return the slaves and property?'

'Sounds like a real challenge of diplomacy to me,' Crassus said.

'That's just what I'm good at,' Crassus said. 'Learned a lot from Lucullus you know. He always took the attitude you should charge in there with all your forces and introduce them to Mars.'

'Hope you haven't learned to crucify your own men sir, like Lucullus,' I said.

Procillus looked at me and decided it was a joke after all and smiled. I departed to my tent and wondered how we would fare.

I began to think of the women in my life: Hypsicratea, whom I had loved and lost and Aripele whom I loved and who was now waiting for my return. I worried in case someone else might steal her away from me but I knew in my heart they could not. I knew she loved me. I wondered what she was doing at that precise moment. Was she thinking of me as I thought about her? I ruminated on the first night I made love to her and how I had followed her to the dingy room she had hired, when I got her back.

I had no one to talk to and it frustrated me. Barbus was good company at times but at other times he drove me to distraction for he was a brutal sort. He was good to get drunk with and we had done a lot of that during the early months of winter quarters, but the legion had hardened him and he had no conscience where violence was concerned.

*   *   *

Within a day's march of the Nervian town, the scouts reported small squads of horsemen staying in front of our marching vexillation. We realised that someone was keeping us under surveillance. There was no contact with our enemy until the following afternoon when the scouts reported a large force of Nervian infantry half a mile ahead. The Nervii never used cavalry, disdaining them for large groups of infantry. They had a reputation for being fierce and warlike, spending much of their time in military pursuits. I wondered if they were a true military society like the Spartans. Perhaps they saw military honour and violent death as an honourable thing. There could be no worse opponents, for such men are hard to kill in battle.

We advanced to a hilltop overlooking a small frozen stream. From there, the land fell away in a gentle amble to a landscape of melting snow interspersed with thorn-encrusted thicket. Grassy tussocks peeped through the snow here and there, but the ground was soft and slushy.

It was a bright afternoon, the snow reflecting the light from a dull Gallic sun imparting little warmth. A light snowfall began as the Nervii came into view over the next rise. They filled the skyline. There must have been four thousand infantry armed with spears and swords. Their round Belgic shields in bright reds and blues seemed the only vivid colour on the horizon; all else appeared bleak and grey.

Our cohorts lined up on the ridge in the usual triple line formation but in close order to take advantage of our shields. A single rider advanced from the Nervian ranks, holding a stave with a green branch tied to it. I watched his slow progress across the stream.

'They want to talk,' I heard Procillus say to Crassus, 'I'll go and see what they want, ask Calvus and Veridius to accompany me.'

The three of us proceeded forward at a slow walk to meet the oncoming envoy; Calvus and I were on foot. We met their dismounted envoy between the two small armies. Procillus looked down from his horse at the Nervian.

'What can we do for you?' he said.

I was puzzled by his query since even I thought this wasn't the ideal way to start diplomatic discourse.

The Nervian stared up at him and said in appalling Latin 'Roman, I cannot talk if I am looking up all the time; your face is hidden by the light. Perhaps I should talk to your horse instead?'

He was a large man clad in a bearskin cloak over a bare chest and wearing the red and green leggings seen on so many of the Gauls. Around his neck, was a string of boar tusks and a silver torque. He wore a helmet with a spike at its apex. At his waist hung a long, heavy broadsword and in his left hand he carried a round shield, decorated with blue enamel and a boss of copper also mounted with a spike. The spear in his right hand was taller than he was and had a crude, by Roman standards, metal spike at its tip. His raven-black hair was tied in plaits; one to either side and a black moustache extending to below his chin, draped his face. He was different in shape to the Gauls whom I had met before, with short bow-legs, a broad chest and long arms. His weather-beaten face had a slightly hooked nose and bristling heavy eyebrows.

Procillus dismounted and stood facing the envoy. It was his turn to look up now for the Nervian towered above him since the envoy was a big man, the bearskin adding to his bulk.

'We come in peace,' Procillus said.

'Roman, you come in peace with Legions of soldiers behind you. Not good for peace.' Again the broken Latin.

'A wise man talks gently but shows his strength. You too have brought an army to meet us although we only come to talk in peace.' Procillus tried to smile but must have felt rather dwarfed and intimidated by the huge warrior who confronted him.

'We talk later in camp of Boduognatus,' the big warrior said.

'No,' Procillus said. 'We talk in the Roman camp or we fight. No other way.'

The warrior contemplated his words then said, 'Yes Roman, to-night in Roman camp. I bring ten men.'

'Very well, but do you have one who speaks our tongue? There is much to say and it would be best to understand everything.'

It was perhaps unwise to insult the man's language but even I was finding the conversation like listening to a three year old.

'We bring a slave and we talk and feast. We bring ox to cook'.

We parted company, each returning to their own side. Our men had already started fortifying the hilltop and I walked back noting with pride how they dug the trenches. I felt our forces would prove more than a match for the Nervians, even though we were so outnumbered. Besides, we had two ala of cavalry and the Nervians had none.

The promised ox was delivered by two warriors clad in a similar way to the man we had parleyed with that afternoon. They drove an ox cart with three oxen, its emptiness conspicuous. The Barbarians were met at the camp gates and there they cut loose one of the oxen and with apparent glee, butchered it in front of our waiting guards. They looked up when they had finished, smiling almost as if to say, 'You'll be next,' and then turned the cart around and headed back the way they had come.

Our cooks prepared the ox meat Cretan style, with a spicy coating and spit roasting it. The officers, centurions and Optios reported to the praetorium as we were expected to host the Barbarian's visit. Arms were allowed since we were not at war in any formal way.

I sat at the front near one of the brushwood fires to try to keep warm. I'd managed to warm up my feet enough to be able to feel them when the Barbarians arrived. The guard-duty troops inspected the guests and showed them to the praetorium where we had arranged some rough seating around one of the fires. I noted that the ten men were all tall, well-built and armed to the teeth. The warriors sat down and I noticed how three of the men remained standing behind the seats of the warriors with their hands clasped in front of them and their legs slightly apart. Their torques and armour glittered in the firelight and their helmets reflected the crackling and sparking flame-light. I had never seen a fiercer band of Barbarians; these men looked almost noble in their bearing unlike the rowdy, unkempt and undisciplined Germans we had fought only months before.

At the end of the semicircle was a man dressed in rags. They held him by a loop of leather around his neck and he held his head and shoulders bowed. He did not speak. The warrior holding the leash pulled the trembling slave to the ground where he knelt in a pitiful pose of abject fear.

Within moments Procillus and Crassus appeared, resplendent in their polished armour and as well armed as the Barbarian guests. They had no intention of letting these fearsome warriors upstage them. They took seats opposite the delegation of Nervians, and smiled in greeting. The Nervii looked at them with contempt. An orderly offered them wine but the Barbarian leader pushed the man away bellowed something in his own language. The slave, without looking up repeated the words, 'We do not drink this poison. Nervii keep a clear head, for no man can be brave if his wits are entangled by this brew that makes men into women.'

The leader looked across the tables at his Roman enemies.

'So Roman, we have come to talk. What you want?' Boduognatus said, for it was he who had first spoken to us in the valley between our two armies.

One of them pulled the slave up and pushed him into the space between the makeshift tables. He bowed and said in perfect Latin 'I have been instructed to translate sir,' addressing himself to Procillus.

Procillus looked at the man.

'You're a Roman aren't you?

'Yes sir I was once, but I was captured and there is no way I can come home.' There was a tear in his eye and he looked down in a hopeless manner.

'You talk more to slave than me.' Boduognatus said with a sneer.

'Tell the noble king that we shall eat first and then talk. Meanwhile we offer him our hospitality such as it is,' Procillus said.

'Perhaps he will be in a better mood with a full stomach,' Procillus said in an aside to Crassus.

Our cooks served the meal but the Nervii ate only sparingly, saying that too much food made the wits sluggish which was no good in battle. Despite this, the seated Barbarians began to relax, although there was nothing relaxed about the men behind the seats who remained in the same posture throughout. When the orderlies had cleared away the remains of the meal Procillus began, his words translated by the slave.

'We have come, Boduognatus, because we have heard you are a great king who rules justly and wisely over his people, a people whose qualities at war are known even to us Romans.' He paused for a moment, then said, 'In your kingly justice we make claim for a crime that was committed against our friends, the Aedui. Three weeks ago a village of theirs was sacked and burned. Slaves were taken and women raped. Rome considers an attack on her friends as an attack upon Rome herself. We do not want war with the Nervii and would prefer to settle this peacefully but war will come if you do not show your kingly justice to our friends the Aedui.'

Boduognatus stood and his impressive figure, illuminated by the flickering firelight, made him appear regal indeed.

'Roman,' he said in his own language, translated by the slave, 'my people are a war-like people. We do not turn our hands to the plough like women. We learn to fight and we live the way of the warrior from our mother's knee until old age. We do not befuddle our wits with wine or German beer for it weakens a man. When we want something, we take it. It has always been so and cannot change. You tell me of a village of these Aedui dogs. I know this village; it was full of things my warriors desired. Why should the strong not take from the weak? You Romans think we are weak and that you can take from us. You would be foolish to try, for we are mighty warriors.'

He turned to his men and thumped his chest with a closed fist and the other Nervii picked up their spears, hammered the ground and called out a battle cry in a fearsome roar.

'You Romans,' Boduognatus went on, 'you come here and make demands, but you are weak. The weak do not take from the strong. We Nervians are strong and give you nothing but your freedom to leave. Your people want to own all lands. You bring armies and you think you can own the land where you fight. We believe the land owns us. It cannot belong to anyone. This land will never be yours any more than it is ours but we will fight for the truth of it. Your blood will feed it and you will become part of it. Make no mistake we are strong and will crush you.'

He sat down again with a smug smile on his face.

Procillus stood up now. 'Boduognatus, you are a great king of a brave and noble people but your tribe and the tribes around you are only a speck of sand on the Roman shore. We number many but send few warriors to challenge you, for although we do not wish war we can wage it and kill all of you in battle. We know this to be true and maybe you have learned enough about us to know it too. Ask the Helvetii, ask the Boii, ask the Suebi. It is no wonder that you brought so many men with you. You know we can crush you. Our history shows that even much stronger armies than the Nervii do not easily defeat us and a Roman defeat is followed by a return with bigger armies and victory, because Rome accepts no defeat. This time, we have not come here to wage war; only to talk and reach a peaceful agreement of compensation for our Aedui allies.'

'What are your claims for compensation?' Boduognatus asked.

'We want the return of the slaves your men have taken; we want fifty herd cows and ten barrels of silver. We also want an undertaking that no Nervii will cross the river to fight the Aedui again.'

'Roman, you make me laugh, you come here with your tiny force and your silly horsemen and give me terms. I give you my terms, tomorrow we fight and I will let one man live to tell your friends of how you died.'

'It would be unwise for you to test the mettle of my men. They are battle-trained and our cavalry know their business. Is there no way that you can see for us to settle this without a war that will crush you?' Procillus said.

Boduognatus, paused a moment and turned and said something to the man on his right. There was an animated conversation and even the men standing behind the chairs chipped in, one of them smiling. Presently, Boduagnatus stood up facing us, looking down at Procillus.

'There is a way, a time hallowed way to settle disputes between warring parties,' the slave translated. 'I have heard that you Romans also have similar laws, or had at one time. Perhaps your champion can fight mine and the winner will get the spoils. If you win we will yield to your demands, but if my champion wins, then you leave all your weapons and provisions here except what you need for your journey back – with your shame written upon your faces.'

Procillus was taken aback for the first time in the evening. He had not expected such terms from this Barbarian. I expected him to say that Rome did not bargain and we would meet them in battle the next day. I heard Crassus at his side whisper, 'We do have a man with a reputedly brilliant sword-arm. He managed to get you out of a German camp and was unscathed after fighting Ariovistus. Why not say yes? At the worst we can fight them anyway and at best we risk one man.'

Procillus still wavered. He gestured to me to approach.

'Do you think that you could take on one of those chaps with your gladius and win?' he asked.

'The Gods will decide that, but if you wish it I'll be glad to try,' I said, for fighting was the one thing I knew I could do; my weak left arm did not matter if I didn't have to carry a shield. As soon as I had spoken however, I began to have doubts. They nagged at me as I watched Procillus rise from his seat. As ever, I wondered if I should have kept my mouth shut. Anything could happen now.

'Very well,' Procillus said. 'Let your man step forward.'

Boduognatus smiled. He turned and gestured to one of the three men standing behind him and indicated that he should step forwards. Both men smiled in silence. The fire flicked a spark at my foot. Of all things, I heard an owl hooting a warning behind me. The smiles on the faces of the Gauls were enough to make me have second thoughts. I was fast but not strong and certainly not as mobile as I had once been. I trusted in the Gods. I trusted also in Meridius. Experience and anticipation he always said. My nerves began to calm as I took possession of my faculties. I kept telling myself I could do this, but doubt gnawed at the roots of my determination like a rat at a rafter. Discipline, mental and physical; I had to draw on my reserves. For Aripele, I had to live.

Chapter XIII

"It is not death that a man should fear, but he should fear never beginning to live." – *Marcus Aurelius.*

I had fought in enough battles and seen enough gladiatorial contests in the arena at home to know that the two techniques are very different. Meridius had trained me well using both long swords and the Roman gladius but there were new factors to take into account here and I was aware of them. For one thing, we both stood in the firelight without armour, bare-chested. Without a lorica or breastplate, any deep cut to the chest would be the end of the fight. The other difference was that we had no shields. I was glad of that as I still found holding a shield up for long with my left arm tiring.

The Nervian facing me was tall, maybe six inches taller than me and lanky but muscular. His bearded face was long and thin bearing a sardonic grin. He looked as if that smile was stuck on his stupid face forever and I wondered whether he was still smiling when he retired to bed at night and whether he got up with it in the morning. On his right arm he wore a single arm-ring and about his neck were a thin silver torque and a sort of necklace. In the flickering light I realised they were human ears on a leather thong. I swallowed hard, for my mouth was arid, but my determination grew. I was not going to let this man take my ears like some butchered beast.

He carried a strange sword. It was very long and heavy. Stood upright it would have reached to the man's shoulder. He swung the weapon sideways and back several times flexing his tight muscles to warm up and resting the tip on the ground in between strokes. He then stepped towards the centre of the space between us, leaving the tip of his weapon touching the ground behind him. He moved in a cat-like and relaxed way. It suggested to me that he was quick rather than powerful. He irritated me. The smile never left his lips. Was he mocking me?

With a speed that took me by surprise, the Nervian stepped to the side. The tip of the heavy sword flew upwards and then down. It arced straight at my bare head. The weight of the weapon added a bone crushing momentum to the enormous blade.

I stepped aside. My anticipation was too sluggish. The Barbarian blade caught my left heel a glancing blow. The pain was searing. I confess I yelped with pain. I had not expected the heavy blade to move so fast. Limping now, my left foot seemed at first unable to take my weight. It was pain rather than weakness. I heard Boduagnatus guffaw off to my right.

Bastard.

My Barbarian opponent continued to smile, weighing me up. My comrades cheered me on, trying to encourage their champion. I saw Procillus swallow in the sure knowledge that he had risked everything on me. The consequences of my death would weigh against him with Lepidus for he knew he had to avoid an all-out war or face the wrath of his legate.

Silence descended. It was a kind of tense anticipation, almost tangible. I could feel it. There seemed to be doubt hanging in the air. It was like some invisible cloak engulfing us all in its folds. I heard that owl hoot again in the nearby ash tree. It irritated me for the discouragement of his call was the last thing I needed. I stepped back a little, waiting for my opponent's next move. I hoped the pain from my heel would settle. I didn't have long to wait.

The Barbarian swung his sword. This time two-handed from left to right. The method was unlike anything I had seen before. The Nervian had stepped forward. The heavy blade still rested on the ground. He used the force and momentum of his body to launch the weapon. It was an horrendous blow. He wielded it in a circle using the weight to propel his body.

The enormous blade swung. The warrior followed. He turned, bringing the blade back almost in a circle. Upwards it flew at first then down towards me. Still limping, I stepped back. I could feel a bench against the back of my right knee. I realised I couldn't back away any further. I hadn't struck a blow yet, to my intense frustration. My painful heel had slowed me down. The length of my opponent's weapon made it hard to get close.

The Nervian stepped back around his sword. He didn't raise it. It was as if the blade was the centre of his game. He positioned the heavy blade to his best advantage and moved around it, until the heavy weapon could be launched at his opponent. He was so light-footed it was almost a dance – a dance of deathly skill.

I was sweating. My heart raced. I knew I had to get past him to gain some breathing space. He moved to the left. I struck with my sword at his right side. I stepped forward despite the pain in my foot. I knew that the pain was better than being laid open by the monstrous weapon I was facing. The Nervian dodged my blow with ease. He showed amazing speed. He skipped around his heavy sword.

The right tactics still evaded me. I had no shield. I could not fend off a blow. I had to rely on parrying the heavy blade with my sword. The size and weight of my enemy's weapon made me wonder if any sword could withstand such a strain.

The Nervian laughed and said something in his own language. It caused a ripple of laughter amongst the watching Nervii. His confidence showed clear. Stationary now, he stood with his right hand on the hilt of his sword, legs apart waiting for me to do something. I responded. I used all the speed I could muster. I stepped to my right and swung my blade from right to left in a two-handed stroke at my opponent's neck.

Had the blow landed it would have taken his head. It never made contact. Again, with astonishing speed, the Nervian sidestepped. His sword was on his left and he lifted the blade upwards in a curving arc. He brought it down with horrendous force. He aimed it at my left shoulder. I stepped back. The tip of the barbarian blade connected with my left hip as it came down. The pain and the weight of the blow pitched me to the ground. The Romans groaned audibly. The Barbarian was making me look slow and clumsy.

I knew it was usual that the one who strikes the first blow wins in these sword contests. Once disabled any man becomes fodder for the opponent. Through the pain, I managed to roll to the side and get up. I could stand only with difficulty now. I was breathing hard. I wondered if my hip might be broken. It would hardly allow me to weight-bear.

Again, my opponent stepped around his blade. There were cries from the Gauls. He brought it down from right to left in a terrifying blow. He was determined to finish the one-sided contest. I parried. The Barbarian sword struck my gladius with arm-numbing force. The ring of steel against steel was like some massive bell pealing in the night. It sent a flock of birds flying startled from one of the overlooking trees. They had slept through all the foolish machinations of the men below. My Hispanic steel gladius, won in fair contest, glinted with a cold gleam in the moonlight.

It stopped the Nervian in his tracks. His right arm had taken the brunt of the counter-strike. He stepped back. His expression revealed surprise and disappointment at the resistance of the Roman sword. I shuffled forwards and parried the next blow, holding the blade vertical before me. Again, as the two blades met, my good right arm took the force without weakening.

This time as his blade fell away, I stepped in close. I swung mine fast. It was a backhand blow. It caught the Nervian on his right arm above the elbow. His enormous sword dropped from his nerveless grip. I had cut his arm to the bone. The laceration bled in a spurting torrent of red to his wrist. I stepped forward again, a little half-step. Following through I whipped up my right arm straight ahead. The hilt of my sword struck the surprised Gaul in the face. He fell to the ground onto his back. I leaned forwards placing the point of the blade at his throat.

He was bleeding out onto the mud beneath my feet. There was little time for indecision. The pain of my hip and my ankle was threatening to make me fall and skewer him but I balanced his life on the tip of my weapon all the same.

I glanced up at the slave. He was looking on with a smile on his face for which I could sense his Nervian masters would punish him later. The Nervians were standing now, outrage and anger on their faces.

'A life for a life?' I said to the slave, 'By Jupiter translate, damn you.'

The slave translated but did not understand the meaning. Boduognatus stepped forwards with a scowl on his face.

'What do you want?' he said, as the slave translated.

'Give me the slave and your man will live,' I said.

Boduognatus paused and thought for a moment, then said in Latin, 'I not care if defeated warrior dies; he is worth nothing now, but he is a kinsman, my sister's son and for that reason no other, I will trade his life.'

'The slave goes free' I said, hobbling back to the bench to sit down. I looked at my sword. There was a deep notch on the edge which I inspected with some disappointment.

Procillus approached. 'Well done Veridius, I never doubted you. Are you badly hurt?'

'I don't know, my left leg feels as if a herd of wild boars has chewed it,' I said, grimacing through my pain. I looked at the man I had defeated. His companions were binding his arm and his face was ashen but he was still conscious. The slave had already removed his halter and was weeping with relief. He knelt before me and looked up and said through his tears, 'For four years they beat me without mercy and abused me in ways I will never tell. You've freed me and I will always be your man whatever happens. Of this I swear, before Jupiter Optimus Maximus and all the Gods.'

Barbus approached and helped me to my feet and we hobbled off to the medical tent followed by the freed slave and he summoned an orderly to tend to me. We had pushed our way through the massed legionaries who had been watching. They slapped my back and said words of encouragement as if I had done something grand. I felt my pride rising. I had defended the honour of the Ninth.

There was a huge bruise the size of a plate over the outer aspect of my left hip. My heel had swollen to twice its normal size and it had taken on a dark-blue hue. There did not appear to be any bones broken. The orderly, our bandage carrier, applied a cold compress – Juno knows there was enough ice all around us after all, so it required neither ingenuity nor imagination.

'A few days of rest, then get going again,' the fellow said, 'but why no breaks I cannot say, it's almost as if your bones are tough as steel.'

At the praetorium the Barbarians had left half-carrying their wounded champion. They had agreed to comply with Procillus' demands. It was a point of law to the Nervians; oaths given over a contest had to be obeyed for the sake of their honour.

I think Procillus mistrusted them for he decided to remain encamped on the hill to supervise the transfer of goods and slaves. He said he expected it to take a month at least and saw to it that the fortifications of the camp were strengthened and made more permanent. He sent his report to our legate explaining the delay in returning and stating how successful we had been. We relaxed into the tedium of a Gallic winter far from home. I missed my woman even more. Surely I would be with her soon? Did I have to lose a limb to go home?

Chapter XIV

"While we stop to think, we often miss our opportunity." – Publilius Syrus.

Procillus marched us in centuries, eight by ten, for as much of the journey as possible. He must have hoped that by keeping us in formation any attacking Nervii would be unable to penetrate our ranks on any side. He posted scouts a half-mile ahead and had small flanking pickets of Gallic horsemen to either side. Three centuries covered the rear of the column and the cavalry rode ahead.

We stowed the baggage on carts drawn by oxen but most of the freed Aedui were walking alongside the carts on their long journey home. Not that there was much for them to go home to. The Nervii had destroyed their village and killed most of the men but they were all relieved to be free.

I still had trouble walking and as a concession I was given a choice between the wagons or riding a spare Gallic mount. I chose the horse; for some reason I felt it would be undignified to arrive back at camp in a wagon.

A chill wind arose when our column halted close to a steep

hill. At its base a small frozen stream cut the stony ground and to the left was a forest-covered slope leading to another hill. We stopped at the entrance to the valley between these two spurs when Crassus rode in from scouting.

Procillus, who was riding near my horse, reigned in and waited for his cavalry commander to report.

'Back so soon Publius?' Procillus said.

'Bit of news for you actually, Gaius,' smiled Crassus.

'Don't tell me the rest of the legion has come to meet us and give us a hero's welcome.'

'Not exactly,' smiled Crassus, 'I think we have some native company hidden in a wood nearby. I was riding back, when I saw a glint of reflected light from that wood on the far slope. There is no reason for such a thing unless it's reflected off a weapon. Can't estimate their numbers but it would be an ideal place for an ambush. We need to consider how to deal with them.'

Procillus smiled back. He dismounted. The two officers assembled and conferred with the senior centurions of whom Calvus was one. I could hear them from my position, mounted close-by as I was.

Crassus traced a map of the valley with the shaft of his spear. 'I think they plan to attack us when we're strung out passing through the valley. We can only march five men abreast beneath the wood and they could break through with ease and take each half of our troops at a time.'

'That's true and the cavalry wouldn't be much use to us mixed in with the infantry. We need to work out how best to deploy in the valley,' Procillus said.

'I can take the cavalry ahead, skirting the eastern hill on our right and then double back out of sight of the wood,' he continued. 'As soon as they engage I can hit them on their left flank while they are facing our troops,' suggested Crassus.

'That's a good idea, but if we can only march five abreast we'll be such a thin line we can't mount much opposition,' Procillus said. 'The worst part is the Aedui and the wagons: they'll get in the way and split our forces in two whenever they pass through the defile. Maybe they could follow on with say, two centuries, and the rest of the men can march through halfway and then deploy as best they can on the hillside opposite the wood. That way we'll be formed up and ready. The wagons can pass through the gap and the men can peel off and follow. If we combine that with your plan then even if they do attack they'll have to come at us from our left and in front and you can take them in their left flank.'

'How will I signal I'm in position?' asked Crassus.

'You could light a fire, there's a little wind but we should see it without difficulty. If I don't see it then I'll give you an hour or so to get into position.'

'Agreed, I'll take some dry wood with me,' Crassus said. 'Good luck my friend, I expect you to be a Hannibal.'

'As long as you don't turn out to be Maharbal we'll be fine,' Procillus said. They both laughed at that knowing, as I did, how Hannibal's cavalry commander had betrayed his friend and commander in the last hour at the battle of Zama. They grasped each other's wrists and smiled encouragement.

Calvus passed the plan to the other centurions and they formed up as planned. We knew there was a fight coming and there was not a man in the vexillation who felt this was more than a job of work to do. Our disciplina demanded silence and order approaching battle and that was how we treated the ambush. We waited half a mile from the valley and removed the leather covers from our scuta. As soon as the smoke from the signal fire became visible, we marched.

I abandoned my horse, tying him to a wagon. I felt I would

rather fight on foot even if I was limping than attempt to fight on horseback as I had tried to do against Ariovistus.

When we reached the defile we marched as if it were a drill. We split into columns of five and proceeded into the jaws of the Barbarian's trap. Halfway into the valley, the first troops cut right and positioned themselves on the slopes of the hill. It was not easy terrain on which to form up but we were disciplined troops – hardened veterans who knew their job. More and more of the cohorts formed up and it must have become obvious to our ambushers we did not intend to string out into the valley.

Half the vexillation were in position when the enemy attacked. Even forewarned, we were surprised at how fast they were. With amazing speed considering the rough ground, the Nervii, for of course it was they, leaped down the snowy slope and began to charge upwards towards our waiting infantry while their missile troops stood behind raining arrows on our ranks. We were in close order with shields almost touching. As soon as the enemy fired their arrows and cast their spears the second rank elevated their shields above their heads protecting the front rank and themselves. The rank behind did the same and the resulting formation was impenetrable to the missiles.

I stood at the right side of my century, shield and sword ready for the onslaught, Calvus stood on the other side. The ranks of the Gauls extended all the way back to the wood and their dark shapes blotted out the snow before us.

'What I wouldn't give for a battery of ballistae,' I thought, as the screaming Gauls came on, their painted faces grimacing and their war-cries filling the air before them.

The Gauls hit our front rank with horrible force. It was made worse by the dense crush of men behind. Our line seemed to buckle from the sheer force of the Barbarian charge. It did not give way.

We were at an advantage. Our short stabbing swords needed much less room than the long Barbarian weapons. The Gauls had difficulty wielding even their axes in the confined space. I engaged two men armed with long swords. I shoved forwards with my shield at one and stabbed with my gladius at the other. The first man stumbled and rolled down the slope and the oncoming Barbarian horde trampled him underfoot. The second man fell, skewered though his leather jerkin with a chest wound. I forgot him as another rushed at me with an axe. He swung it horizontally. I stepped back. I caught him on the arm as the blow flew past an inch from my midriff. He howled and dropped his weapon. I cut his throat then with my blade and he fell only to be replaced by another, this time with a spear. I backed off and the legionary to my left hamstrung the spearman. I wetted my blade again in Barbarian blood.

Our front rank began to fall back a little from the sheer weight of numbers confronting them. They stabbed and pushed, stabbed and pushed, until their arms must have felt like leaden weights and their legs wobbled beneath them. The fighting churned the snow to a red slush about us. All through the din of sword on sword and shield on shield, the press of Barbarians screamed their chilling screams. The cries of men dying and the wounded begging for help mixed with the terrible sound of those inhuman Barbarian war cries. The smell of blood and worse stank in my nostrils.

Our front line began to move backwards. The second rank began to move forward as best they could to replace men who were dropping back in exhaustion. The Barbarian bodies began to pile up in front of our line. The enemy didn't care, the climbed on the bodies of their comrades, they shoved the dead and dying aside, eager to kill us. In the corner of my eye, I could see how through the southern end of the valley, the remaining centuries began to move into the gap. They were attacking the right flank of the Barbarian horde now. With the huge numbers and the narrow gap through which we had to fight, their attack made little difference at first. The Nervii were big and savage but they were brave too. I understood what Boduagnatus had said. These men lived for battle. They had no fear. All they wanted was the glory of dying in the fray, sword in hand. And we obliged them. On they came; wave after wave until they stepped back, as always happens in a battle. It is kind of natural pause seconds long only, but enough to recuperate and then fight on. The Barbarians behind pushed forward and filtered through the ranks of the men at the front to meet our advance. Each time we advanced and they repulsed us.

The battle reached an impasse. We ceased to give ground, stabbing with our gladii. The Barbarians swung their weapons as best they could. The Barbarian dead piled up in front of us. We had to stand on their corpses now to reach our enemies but still they came on. Their numbers seemed never to decline.

Still fighting in the thick of it I heard a sound above the din of the battle. It made me smile as I jabbed, shoved, and parried. It was a single horn blown from the north. The sweetest sound I have ever heard. Our equites had come. The terrain suited them. The gap, although narrow, fitted their wedge formation like a glove. They burst upon the enemy flank like a crashing wave that batters the shore in a gale. They wielded their spears and grimaced. The Nervii were now beset on three sides. The men at the centre of the crush could hardly move, pinioned as they were by their own warriors.

Our cavalry cut into the press with Crassus at their head. He was stabbing left then right with his spear. I saw it lodge in the chest of a huge half-naked warrior. I watched as he turned his horse and drew his sword. He was hacking and stabbing in fury;

maniacal, unreasoning and fearless. He looked invincible astride his mount above the sea of enemy heads. Never still, he circled his horse. The beast kicked and bit and no one could come near.

The horn sounded the retreat and the equites fell back to reform and wait for their mounts to gain some breath. A blown horse would be no use in that press of slaughter. The Barbarians attacked with renewed vigour but I could see that at last their ranks were depleting. They still outnumbered us but we had slaughtered so many I was sure they would run.

Crassus charged again. This time, the huge Barbarian mass crumbled before the onslaught. The men nearest the wood began to fall back. The wedge of horsemen sensed the enemy flagging. They pressed on. They drove the Nervii before them. Our front rank moved forward now and began a slaughter.

I took a man's arm with a forehand cut. I threw another down with my shield and the advancing century trampled him into the mud. A big bear-skinned hulk of a man stepped up, but the ranker on my left unbalanced him with his scuta. My blade descended point first into his throat and he died screaming. I moved on. So it was – we advanced over bloody gore and blood-slicked corpses, some still writhing in agony, others limp and pallid in death. The gods of the Nervii had deserted them. The Barbarians could stand no longer. They turned and fled like rats from a fire. They dropped their weapons. They ran before the merciless discipline of our two cohorts. We made no sound as we continued hewing this human corn that bled and died before our scything wrath.

The Barbarians broke up and although most melted away into the treeline, some did not. Here and there groups of Nervii tried to form a ring of shields but the riders were everywhere and, beset on all sides, these last warriors threw down their weapons and begged for mercy. The equites rode among them slashing with sword and stabbing with spear, cutting down any who resisted.

It took only a short time for the battle to end, leaving hundreds of Nervii dead on the field and hundreds more captured or wounded. Every jubilant Roman present cheered our success and every man was smiling and waving his arms in the air in triumph. We were allowed to voice our feelings at last.

Chapter XV

"He who is brave is free." – Seneca.

The return of the vexillation was a moment I will remember for the rest of my days. We approached the Ninth Legion barracks and the guards threw the gates open wide. The Legate rode out to meet us. He greeted us in a formal way then slapped both Procillus and Crassus on the back as they rode smiling into the camp. The men of the Ninth lined the Via Praetoria and they cheered and shouted; five thousand men cheering their comrades who had returned from a great victory. It was not the size of our battle that was impressive afterwards; it was the manner in which we had won.

Seventy-five men were lost from our ranks but nine hundred of the enemy were dead, six hundred wounded or captured and the remaining Nervii had fled home to their land in shame. We had freed the Aedui slaves and we had forced Boduagnatus to pay the Aedui compensation after taxation by the legate for it was after all an expensive war in Gaul.

The men had erected a podium in the Praetorium and Titus Lepidus gave a speech in praise of his men and his achievements.

Lastly, he honoured both tribunes with oak-leaf crowns and to my profound and puzzled embarrassment he summoned me to the rostrum too.

'This man has shown himself to be a champion of the legion and it is with great pleasure that I award an oak-leaf crown to Aulus Veridius Scapula, Optio of the First Century Second Cohort.'

There were loud cheers and I didn't know where to look. I had been lucky enough to gain two oak leaf crowns in one campaign. I learned later that the only man to do that before had been Gaius Julius Caesar when he was a young man.

That night there was a celebration in both the officers' quarters and among the enlisted men. We became a camp full of drunken soldiers but apart from a few small-scale brawls nothing bad happened. The unlucky ones were on guard duty and since sleeping on guard duty attracted a death penalty there was no wine consumed on the walls of the camp that night.

'Aulus,' Calvus said, slapping me on the back, 'you realise you're well on your way to centurion now'

'But I thought it would be many years yet,' I slurred.

'You're right but you have to start slowly. Your rise to optio and two oak leaf crowns at your age will make it certain you'll get promotion in a few years. All you need is a few more battles and a few of the centurionate to die and your elevation to our ranks is certain. Trust me.'

I awoke next morning with a hundred equites charging through my head. Each time I raised it the room spun and an overwhelming feeling of nausea overcame me making it all but impossible to get up.

I had a double space in the barrack room and I was glad of it. Fewer fleas and less smell from other bodies made life a little more bearable than for the other soldiers. Not that I was unable to rough it. I had slept in all kinds of places since I joined the legions.

It was one of the hardening aspects of military life that allowed the legionaries to move fast and bed down anywhere. Not with a hangover however. Not with the grandfather of all hangovers like this. Not the one I suffered that day. I lay still and hoped it would be over by mid-day. I closed my eyes but sleep would not come. I wished I had an orderly, like the centurions; at least I could get something brought to me instead of fending for myself.

There was a scrabbling noise at the leather door to my room. I managed to look up. It was the Nervii's released slave. His name was Gliconius. I thought he had put on a little weight since we had freed him. His grey hair and the lines about his eyes testified to the hardness of his life with the Nervii. I never managed to get him to speak of it but I could guess. He had been a servant to a rich merchant before the Nervii killed his master and took him prisoner. Keeping him alive was unusual but the Gauls are not like the Germans, who torture their prisoners to death. He must have had an iron constitution to have survived the beatings and the bad treatment. Our legion had now taken him in so he functioned as an orderly and we paid him at the normal rate. He had few duties for he was not assigned to anyone yet.

'Dominus, I have brought you some honey and water, I thought that if you had overindulged last night you might need it.'

'Well thank you,' I said.

I sat up and wished I had not. The room spun and my head hurt. I drank the honeyed water and began to feel a little better.

'If you wish, I can act as your orderly until they find me some other duties. There isn't much to do here in camp and I owe you my life.'

'You don't owe me your life. Maybe your freedom, but not your life. A simple thank you would be enough. I do appreciate your kindness this morning however. I think I was poisoned last night. I remember Calvus slapping me on the back but that's the last thing I recall.'

'Most understandable Dominus,' he said.

'Tell me Gliconius, what will you do with your life now?'

His face changed. It was not a scowl but close to it.

'I live now only to see Caesar defeat the Nervians and kill every last one of them. They killed my daughter who was all I had. They did it in front of me and for sport. If Caesar wipes them out, I will celebrate. I want to stay with the legion, I want their blood.'

'I can understand that, but I don't know that Caesar will do what you want; he is determined to take over in Gaul and to do that he can't afford to wipe out whole populations of the natives.'

'I will still stay with the legion to see them defeated; it is all I have left now, a wish for revenge and perhaps to repay you for what you did for me.'

He left almost as fast as he had entered. I was sorry I had stirred up all that emotion and felt I should have realised what my question would do. I had been clumsy.

Time passed and the cornua sounded for the start of the day. This was a drill day. Tomorrow was a weapons practice day and we had five such days then a break for one day then a cross-country marching day in snow. The lucky ones had to do patrols but it was more usual to send cavalry who could move fast and gather information with speed.

I almost fell from my straw pallet. I rousted my men and when all were assembled sent a man to inform Calvus that the century was ready for inspection. The day had begun and for once, I was glad there was no fighting, my head felt as if it was twice its normal size and it seemed to have difficulty staying on my shoulders. Calvus appeared, looking fresh as a watered plant and with a smile on his face. It was a drill day.

The same pattern of training and tedium continued,

interrupted from time to time with permission to go into Bibracte and our men often returned drunk and satisfied after visiting the whorehouses and taverns. I skipped the whorehouse most of the time. I found it hard to enter there without thinking of Aripele waiting in Rome for my return. At times, however my resolve weakened. I was a young man and tempted by my vigour like any other.

Both the tavern and the whorehouse had become a developing industry over the winter as the presence of the two legions made both trades essential for the release of the inevitable built-up tension in such a large group of fighting men.

The two legions mixed little unless they came across each other in town and then there was in general a friendly rivalry. Often there were drunken brawls but if the culprits were caught, they could face a ban from visiting the town, which was the main reason behind the peaceful repartee rather than fighting.

Thus, the winter passed with training, marching, weapons practise, wine and women. The men longed now for battle and wondered what was going to happen once the Proconsul returned as expected. That seemed to never happen. Caesar, we were told, had faced interminable delays in receiving payment and late snowfall delayed anyone crossing into Gaul across the high mountain passes. It was no consolation to hear Procillus complain that if Hannibal could cross in winter, what was stopping the General in spring?

Return he did however. As soon as the Alpine passes could be negotiated, Caesar came back to his men with two fresh legions- raw recruits. Ballistae and archers followed behind; at last, it was time for war.

Chapter XVI

Chapter XVI

"Anger is a momentary madness, so control your passion or it will control you." – Horace.

Spring brought warmer weather but all the same we lived in a sea of mud. There was some sunshine at least, but most of the time it poured. The rain fell in sheets and turned the ground into a mud-mire beneath our marching feet. Despite the mud, our veteran legions were glad of the respite from the bitter cold and icy weather of the long northern winter and we were happy to be working again. We marched north now that cavalry skirmishes had established the nature of our Belgic enemy. Caesar was always a careful, but never timid, tactician and had taken time assessing his foe, using his equites to hit and run, hard and fast. The Belgic tribes had armed themselves over the winter in response to the ever-growing threat of Roman dominance and the insult of the defeat by Procillus and Crassus in the winter.

The Belgae were a loose confederation of tribes including the Bellovaci, Atrebates, Nervii and Suessesiones among many others. We had established a huge camp on a hill bounded to the north by a swamp and to the east by the river Aisne. Six legions were camped upon that hill supported by four thousand auxiliaries and large a number of ballistae. Trenches with wooden stakes in their depths defended the whole area of the camp and the river contained sunken spikes to make crossing even more hazardous for any attackers. Perhaps Caesar was a romantic, for he always referred to the wooden spikes we set in the trenches as 'lilies'. There was nothing romantic about their effects though – they skewered the attacking foes that fell before us, like a cook spit-roasting chickens.

I stood on the wooden wall-walk and looked out onto the valley below. This was a good site to defend. The trenches zigzagged in front of the walls so an attacking force would only be able to approach in small numbers and they would face the ballistae firing heavy bolts capable of killing several men at a time. The archers had practised using their weapons from the walls and had good lines of sight all around our camp wherever the attack might come.

No wind stirred the early morning mist and apart from a thrush calling and the sound of the rushing river below, the camp was silent. A clear sky arched above me but the sun had yet to cast any warmth on the misty green landscape below. I wished for some warmth. At home I would have had the sun on my back, but this was Gaul – a grey muddy expanse of enemies and war. As I looked out at the hazy expanse before me, I missed my woman. Aripele; how was she? I had only received the one letter and I missed her more with every passing day. The papyrus of her letter had long since split into several pieces and it was now all but impossible to read. I tried to piece it together again each day, but all I could do was read a few strings of phrases.

Like most of my companions, I longed for the hot sunshine of home, the cloudless skies and in my own case, the rush and tumble of the forum and streets of Rome. I was up early today however, unable to sleep. The proximity of the enemy always did this to me. I felt restless and could now put my mind to little apart from the forthcoming battle.

Scouts had brought news of a vast force, a confederation of a dozen tribes gathering across the river. The Nervii would be among them I knew that. I also knew they had vengeance in their hearts after having given way in the matter of the slaves and silver. Despite this, we had fought and won so many times against similar foes I had begun to think the Roman army was invincible. I wondered whether this was because of our General or whether it was because Roman discipline and order could conquer all. If Caesar said fight, then we fought to the last man – for we loved him. We were his loyal army and would follow him to the gates of the underworld if we had to.

I heard a whistle below. It was Calvus.

'Aulus, get down here.'

'Problems?'

'You're in deep shit my friend.'

'What do you mean?'

'You are in deep and smelly excrement, that's all.'

'What's all this about?' I descended the wooden steps and joined him.

'Legate wants to see you and you'd better tell him the truth or you'll sink.'

'Now? The bloody Gauls are about to attack, sir.'

'I don't know all the details but the Legate said it was about stealing. He didn't look best pleased.'

'I haven't stolen anything.'

'You can explain that to Cicero. I believe you but he may not. Off you go.'

I made my way to the Via Praetoria and found the Legate's tent. I waited outside and his orderly came out.

'Veridius Scapula?'

'That's me,' I said smiling; I had after all, done nothing wrong. If it was about Marcus' tent, I knew nothing could be proven.

'In there,' the man said.

I entered and there was Cicero with a centurion I did not know. He looked up with a frown.

'Optio Veridius. You have some explaining to do.'

'Yes sir, anything you say, sir.'

'Centurion Bassus of the Tenth has passed some information to me that is of extreme concern. You are of course innocent until proven guilty, but I think you have to explain why you have taken money from the legion under false pretences.'

'I have taken no money sir. I'm no thief.'

'Do you deny that you were paid an advance on your pension by Gaius Procillus just after the Cataline defeat? It's entered on the legion records.'

I thought hard. Of course, Procillus had helped me out with an advance. That was before I had re-joined the legion.

'Yes sir. At that time, I had been pensioned off because of an injury. The injury got better and I re-joined my unit sir.'

'According to our legion records you are drawing pay at the same time as you are drawing a pension. That is stealing, Veridius.'

'But my pension was cancelled sir.'

'If your pension was cancelled what were you doing drawing funds from the legion through Procillus?'

'But it wasn't cancelled then.'

'But you didn't pay the money back when you re-joined did you?'

'Well, err... No, I forgot, sir.'

'You forgot?'

'The legion owes me two years back pay anyway. You can take it out of that sir.'

'That's not the point. The sum is paltry. It's the principle of the thing. As things stand, you are guilty of embezzlement of legion funds. Drawing a pension in Rome at the same time as you are enlisted and being paid as a recruit is illegal.'

'But I don't get a pension as well sir.'

'You are down in the legion records as being in receipt of a pension. Do you deny that you went to arrange a pension?'

'No sir, but...'

'You have distinguished yourself twice as a soldier in this army so I don't intend for you to be harshly punished. The usual sentence is two years on the galleys.'

'But...'

'Silence. You will speak when I give you permission. I will be lenient. You are dismissed from the legion and you will leave with the wounded after the battle. Is that clear?'

'Yes sir. Permission to speak?'

'Well?'

'If when I return to Rome I can prove that my pension was stopped as soon as I re-enlisted will you allow me to re-join sir?'

'I will reconsider the matter. How could you let us down in this way? I thought you were cast-iron.'

'I am innocent and will prove it.'

'You'll have to wait until the legion gets back to Rome won't you?'

'Yes sir.'

'Centurion Bassus told me you would try to wheedle your way out of it. He wanted you sent to the galleys. If it wasn't for fastidious and attentive centurions like him this army would founder.'

'Yes, sir.'

'Dismiss. Oh and by the way. I have never in my career had an enlisted man make a fool of me in front of my superiors as you did that night in front of the Proconsul. I would have had you whipped not given you an oak-leaf crown I can assure you. In my opinion the legion is better off without the likes of you.'

Stung by his words, I returned to the walls wondering how I could have landed myself in such a stupid position. I was not comforted by the fact that Bassus had something to do with it. It must have been part of his revenge but I had no clear idea how to get back at him.

Had someone altered the ledger entries? No. On the face of it, it was all true, but it was not the way it looked. If I could get the records from Rome, it would show that Quintus had cancelled the pension, but Rome was a long way away.

I supposed they expected me to fight, for the battle seemed imminent. Was I now a civilian? Had they discharged me? I did not understand what was happening. I waited on the walls unable to believe how events had turned against me.

The wait was over sooner than we expected. The first indications of the battle to come were dark shadows in the mist at the edge of the river. Within moments, there were thousands of visible shapes entering the water at its most shallow point. The thousands continued to build up and as the mists began to lift, the enormity of the attacking army became clear. There must have been seventy thousand or more Barbarian troops and their pennants and standards floated above the human sea like sails of ships in a gargantuan fleet. There was a flanking force of horsemen numbering several thousands on each flank. The sheer numbers were startling.

I had to be part of this. I had a strange, surreal feeling as if the interview with the Legate had not happened. No one knew about it yet so I supposed I was to fight. Even if I were just a Roman civilian the legion would expect me to fight now, so I relaxed back into my role as optio.

The hidden wooden spikes in the river slowed the Barbarians' progress and I could hear cries of injured men and horses as they floundered in the water. The initial defences did not hold them long and they swept across that river like a tidal wave, leaving bodies and wounded men to float downstream. They attempted to jump across the trenches around the perimeter. The 'lilies' as Caesar was fond of calling the sharpened wooden trench spikes, transfixed many as they fell into the trenches below. Those trenches filled with men and corpses, for the press from behind was so great. Our ballistae, firing their three-foot iron bolts, cut swathes through their lines creating gaps though they filled up almost at once.

We had time to muster and our archers and infantry lined the solid wooden wall. The enemy tried to place ladders – crude lengths of wood with tied crosspieces for rungs which bent under the weight of the Barbarian soldiers as they clambered to their death at the hands of the defenders.

Our century was protecting the walls at first but there was little hand-to-hand fighting to do at this stage since the lads pushed down the Barbarian's ladders with long poles we had adapted for the purpose. The Barbarians piled timber high enough for the attackers to climb up the slick surface and then the real fighting began. We cut and stabbed them with our swords and they made little progress for several hours.

The Belgae were able to loosen wall timbers in two places and the resultant breaches filled with men then with bodies as we kept the attackers at bay. Blood ran red, men screamed, men died and all the time the massive press of Barbarians pushed on, seeking no quarter and giving none. Detached from the ramparts, Calvus rested us and we stood in the compound behind the wall with raised shields to fend off the enemy arrows. The battle had raged. For almost four hours we fought then rested, then fought again, but there was no sign of the attack stalling

At the breach before us we could see them. They were pushing through by sheer attrition. They called their war cries and grimaced as they did so. I saw some in bear-skins, some wearing captured loricae and witnessed how these staunch attackers screamed in their determination. Septimus, centurion of the first century, was hard pressed. He was fighting off three Barbarians, armed with spears. I saw Calvus run forward and the resulting clash threw down two of the spear-warriors. Septimus took the other with a quick thrust of his gladius. I took it upon myself now to throw the century forward into the gap in the wall. The first century was giving way before the onslaught and their numbers had dwindled.

We pressed forward with such vigour and strength the Barbarians fell back despite the press of men behind them. A wall of dead lay before the breach. Barbus leaped on to it. Calvus and two more legionaries joined him. The Nervii screamed a battle cry and stabbed at their legs hoping to dislodge them. A legionary fell back from the wall of bodies, his foot almost severed from his leg by an axe stroke. Cruel blades finished him as he lay among the dead. Even in that cacophony of screams and ringing steel, I heard him scream. Another replaced him and stood shield to shield with our centurions. They were cutting, thrusting pushing and killing. The Roman shield wall began to expand as more and more of my men joined the fray in the wall's gap. The huge numbers of attackers slowed our progress. We had begun to fight our way out. Soon a group headed by Calvus and Barbus, who stood shield to shield, became isolated outside the walls. Axe-men on one side of the gap assailed them. I watched as they formed a ring of shields. The barbarians hooked their axes on the shield rims.

Others behind reached forward, weapons battering, but our men knew their business. The gladii flashed. The blood ran. The dead piled up. The surrounded Romans fought like Gods but it was not enough. They fought myriad assailants. Our men's numbers were dwindling. I realised they were moments away from the enemy swallowing them up and trampling them underfoot.

Septimus, seeing his friend in trouble, grabbed me and with a handful of men went to their aid. We cut through the Barbarians like a wind in the corn. My gladius sliced and stabbed. None could stand before me. If ever my good right arm was needed it was now. A rage had filled me. My weak shield arm bothered me no longer and my good right arm moved with a speed and ease even Mars would have praised. It was as if the sounds and the smells of battle possessed me. I became part of it. I flew. I shoved men to the ground and my comrades killed them. I took on a massive bear of a man. He weilded an long axe. He sung it in circles above his head. None could come near. I ducked and felt the wind of the blade as it passed above my head. I got him in the chest. As he fell away I almost lost my grip on my blade, but Fortuna protected me that day. Septimus stood by my side. He fended off the enemy as I drew my blade from its bloody home.

We reached the isolated men. The ring of shields opened and we joined them, fighting all the time and surrounded by our foes. Together, we fought our way back to the walls. It was a slow retreat, back to safety. We killed man after man on the way, for the Gauls pressed us on all sides. Calvus had lost his helmet and an axe wound on his leg bled into the greave on his calf. His breastplate was now red with blood, brains and other human debris from the Barbarian dead. He looked like some mythical Fury from the underworld. Septimus supported him but even he was not unscathed. A long rent in his lorica, oozing gore testified to that.

In our progress, a few yards from the walls, the Gauls were still two or three men deep blocking our retreat but I heard our men launch a sally through the wall-gap. The Barbarians screamed as our lads poured out and the nearest enemy were caught between Scylla and Charybdis wrought of Roman steel.

We fought on. Hours passed. Fight then rest, rest then fight. The east side of the walled camp was now so clogged with dead that even the most limber of the Barbarians had trouble scaling the wall of corpses. The trenches outside the camp had filled to the brim with dead and blood was everywhere. It was as if the world was made of blood and mud. As I sat in the mire resting between assaults, I wondered where all this blood would go, soaking into the land. Was the earth never slaked?

And still they came on. There was no end to them and they died in droves. The tiring haul up the slope with full battle gear seemed not to daunt these doughty Barbarian warriors. But we were trained to a man. We stood our ground, repelling wave after wave of screaming tribesmen. The Roman archers turned the tide in the end. Their arrows flew like clouds above the Barbarian horde whose small round shields gave only partial protection. No army could withstand such flying death. The arrows flew and the din of battle began to falter at last. The Barbarians fell back. This was an orderly retreat and not a rout. On this day there was no following up with a cavalry charge for it would have been suicidal in that vast press of remaining enemy.

The fourth cohort of the Ninth had been held in reserve and they charged at the retreating enemy inflicting further casualties but they were careful not to become trapped. They returned, backing away as soon as they reached their maximum safe distance.

All around the east wall the story was the same. Heaps of dead and most were Barbarian tribesmen. Although it had been a bloody and hard-fought battle there were smiling faces now in the camp.

I felt the pride of a real fighting man. To fight, to vanquish, to survive. I even felt proud when directing the clearing up operations after battle. The men dragged Barbarian dead and piled them up near the river. We burned our Roman dead with honour, and all booty taken from the dead Barbarians was pooled to add to the legion's wealth. The medical orderlies ran from place to place to bear away the badly wounded and to tend the injured, and the legionary engineers repaired the wall the same evening.

I found Calvus at the surgeon's tent. He was having his thigh stitched at the time.

'Aulus, my friend. I thought I was leaving for Elysium. I praise Jupiter you came to our aid with Septimus.'

'Me too, my friend. We gave them a beating, didn't we?'

'We did indeed. Oh, I nearly forgot, what did the legate say? Ouch.'

What had happened then dawned upon me. I was no longer a soldier. I was to leave and that was the end of it all.

'Calvus, they think I've been claiming a pension at the same time as drawing my pay. It's all a mistake, but I can't clear it all up until I get to Rome. That's where the records are. The Legate has sent me home.'

'What?'

'Sent me home.'

'He can't do that.'

'Well the alternative would be to be sentenced to the galleys.'

'I'll see about this. Don't you worry; old Calvus will sort it out.'

'I wish you could, but I don't think there's anything you can do short of getting the records from Rome.'

'I'll go and see Procillus maybe he'll be able to fix it. Don't you worry my boy. Sweet Persephone in the underworld. What are you doing?'

The orderly stitching Calvus' leg ignored him and carried on.

'If the centurion would just sit still it wouldn't be so painful.'

'Damned Greeks.'

*   *   *

It was a strange afternoon. I felt like a discarded old tunic, unwanted and worn to a ravelling. The spring sunshine was trying its best to appear behind shapeless clouds but failing in its efforts. There had been a sudden heavy shower after the battle, leaving the ground muddier and soft. It squelched underfoot as I looked for Procillus. I found him in his tent near the Via Praetoria.

'Excuse me sir.'

'Aulus. Glad you got through that. No injuries?'

'No sir.'

'Good, I've got some things I need you to do,' the Tribune said.

'That's just it sir. It seems the Legate has discharged me.'

'Discharged you? For the whole day?'

'No sir, permanently.'

'What?'

'You may recall how I borrowed some money that day when the legions defeated Cataline.'

'Yes.'

'It was an advance on my pension.'

'What of it?' He looked uncomfortable.

'I cancelled my pension later and didn't think that I had to pay the money back, because the legion owed me two years pay for the time I was in Pontus.'

'You did what?'

'I forgot. I cancelled my pension but the records of that are in Rome because it was only just before we left. Quintus Cerialis arranged it all for me.'

'So they've thrown you out?'

'Yes sir. I can't prove I'm not drawing a pension at the same time as drawing pay, I would need access to the records office in Rome to prove it.'

'Why didn't the Legate merely shelve the matter until we got home?'

'I don't know sir. I think he doesn't like me anyway. Can you speak on my behalf?'

'I'll try to but if Cicero has made his mind up and it's official, there may not be much I can do you know. I'm only a tribune.'

'I'd be very grateful.'

'Aulus, after what you did for me, I'm the one who should have the gratitude. I will go to Caesar himself if I have to.'

I walked from the tent with my heart sinking. I felt as if I knew nothing would be the same now. No military career, no amulet. I felt like a man in a cell – brick walls all around and nowhere to turn.

Chapter XVII

"The high-spirited man may indeed die, but he will not stoop to meanness. Fire, though it may be quenched, will not become cool." – Ovid.

Procillus looked sideways at me as we walked across the Praetorium through the mud. There was a smell of dead bodies hanging in the air, for the wind came from the direction of the river. It was still cold despite the spring sunshine.

'I'm sorry Aulus. There was nothing I could do. The evidence seems to be solid. The ledgers record the payment you received from me and then they show nothing about it being paid back. The problem is that the clerk who wrote it put against the entry that it was a pension advance. I don't even remember telling him it was for that reason but it's quite clear on the scroll.'

'You don't think anyone could have changed the entry?'

'No, it was written in the same hand, I'm certain.'

'Forgery?'

'You would need an expert to say. We don't have such experts in hand-writing in the middle of the Gallic wars.'

'No, sir.'

'You don't need to call me sir now, do you?'

'No sir.'

'For Jupiter's sake, Aulus. I can't do anything about it. You'll have to get the evidence once you get back to Rome.'

'I realise that. I'm just disappointed because I wanted the career badly. I can't even join another legion when I get home now.'

'Cicero was adamant. A dishonourable discharge was all he would consider and that means, as you know, no pension.'

'I realise that.'

'Aulus I want you to take this.'

He reached into his pouch and produced a scroll, which he proffered.

'It's a letter to my uncle. He's the legate of the Town Guard. He'll give you a job. I have mentioned to him how all this came about. He's a good man. You can trust him. He has Pompey's ear. They fought pirates together and Pompey has never forgotten it.'

'Thank you sir. I pray Fortuna will smile upon you and all your house.'

'I'll miss you Aulus but at least you know you have friends in the Ninth if ever you need them. I owe you my life for Jove's sake. I will not forget.'

We clasped hands and he walked away. Junius had always liked him and I understood why. He had a way with his men. It was familiar but everyone he commanded knew who was in charge. We all knew to call him 'sir' but it was because he earned it. Respect isn't given freely in the legions.

I looked down still feeling dejected. I knew Bassus had cooked up the whole thing but had no way to prove it. I needed documents from Rome and there was no way I could pay to have them brought to Gaul. It would have cost a fortune. We parted at my tent and I sat outside in the drizzle. It made my cloak damp and heavy but sitting in the musty leather tent in semidarkness was not appealing either. It was too damp to light a fire.

I was due to depart the following morning and had no duties and no responsibilities. Barbus had already been promoted into my place but I did not begrudge him that. He was a good soldier and a good friend. Manlius had been made decurion. He was a big man with no brain and I found it hard to understand his promotion. He was built heavy and brutal and in a fight on a battlefield he was ferocious. I had never thought of him as promotion material but there again it was nothing to do with me anymore.

Bored, I decided to walk around the camp. It was a sort of farewell gesture. Bitterness arose in me so I had to keep busy to prevent my feelings from festering.

I reached the south gate and went outside. In the distance I could see groups of soldiers drilling and there was an ala of cavalry training across the other side of the river, too far away for me to see any details. I sighed. I loved the legionary life. I had no idea what I would do in Rome.

I knew I had to try to get the amulet but even if I obtained it and became rich, this life would never return to me. It was the end of a chapter and even the recompense of seeing Aripele did not replace the sheer joy of being with my brothers-in-arms, on foreign soil, fighting to establish Roman ways in a Barbarian country for the glory of our city and nation.

Rome was everything and nothing in many ways. It was all we strived to achieve yet it was more an idea than a city. An idea we all carried with us deep inside our beings whether we were humble enlisted men or noble officers. It was the common bond and our sole reason and purpose. Rome was the Legion and the Legion was Rome.

'Well, well, well. What have we here?'

It was a high-pitched Sicilian voice. I continued to walk and ignored it. I wanted him to feel foolish.

'You're a civilian now.'

I continued to ignore him. I walked a bit faster, knowing he was following and he was limping. I reached the wall around the corner from the gates. There was no one around. I turned. I would not give him the satisfaction of thinking he had rattled me.

'I suppose you mean that if you kill me there's no court martial.'

'Aren't we the clever one?'

'Is that what this was all about? I've been unjustly accused and thrown out so you can have your pathetic attempt to kill me again? I can kill you without even looking at your fat face.'

'I thought that might be possible after our last encounter. That's why I brought some friends.'

He whistled. I was surprised by its loudness. He placed two fingers in his mouth and blew. It irritated me more than anything he'd said. I had never in my life, try as I might, been able to do that and it rankled.

Four men appeared from around the bend in the wall. Each was large and each held a sword and shield. I was unprotected apart from my gladius and the knife Polymecles had given me when I left Sinope.

'Think you can fight five of us?'

'Well, Bassus, there are many ways to do that. In case you missed it, Meridius trained me well. He was a man so far above you in nobility and swordsmanship you would never understand his integrity. I killed Asinnius because he was treacherous scum and that's what I'll do with you. I'll think of my teacher Meridius and smile when your head leaves your shoulders.'

I was boasting, truth to be told. I knew I couldn't fight five men. What Meridius had taught me was that if you are confronted by more men than you can kill with ease, run away. That way you can string them out and kill each one in turn without ever taking the risk of anyone coming behind you.

I ran.

I was used to running. I started most days with a one hour run and it gave me stamina and strength. I ran towards the swamp area to the north of the camp. Not fast, but fast enough to let a man with a shield and lorica begin to tire after a few minutes. I was unencumbered. I had no armour and no shield. I could use speed and they had armour, shields and helmets. It would not help them.

After about five minutes, I stopped and turned. They were still running but now they were two abreast. The second pair was not far enough from the leaders so I turned as soon as they came close and jogged away. I had not seen Bassus. He was not a runner with his fat paunch in any case and I knew he could never keep up. I had spent years in the Subura picking my targets when I was stealing food. The fat ones were always best. I would wait until they bought some food and then snatch it and run. They never would run after me because I was young and fit and they were carrying too much weight. I realised that when all this was over, if I was still alive, I would have to go all the way back to get Bassus.

We must have looked very strange to any observer. One man running pursued by panting, tiring, heavily armed men in the cold and muddy Gaul afternoon. The chase continued up to the marsh about a mile-and-a half away. I was jumping from one green tussock to another and once the tussocks were too far apart, I turned again. The foremost man must have been very fit. He was a long way ahead of his friends. He was unwise. If he had possessed any common sense he would have waited for the others. As soon as he came close enough and before he could gain his breath, I ran at him. He had to stop and he used his shield to protect himself. It didn't help him; he'd stopped in a deep, boggy puddle. Fighting when you can't move your feet is a frightening prospect, as any soldier will tell you.

I ran past him rather than straight at him. As I passed, I struck a blow at his left side where he held his shield. I hit the shield but it did little. I was still on firm ground, since I had jumped onto a green patch. I jumped onto the next green patch and he turned so slowly with his feet mired in the mud I almost felt sorry for him. His back was exposed and since I had circled him to his shield side, he couldn't use his sword. I jumped, almost flying, stabbing with my sword. It was over in seconds. My gladius entered the soft area between the neck and chest. He fell groaning. He was as good as dead when the second man was near enough to reach me.

I faced my next opponent with glee. It was not the battle rage that grips us in the heat of war and drives us on to unreasoning and ferocious killing but it was some lesser cousin of that. I smiled as the fellow approached. I felt such confidence. I was a killer. Natural and born to it. He might kill me, but then it would not matter. All I wanted at that moment was his blood on my sword.

The muddy ground didn't bother me at all. I stepped forward as he came to a halt. He was taken aback by the ferocity of my assault. It was what I had intended. Imagine running for ten or fifteen minutes carrying weapons, shield and armour to be confronted by a man who, unencumbered, flies straight at you wielding a sword and never ceasing in his parries and ripostes. I hammered blows on his shield. He began to back away. Thrust, swing, stab, parry. It was a blur of motion. He was still stepping back.

He tripped as he retreated and I was on him in a second. He stabbed upwards. I parried. He fell to the ground and I stepped on his sword arm. He held his shield to protect himself but I kicked it out of the way and stabbed at his head. My blade pierced his left eye and he screamed. I pushed harder and he was silent. I knew he was dead as I backed away from his twitching body. I looked up. The remaining two had slowed, realising they had to keep together and they had to get their breath back. They were facing a demon. A killing Fury from Hades.

I could feel my blood coursing. My head throbbed, my muscles ached to be used and I screamed at my enemies. I don't know whether it was words or some animal cry, but I know I screamed. I came on.

I cannot explain it. Perhaps it was the scream; perhaps it was the look on my face, I don't know. They glanced at each other and they ran. They both dropped their shields and ran as fast as they could away from death – away from me. I gave chase in my confidence and rage. I caught one of them and stabbed with the gladius into his back. He fell but it was not a mortal wound, I knew that.

The last of the four managed to run for precious minutes but when he turned to see where I was. I was right on top of him. He held his sword in front of him and I could see from the expression on his face he was terrified. I had no blood on me and I don't think the look on my face could be anything like as terrible as it might have been if this was a real battle, but he was terrified all the same.

He surprised me by kneeling before me and throwing away his sword. He began to beg. It was pathetic. He cried and told me of his children, his wife, his family, as if it made any difference. He had chased me. He had been paid to kill me yet he expected mercy. Was I a fool to be tricked into a position of vulnerability? Would he have spared me?

'Name?' I said.

'Quintus Servilius. Please, I have a family, please don't kill me.'

'You're pathetic. You were trying to kill me.'

'Please I'll do anything.'

'Anything?'

'Yes, yes.'

'Then get up and die like a man. I can't kill a snivelling, crawling, wreck like you. Get your sword and face me like a man.'

'Please, I'm sorry.'

He tried to hold my leg.

'Look, Quintus Servilius, you took money to kill me. Why should I spare you? How do I know you won't try to stab me in the back another time?'

'Please sir, I won't. Only let me live.'

He was crying now. He saw his death.

'Pathetic,' I said and kicked his supplicant hands away. I began the long walk back to the camp. I had calmed down and I was sick of the killing then. I should have realised that violence was an integral part of me. It was the battle lust, the rage, the fire in the shade that compels us and draws us into battle when times demand it.

In that moment though, it all went away. I was nauseated by it. All I wanted was to go home to the arms of my woman, to a little comfort, a little wine and the amulet. But I needed the amulet; I needed my revenge and I wanted it because of my dead parents whom, as I walked back to the camp, I swore to avenge. An enigma, a dichotomy of emotion. I wondered how any man could cope with such things.

Bassus had disappeared from view. With luck, I would never see him again.

BOOK III:
THE AMULET

Chapter I

"Love conquers all." – Virgil.

Ostia had not changed while I had been away in Gaul. The principal shortcoming of the port of Rome was it was too small and everyone was aware of it. I did not envy the harbourmaster having to try to arrange berths for the incoming ships with their cargoes and the hardship of managing the off-loading. I supposed that keeping the ships moving was the way to do it and even I knew that unless they expanded the port there would be difficulty getting anything done with efficiency.

I stepped off the ship and made my way to the road leading to Rome. In doing so, I contemplated what had happened and how it had affected my life. I had hoped to get promotion and end by being "the distinguished soldier" who could have made my father proud. Now, all I had become was an optio with a dishonourable discharge, hoping to prove my innocence. Quintus Cerialis was my best hope. His influence at Legion Headquarters might make a difference.

Procillus had given me that letter of introduction to his uncle who was tribune of the Town Guard, but I viewed the whole thing as a disappointment. The Town Guard was full of injured old soldiers and those who were not good enough to join the legions. Jupiter knows that joining the legions required little enough of a man, so what the Town Guard would be like I could only guess.

All my friends and supporters had tried to reverse the decision to discharge me. Cicero would not listen and when Procillus requested an appointment with Caesar it was refused at first. He then heard Caesar had left camp to negotiate with some local kings and would not be back for weeks. They sent me home before Caesar returned. When I weighed up the disappointment of my failed military career against the thought of seeing Aripele again I felt it restored the balance.

It would be half a day's walk to the city. I knew the way well enough and   recalled the day when she and I had ridden to Rome with our thoughts on a happier future for her and a chance of revenge for me.

In one sense, I was looking forward to coming home. I had my woman waiting for me and I thought the amulet would still be in Rome. Thinking of her gave me a warm, almost comfortable feeling inside. I longed for her, craved her voice, her hair. Absence had enhanced my feelings and I knew now she was the only woman for me.

The possibility that Marcus already had the deeds worried me but I did not think it likely there had been time for him to get them before he had been back in the legion and on his way to Gaul.

An old man was walking next to me going the same way.

'Soldier eh?' the old man said. He looked sideways at me with a toothless grin, all gums and grey stubble. He wore a once-white tunic and his sandals were neat and new. He held a stave in his hand and walked with a stoop.

'Well I was a soldier but now I'm to join the Town Guard in the city,' I said wishing the man would go away.

'Town Guard eh? Not much fighting to do there.'

'No.'

'I was a soldier once, then a gladiator.'

'Gladiators are slaves, aren't they?' I said, with manifest disinterest.

'Most of them are, but you can get work fighting for money in the arena if you put up a good show. You risk your life, but the money's always good.'

'Maybe I should try it.'

'Go to the Scholae Rotundum near the circus and you'll find the gladiator school. Ask for Titus and say Vibius sent you. He'll give you some advice. Don't blame me if you get killed.' the old man said, still smiling.

'Believe me; if I get killed I won't be able to blame anyone.' I said.

We walked most of the remaining way to Rome in silence apart from a little small talk. I knew being in the Town Guard would not hold much interest for me but I would need employment while waiting to get the legion to re-instate me. The thought of fighting in the arena seemed more attractive, but I was uncertain whether I had the skills or confidence.

At the gates at the end of the Via Appia, the old man asked me if I had a place to stay.

'Yes. I have a woman in Rome and a friend whom I can stay with.'

'My name is Vibius Arbrucius. If you need any help while you're here, let me know. I have a stable and rent horses from time to time, although I don't need the money now.'

He told me where to find him as we were about to part at the Porta Appia.

'Look there.' Vibius said.

'Where?'

'Over there to the right, beyond the Circus Maximus. Smoke. Doesn't look like good news; hope it doesn't spread.'

We walked together towards the black, billowing smoke. The origin was a tenement building on a side street, off the Vicus Patricius. There was smoke flowing from a window on the top floor and a stream of panicking men and women fought to exit, but all at the same time. They pushed and shoved and clambered.

A house fire. It evoked sombre thoughts in me. I could feel sweat on the back of my neck and my heart beating fast as memories came. It took my mind back to the day when my parents were killed under similar circumstances. I had run up and down outside, panicking and crying, looking for my parents. I tried hard not to think about it. It was too painful.

The buildings of most of the poorer quarters of Rome were built of wood. There were no fire fighters and there was every likelihood that if fire took hold in one place, then it could spread with ease through the entire city. We watched as the flames grew higher. A few of the tenement's occupants were gathering water and throwing it at the building which was as much use as sneezing at it.

Out of the corner of my eye, I noticed a covered sedan chair carried by four Nubians of enormous stature. A servant running beside the sedan unfolded the steps and opened the door and a large man dismounted. He was tall with thin arms and legs but had a very fat pendulous waistline. He sported gold-decorated sandals and he wore a magnificent decorated tunic with a green embroidered border.

'Hold fast, dear friends, for Crassus is here,' the man said. 'Who owns this unfortunate building? Where is he?'

'It is my building, my lord,' a small Greek said.

'You poor fellow, it is such a shame that no one can put out these voracious flames,' Crassus said, slapping the man on the arm.

'I must say I could use a site here for a storage building. Would you care to sell it? I won't pay much of course – it is hardly prime real-estate when it's on fire is it?'

'Sell it?' the Greek said. 'What would you offer? I stand to lose everything if it goes up in smoke.'

'I could manage five hundred sestertii but that is my first and only offer. Take it or leave it,' Crassus said wearing a benevolent smile.

'But I bought it for fifteen thousand only five years ago. It's robbery.'

'My dear fellow, if it goes up in smoke it won't be worth anything to you will it? It's only of value because I can build here and use the space once the building has burnt down, but of course if you can't accept the offer then I will go.'

Crassus was still smiling as if he was doing the Greek a big favour and turned to get back into his sedan chair.

'No, all right I'll sell,' the Greek said.

Crassus passed the man a purse, which must have contained the exact sum and smiled again.

He's all smiles this chap, surely only a fool would trust him.

Crassus clapped his hands and the servant ran around a corner twenty feet away. Suddenly, as if by divine intervention, fifty or so men appeared, all had buckets of water and they ascended the stairs and formed a human chain to the pump in the street outside. In only half an hour, they put out the flames, which had thus only gutted the top floor.

'Remarkable luck for Crassus his clients were around the corner with buckets isn't it?' the old man said from beside me.

'Even luckier his clients knew where the water pump was and that only the top floor was actually on fire,' I said.

'That Crassus makes a living setting fires and getting rich by buying the properties.'

'I'm surprised. I know his son Publius. He's honest and brave. Does this Crassus chap do a lot of that?' I asked.

'Yes all the time, it's how he made his fortune. He's one of the richest men in the Roman world and his fingers dip into everything.'

'I thought he was a famous general and defeated the rebel slave, what was his name? Spartacus?' I said.

'Famous crook more like it. He took all the credit for putting down the slaves' rebellion and all the time it was Pompey who did the fighting. Crassus crucified them all right, but he didn't do any actual fighting. He walled in the rebels and waited for Pompey. Crassus couldn't fight his way out of an orgy.' Vibius said.

'A man on board the ship said he was going to raise legions to conquer Parthia.'

'And what does he want to do that for? He already owns half of Rome and doesn't need more money, however rich the Parthian plunder is. No, if he wants a war it's because both Caesar and Pompey are famous as generals and he isn't, that's all,' Vibius said.

'Will the Senate let him?'

'Who can tell? I think the three of them secretly control the whole Republic really.'

'Who?'

'Caesar, Pompey and Crassus. Wouldn't surprise me if they wanted to become emperors. Don't trust any of them. Well, I'll see you around I suppose.'

'Go with Mercury.'

We parted company and I made my way to the Quirinal and a homecoming. The feel of the cobbles under my feet and the rank smell of the central gutter evoked memories of my youth. Memories of thieving, danger and even hunger. Whatever happened I was sure I was better off than if I had never joined the legions. I wondered if Quintus could, in truth, swing it for me. If I re-joined they would send me back to Gaul with the new recruits. I had to get my hands on the amulet first, but how?

I didn't take the usual route along the Vicus Longus as I had already walked halfway up the Vicus Patricius to watch the fire. It turned out to be a longer walk than I had planned. I passed the house of Marcus Mettius. I stopped and looked at the gate lodge. The gate was shut and a man stood there. I knew him. It was Cerberus, the man who had turned me and Gennadius away after I had cremated my parents. He was pacing up and down, a frown on his thin face. Tempted, I almost crossed the roadway to tell him who I was, but thought better of it.

Instead, I gazed at the house. It took me back to the days when I had attended lessons there as a child. That had all ended when I had a fight with my cousin and knocked him out. He was a bully and was always picking on me. His furious parents banned me from their home.

I peered at the villa. All looked much the same as when I had been there as a child. The high wall and the ornate gate with the janitor's lodge. I knew there was no one there however, since both of Marcus' parents were dead and he was away in Gaul. I wondered if it would be easy to break in. If there were only slaves and servants in the place there would be no one in the upstairs bedrooms like last time. I could get in and search with ease and undisturbed.

There was something odd about the thought. Searching dead people's things was not something I wanted to do. It was not any kind of delicacy of conscience but it was because like all Romans, I dislike dead bodies; dead things. There is something that feels unclean about the dead. It is innate in me. Even purification by the Libitinarii, our priests of the dead, failed to make such things palatable to me.

Whatever it took I supposed I would do it, since the amulet

had been so central to my life and it had meant more to me than its financial value. My father's hand had passed it to me and that alone was worth taking risks for. There was revenge too. Revenge on Marcus and his whole gens. I knew I would stop at nothing to obtain that. The Mettius Costa family was becoming an obsession. It possessed me. I had to have revenge and if it meant burglarising the Mettius house once more then it was a risk worth taking. There was no hurry though. Marcus would be in Gaul for years yet.

Chapter II

"If you wished to be loved, love." – Seneca.

Although it was a warm, almost balmy early spring night there were not many people abroad as I reached the house of Quintus Cerialis on the Quirinal. The air was humid enough for the cobbles beneath my sandaled feet to feel moist. I felt my pulse quicken as I rang the bell. I was sweating. She would be there. She would be home and I pictured in my mind how I would take her in my arms when I entered.

I stood and waited. Nothing happened. I waited more. The house was empty. Where could they have gone? I would have expected Quintus to be at home at least, for he seldom went out and Aripele in her letter said that she was making tapestries, would she not be doing that in the evenings, waiting for me to come home?

I think perhaps that in my mind I had slipped her into the role of Penelope, the long-suffering wife of Odysseus waiting for the return of the wandering hero. This was no hero's return however. I had no desire to tell anyone how I had been ejected from the legion in shame and ignominy. Two oak-leaf crowns and rapid promotion then out on my ear. It made no sense. I was sure Cicero had it in for me. That laughing episode in his tent to a man with no sense of humour perhaps had been offensive. It might of course, have been the way I had answered back before Caesar interrupted.

I tried the bell again. After a few minutes I realised it was pointless. Ringing a bell when there is no one home is depressing. I waited a few minutes more and sat on the step. Neither of them knew I was coming so I had no right to complain but I couldn't understand where they could be. It was early evening and I could feel the rumblings of hunger deep inside me.

I decided to find somewhere to eat and then return to keep vigil on the doorstep, so I hid my gear near the doorway and crossed the street. I dared not risk being seen to bear weapons in the Pomerium. Like all streets in the Quirinal district, it was wide with smoothed flat cobbles and no central channel. People in this area did not empty their chamber pots in the street. There were water channels for such things inside the estates and in the grounds of the big houses for that sort of thing. No wonder the Tiber smelled the way it did.

I made my way to a little tavern on the edge of the Forum Romanum. I sat outside with a jug of wine and ate some bread with a fish stew, hoping the fish had not come from the Tiber. In Rome one has to be careful what one eats. I dipped the bread in the stew and thought about Aripele. I thought about how we had met in the streets of Pontus after my return there from Armenia.

How strange the Fates are. They spin our future and we know little of what is to come. Had I known that I was meant to be with Aripele I would have gone straight to her but the Gods dictate our paths in the end, however tortuous they may become.

The forum was busy. I watched as some young men passed, laughing and pushing each other. One of them bumped into my table and looking in my eyes, he apologised fast, as if I might pick a fight. I didn't care – I even smiled at him. He passed by, still grinning and japing with his friends and I wished I had that kind of life – where the future was clear and the past was unsullied.

The wine was good. It was a dark, rich, fruity wine that smelled and tasted of cherries. It must have been a good year. I spilled some drops as I finished the jug and it stained my tunic. I swore under my breath. It would not be an easy stain to remove by any means at my disposal. In my partially inebriate state, I thought perhaps Aripele would have a way of removing it. Where had she been? I stood and staggered a little as I made my way back through the dark streets. It occurred to me I had been unwise to drink so much when I knew Rome wasn't safe at night. I had no real weapons on me. I had left my gladius hidden with my things at the house on the Quirinal and all I had was Polymecles' knife secreted at my back.

The heat of the night was oppressive as I walked to the house. I heard a faint noise of sandaled feet moving with a gentle tread behind me. It was a simple, almost reflex movement to draw the knife and turn.

'Aulus?'

'What...?'

'It's me. Aripele.'

She ran towards me and in my embarrassment I fumbled the knife and it fell to the cobbles at my feet with a clatter. I took her in my arms. That reunion was everything I had wanted. It was made more urgent by the length of time I had been imagining it. We kissed gently and then passionately even though such expressions of affection are not considered polite in Roman society.

A soft cough behind us made me break off.

'Maybe you should reserve that for when we get back?'

'Quintus you old war-dog.'

I raised my right arm and had an arm around each of them.

I hugged them both, to Quintus' surprise. I was home. I was where I had longed to be for more than a year. Even Quintus was a welcome sight, his scarred face brightening with a smile of genuine pleasure. I picked up the knife and hid it away and we walked together to the house.

'Where have you been?' I said

'We've been to a tavern called the Old Gaul in the Subura,'

'I wouldn't let her go on her own,' Quintus said. His speech sounded a touch slurred.

'Why go to the Subura? It's risky.'

'We went to see Junius.'

'What? What about his wife?'

'Aemilia was there too. She is such a lovely woman. Junius has been telling us and everyone in the tavern, I might add, about his adventures in Gaul. They've renamed it. It used to be the Old Soldier, but since Junius' returned everyone comes there to hear his first-hand accounts of the great battles he's been in. He's named it The Old Gaul.'

'So now he's an entertainer?'

'Yes. The place was packed. Everyone wants to know what is happening in Gaul. We get news of Caesar's great battles but not many first-hand accounts,' Quintus said.

'He's all right is he?'

'Yes,' Aripele said as we entered Quintus' house. 'He'll be so pleased to hear you're back. Are you just on leave?'

'It's a long story; I'll need time to tell it.'

'Not tonight then,' Quintus said, 'I'm off to bed. I know when I'm not needed,' he slurred.

He left us holding hands in the atrium. We looked at each other for a moment and then she led me to the room off the peristylium she was still occupying. It was a long, sleepless, happy night.

*   *   *

We sat at our usual table in the corner of the Old Gaul tavern. The weather was sweltering, baking and dry outside making the cool of the tavern with its thick walls, a pleasant relief. Junius poured us some more wine and we watered it ourselves to taste. Quintus used only a dash of water. I was more generous with it, wanting to keep a clear head. I waved away a fly that was buzzing around my head with irritating persistence and I smiled to my companions.

'The time has come to get the amulet. I can't leave it any longer.'

'Not that plan of yours again,' Quintus said.

'Yes, it could make us all very rich.'

'But you said the house was impossible to break into, after your last attempt,' Junius chipped in.

'That was before I realised I had to do it. If Marcus gets his hands on the amulet for long enough he'll work out where the deeds are and all will be lost,' I said, fiddling with my half-empty cup.

'How do you propose to do it?' Quintus said.

'Hey, look at her. Did you ever see…?' Junius began.

'Concentrate will you?' I said.

'Sorry, it was just…'

'Do I have to sit here and listen to this? Say something or I'm off,' Quintus said.

I described my plan in a few words.

'Sounds dangerous to me. I can't see what use I'll be to you with one arm.'

'I can't understand you Aulus. You've been back weeks and you should have done this as soon as you got back,' Quintus said.

'I've taken my time so I can get my life together again after Gaul. You know what it was like after I got back.'

'I can't help it if the legion won't take you back. At least they've rescinded the dishonourable discharge. It does mean you'll still get a pension.'

'If this comes off I won't need one.'

'When do we do it?' Junius said.

'There's a full moon at the moment, better to wait a week or so. It may be that bit darker,' I said.

We left the matter there and drank our wine. Junius went back to serving his customers and left the two of us talking. Quintus and I reminisced about army life. I learned much from him. He had ten years' experience as a centurion and two as prefect. When I learned about the circumstances of his last battle I realised he was not only courageous but had been a skilled and fierce fighter in his time.

We walked through the dark streets wondering whether Fortuna would smile upon our venture and produce the amulet. It haunted me. I even dreamed of it that night. I couldn't understand why I had delayed – perhaps I was trying to avoid the disappointment of not finding it in the Mettius residence.

The following night we walked past the Mettius house. It was a vast property and therein lay the problem. The extensive grounds made discovery in approaching the house a strong likelihood. We could hear dogs in the grounds too. I doubted there would be many armed men since Marcus was away and perhaps still suffering in his mind from his German capture. He would still be with the legions and they never sent soldiers home, unless it was for physical disability. Mental scars counted for nothing.

The house had once belonged to Marius. After Sulla had defeated him, he gave the house to Marcus Mettius Senior as a reward for his loyalty. Soon afterwards, Sulla began his proscriptions. He executed half the patricians in the Senate, including my grandfather. They spared my father because his sister was married to Mettius. Father was in any case only a jeweller and posed no political threat to anyone.

There was a high wall surrounding the grounds and I knew the layout of the house because of the time I had spent there as a child, taught by Gennadius the Greek tutor. In any case I had broken in once already. I was uncertain which rooms upstairs would be in use, since the sole living owner was Marcus and there would be no one in residence. It did not seem probable there would be many slaves there either, apart from the ones maintaining the house.

Chapter III

"It is not because things are difficult that we do not dare, it is because we do not dare that things are difficult." – Seneca.

The stars were hidden from view by some light cloud and it made it a dark night. The air was still hot and humid, for summer is always so in Rome. I could hear an occasional sound of voices on the other side of the wall despite the hour as I waited with a rope coiled over my shoulder. My heart was thumping against my ribs but my mood was elevated. What was it that Procillus used to say? Positive attitude.

At last, I had a chance of getting my inheritance and it felt exhilarating. The alley in which I stood was deserted. In the small hours only a fool or a thief would be abroad in Rome in the tiny alleys that bounded such properties.

It was the waiting that got on my nerves and I became as nervous as a virgin on her wedding night. A moment later I heard it. There were shouts from the far side of the surrounding gardens. Cerialis and Junius had done their work. I could smell the fire from where I stood. If I could detect it, I was certain that the occupants of the house could too. There would be widespread panic.

Starting a fire was a dangerous business in Rome. This was

not only because it might set fire to the entire city but also because the penalty for arson is to be burned alive in the arena. It was not a pleasant prospect and I understood how much my friends had risked to give me this one chance.

I threw the rope over the branch of a tree standing in the garden. I pulled. The knotted end wedged on the branch. I tested its firmness and climbed up. I looked down. I saw two hunting hounds, big dogs, looking up at me in silence. The look in their eyes was one of eager anticipation. I threw them each a piece of meat, big enough to satisfy any such beast. I climbed down unobserved and with some regret killed both dogs while they fed. I could not take the chance that either would chase me like last time once they had finished their meat.

I crossed the garden moving silent and fast from tree to tree until I came to the wall of the peristylium. It was in that colonnaded garden where most of my lessons as a child had taken place. Nostalgia pricked me. Although Marcus had often bullied me there had been many happy times too, learning about Greek heroes and battles fought in history.

I climbed the wall without difficulty. All along, I could hear the sound of people shouting, running and I could sense their panic. The peristylium was empty. I crossed in silence to the stairway leading to the upper floor. I reached the stairs. I heard a sound behind me and I turned. There was no one there and I sped up the stairs. I did not expect armed resistance but was well prepared for it.

The slave had lit oil lamps that stood on low tables in the corridor from which the bedrooms opened. There were four doors. It was cool inside and there was a fusty smell, perhaps from lack of use. The lamps flickered and threw spectral shadows across the narrow passageway. I was not expecting anyone to be there but drew my sword in any case.

I crept along the passageway trying not to make any noise.

All the previous burglary I had done as a youth was in empty or almost empty houses. This was not the same thing at all. I was sweating. I was jumpy. All was still and quiet.

It was then I saw him. There was a man with his back to me, looking through the doorway of the room at the end of the corridor. The fellow was in all likelihood observing the fire my friends had started. He was oblivious to me.

I was undecided. Kill him? Knock him on the head?

I stood motionless for what must have been minutes. The man did not move. Could I get close enough to overpower him and avoid killing him? I had no wish for slaughter. The people in this house were not my enemies; it was their master who was guilty.

The man before me was not tall but wiry with grey hair tied back in the nape of his neck and he was no youngster, for he was balding at the crown. I decided to creep forward and hit him with the hilt of my sword in the hope of stunning him.

It was then he turned. I looked him in the eye and he knew. He saw his death. It was Cerberus. He who had tortured my parents. It was he who had burned them alive in that building. He was the one who turned me away at the gates that night and later sold the ring my father was making for the Chief Vestal.

Anger rose in me. Rage. I wanted his dead body on the end of my gladius. I wanted him to writhe in pain. Pain like he had caused me. Pain like he inflicted on my parents. He had taken away my family and left me homeless and destitute on the streets of Rome. But Rome takes care of her own. There is always a way to stay alive. A way to grow. Even if it means sinking to join the dregs of humanity, you can stay alive in Rome.

I stabbed with my sword. He sidestepped and I realised I had been hasty. He had a knife. He drew it in a single fluid motion. Holding it parallel to his wrist it was hard to follow. He swung it very fast, backhand at my face. It caught me on the tip of the chin. How an old man could do that had me wondering. I realised he was not the old janitor I thought he was. That was a gladiator's trick. I realised now I would have to kill him. I wanted him to know who I was.

'remember me Cerberus?'

'I remember you. You're the poor relative. You eluded me for years in the Subura. I found you though. Hiding in the Ninth Legion. Marcus always was an incompetent. How he failed to kill you I cannot guess.'

'You killed my parents.'

'No, the fire did that, but it was a merciful release after what we did to them. They squealed like pigs you know. Pigs.'

He was goading me and it was working. I began to feel almost dizzy with anger. I thought my brain would burst with it. Father's voice in my head said, 'Never lose your temper like that again. It makes you hasty and you will do silly things.'

I stepped back. Cerberus shouted.

'Up here there's a burglar.'

To shut him up I swung my gladius at his head and realised my mistake at once. He was very fast. He stepped forward into my raised arm and my wrist hit his head instead of the blade of my sword. He raised his knife to stab me in the armpit. My sword flew from my hand as I hit him. I fell to the left and the knife shaved through my tunic catching me another superficial cut on the back of the armpit. I rolled against the wall and my hand scrabbled for the sword.

Fast, he knelt. He raised his knife. His left hand reached for my throat. My hand found the sword. I held it by the blade. There was no time to find the handle. I punched with the blade in my hand. I hit him on the temple. It was not as hard as I wanted, but it was hard enough.

Meridius had taught me that there is a thin area of the skull at the side, low down above and in front of the ear where a blade can enter with ease. I found it.

I let go of the sword and grabbed his right wrist as it descended. He cut me again as I did, but the look on his face told me he was dead. It took a moment or two but he began to crumple and fell across me as I held his knife hand away. His limbs went to his sides and his legs stretched out beneath him. All his limbs were stiffened as if he was standing tip-toe with his arms by his side. He was twitching too – a dance of death. I had seen it often enough before but this time, shaken though I was, it brought me pleasure. The first step in my revenge.

I pushed his fibrillating body off me. I felt as if I was cut all over. Blood ran down my fingers and dripped onto the floor.

I left him there. I had cut my right hand on my own sword and it was exquisitely painful but no tendons were severed, so my fingers moved well enough. I entered the room. It was a sleeping chamber. It was empty. I turned and dragged the still twitching Cerberus into the room and began my search. I went into the corridor and listened. No one came so I supposed no one had heard his call.

Re-entering the room I looked around. There was a cot in one corner and a table with two chairs but no chest, no boxes and without question, there was nowhere to hide anything. I went to the next room aware that time was short.

Again there was no sign of the amulet. A chest in the corner contained some women's clothes and as I lifted them out I recognised my aunt Livia's red gown. It was the one she wore on the first day I had begun my lessons in this very house. It smelt of flowers. I almost felt sorrow. The feeling left me almost as soon as it had arisen. I recalled how she had refused to let me in after my parents died. She was as much a Mettius Costa as the rest of them. And the amulet? Nothing. No trace.

I searched the other bed-chambers but found again found nothing. Either it was not here or it was hidden so well it would take me a month. I realised how stupid I had been. The chance of finding such a small item in the dark was remote. Quintus had told me so, over and over again, but I had insisted I would find it.

I began to get angry. Angry with myself for my stupidity. Perhaps I should face up to the knowledge that it was gone forever. In desperation, I went back to the first room. Maybe there was a secret niche or even a doorway.

There was a faint, green, glint of light from the body – a momentary flicker no more. A reflection of the flames outside perhaps. I licked my lips. It was a reflex, anticipation.

I crossed to the dead man. Around his neck was a cord. I grabbed it and pulled. The amulet was there. Marcus must have had given it to him for safekeeping. Had I known, I would have wanted to kill him twice. I looked at the little jewel in the palm of my blood-stained hand. It was oval, green and bound with silver wire. My father had dovetailed two green stones together and bound them close. I tied the double leather thong around my throat and it felt like coming home after a long journey. My heart leapt.

It was obvious. A band of Corsairs had once captured me in Pontus and they had missed the stone. It hung in such a way it was concealed below my tunic neck-line. No wonder I had not seen it during the struggle in the half-light. And it was mine again. I smiled as I made my way down the stairs to freedom and perhaps wealth.

I heard people approaching. They must have put out the fire already or else I had tarried too long. I bounded across the peristylium and scrambled up the vine that climbed its corner. I was in the garden outside in no time and running for the wall. I used the tree and my rope to climb up and I dropped to the ground outside. I coiled the rope and slung it over my shoulder. I ran.

I ran away from the Quirinal as we had arranged and headed for the Subura. It was dark and I hoped no one would spot that I was armed.

Reaching the Old Gaul I was breathless and smiling as I entered. It had taken only ten minutes, running fast. I hid my gladius at the back of my tunic slinging it from its cord and approached Quintus who was at our usual table.

'Well?' he said.

'Very well.' I said. I couldn't stop grinning.

'Junius,' Quintus said. 'More wine. If that look on Aulus' face means what I think it does, then we're celebrating tonight. Oh yes, definitely celebrating.'

Chapter IV

"The more laws, the less justice." – Marcus Tullius Cicero.

Marcus Tullius Cicero was a wizened little man. For a great orator and lawyer he looked unimpressive. That is, until he opened his mouth. The voice it emitted was deep and resonant. He intoned every syllable when he spoke and he had a faint Sicilian accent. He looked us up and down in an almost disdainful way but there was a twinkle in his eye. It suggested he was not as serious as his humourless brother Quintus, who had discharged me from the Ninth.

He showed us in and we lay on couches in his triclinium, watered wine and figs on the table before us and a cool breeze wafting through the entrance to the peristylium. There was a faint odour of food cooking but he offered us nothing else to eat, despite loud rumblings from my stomach. An audible embarrassment, but one controllable by a mouthful of figs.

'So you want to establish title to these lands do you?' he said, reaching for his cup. He wore a white tunic brushed with chalk to seem bright and clean. The tunic had a red border showing his Equestrian rank.

'That's the idea, Senator,' I said.

'The documents look authentic. They are certainly pre-Marian. You inherited them then?'

'Yes, but they were hidden by my father and I have only just managed to locate them.'

Marcus Tullius shifted on his couch. 'Locate them?'

'Yes,' I said. 'My father was a jeweller. He etched the location in just a few words of Etruscan inside the bulla he gave me when I was young.'

'You read Etruscan?' He leaned forward and a look of surprise lit the lawyer's face. 'Is there no end to the talent of this old war-horse?'

'Err... No. I can't read Etruscan but there are still some academics at the Pollio Library who do. You only have to go to the Etruscan section.'

'Just like that?'

'Not quite. We needed someone discreet. It took a lot of following around and making enquiries. The bulla was in two halves and once the wire holding it together was unravelled the words were inside on the two faces. Shrine – back – three forwards, two right.'

'I don't understand,' Marcus Tullius said.

'It was simple in the end. Stand in the courtyard with your back to the shrine, three flagstones ahead and two to the right. I got it wrong at first but Aripele has a good head on her shoulders and we found the deeds in a small lead chest, buried underfoot all those years.'

Marcus Tullius sat back and smiled that thin smile of his, like a knife cut across his face. 'What made him hide the deeds?

I had no intention of telling him the whole story so all I said was, 'He was getting old and he often hid things in those days.'

'Well old people do that sort of thing. Always hiding things away. Do it myself sometimes you know.'

'How long would it take to establish my rights?'

'With the right funding I would estimate approximately five years. We have to first establish the authenticity of the documents and that can take two years the way the courts are working now. After that there has to be ratification by the Senate, then the Land Commission. After that, notice has to be sent to all the existing tenants of the property that you wish them to leave. Then you can start to use the land. Such things have been known to drag on for considerably longer. The Senate Land Commission only sits once a year and they sometimes leave things over to the next meeting if there is a lot of business.'

'Is there no way to shorten the procedure?'

'Well we could bribe members of the Commission but it will cost.'

'How much?' I had a sinking feeling in the pit of my stomach.

'With deeds of this nature I would suspect I could do this for you with ten thousand sestertii. That's not including my fee of course.'

'I can't raise that sort of money.'

'Perhaps it explains why your father never claimed the land.'

'Aulus, it's hopeless,' Aripele said.

'No it's not hopeless,' I said. 'We will just have to raise the money. I have some ideas.'

'Do you wish me to act for you?' Cicero said. He stood up then indicating that the meeting was over.

'I can't pay you. I had hoped I could pay you once the claim is settled.'

Cicero shrugged his shoulders putting his hands out at his sides.

'You can't expect me to work for nothing. I have to eat like anyone else.'

'No, I understand. How much do I need to pay you to get the land?'

'If you want to wait until it goes through normal channels then I will charge a thousand and the rest will cost perhaps fifteen thousand sestertii.'

'But that's a fortune.'

'Well money craves money.'

'I'll save it and contact you as soon as I have some of it. Can you start now?'

'If you guarantee to pay my fees as first priority I will make some initial enquiries.'

'You are most kind.' I said.

Aripele and I walked away, both of us wondering how we would raise the money.

'He's a crook,' I said.

'No, he's a lawyer. You won't get a better one in Rome that's why he's expensive. He needs the money for bribes. The corruption in this place knows no bounds,' Aripele said. 'Why it's almost like working in a whorehouse.'

It was then I saw Vibius, the old man I had met at Ostia. He was standing with a street vendor who was selling tunics from a stall.

'Vibius.'

'Aulus Veridius. How pleasant to meet you again. Is this the charming lady you were coming home to, all those months ago?'

'Yes, we are to be married. Aripele, may I introduce Vibius Abrucius, he's an old soldier and ex-gladiator.'

Vibius bowed to Aripele.

'Less of the old.' Vibius said.

'I am most pleased to meet you,' she said.

'You must be from Pontus or Bithynia?'

'Why yes, how did you know? I'm from Sinope.'

'I never forget an accent. I was there fifteen years ago when our Roman legions first appeared, to trouble your poor people.'

'We were troubled by Rome long before that.'

'Yes but not in Pontus itself. Well never mind. I'm pleased to encounter you both.'

'Vibius,' I said, 'I need to raise a lot of money in a hurry. You said that gladiators are well paid here in Rome.'

'Well they are for what they do, as long as they're successful. The real money is on the betting. You can't bet on yourself of course. That would be illegal. You could, however, ask a friend to place your bets for you and get the money after the fight.'

'Where are the bets placed?'

'Well you have to know who to approach. The games are a religious activity and as you no doubt know, any betting is illegal at the arena. I do have some contacts if you want me to help you. I don't need money so I don't mind helping for only a small percentage.'

'I'll contact you later if it's going to be viable. Are you still in the same place?'

'Yes, but don't forget, go to the gladiator school and tell them I sent you.'

'Many thanks. I'll think about it.'

We parted company. I looked at Aripele.

'I know what you're going to say and there's a risk but we have to get that money.'

'I know. You will be safe enough. I've heard from Hypsicratea how you killed two brigands as if they were nothing.'

'Brigands aren't gladiators. I'll manage though, with some practice.'

'If you get killed, I don't know what would happen to me.'

'It's the same risk as going to Gaul you know, just closer to home.'

'I'd rather we were together and poor than you dead and me alone.'

'I can join the Town Guard first and at least we will have some money coming in.'

'Good. I think Quintus doesn't have very much left now. We've cost him some money just staying with him.'

'Don't worry I'll make it good.'

'My tapestry business is making money, but not thousands.'

'I know. I'll have to make some big bets.'

'We'll manage. The Gods will favour us I'm sure. They haven't deserted us so far.'

'Don't put too much faith in the Gods. They can play tricks for their own amusement.'

'So can I,' she said with a wistful smile on her beautiful lips.

*   *   *

The walk to the baths refreshed me. I stopped at a barber's stall near the forum and chatted with the barber about the local politics while I had my shave. I was beginning to warm to the idea of being in Rome. I had always loved our big city. I enjoyed the bustle of constant activity day or night. I liked the fact that almost everyone spoke the same language as me and I never had problems communicating. I knew my way around and where to buy things and who to approach for advice.

At the Thermae Decianae, I cleaned up. I bathed and took a short time in the steam and then after visiting the caldarium I was dried and oiled and scraped. I donned my clean tunic and set off to the headquarters of the Town Guard.

There was a pretentious slave at the door who insisted he was told my full name and rank and where I had come from. The questions continued until I grew impatient, pushed past him and entered the low building at the Esquiline Gate. I came to an office and knocked on the door then entered the room. At the desk was another slave, who looked Greek and serious and who said, 'Unless you are announced you will not be seen.'

'I have come to see the Commander and would appreciate it if you would kindly announce me. If you won't do so, I will have to go in unannounced. Is that clear?' I said.

The slave looked at me pondering for a few moments and then said, 'You seem to be very new to the system. This isn't Gaul or Africa and there is no hurry at all. No one is going to invade the city for the moment so I suggest you sit down and allow me to take some details. Then and only then, will I disturb the Commanding Officer of the Town Guard. Is that clear or should I say it again? I can always leave you waiting until mid-day if you cause me trouble.'

I began to realise the slave was right, there was indeed no hurry to start this miserable posting as what I saw as only a military janitor.

I sat. I waited. The slave asked me a few questions and copied down the answers. He asked for the letter of introduction that Procillus had given me before I left Gaul. I handed it to him with a feeling of reluctance. I felt that it was important to me but I don't know why. It was only a letter. The slave stood and turned in a stiff manner and went to a door and knocked. There was a muffled reply and he went in.

A moment later the door opened and a small plump man dressed in the semi-military uniform of an officer of the Town Guard came out.

'My dear chap, I'm so sorry if they kept you waiting, I'm the Commanding Officer here,' the man said.

We shook hands and I introduced myself.

'I'm Gnaeus Valerius Procillus, Senior Tribune. I report directly to General Pompey but not very often I'm afraid.'

His broad grin was disarming and I began to like this short, plump, balding officer already. I followed him into his office. It was a tidy place with everything neatly arranged. Piles of scrolls sat patiently on the desk and a jug of water or wine waited on a small adjoining table.

'My nephew told me in the letter to look after you. He describes how you saved him from torture and death. He has a high opinion of you as a soldier.'

'It was kind of him to say so but it was much less heroic than it sounds.'

'My intention is to place you in the guard as a centurion.'

'Is that the same as in the regular army?'

'Well sort of. It's not a job with much status I am afraid. No-one is particularly interested in what the Town Guard does, not even Pompey.'

Valerius looked at the papers on his desk and said, 'I must say I don't quite know what to do with you, all we have to offer you is the usual routine of guarding the Gates and ensuring the men are capable of defending them if necessary. We certainly don't drill them or do weapons training like in the regular army. They would fall about laughing if you tried.'

'Am I allowed to train them then?' I asked.

He smiled. 'Well yes, if you want to. You will have about twenty men and an optio and there is no reason why you can't try to lick them into shape. I should warn you though, the shifts are short and this is an easy job even for soldiers who have seen better days and are close to retirement.'

I wondered whether he was describing himself or his men.

'I will ask Barbato to show you around. By the way don't ask why he's called Barbato, he's as hairless as an egg and I think his first master was making a joke when he named him,' Valerius said smiling.

He picked up a small bronze bell from his desk and rang it.

The first slave that I had encountered showed me out to wait in the antechamber. Soon a small, aged, bald man appeared. He walked with a stoop and was continually wringing his hands.

'Would you kindly come with me sir,' he said in a squeaky voice and looking at the ground. 'I will show you to your post at the Servian Gate and introduce you to the men. I hope you will be happy here.' The slave talked in a resigned monotone suggesting that what he meant was that he was'nt happy here but hoped that I would be.

I began my job with an enthusiasm that was quite unlike anything the Gate Guard had ever seen before but the men's response was so unenthusiastic it took very little time for me to realise that training them was going nowhere and that weapons drill would be hopeless. They were the laziest, most unkempt and unfit collection of men I had ever seen. Over the subsequent months, my keenness wore down and it all became a drudge. It was the most boring time of my life.

*   *   *

'So you're a killer are you?' the large, bearded, barrel-chested man said. 'Been a soldier and now you want to fight in the arena?' He laughed. His voice was deep and booming and his laugh made me think of thunder.

'I know how to fight if that's what you mean. I grew up in the Subura and then trained with the Ninth Legion.'

We stood at the edge of a large high-walled courtyard where ten men were practising various techniques of gladiatorial fighting. They sweated in the sunlight and their wooden weapons struck each other with a dull clicking sound. The only man present wearing armour was a huge armed Numidian guard standing in one corner. His gaze embraced the yard and he gave the impression he was ready to put down any hint of trouble from the ten gladiators.

'All right Aulus. Let's see what you can do,' the big man whose name was Titus said. He had run the gladiatorial school for many years and seen fighters come and go and it came as no surprise to me that he was an expert at picking fighting men.

I was given an ill-fitting helmet and a wooden gladius and one of the practising gladiators was called over.

'Cadonus, this chap has been killing your relatives in Gaul for the last year with Caesar. Now he wants to kill you in the arena. Want to show him how it goes?' Titus said with a grin.

I studied my opponent. I wondered what I was being set up for. I thought back to the campfire in Gaul and the fight with the Nervian champion. Perhaps this man was similar.

Cadonus was enormous. He stood a head taller than me and had a shaven head, gleaming with perspiration. In his hand he held a wooden gladius which in his enormous grip looked like a knife and his expression was less hostile than I would have expected judging by the scars on his face and the flattened, broken nose.

'Actually, you don't want to pay attention to the goading,' the giant said in near fluent Latin. 'He does it to wind you up so you can't fight. If you lose your temper here, you're finished. Ready?'

I nodded and we faced each other. I made a swipe with my wooden sword from right to left. As my gladius swept past to his right the big Gaul stepped forward to my right side and instead of striking with the blade put his right foot behind me and pushed. I pitched over backwards and ended sitting on my buttocks looking up. He had taken me by surprise but I managed to parry the Gaul's blade as it descended towards my head with astonishing speed. It woke me up.

I rolled away and cat-like sprang to my feet. In one movement I thrust at Cadonus with the wooden sword then swung clockwise in a three hundred and sixty degree arc and caught the Gaul square on the left shoulder. I struck another blow at the right shoulder fast and the Gaul grunted as the wood made contact.

'All right, that's enough,' Titus said. 'What do you think Cadonus?'

'Not bad at all,' the big Gaul said. 'Quick enough. I think we can use him if he gets a bit of practice.'

Titus smiled at me, 'He was playing with you. He is as fast as you are and could do much better than you saw. He has sixteen wins in the arena and the crowd love him. He earns me a fortune. Pray to Mars you never have to meet him in the games. Each night after work come here and practise. If you get good enough you could be in for a private contest in six months but only if you train every day.'

I was walking away when I heard Cadonus say, 'He could be god-like that man.'

I smiled to myself. I was still a fighting man.

Chapter V

"It is not by muscle, speed, or physical dexterity that great things are achieved, but by reflection, force of character, and judgment." – *Marcus Tullius Cicero.*

It was a roasting hot day. The unrelenting sun beat down from its clear, blue, cloudless sky. It baked the surface of the arena to a plane, golden crust corrupted here and there by brown-stained patches where blood from previous contestants percolated through the overlay of clean sand.

The crowd, seated in the heat of Rome's only amphitheatre buzzed in anticipation. It had been built by Scribonius Curio and it doubled for an arena or a theatre. The wine salesmen with their half amphorae of watered wine criss-crossed through the packed, sweating citizens. The rich, the poor, the elated and dejected all focused for this moment on one point in Curio's massive cauldron of fervour and death. In the senatorial box sat two senators whose expressions betrayed their desire to witness a display of gore in the name of the Gods and the birthday of their nephew. The nephew was in the cool shade of the atrium. After greeting the crowd, he had only managed to stay an hour in the heat. Death was unusual in the arena – gladiators cost a lot of money after all, but this was a special celebratory bout to the death.

Nice birthday present.

I stood with legs apart and my light bronze shield on my left arm. I could smell the new leather of my full-arm grieve as I gripped my sword in my good right hand. I waited. I was trying hard to focus but I'd stood in the sun for long minutes while my opponent strapped on his greaves. Although I could feel the tension in my body, an odd picture of a cool cup of wine and Junius' tavern in the Subura flashed through my mind.

I could kill for a cup of Falernian.

The thought brought a smile to my lips. I really was going to kill for that cup of wine. As silence descended, I began to focus. I had done this four times this year and had it not been for the fact that I still needed the money I would not have been there. I was foolish enough to have bet a month's pay and half of our savings on this one. If I lost I wouldn't need money anyway apart from paying the ferryman. If I won, we would be halfway there.

My opponent came from a provincial gladiator school. He was a large man and muscular. From the way he stood forward on the balls of his feet I assessed him as fast. His right hand held his round shield and his left wielded a wicked looking, curved and decorated sword. A Thracian and left handed.

I tried to appear impassive. I glanced above my opponent at the crowd. I could see the tension in capital letters on their faces. One man licked his lips in anticipation and another drank from a jug but they all stared, sweating, into the arena. There was some kind of animal instinct which seemed to bind them all together. A thirst for gore and a gratitude to the Gods for a life continued. For me, I needed the money. There was a risk I would die but I had little to lose. Years in the Town Guard can do that to a man. This was the nearest thing to excitement I had, apart from my life with Aripele. The bouts always caused a row but I understood her. Despite all Aripele's arguments to the contrary, I needed the money and anyway, life without risk is no life at all. She said I was selfish and perhaps she was right.

Someone in the crowd booed. A couple of catcalls followed. The Thracian shuffled forward with quarter steps, right foot forwards, shield held a half arms-length from the body. He held his sword back. I didn't want to take too much of a risk and felt I should try to finish this as fast as I could. If I could.

I stepped forward with my left foot. I side-stepped fast with my right. I brought my left foot forwards again. The Thracian hooked at my head with his shield. He missed. I had stepped past to my right again. I knelt, smashed my shield upwards onto the Thracian's sword and with the point of my gladius stabbed into the back of the Thracian's left knee. I rolled away fast and stood to assess my handiwork. A smile flickered across my lips.

First blood.

This was not some sort of cruel sport. It was a religious offering. The Thracian and I were both offering our lives to the Gods. We both accepted the risk when we swore the gladiatorial oath. We were passive; run by the gladiator school we knew whether we lived or died, the contract was what mattered. Each of us hoped we would not be the one dragged feet first from the arena but we both knew the consequences of any mistake. The Gods were looking down at us and they would choose either of us today with the same ease as they would let a child get a fever tomorrow or a man die in a street brawl next week.

The Thracian was limping now. Blood trickled down his left greave. The artery at the back of his knee was pushing small jets of blood onto the hot sand. He must have realised that it was now vital to engage me before his strength began to ebb as he bled out.

Watch out for the left hand.

I circled to my opponent's left with fast, small side steps. I knew he couldn't step forward with confidence since he couldn't rely on his injured leg. It was a question of finding my opportunity now. Left-handers always made the same mistake. They thought only of attack against the unshielded opponent's right side. Hobble them and they become easy prey.

I had slowed my opponent down and could now come at him from his unshielded sword side. The Thracian would have no chance to strike with his small shield, let alone ward off my gladius. I stepped forward again, fast. Shield up, I deflected the Thracian's sword. I stabbed in a blurring hook-like arc, fast as a snake. I used the twisting strength of my back muscles.

This time my blade penetrated behind the breastplate between the ribs. The blade sank in to half its depth. I withdrew it and there was a gush of blood. The crowd roared. Some stood raising their fists in excitement. I stepped back. The Thracian fell to his knees, breath rasping. He was coughing blood. He slumped forward with a surprised look on his face and lay still. Blood trickled from his mouth as well as the small entry wound in his chest. Crimson stained the arena's sand once more.

This time Fortuna was smiling at me. This time but for how many more?

*   *   *

I arrived home and Quintus' new slave opened the door. His name was Statius and Quintus had picked him up cheap at an auction. We had gone halves on the cost, Quintus and I. Statius had only cost two aurei – a hundred sestertii each, because of his age. The fellow's previous master had died intestate and all the man's goods were sold off to boost the coffers of the Senate and People of Rome. Statius, an old man, limped from a hip disease he had acquired as a child which was why he only cost two-thirds of a more useful slave. He had few good qualities apart from a fierce loyalty to Quintus. His loyalty was borne of the kindness with which Quintus treated him, in sharp contrast to the way his previous owners had.

'Has Aripele retired?' I enquired.

'Yes master,' replied the slave. 'Will that be all?'

'No it won't be all,' I said. 'A cup of wine and a snack would be a reasonable way to greet your master when he arrives home after earning your keep.'

'Yes master. There isn't much to eat apart from some nuts and dried fruit, I'm afraid. The mistress threw your food out because she said you were too late for it.'

'How about the wine then?' I said.

'Yes, master.'

Statius hobbled away to do my bidding.

I stood and looked up at the sky. A clear cloudless view of the stars greeted my eyes and I sighed as I began to relax. I had a good view of Orion, my favourite constellation for which I had always felt some kind of affinity.

I felt I was wasted. A good soldier, good at the business of killing in the front line and commanding my own men, twice awarded an oak-leaf crown. Was I not worth more to the Gods than this miserable existence on the walls and gates of the city? I could hardly support my wife and future children as well as pay the lawyers on this pittance from the city administration supplemented by killing in the arena. It was no life for Aripele or me. I was however, very happy being with her. It was almost contradictory.

I thought about the amulet. Although it might have been a way of obtaining wealth, had it mattered? There were other things that were perhaps more important. Love and life with a woman who meant everything to me. I had the deeds but no means to use them.

Statius brought a small jug of watered wine with a wooden cup on a tray and went off to his straw palette, leaving me alone in the peristylium; I knelt before the domestic shrine in the sheltered corner of the courtyard and poured a small libation to Mercury, our House God before seating myself on the stone bench before the fountain.

I remembered the first time I had been there. I was just a youth then and Quintus had caught me trying to burglarise his home. He had tied me up and frightened the wits out of me. I smiled as I recalled it. He had threatened me with the galleys or the legion knowing full well which path I would take. He was a good man Quintus. In a sense, I owed him everything, yet he asked for nothing but friendship.

Soft sandaled footsteps approached behind me. I smiled with pleasure as I turned, cup in hand.

'You're late.' she said.

Her anger erased the smile from my lips.

'You could be dead for all I know. You could have sent word you were all right. I've been worried sick and you stink of wine.'

'I'm sorry my love but after the fight I stopped at the Old Gaul for a small libation and one thing led to another. A man must have male company sometimes.'

I felt I was struggling harder now than when I was in the arena.

'Well at least you're here now I suppose, but you must send word, I've told you so many times. I get so angry'

'I made a lot of money. We'll soon be able to realise our ambitions and pay Cicero.'

'Is that all that matters to you?'

'No, but you matter so much to me I want this for both of us. We'll be free of this dreary existence.'

She put her arms around my neck and I reached forward kissing her lips softly. My hands settled on her warm and fluctuant hips.

'Let's go to bed before Quintus comes down,' she whispered.

We left the courtyard hand in hand and I forgot the wine, a smile dawning on my lips.

    *   *   *

It seemed as if making love to Aripele was the purest unbridled pleasure I found since I had left Pontus. I felt as if it was fulfilling a dream. She was beautiful, she was kind and she loved me. I often pondered how lucky I was to love and to be loved. For me, once friendless and alone in Rome, it was the greatest and most noble thing in my life. Since I had returned to Rome, I had enjoyed few pleasures apart from this queen among women. The arena fighting, the Town Guard – neither gave any pleasure. She made it all pall into insignificance. Even now, many years later, I find it hard to comprehend what she saw in me.

I was sweating in the heat of the summer night. I shuddered as I finished. She held me tight, her cool hands caressing my moist back in soft circles.

'I'm sorry; I was hasty,' I said. 'I was desperate that's all.'

'It's alright my love, I have things on my mind anyway,' Aripele pulled her head back a little and looked at my face.

She smiled an enigmatic smile.

'There's something I need to tell you.'

I rolled away from her in the gentle lamplight and settled on my side with my head propped on my hand. I caressed her with my other hand tracing the outline of her breast with my fingers.

'Not the tapestry business again?'

'No not that.'

'What then?' I looked into her dark and glinting eyes. The half-light of the bedroom hid their colour but they seemed as alive as ever I had seen them.

'Don't you know?' she whispered.

I stared at her wondering what she was hinting at. The thought burst on my brain like a flash of divine lightning.

'You're not... are you?' I said.

She looked at me and smiled. Her expression was one of both triumph and happiness.

'You're...?'

I gazed at her in silence for a moment.

'Oh, Aripele, I just don't know what to say. It – it's wonderful. Are you sure? You're quite sure?'

'I saw a doctor at the temple of Ceres near the Castra Urbana. He was a Greek and he examined me and swore it would be a boy. He said he could tell from the shape of my parts.'

'He did what? You didn't let a Greek...' I was sitting up now.

'How on earth do you think a doctor diagnoses pregnancy? You silly man.'

'Well ... I don't know. I don't know about such things. You're sure he's right?'

'Sure as can be, Aulus,' she said. There was laughter in the voice and something more.

'I don't know what to say. It's amazing, incredible.' I said.

'You're such a man Aulus; you can't express any feelings using your mouth. The only part of you that expresses real emotion is best not talked about,' Aripele said with a smile.

'Well at least it works properly.' I said.

I couldn't stop myself smiling for weeks afterwards. In fact, I even smiled on my way to work which my subordinates seemed to find disturbing. It was the most momentous occasion in my entire life and for once it depended not on my strength and skill but on my love for Aripele.

Chapter VI

"This is the very perfection of a man, to find out his own imperfections." – St. Augustine.

'How long?' Quintus said, as we sat in the Old Gaul.

'About six months she tells me. It's all a mystery to me.' I sniffed my undiluted wine and added two parts water.

'I don't see how you can say that. It wasn't a mystery when you got her up the duff.'

'Well no, but I don't have any experience of being a parent.'

'No, nor have I. Wonder if it will be a boy?' Quintus said, raising his wine-cup to his lips.

'Aripele thinks it will be. She says her physician said it would be.'

'How would he know?'

'They know things like that from looking at the woman's parts.'

'You mean you let one of those Greeks look at your wife's privates?' he was frowning now.

'Well he is a doctor.'

Quintus said, 'Don't trust them myself. You need your head looking at.'

'Better than looking at my privates I suppose.'

Cerialis looked at me and he gave a gentle laugh then slapped me on the shoulder.

'That sense of humour must have got you into a few messes in the Ninth.'

'Well it did once with Caesar.'

I told him my story and we both enjoyed the feeling of reminiscing. Even at my young age, I had stories to tell. Cerialis told me of his time in the legion and we passed a good evening.

'I'm going to stop fighting in the arena,' I said. My speech was a little slurred from the wine.

'About time you came to your senses. It's all very well getting a reputation for killing in the festivals but the risk is high. Only one in twenty survives more than ten bouts and you've had fifteen.'

'I'm good for a few more, if I want to. The practice keeps me fit and well trained.'

'Not for the army. Individual skills aren't needed. You have to work as a team or you're dead, my friend.'

'Centurions don't fight as a team,' I said.

'No they don't. Look what it did for me.'

'Maybe you're right. All the same I can't risk my life for money, now I have a child coming.'

'Glad to hear it.'

'Aripele wants to call him Quintus Veridius Scapula. Sounds good, although Quintus isn't a family name of ours. We're mainly Aulus and Gaius and Julius in our family.'

'Why Quintus?'

'After you; you old git.'

'Me?'

'Yes, we owe you a lot. Since we came to Rome you have been a good friend to us both and Aripele says you have been like a father to her.'

Beaming now, Quintus said, 'Well I don't know what to say. I'm deeply honoured, my friend. I'm proud to know you both.'

'You didn't think so the first time we met.'

'No I wanted to frighten you into becoming the man you are now. I only doubted you when you pissed yourself.' He chuckled.

'You made me into just that. I'm grateful for that too,' I said.

'Let's get back.'

We stood to leave. There were two soldiers sitting drinking at the doorway as we took our leave of Junius. I looked and smiled at one of them. He looked back at me and smiled. His face looked familiar. His lorica was dusty as if he had ridden a long way in haste. His companion, a thin fellow with dark staring eyes, looked up and smiled too.

'Quintus Cerialis?'

'Yes,' Quintus said. He turned and put his right hand behind his back. It was a nervous gesture. He always kept a hidden knife and his caution had kept him alive so far, so I supposed it must have been of value.

'Can I buy you a cup of wine sir?' the first soldier said. He had a sun-burned face and small scar on his forehead that beamed red, perhaps from the wine he was drinking or maybe it was fresh.

'Who's buying?' I said.

'I'm one of Pompey's advance guard. Haven't you heard? The Eastern Legions are coming home.'

'That's nice for you all. Soon the city will be full of drunken soldiers. What's that to me?'

'You're one of the heroes of the legions. Men still talk about you with awe, even in the Fourth Gemina, to which I belong.'

Quintus smiled.

'Twice honoured in one night and not an *as* richer.' He began to laugh at what he felt was the irony.

'The legions are coming home?' I said.

'Yes, Pompey has finished his campaigns in the east and he's coming home to a triumph, assuming the Senate grant him one.'

'Seems unlikely they won't,' I said.

'Indeed,' the first soldier said.

'How long before they arrive?'

'Probably four or five months I would guess.'

We had to stay; had we left, it would have been insulting. We drank more wine and we swapped stories as only soldiers can. Pompey's victory had been complete. He had quashed all resistance. He had taken Pontus back and subdued Armenia. He had allowed the Armenian king to keep most of his country but had exacted a fabulous price for that.

The hour was late when we left. Threading our way through the raven-black night we betrayed a slight stagger imbued by the wine and I wondered if Pompey's triumph would be as grand as expected.

*   *   *

It was a lazy day for me and we had nothing in particular to do. I had no duties for five days and Aripele and I were hoping to go to the country for a rest. Aemilia's father owned a small estate and winery near Ostia where he had a vineyard and he and his wife Flavia, had invited us to escape the stress of the city. Statius had passed me the note with his usual humourless expression and waited in case there was a reply.

'No, nothing,' I said. 'I'll write a reply later.'

He turned and made his way to the vestibule to inform the messenger from Ostia.

I began to ponder in silence. There might be consequences to my raid on the Mettius residence. It could turn out to be a full-scale feud now. Marcus would not take it well that I had the deeds even though I had been unable to use them like my father before me. The difference was I had no intention of being caught like my parents. Once warned, I was not a man to ignore such knowledge. History would not repeat itself this time. What could he do anyway? He was with Caesar's army and I was in Rome. Even with his money his reach could not be that long. Aripele stirred me from my reverie.

'When will Pompey's legions come home?' Aripele said.

'About four months' time, the soldiers in the tavern said.'

'Four months.' Aripele said, 'We'll see the celebrations. I hear there are parades, free food, and street parties. It will be such fun.'

'Well, yes it will be.'

'You'll see friends from the legions.'

'No, not really. I never made many friends in the legions in Pontus. Lucullus had Junius and me spying on them, so I was not the most popular of soldiers. They'll bring back Armenian and Syrian prisoners who they'll strangle in public for the amusement of the crowds. It isn't very nice you know.'

'I saw a ritual strangulation in the square outside my parent's home when I was only six. Mithridates had captured a Roman spy and condemned him to public execution.'

'You never told me that.'

'You never asked. He was a cruel man Mithridates.'

'I'm glad I didn't stay. Let's hope there are none of your countrymen amongst them.'

I thought of Hypsicratea then. I wondered where she was. I wondered what she was doing. I had left her to her fate but I reasoned it would have been fruitless to have stayed. It would have cost me my life. Mithridates would not have tolerated even a single Roman in the palace or even the city. She had refused to come with me. It was surely not my fault. Guilt still nagged at me though. I had always known that she may have been sacrificing herself for my safety but I had never wanted to admit it to myself before now. The coming triumph had somehow stirred up a lot of memories buried in my mind since I left Pontus with Aripele.

My mind returned to the present with a wrench.

'You think I care? The Pontic men I remember paid to use my body. It hasn't exactly endeared me to any of them. There was only Junius in those days who ever expressed any affection or respect.'

'Now, now. There's no need to get worked up. You're here with me now and we have more to think about than our past. We have a future.'

I put my arm around her. We were in the peristylium sitting on the little stone bench in the fading sunshine as autumn began to descend upon us.

'You know,' I said, 'I look back on that time with regret in one sense, that I left Hypsicratea to the returning king, knowing he might find out about my relationship with her. I found you though and I would never want to change anything.'

'Nor would I. Our little Quintus would not be arriving if it had been different would it?'

'No. I owe it to him to find the money to pursue the amulet's legacy. I understand now why my father wouldn't sell it to Marcus Mettius senior. It is all that is left of our family and it must go to family.'

'It's almost as if it's a race. The winning family will get the inheritance.'

'It is not their inheritance. Marcus has no legal claim. It is a piece of land that's always belonged to the Veridius Scapulae and it will always be so.'

'All right, there is no need to become so emotional about it.'

'I'm not emotional. It's a matter of family honour and I will teach that to my own son when he's old enough.'

'Aulus you've changed. Just the knowledge that you have a son on the way seems to have made you more serious.'

'Maybe that's what it does to a man. I can't read the future but I must try for the sake of my unborn son. It is now my duty to preserve the name of my family and to protect him and you,'

'I notice you put him first.'

'What would he be without his mother and what would I be without you?'

I leaned forward and kissed her mouth softly, so softly, my lips more gentle than usual. She was the mother of my unborn son. I wanted to handle her with care.

If I could have read the future as I boasted, I might have held her closer.

It was the Fates again. Spinning, spinning.

END

To Be Continued...

The tale of Aulus Veridius Scapula and the amulet
continues in Amulet III – The Parthian Shot.
The fight against the house of Costa goes on in Rome
and later in Parthia where Aulus finds the legions of Rome
less than invincible.
Below is the first chapter...

AMULET III
BOOK I: ROME

Chapter I

"I love the name of honour, more than I fear death." – Gaius
Julius Caesar.

I held Quintus' little hand in mine as we walked along the
Vicus Longus. When I looked at him I felt a pride I had never felt
in any part of my previous life – a father's pride. He chattered.
When he was happy he chattered a lot. I tended to switch off
at times replying with 'yes' or 'no' and not listening with full
attention. On that particular day he was talking about his first day
at school. With many 'umm's' and 'ah's', he explained in intricate
detail about his teacher and the other children. He was excited and
pleased with all of it. In short, my son, Little Quintus was a delight.

He had sandy hair and a freckled face. Neither my wife
Aripele nor I had been able to understand it because she had hair
the colour of cinnabar and mine was dark brown. We often joked
that he must be a throwback to my great grandfather who had
been a Consul and a General in the army of Marius for he had been

a man with sandy hair but in truth, we could not fathom how it had come about.

At the age of eight, Little Quintus had just started school. We had begun our son's education at home. He progressed well, reading a little simple Latin and Greek but we had realised that he needed to mix more with others his own age so we had enrolled him at a good school near the Scholae Rotundum. The school was expensive but worth it even though the school was opposite the gladiator school where I had trained, nine years before. The irony did not escape me.

I noticed the huge oaken door of the gladiator school as we passed. I remembered my first day there. The memory brought back the smell of sweat in my nostrils again. Gladiator schools smell like that, you know. Titus Gallo, the school's owner, had been a gladiator himself but he was no slave. He was big and fast and it had stood him in good stead for he had risen through the ranks of the gladiators; in the end, becoming rich. I recalled how Cadonus, a big Gaul had sent me sprawling with his wooden gladius when they tested me to see if I could really fight. I know I impressed them.

As my son and I walked, the streets became less crowded and instead of constantly having to sidestep to avoid people, walking became easier once we passed the Esquiline on our right.

On this particular day, his first day at school, I elected to take Little Quintus there and bring him back since it seemed to me that it was a father's duty and not something to delegate to our house slave, Statius. Poor limping Statius. He came cheap at two aurei, because he was old and limped badly from a deformity of the hips. He was a faithful slave though and we treated him well despite his shortcomings.

Quintus and I were both breathing hard since the walk up the Vicus Longus, the main road from the Forum Romanum leading northeast, was steep and we were walking fast considering the heat and the cobbles that tilted our sandals as we walked. It was easy to sprain an ankle or trip on even the best of our city's streets. There were traces of straw and horse dung filling the cracks between each cobblestone beneath our feet but the smell for once was tolerable. When the wind blew from the west, it brought the smell of the Tiber with it laden with the odours of the sewage that drifted from Rome to the sea – never an engaging prospect.

We walked, hand in hand to where we turned off to climb the Quirinal where we lived. The sinking summer sun still held a sticky warmth and I was sweating a little beneath my tunic. My hands were damp and I remember the feel of his little fingers enclosed in my rough, calloused grip. There is no feeling like the touch of another's hand when it belongs to someone you love.

Quintus Cerialis owned the house but we lived with him as his guests and Aripele looked after his household. I contributed to the finances from my wages as a Centurion in the Town Guard. It worked well, but we all knew it might not last forever. My son had come by the epithet "Little" because, naming him after the scarred veteran Prefect of the Ninth Legion had made it hard to know who was being addressed in conversation.

'Father, tell me about the battles in Gaul,' Little Quintus said.

'No, you've heard all about my time there over and over again.'

I smiled as I spoke of course. His high-pitched voice usually made me smile from the sheer pleasure of his company. I was a doting parent you see.

'Please father. Did you really fight with the Great Julius Caesar? I've told all the other boys about you.'

'You shouldn't have done that. I keep telling you. Quintus Tullius Cicero was the Legion's Legate and Caesar had control over him. I did meet Caesar once though.'

'I heard you and Uncle Quintus talking about it. Did Caesar really laugh like that?'

'Yes he did, but he was usually a serious man. By the way, you shouldn't eavesdrop. Listening to other people's conversations is rude.'

'Which battles were you in?'

'Never mind. I've told you the stories so many times.'

'Oh.'

'Well, I can tell you, he's still fighting. The barber who shaved me this morning tells me that Caesar has embarked for Britannia.'

'What's that, Father?'

'It is a dark and mysterious country separated from Gaul by a wide sea or river. It's full of mists, ghosts, and witches. We don't know how big it is. It could be an island for all we know.'

'Why would anybody want to conquer such a place?'

'I heard Caesar is very fond of pearls and the oysters in the sea around Britannia are full of them. It can't be to get gold or slaves; the savages there have little to offer in that respect and they make poor slaves.'

'How many Legions has he taken?'

'Never mind now, we are almost home.'

'But father...'

'Enough. You'll drive me to distraction.'

I still smiled as I spoke, after all the past tribulations in my life, I had become a patient and tolerant parent. We stopped then as we had reached the gate of our home. The house was small by Quirinal standards. The entrance had a shop front; a baker's shop. We liked that because it allowed us ready access to fresh bread and the smell of the shop was a delight in the early morning. It seemed quite a privilege to awaken in the morning to the yeasty smell of fresh baked bread.

Our home was singular, for it was the only one in the wide

cobbled street with shop fronts. Shop fronts were uncommon here where the residents were rich people with big houses. Quintus Cerialis had picked up the house cheaply when the owner died leaving it in a dilapidated condition. He had worked hard and spent most of his pension restoring it. Since then Aripele had opened a tapestry shop and because the tapestries were unusual – in the Pontic style, they sold well to the wealthy passing trade.

The vestibulum was a small entrance hallway between the two shops. A predecessor of Quintus' had a guest, perhaps after a grand meal, who had left graffiti behind on the wall: *"I love your food but your lips are sweeter."*

Underneath, in a fine and feminine hand was scrawled, *"If you must taste them in front of my guests I won't invite you again."*

The Vestibulum led to the atrium where we often sat and talked, listening to the sound of the rainwater splashing into the impluvium, the pool in the centre of the open-roofed room. None of us had enough money for the usual decorations most Romans kept in the atrium. We had no golden statues or ornaments but Aripele had made some fine tapestries depicting tigers and elephants which we hung there adorning the walls.

I was about to ring the bell when a low voice behind me made me turn my head.

'Veridius Scapula?'

The voice belonged to an unprepossessing man of medium height and I didn't like the look of him. He was my age, maybe mid-thirties, broad and squat in the frame. Squat seems the right description for his arms were long and his legs bowed. There was something odd in the slow, relaxed way his limbs moved, for it was out of place. It reminded me of the very fit gladiators with whom I had mixed in my time in the arena. His face reminded me of a toad, with a protuberant mouth and bulbous eyes blinking as if he had emerged from some dark place into the sun. Around his neck was a copper ring, which in Greece, indicates a slave.

'Yes?' I said.

'You him?'

'That's why I said yes, don't you think?'

'I have a message.'

'Well?'

'I am Adonis. My master wants you to come.'

Adonis was as likely a name for this ugly man as it was appropriate. I never liked the fashion prevalent then in Rome of calling slaves by the names of Greek heroes and Gods. It seemed facetious to me; as a child, I had a Greek tutor and I learned enough about the Greek heroes to admire them. To call slaves after true heroes like Leonidas or Themistocles seemed insulting to their memory.

'And who is your master?'

'Your cousin, Marcus Mettius Costa. He has returned from the war and wants to see you. He says to come alone and unarmed, this evening.'

'You have delivered your message now go. I don't think I have any desire to visit Marcus. You can tell him so.'

'Your child?' Adonis said looking at little Quintus. Quintus smiled back at the man. Children don't read these things like we do. Adonis betrayed a malevolent smile. I half stepped between my son and the presumptuous slave.

'For a slave you seem to need instructions in manners,' I said.

'Well, you need to take care of him; anything could happen. Rome is a dangerous place.'

'Are you threatening me?'

'No. My master wants you to come and I think you might find it wise to obey him.'

He had a thick Greek accent but I could understand him easily. His thinly veiled tone of aggression annoyed me.

'Obedience and subservience is the clothing of slaves not Roman citizens, you would do well to remember it. Marcus is no more my master than you are a free man.'

'All the same, my master expects you this evening.'

He turned and walked away, with a slow, easy, loping gait. I had it in mind to whip him but assaulting another man's slave was not acceptable by law so I let him go.

I rang my doorbell feeling angry. My hand evinced a faint tremor and I think little Quintus noticed for he was silent for a change and looked up at me perhaps wondering what it all meant.

Statius opened the door. Quintus and I had purchased him together, ten years before and he was old then. He limped like a hobbled horse and his previous owners had mistreated him. To say he was surly was an understatement but he was always loyal and discrete.

He smiled when he regarded little Quintus. I never understood how a grumpy and sometimes bitter old man like Statius could have such a good relationship with my son. Little Quintus adored the old man and often spent time talking to him. We never objected for the old man spoke good Greek and little Quintus had picked up quite a bit of that language from Statius.

'Is the Mistress in?' I enquired.

'Yes master. She is in the triclinium.'

'Would you see to Little Quintus please?'

'Yes master,' he said and smiled at Quintus as he reached forward to take his hand.

I almost swore; he always reserved those rare smiles for my son. It made living with Statius irritating.

I walked through the atrium to the peristylium and crossed

the colonnaded garden to the triclinium where we entertained. I hoped we did not have guests. I should have asked Statius.

I entered the room to find my wife sitting in a chair opposite a small, wizened man with short grey thinning hair. Statius should have told me. I decided to have words with him later.

Our guest, Marcus Tullius Cicero had some little wine stains on the front of his expensive toga and he had wine and water in jugs in front of him on a low table. His wrinkled hand gripped the clay cup with blanching knuckles as if I might take it away from him. He smiled a furrowed smile as I entered.

'Marcus. How good to see you,' I said.

'Aulus, I am so pleased to see you again too,' he said, standing up. 'Your lovely wife has kindly been entertaining me with tales of far off Pontus and the exploits of Mithridates; I would hesitate to call him "The Great", of course.'

We clasped wrists and Aripele fetched another cup for me. I reclined on the divan next to Cicero. It was customary for ladies to sit in chairs while the men reclined and although it was not usual for us to be so formal in our household we knew Cicero was a little old-fashioned and we also knew him well enough to recognise that.

'How are your funds mounting up?' Cicero said.

'Well, Aripele is the keeper of the finances these days. I earned a lot through fighting in the arena but when little Quintus was born I had to stop as you know. I could not risk leaving him fatherless. The tapestry business seems to be going well though, isn't it Aripele?'

'Yes my husband, we are saving like Egyptians. Two more years and we will have the money.'

'That's marvellous,' Cicero said. 'I am so sorry about my fee being so exorbitant but a man must eat you know.'

'My dear fellow. If you lawyers ate everything you earned

you would have to be wheeled around the streets in barrows for you wouldn't be able to walk.' I said.

'How can you say that? I have not charged you a copper *as* yet, have I?'

'Marcus, it is an investment for you. You know the land I inherited is worth a real fortune. A percentage of that is a huge reward if you can re-establish my ownership.'

'I know that and for once I mean it when I say I trust you.'

'You have the deeds safe?'

'Of course. They're locked away with my will, in the House of Vesta. They are probably on a shelf next to the wills of the wealthiest people in Rome; perhaps even that of Crassus himself.'

'Does he really intend to go to Syria?'

'It seems so,' Cicero said.

'What on earth does he want to do that for? He owns half of Rome and can't possibly need wealth,' Aripele said.

'Well,' Cicero said, his eyes narrowing like a conspirator, 'I hear he thirsts after a triumph and wants to be known as a General like his co-triumvirs.'

'That's silly,' I said. 'He can't compete with either Caesar or Pompey on that level. The man is a fat money-grubbing fool,' I said.

'Don't underestimate him,' Cicero said. 'Did you know he fought and defeated Marius' army at the gates of Rome when he was younger? Sulla praised him for that you know.'

'That was only possible because of the superiority in numbers. Marius was a great man. Crassus didn't even defeat that slave army led by what's his name? Spartacus. All he did was surround him until Pompey came and did the job for him.'

'Isn't that the point?' Cicero said. 'You need look no further for a motive. He knows quite well he has never had a genuine military success and now he wants to redress the balance. I think he believes that if you throw enough talents of gold at a thing it will happen.'

'Well I'm glad I'm out of all that now. I'll never have to face another man in armed combat again if we can just get the deeds to my inheritance established in law.'

'Who knows what future the fates spin for us, my friend?' Cicero said.

'Indeed. Was this a social call? A pleasure of course either way,' I said, glancing at Aripele.

'Marcus came to see Quintus actually,'

'Oh?'

'Yes,' Cicero said, 'He has asked me to find out about the boundaries to his property and I was hoping to catch him at home.'

'Unfortunately Quintus has gone to the Subura to meet an old friend. They were both in the Ninth together, all those years ago,' Aripele said.

'That being so, my friends, I must depart. There is a dinner I have been invited to at the house of Clodius Pulcher and I don't want to miss that. The man's a scoundrel but his guests are always amusing.'

'Perhaps you would have time to dine with us some time?' Aripele said.

'I would be delighted. If you send word through your slave I will be able to make a space in my schedule. You must tell me more of your famous military past Aulus. I am always fascinated by your account of the Cataline conspiracy.'

'Now, Marcus, you know quite well my only participation was sitting and watching, tied to a horse on a hilltop.'

'Yes, but the first hand accounts I have heard are all so different from yours you know. According to the military commanders and Generals I've heard, Cataline was killed running away, but you always seem to say he fought like a true Roman.'

'He did that. All his wounds were at the front. Well, perhaps it would bear telling again then if it amuses such a great man as you.'

'You are most kind,' Cicero said, taking his leave with a bow.

When Statius had shown him out, I told Aripele about the messenger from my cousin Marcus.

'How did he get back to Rome when Caesar is still fighting in Gaul?' Aripele said.

'I don't know. Many of the Military Tribunes enlist for a few years and then they come home to start their political careers. Must say, I don't recall Marcus having any political knowledge or aspirations. He was always a fool as a child and a foolish man when he had grown up.'

'You can't go you know.'

'Why?'

'It's a trap. Isn't that obvious?' Aripele said. She reached for her cup of watered wine and took a mouthful, thinking.

'Why would he kill me? If he did, he couldn't get the deeds anyway. You would inherit them and he would be no better off. If he wanted revenge he would hardly invite me to his house. It would be too obvious.'

'I don't trust him. Considering he left you for dead in Armenia and he and Bassus, that awful lackey of his, tried to kill you in Gaul as well he can't be asking to see you to make peace.'

'Look, my love, I think I should go, but I'm inclined towards caution and won't go without back-up. It's a pity Quintus is out.'

'He's not out.'

'But you told Marcus Tullius he was out.'

'Quintus is avoiding him.'

'Why? Marcus is such a pleasant fellow considering he's a Senator and the best lawyer in Rome.'

'You amaze me at times Aulus. Quintus owes Marcus Tullius

a fee for the land registry inspection on this house and he wants to avoid paying him. Cicero only came round to get the money.'

'Oh,' I said.

'Will you still go?'

Well as long as Quintus comes along; even if he waits outside I'll feel a lot more comfortable.'

'Why go?'

'I'm curious to hear what he has to say. Maybe I want to gloat.'

'There is no reason to communicate with him at all. Don't go.'

She stood then. She crossed the room and sat beside me placing her hand on my shoulder. She said, 'Whether his father killed your parents or not this family feud will only lead to bloodshed.'

'It's a matter of honour, Aripele. He thinks I'm weak and he can come with his Patrician money and take anything he desires. I won't let him. If I could kill him for what his family had done to mine I would.'

'It's all so dangerous Aulus. Anyway, his death won't bring back your parents. You can't erase the past by violence today. I know you want revenge, but what if he kills you? Or me and Quintus? That slave threatened to do just that didn't he? Don't go, let him rot.'

'Look, I'm not scared of him and I won't let him think I am.'

'Who cares if he thinks you're scared of him. I know you for the man you are. Does it matter what anyone else thinks?'

'It matters to me. It's to do with family honour, anyway I swore an oath. I have to go.'

'You stay down here then, if I can't persuade you. I'll go and ask Quintus. I just have a bad feeling about it. Oh by the way, how did Little Quintus get on?'

'Fine; just fine. He chattered all the way home about the other children and the Greek history he learned. He is quite a bit bigger than the other boys you know, bigger than I was at that age.'

'Yes. I'll go and see where Quintus is hiding.'

I stared at the mosaic on the floor. It was a large green fish surrounded by vertical weeds. I remembered how burglars had ripped it up when I had first come back to Rome from Pontus all those years ago. I looked back at the fight that Quintus, Junius and I had with those attackers in the atrium after I had found Junius again. It seemed a world away, an eternity.

Now I had a real future. In two or three years we would have enough money for the bribes and legal fees necessary to re-establish ownership of a huge estate near Ariminium. It was my inheritance, taken from my family by Sulla when he reduced my family to poverty and had my grandfather killed in his proscriptions. The estate had included half of the city of Ariminium and the rents and land sales would make us wealthy, beyond our wildest dreams.

We only needed that little bit more money and my inheritance would be realised. I recollected the moment when my father had told me about it; how he had hidden the deeds and written their whereabouts on the amulet. Marcus Mettius had stolen it but I had retrieved it and got the deeds in the end while he was away in Gaul. I reached to my neck and felt the silver wire that bound its two halves together. I thought of my father then. I missed him.

I began to think of both my parents. I saw a small boy with his hand on the workbench my father used for his jewellery making. I remembered the feel of the pitted oak surface and the smell of the charcoal burner he always used to smelt the gold. My eyes began to close, eyelids heavy, flickering; I must have slept.

Also by Fredrik Nath:

Roman fiction:

Galdir – A Slave's Tale

Galdir – Rebel of the North

Galdir – Protector of Rome

Galdir – Oathbreaker

Amulet I

WW2 Adventure:

The Cyclist

Farewell Bergerac

Francesca Pascal

The Fat Chef

The Evil That Men Do

All available from Amazon uk and .com.

You can see all of Fredrik Nath's books on:

http://www.frednath.com

Fredrik Nath is a full-time neurosurgeon based in the northeast of England. In his time, he has run twenty-five Great North Run half-marathons in twenty-six years , trekked to 6000m in Nepal, done a 4000m tandem parachute jump and crossed the highest mountain pass in the world.

He began writing, like John Buchan, "because he ran out of penny-novels to read and felt he should write his own." Fred loves a good story, which is why he writes.

Catch Fred online at:
www.frednath.com

20900965R00223

Printed in Great Britain
by Amazon